CADUCEUS AWRY

To Rick
Best wishes!
Tom Milhorn

CADUCEUS AWRY

H. THOMAS MILHORN

Writer's Showcase
presented by *Writer's Digest*
San Jose New York Lincoln Shanghai

Caduceus Awry

Published by Writer's Showcase presented by *Writer's Digest*
an imprint of iUniverse.com, Inc.

For information address:
iUniverse.com, Inc.
620 North 48th Street
Suite 201
Lincoln, NE 68504-3467
www.iuniverse.com

ISBN: 0-595-12883-1

Printed in the United States of America

CHAPTER ONE

He had had hangovers before…on occasion terrible ones…but this one didn't make any sense. He had consumed only three drinks at most the night before.

Or was it four? It was hard to think clearly. His thoughts were jumbled.

He eased his feet over the side of the bed and sat there holding his head in his hands. Unlike most nights he had slept soundly, awakened only by the throbbing pain in his temples. He closed his eyes tightly for a moment in an attempt to clear the fog from his brain. It refused to budge.

As he raised his head, the vodka bottle sitting near the center of the antiquated dresser at the far side of the room caught his attention. Just the thing for this damn headache, he reasoned.

He stood, then quickly walked across the worn carpet. The thin rays of sunlight from the small window above the head of the bed faintly illuminated the clothes scattered about the floor, the ashtrays that should have been emptied days ago, and the overflowing wastebasket in the corner of the room. Already the air conditioner strained to keep up with the rapidly rising temperature outside.

Approaching the dresser, he reached out and took the bottle in his hand. His heart sank…it was empty! It had been half full when he came home from work yesterday. Where did it go? He certainly didn't remember drinking it. His thoughts began to race. Could someone have been in his apartment while he was asleep? If so, who? How did they get in? What did they want? Why didn't they wake him? Where did they go?

As a wave of nausea swelled in the pit of his stomach, his frustration quickly turned to anger. He drew the bottle back to a point just above his right ear and hurled it at the far wall as if he were throwing a bullet pass to a wide receiver running a curl pattern. It struck the wall with a loud crash and shattered into a hundred pieces.

Abruptly, movement drew his attention back to the bed. The form previously hidden by the sheet had suddenly bolted upright. Clasping the sheet tightly to her breasts with both hands, she appeared to be in her mid-thirties. Her platinum-blond hair was badly tousled, and her heavy mascara and bright-red lipstick were smeared. Her eyelids appeared heavy, as if from sleep and too much alcohol. He had never seen her before in his life.

"How the hell did you get in here?" he asked gruffly.

"I came with you. We met in the bar last night," she responded, rubbing her eyes in an attempt to get the sleep out.

"What bar?"

"The one on Webster Street. What's wrong with you?"

"You were at Alfredo's?" he asked, ignoring her question. "Why don't I remember you?"

She leaned forward with a frown on her face. "Mark, what do you mean you don't remember me? We had sex for an hour last night before you rolled over and went to sleep. Are you crazy?"

He didn't answer her immediately. Something was terribly wrong. How could he have sex with someone for an hour and not remember it? For a moment he wondered if he were crazy.

"I don't know," he said finally, shaking his head from side to side in another unsuccessful attempt to clear the fog. He gathered her clothes up from the floor and walked to the foot of the bed with them in his hand. "Look, ah…what's your name?"

"Marsha," she responded, nervously shifting the sheet higher. Her eyes flickered over the room, then back to him. "I told you that last night."

By now he was sure that she thought he was some kind of lunatic. "It's okay," he said more calmly. "I'm not going to hurt you. My head's just a little fuzzy. I'm sure I'll be okay in a few minutes."

He laid the clothes on the bed at her feet and tried to muster a weak smile to reassure her. When she didn't respond, he stepped back out of the way. She immediately brushed the sheet aside and got to her feet...naked from head to toe. The fullness of her firm-appearing breasts was a dead give away that she had silicone implants. She pulled her red, bikini panties out of the pile and quickly lifted a foot to slip them on.

Embarrassed by his own nakedness, he searched the room with his eyes until he located his white Jockey shorts under the edge of the room's only chair, an old cane-bottom rocker that needed painting. He retrieved the shorts and put them on, keeping his back turned to Marsha to give her a chance to get dressed with a little modesty.

"Last night you said you were a plastic surgeon," she said in a voice that sounded more at ease. "I figured you were bullshitting me. This dump sure doesn't look like it belongs to a hot-shot doctor."

He turned back in her direction just as she tucked her white, cotton blouse into her blue mini-skirt. A black purse was cradled loosely in the crook of her left arm and a pair of white pumps dangled from her hand.

"I'm a plastic surgeon," he said quickly. "Or at least I was. I work in the Emergency Room at Charity now, but it's only temporary."

"I know the place. I went there once a few years ago. Thought I had the clap. The doctor that took care of me was an Iranian or something. I couldn't understand a word he said. Why in the world do you work there? The place is the pits."

"Believe me, it's not by choice. It's the only place I'm allowed to work."

"What do you mean? I thought doctors could work anywhere they wanted to."

"They can if they have a license. The Board of Medical Licensure took mine four months ago." He nervously ran his hand through his hair. "Look, I'm sorry about all this, but I think you'd better be going."

"Did you lose your license because of your drinking?" she asked.

Before he could answer, she halted his response with an upraised hand. "I know, none of my business."

He nodded, then stepped aside to give her a clear path to the bedroom door. Taking the hint, she put her shoes on, reclaimed her large gold-colored earrings from the bedside table, and crossed the room, gingerly stepping over the larger pieces of glass in her path. She opened the door, then glanced back at him.

"Good luck, doc," she said with a compassionate look on her face. "I think you're going to need it." She passed through the door and eased it to behind her. Seconds later he heard the door to the apartment close. Finally, the fog in his brain began to clear.

"Shit," he said aloud "It's happened again."

He had had memory lapses before…two of them, each occurring after a bout of heavy drinking. The first time his memory failed him, he didn't remember an argument that had ended up in a shoving match at a party. He woke up the next day with sore ribs and not the slightest idea why. A three-hour period of time was completely missing from his memory. A friend who had been at the party told him about the scuffle. At first, he had been concerned about the episode, but he refused to believe it had anything to do with alcohol. He attributed it to having had a hard day at work and being tired.

His second memory lapse had concerned him more. One morning when he unlocked the door of his car to go to work, he had found a loaded gun on the front seat…a Smith and Wesson thirty-eight-caliber revolver. He had quickly smelled the barrel and been relieved…it had not been fired. The gun was still in his bedside table where he had placed it two months ago. Despite wracking his brain numerous times over the episode, he never had been able to figure out who the gun belonged to, or how it got in his car. Alcohol amnestic syndrome, Dr. Barkley had called such memory lapses when he was in the hospital. In the few Alcoholics Anonymous meetings he had been to since, they simply called them blackouts. It didn't take long for him to convince himself that, even if alcohol were the culprit, it wouldn't happen again if he were careful about how much he drank.

He couldn't believe he had picked up someone in a bar. It wasn't like him. He wondered what Marsha was like. Was she sweet and kind, or bitchy like his ex-wife, Joanna? Did she make a habit of getting picked up in bars, or had this been a one-time thing for her? Was she divorced, or never married? Did she have children? He wondered if they had discussed those things, and more, the night before. He didn't have a clue. His mind was still a blank.

Putting Marsha out of his mind, he glanced at the clock on the bedside table and registered the time with dismay…six thirty. "Damn! I'm going to be late again," he muttered in disgust.

He hurried into the bathroom where he clicked the light on and stared at the mirror. He looked every bit of his forty-two years. His hazel eyes were puffy and red, and he badly needed a shave. He didn't like what he saw, and he detested what he had become. For most of his life he had had it all…a consensus All America quarterback at the University of Georgia, a lucrative plastic-surgery practice that he loved, and a wife and daughter that he adored. When his life began its downhill spiral, he never dreamed that things could go so bad so fast.

He opened the medicine cabinet, took three aspirin tablets from a bottle, and swallowed them with a gulp of water. If two were good, then three had to be better. After following the aspirin with a Dramamine, he hurriedly combed his hair, brushed his teeth, and shaved. No time for a shower this morning. He knew Stottlemire would be angry because he was late again. He hoped Dr. Billingsworth wouldn't find out. He didn't need another bad mark on his record. He re-entered the bedroom and slipped on a pair of blue jeans that showed signs of wear at the knees, followed by a gray T-shirt that he had worn for the past three days and a pair of dingy white tennis shoes.

As he exited the apartment building and trotted down the steps to the street, the hot muggy air hit him in the face like an oven. The temperature again was predicted to reach a sweltering hundred degrees as it had done the past five days. He stared at his ancient, green Porsche, parked by the curb in a tight line of cars. An ugly dent marred the front fender, the paint was peeling in a large area on the hood, and a foot-long crack crossed the passenger-side of the windshield. He needed a new car. Too bad he couldn't afford one. The divorce had seen to that.

Because Judge John Clemmens hadn't believed his story about the tall, tanned man in the light-blue suit he had seen kissing Joanna on the balcony of the Starlight Motel, she had gotten almost everything in the settlement…their large brick house with the tall white columns in Buckhead, most of the considerable financial assets, and, of course, custody of Lisa, their eleven-year-old, hearing-impaired daughter.

Now thirteen, Lisa had inherited her mother's blond hair, blue eyes, and perfect complexion, and was beginning to develop her well-proportioned figure. She too would be a head turner. Fortunately, she hadn't inherited her mother's nasty disposition. He missed her.

Shortly after the divorce, to make it more difficult for him to see her, Joanna had placed Lisa in Briarwood Academy, an exclusive college preparatory school in Valdosta, 220 miles south of Atlanta. Most of the time she refused to let him see her when she came home on holidays and on an occasional weekend. Needless to say, he was bitter as hell about it.

He plopped on the worn seat and sat there for a moment with his head down. God, he felt bad. He knew it was going to be another miserable day.

Just as he turned the key in the ignition, the curtains in the window of the apartment just to the left of the building entrance closed abruptly. He sat there for a moment staring at the curtains. It was obvious that someone had been watching him. He thought it was strange, but he had more pressing things on his mind.

————————

In another part of town, Audrey Touchstone, wearing a faded blue housedress and no makeup, finished putting the breakfast dishes in the dishwasher and eyed the coffee pot on the stove. She wished she could have a cup, but she had been told not to eat or drink anything after midnight. Breakfast she didn't miss. She seldom had time to eat it anyway.

She had just celebrated her thirty-ninth birthday when she noticed the pain in her left breast. A mild discomfort at first, the pain had gradually intensified until she couldn't sleep on that side. That was when she discovered the lump. Her mother had died of breast cancer at the age of forty-one. Audrey was terrified.

Her husband, Raymond, had been laid off at the mill six months earlier. His boss blamed the cutback on the over-supply of steel by the Japanese. American companies could no longer compete, he had said. Because Raymond lacked a formal education, his job in the machine shop at Winthrop Steel was all he knew. He had worked there for twenty-two years, ever since he graduated from high school. Despite his intense effort to find another job, he had been unsuccessful.

Audrey had said nothing to him at first about the lump. She hadn't wanted to add to his worries. Then, last night, she couldn't put it off any longer. She had had to tell him. It had taken her a week to get up the nerve. She hadn't been sure how he would respond. He had always been proud of her figure, despite the fact that she had put on a few pounds since the birth of her children. Would he still love her if she had to have a mastectomy? He had never been very affectionate. Would he be even less so if she were deformed?

Their daughter, Betty Sue, was fifteen. She had been told everything. Clinton was only nine. There was no need to upset him. He simply had been told that his mother didn't feel well and had to go into the hospital for some tests. It wouldn't be a lie, at least not entirely. She would have some blood tests done…electrolytes and a blood count. The biopsy, too, would be a test. Dr. Todd Wilson, her surgeon, had explained to her that while still under anesthesia, a small piece of breast tissue from the affected area would be frozen rapidly and sliced into ultra-thin sections by a microtome. Then the pathologist would search the thin slices for cancer cells under a microscope. Finding any, he would report back to Dr. Wilson in the operating room who would remove her breast and dissect the lymph nodes from her armpit, or axilla as Dr. Wilson had called it.

At first she had been apprehensive about being operated on by a doctor she didn't know, especially since four of the seven surgeons on staff at Charity had names she couldn't even pronounce. Dr. Wilson's name had simply been next on the indigent rotation list. After she met him she was pleased. He seemed like such a nice young man. His easy-going demeanor had set her at ease almost immediately.

She worried a lot about not having health insurance. They lost coverage when Raymond lost his job. Fortunately, no one in her family had been sick, that is up until now. She felt awkward about going to Charity. They were proud people who had always paid their own way. They had never been forced to accept help before. Things had to get better. Raymond would find a job. She was sure of it. It was only a matter of time.

She eyed the clock on the microwave and sighed deeply. It was time to head to Charity…and her surgery.

———————————

As Mark pulled away from the curb and eased into the steady flow of traffic on South Cobb Drive, guilt over the hostile way he had acted earlier began to work its way into his mind. His angry outburst was uncharacteristic. He would clean up the broken bottle as soon as he got home.

When he was growing up, his mother hadn't tolerated such open showing of anger. One was supposed to resolve one's anger by rationally confronting the object of the anger in a civilized manner. It had been drilled into him. Many times, however, when he was particularly frustrated over something, he had gone out in the woods behind their house, out of sight of his mother, and vigorously thrown rocks at an old oak tree that he pretended to be the object of his inner turmoil.

As a child he often wondered if his father, a very intelligent but quiet man, did the same sort of thing. A number of times he thought of asking him, but never did. He knew he would merely sidestep the question, as was his habit. His mother never caught him throwing the stones. They would have discussed it in a rational manner if she had. He often wished that she would lose her temper and whack him, but she never did. He blamed his irrational behavior with Marsha on his headache and made a vow to do better. He would apologize to her, if he ever saw her again.

A mile later, he picked up speed, headed down the on-ramp, and merged with the fast-moving traffic on Interstate 285 that circled the city, headed for the Interstate 20 and the complicated maze of interchanges known locally as Spaghetti Junction. The white letters of a large, green sign above the highway declared **Downtown Atlanta, 10 Miles.** Traffic got heavier and heavier as exit after exit dumped its multitude of cars and trucks onto the four southbound lanes. Thanks to the Dramamine, his nausea finally began to ease. Unfortunately, his head continued to throb.

He lit a cigarette, took a deep drag, then glanced at his watch. It was seven o'clock.

"Damn," he said aloud. It was time for him to be arriving at work. He knew Stottlemire would be watching the clock and wondering where the hell he was. He would just tell him the truth…he over slept. He wouldn't tell him it was because he drank too much the night before. He certainly wouldn't tell him about Marsha.

Marsha had been right. Alcohol had cost him his license. He had been too embarrassed to admit it to her. He hadn't always been a heavy drinker. After the divorce he seemed to sink deeper and deeper into the black abyss of depression. Despite the bad things Joanna had done to him, he still loved her. God knows he didn't want to. He couldn't help it. He just did. Alcohol dulled the pain of his loss, he told himself. It had become his way of coping, and he made good use of it.

Since the divorce, alcohol had caused him some minor problems, at least to his way of thinking. He had found it necessary to cancel surgery a couple of times because he was too hung over to make it to the hospital, and one weekend when he was supposed to pick Lisa up at her school he didn't make it until the next day. For the most part, though, he had handled his drinking pretty well...until he showed up in the operating room one morning high on Johnny Walker scotch.

"As of this moment, you will no longer be allowed to practice medicine," Dr. Allen, the Chairman of the Board of Medical Licensure, had said at his brief hearing.

Dr. Allen's words had hit him like a brick. The most he had expected was a year of probation. He had been completely devastated. Plastic surgery had been his life. He had lived it and breathed it. He had come to work early, stayed late, and looked forward to coming back the next day. He felt like his life had ended.

Successfully maneuvering Spaghetti Junction, he headed north on Interstate 75 toward the heart of the city. He quickly crossed under Martin Luther King Jr. Drive, and then the railroad tracks. Ebenezer Baptist Church was two blocks off to his right.

As the red brick buildings and white-blossoming dogwood trees of the Georgia State University campus appeared off in the distance to his left, he made a right turn onto Magnolia Avenue, a main thoroughfare in the less desirable section of Atlanta. Pawnshops, empty storefronts, and run-down apartment buildings, many not more than tenements, dominated the landscape. Whites had begun moving out of the area after the advent of integration and forced busing in the early 1960s. The area now was almost totally black. Every evening, about the time he gets off work, prostitutes and drug dealers wearing digital pagers begin coming out to look for potential customers.

When a break in the heavy traffic occurred, he turned left and pulled through the gate of the six-foot-high, chain-link fence that surrounded the parking lot. He drove past a dozen rows of what seemed like every make and model of automotive transportation and took another left. The worn tires of his creaking, old Porsche made a whirring noise as they rolled over the still-sticky asphalt of the recently repaved surface. The acrid smell of creosol permeated the stagnant air and burned his nostrils. Finally, half way down the row he pulled into the only remaining space next to the aging, brick building.

Leaving his car, he hurriedly walked to the gray, metal door. Three-inch, white letters stated **Side Entrance** and identified the structure as **Greater Atlanta Charity Hospital.**

The hospital, known by everyone in Atlanta simply as Charity, was built sometime in the early 1930s, he had been told during his brief orientation. As a WPA project, its purpose had been to furnish free medical care to the multitude of indigent patients created by the great stock market crash of 1929. Despite its age, it was still an impressive structure. The white-columned original building, which now served as main entrance, lobby, and administrative offices, more resembled a Southern Baptist church than a modern-day hospital, although it lacked a steeple. Because the need for additional space had grown over the years, the city constructed a modern six-story building behind the original building in the mid-1960s. The contractor had made an obvious attempt to match the original red brick, but fell far short. The city made renovations from time to time, but for the most part the building had been allowed to run down and, in general, stayed in a state of disrepair.

Rumor had it that the city council, on a number of occasions, had tried to close Charity, an act abhorred by the administrators of the more affluent hospitals in the city. They feared that, if Charity were to close, hoards of nonpaying patients would fill their hospitals. Under pressure from the affluent hospitals' powerful lobby, the motion always failed by a vote or two.

Closing the door behind him, he proceeded down a narrow hallway, which eventually divided into three larger ones. A small, black, white-lettered sign hanging from the ceiling indicated that the hallway to the left led to Administration, the hallway straight ahead to the lobby, and the one to the right to patients' rooms. He looked at his watch, took the hallway to the right, and quickened his step. His headache finally began to ease.

As he passed from the older building into the newer one, the lighting suddenly got brighter. Patients' rooms appeared on either side of him, and hospital sights and sounds surrounded him. Finally, he came to the end of the hallway. A sign on the door in front of him declared **Authorized Personnel Only.**

He opened the door and entered a small office. A gray metal desk, paint chipped in several places, sat against the wall to the right. A white wooden bookcase filled with books and journals of various sizes and colors occupied the wall behind the desk. The desk sat just beneath a small dirty window with a cracked pane. A matching gray metal cabinet about shoulder high, and with equally chipped paint, sat just to the left of the bookcase.

He hurriedly disrobed, took a set of green scrubs out of the cabinet, and put them on. Then he opened the door opposite the one he had come in and entered the city's busiest emergency room.

CHAPTER TWO

Despite the early-morning hour, the place was already a zoo. Nurses and orderlies scurried in and out of the sixteen examination rooms that lined the four sides of the large central area. An infant with an I.V. in his hand in a room on the far side of the area cried loudly. A young pregnant black woman in a room to Mark's left screamed, "Oh Jesus! Oh Jesus!" as her labor pains intensified. In a room just to his right, an elderly man sat on the side of the examination table with his head down, apparently in a daze. His face was heavily crusted with dried blood.

Sitting in a chair in the counter-high, circular Nurses' Station in the center of the area, a middle-aged, black nurse scribbled on a chart. A young, white ward clerk just to her left transferred doctors' orders from Emergency Room forms to laboratory slips. The smell of astringent disinfectant permeated the room.

Mark glanced up at the clock on the wall above the stretcher entrance. It was seven-thirty. He took a deep breath, then started toward the Nurses' Station, ready for another day in the hellhole of medicine...Charity Emergency Room.

"Dr. Valentine, where the hell have you been?" a gruff female voice demanded impatiently. "You're thirty minutes late."

He recognized the voice immediately. Mattie Johnson had worked in the Emergency Room at Charity for over thirty years, ever since she graduated from the diploma school that the hospital once operated.

Such programs now no longer existed, having been replaced by baccalaureate programs in colleges and universities.

Unlike many diploma nurses, Mattie had never seen the need to upgrade her di-ploma to a degree. Doctors who knew her would tell you quickly that she was a real nurse, a much better one than most of those highly educated nurses who referred to pa-tients as clients. Her hard work and natural talent for nursing had earned her the head nurse's job at Charity Emergency Room after only three years, despite the fact that posi-tions of authority at that time were usually reserved for white nurses. He turned in her direction

Mattie stood just outside examination room 12 with her hands on her hips and a stern look on her face. Her starched, white uniform and matching nurse's cap, which had long since gone out of vogue, made her look like an image from the past. Her silver-framed bifocals, as usual, hung at her chest, supported by a gold chain around her neck.

"My alarm clock didn't go off," Mark offered apologetically.

It was obvious that Mattie wasn't impressed. He had given her the same excuse twice before in the past month.

"Stottlemire's fit to be tied," she said sternly. "He only got two hours sleep last night, and he's eager to get home and go to bed. Now he's had to wait for you again."

"Where is he?"

"In the orthopedic room."

Mark sighed deeply, walked around the Nurses' Station, and headed for the orthopedic room.

Eric Stottlemire had been head of the Emergency Room at Charity for eight years, ever since he finished the Emergency-Medicine residency program at Emory. He and Mark worked twelve-hour shifts, seven AM to seven PM, as did the nurses. Stottlemire preferred the night shift because that was when the automobile accidents, stabbings, shootings, and general mayhem usually occurred. Mark didn't like working at night, so the day shift suited him just fine. He knew

Stottlemire would be angry because he was late again. He didn't blame him. He would be too if the situation were reversed.

Entering the orthopedic room, he found Stottlemire putting a spica cast on the forearm of an adolescent boy. Stottlemire wore a white lab coat. A gray Litman stethoscope hung around his neck. He was no more than five-feet, eight-inches tall and weighed only 150 pounds. His pock-marked face gave evidence of the severe cystic acne he must have had as an adolescent. His reddish-brown hair was more unruly than usual.

Mark's initial impression of Stottlemire had been that his sharp tongue and holier than thou attitude was merely a compensation for his lack of height and acne scars. Now, after knowing him for three months, he was convinced that his initial impression had been correct.

"I'm sorry I'm late," Mark muttered. "My alarm clock...."

"Save it for someone who believes it," Stottlemire said without looking up. He began applying another layer of the wet, plaster-impregnated gauze to the boy's arm.

"I'll finish that," Mark said, reaching for a roll of cast material.

Stottlemire held up his hand, palm toward Mark. "No! I started it. I'll finish it," he said coldly.

Mark dropped his head and stared at the floor. "Suit yourself," he said, truly feeling bad that he had made Stottlemire stay late again. He would be on time from now on, he promised himself. This wouldn't happen again.

Leaving the orthopedic room, he walked back to the Nurses' Station and began looking at the large number of clipboards, each containing information about a yet unseen patient. The charts, as they called them, sat in individual rectangular holes in a rack on the counter top. The elderly man with the bloody face had been admitted, the pregnant woman had been wheeled off to Labor and Delivery, and the mother of the crying child had gotten tired of waiting and left with him.

Mark picked up a chart with the number two written in felt-tip pen in the upper right hand corner and turned to Mattie who had just entered the Nurses' Station.

"Who's going to help me today?" he asked.

Mattie sighed. "Lena called in sick again this morning. I haven't been able to get anyone to replace her, so it looks like you're stuck with me."

He was delighted. He loved for Mattie to assist him. She had been an emergency room nurse for so long she knew exactly what he needed, sometimes before he did. He proceeded to examination room two, chart in hand and Mattie close behind him.

"What do we have here?" he asked, talking aloud to himself as he silently read the chart. "Eight-year-old black male with an earache. Temperature 101.5 degrees."

The boy's mother, a grossly overweight young woman, sat in the corner of the room with an infant in her lap sucking on a dirty pacifier. Another child, a girl with pink-ribboned pigtails, who appeared to be three or four, clung to her side. Mark introduced himself to the mother, then looked at the chubby boy perched on the end of the examination table. The Chicago Bulls T-shirt he wore looked as if it had never seen the inside of a washing machine. The dirty tennis shoes were high-tops, laced only halfway up. His baggy pants came down to his knees. He had an apprehensive look on his face.

"What's the matter?" Mark asked, patting him reassuringly on the shoulder.

Without a word, the boy pointed timidly to his left ear.

Mattie slipped a small, plastic speculum on the otoscope and handed it to Mark. He inserted the speculum in the boy's right ear and looked at the eardrum through the otoscope head.

"Normal," he said. Then he walked to the other side of the table, gently inserted the speculum in the problem ear, and looked at the eardrum. It was red and bulging.

"He's got an infected ear," he said to the mother as he handed the otoscope back to Mattie.

Mattie took the speculum off the otoscope, tossed it in the garbage can, and replaced the otoscope in its holder on the wall. Mark pulled a pen from his shirt pocket and scribbled his findings in the chart. Then he pulled a pad from his pocket, wrote a prescription, and handed it to the boy's mother.

"Give him one of these three times a day until they're all gone," he instructed, skeptical that she would actually do so. In his experience, mothers who brought their children to Charity usually gave them medication until they didn't appear ill anymore, then they stopped. A week or two later, the children often ended up back at Charity with the same complaint. He felt sorry for them. Most were from single parent families, uneducated, and unemployed. He knew that they had a good chance of growing up to be just like their parents. Welfare recipients breed welfare recipients, staff members at Charity were heard to say from time to time. Little changed from generation to generation in that area of Atlanta.

Mattie gave some last minute instructions to the boy's mother while Mark examined a young woman's sprained ankle in the next room. As he came out of the door, Mattie cut him off.

"Dr. Stottlemire just left. He called Billingsworth," she said, concern showing on her face.

"Shit!" Mark said aloud.

Heads were still turned as he walked back to the Nurses' Station to get another chart.

Despite his anxiety about the prospect of being called on the carpet by Billingsworth, he admired the man for what he had accomplished at Charity. Shortly after coming to the hospital as its director, Billingsworth had discovered that the hospital had a major problem...medical care was atrocious. Few staff doctors spoke without a heavy accent of one kind or another. Many were foreign medical graduates, known as FMGs, who were studying to take the examination to obtain a Georgia license for the first time, had already failed it a number of times, or simply had chosen never to take it. Like Mark, they worked at Charity under a special, limited permit granted by the Board of

Medical Licensure called an institutional license. Because of the low rate of pay, long hours, and poor working conditions, it was the only way hospitals like Charity, which catered to the poor and indigent, could get, and keep, adequate numbers of doctors.

To attract first-rate physicians, Billingsworth, on his arrival, had instituted a policy which allowed physicians with bonafide Georgia licenses to supplement their relatively low salaries with income from the care of Charity's limited, but growing, number of paying patients. Using his connections at Emory, he had pursued some of the brighter, more dedicated young physicians as they finished their residencies and enticed several of them to join the medical staff at Charity. Eric Stottlemire had been the first to come on the payroll.

By noon Mark had gotten things in the Emergency Room pretty well under control. He had taken care of the true emergencies, and the fifteen or so remaining patients could wait. Mattie had sent a clerk to the cafeteria to get him some lunch, and the clerk has just delivered it to the Doctors' Office.

He was especially hungry since, in his haste to get to the hospital, he had skipped breakfast. He slumped into the executive chair behind the desk. The Styrofoam container sat on the desk in front of him. The aroma of country fried steak, mashed potatoes with gravy, and peach cobbler filled the room. As he reached for the food, the telephone rang. The shrill voice on the other end of the line was unmistakable.

"Dr. Valentine. This is Edna. Dr. Billingsworth wants to see you in his office immediately." She quickly disconnected.

"Damn!" Mark said, pushing the chair back from the desk. "Four years of medical school, three years of general surgery residency, and two years of plastic surgery training for this. What a waste." He briefly thought about delaying the trip to Billingsworth's office long enough to eat lunch.

Billingsworth could wait!

Sanity quickly returned. He was in too much trouble already to push his luck. He glanced at the Styrofoam container, hesitated, then headed for Billingsworth's office.

———————————

Audrey Touchstone had had her breast surgery and been delivered to the Recovery Room on the second floor. On awakening from the anesthetic, she immediately felt through the hospital gown for her left breast. As her hand touched her chest, she winced in pain. At the same time, she was relieved…the breast was still there. Maybe she didn't have cancer after all, but she couldn't be sure. Dr. Wilson had promised to come to her hospital room and talk with her after the surgery. She was still worried to death about the outcome. Hopefully, he would arrive soon. He had promised to be honest with her, regardless of what he found.

A few minutes later, a young white-clad orderly approached her. "Time to go," he said, reaching for the gurney. He wheeled her out the Recovery Room door to the elevator, which delivered her to the fifth floor. Then he pushed her down the hallway and into her hospital room. Two nurses followed them into the room and helped him transfer her from the gurney to the bed. The nurses and orderly promptly left.

Feeling tired, she closed her eyes and thought about Raymond and the children. He had been there that morning before she went to the operating room, but had had to leave to go to another in a long line of fruitless job interviews. Despite the fact that it had been only a few hours since she had seen him, she missed him. She missed the children too. She felt sad that Raymond hadn't been able to be there with her when she came out of the operating room, but she understood.

At the sound of a light knock on the door, she opened her eyes to see Dr. Wilson come through the door wearing a white lab coat over his green scrubs. His white, surgical mask hung down against his chest, supported by two of its four straps around his neck. Of average height, he had a pleasant face and a head full of bushy, black hair. Audrey thought he looked awfully young to be a surgeon, but a lot of people looked young to her these days.

"Good news," he said in a pleasant voice as he sat down in a chair by the bed. "The tumor was benign."

"Benign. What does that mean?" Audrey asked, still a bit groggy from the anesthesia.

"It means that it wasn't cancer. It was a fatty tissue tumor called a lipoma. We removed it all."

She closed her eyes and said a silent prayer, thanking God that she wouldn't die from breast cancer as her mother had done. Her worst fear wouldn't come true…her family wouldn't have to do without her. From now on she would have the annual mammograms she had read about in one of her woman's magazines.

She opened her eyes and looked at the needle in the back of her hand, then followed the plastic tubing to the pump, and beyond that to a bag of clear fluid hanging on an I.V. pole at the head of the bed.

"How long do I have to have this in?" she asked expectantly.

"For the next eight hours," he replied. "It contains a prophylactic antibiotic to prevent infection."

"Can I go home then?" she asked.

"Not quiet that fast. The surgery was more extensive than I normally expect for a lipoma. I had to dissect out a number of extensions of the tumor from in and around the chest wall muscles. I want to watch you overnight…in case there are any complications."

"Do you expect any?"

"Not really. It's just a precaution. If everything goes okay, I'll let you go home first thing in the morning."

She thanked him for his kindness, and, as he left the room, her thoughts turned back to her family. Raymond would bring the children by later. She looked forward to telling them the good news about her breast. She thanked God for Charity. She and Raymond probably would have had to mortgage their house if they had been required to pay for the operation.

There was no doubt in Mark's mind why Billingsworth wanted to see him. It had to do with Billingsworth's determination to keep the good ship Charity running tightly. He felt like a high-school student who had been called to the principal's office for being tardy again. He dreaded facing him. Billingsworth didn't tolerate screw-ups, as he had learned on a couple of other occasions.

When he arrived at the outer office, Edna was sitting at her desk filing her orange fingernails, which perfectly matched her orange hair and the large polka dots in her green dress. Half-glasses perched precariously on the end of her bird-like nose.

"He's waiting for you," she said, waving toward the door to Billingsworth's office.

Mark took a deep breath, gulped once, and entered the room. Billingsworth sat behind a large, oak desk with a stern look on his angular face. His dark-blue suit, white shirt with thin blue stripes, and burgundy tie were perfectly color-coordinated. His black hair, graying at the temples, gave him a sophisticated appearance. He looked every bit the executive he had become.

Stacks of requisitions for pieces of equipment, which were unlikely to be purchased because of lack of funds, sat on one end of the desk. A half-full coffee mug with his name on it, a gift from a pharmaceutical representative, sat at the other end. Rows of gray filing cabinets lined the wall to the left. A large picture of a lake with pine trees surrounding it and snowcapped mountains in the background decorated the wall behind the desk…no diplomas, residency training certificates, or medical licenses. Billingsworth had put all that behind him when he became the Hospital Director. He waved toward the chair directly in front of the desk. Mark took a seat.

Billingsworth removed his glasses and laid them on the desk. "Mark, what am I going to do with you?" he asked, obviously not expecting an answer.

Mark looked down at the floor and didn't respond. His palms began to sweat.

Billingsworth continued. "At first, you worked hard and did a real good job. You even impressed Mattie, but here lately you've started to slip. This is the third time you've been late in the past month. Stottlemire is out to get your scalp. You know I have to put this in your record."

Mark slumped further into his chair as a dark cloud of depression settled over him. He knew Billingsworth was right. He owed him a lot. Three months earlier, when he was discharged from the Chemical Dependency Unit at Ridgeview Psychiatric Hospital, Billingsworth had talked the licensure board into letting him work at Charity on a limited, institutional license. Billingsworth was to give the board a written report and testify about his progress in person at his appeal hearing, now eight months away. Billingsworth was the key to getting his license back. The doctors on the licensure board were almost certain to follow his recommendation…good or bad.

"I'm trying Ed," Mark said. "I just can't seem to get it together. Things just seem so hopeless since the divorce. I thought I would feel a lot better by now, but I don't."

"Mark, your fate is in your hands," Billingsworth responded as if he hadn't heard a word Mark said. "Your future as a physician in this state depends entirely on you. Somehow you've got to pull yourself together and get on with your life."

Mark felt even more uncomfortable. He shuffled his feet. "I know. There's not a day that goes by that I don't think about it, and I try Ed. I really try."

"Damn it! You need to quit trying and just do it. It's up to you. I've done all I...."

Suddenly Billingsworth bent forward and clutched his hand to his chest, his face contorted with pain. Beads of sweat broke out on his forehead. Mark quickly leaned across the desk, and touched his shoulder.

"Are you all right?" he asked with genuine concern.

"I'll be okay in a moment," Billingsworth assured him, removing his hand from his chest and sitting up straight again.

It was clear to Mark that Billingsworth was still in a great deal of pain. "It's your heart, isn't it?" he asked, already sure of the answer.

Billingsworth nodded his head, then he reached into a desk drawer, pulled out a small brown bottle, and opened it. He took a small, white pill from the bottle, put it under his tongue, and waited for the pain to go away. Mark sat back down and waited for the agony in Billingsworth's face to dissipate. A few seconds later, he appeared more relaxed. Mark knew the nitroglycerin was working.

"When did you start having heart problems again?" Mark asked.

"About a month ago," Billingsworth replied. "Exertion or anger usually brings the attacks on, but sometimes frustration does. I had to give up my exercise program at the fitness center. I just couldn't do it any more."

"Have you talked to your cardiologist?"

Billingsworth leaned back in his chair. "He wants to do a cardiac catheterization."

"You don't sound very enthusiastic about it."

"I'm not. He thinks I'm probably going to need a coronary artery bypass graft. I'm not ready to have my chest cracked."

"What does Martha say about it?"

Billingsworth's gaze dropped to the nitroglycerin bottle. "I haven't told her yet."

"Ed, don't you think she has a right to know?"

Billingsworth swept the brown bottle back into the drawer and cleared his throat. "Mark, I didn't ask you to come here to discuss my problems." He settled his glasses back on the bridge of his nose, then picked up a report from his desk and stared at it. When Mark didn't move, Billingsworth glanced up at him. "That's all, unless you have something else to say."

Mark rose slowly and reluctantly. Billingsworth's eyes dipped back into the papers in his hand, but it was obvious he wasn't reading. At the door Mark stopped and waited. Billingsworth couldn't help but notice his concern. After a moment, without looking up, Billingsworth said, "I'll tell Martha tonight."

Mark nodded his approval, then headed back down the long hallway toward the Emergency Room. Billingsworth was a good man. He had gone out of his way numerous times to help people that others had given up on, including him. As a result, he felt a special bond to him. He hoped Billingsworth would be okay. He would call Edna later to check on him.

Entering the Doctors' Office, Mark plopped in the chair behind the desk and reached for the Styrofoam container. The food was cold. By this time he was so hungry it didn't matter. He gulped the food down, then he leaned back in the chair, propped his feet up on the desk, and lit a cigarette.

He knew he could quit drinking any time he wanted. He wasn't an alcoholic. Indeed, he had quit twice in the past three months. The first time, he didn't drink for a week. The second time, he stayed sober three days. He was aware that it was becoming more difficult for him to abstain. He promised himself that in the future he would do a better job of controlling his drinking. He could see where it might get to be a problem.

CHAPTER THREE

As Mark re-entered the Emergency Room from the Doctors' Office Mattie met him with a chart in her hand. "I think you'll want to see the patient in room eleven first," she said.

"What's the problem?"

"Severe abdominal pain. He looks like he may need a surgeon."

Mark quickly walked to room eleven where he found a dark-haired man with a handle-bar mustache lying on his right side with his knees drawn up to his chest. The man appeared to be about his age, but shorter and a good twenty to thirty pounds heavier. His face was contorted with pain. Mark introduced himself. The man, a Rufus Askins, did the same.

"When did you start hurting?" Mark asked.

"About an hour ago," Mr. Askins responded through gritted teeth. "I was okay when I woke up, then all of a sudden this pain hit me like a hammer."

"Show me where it hurts."

Mr. Askins stretched his legs out, moaned with pain, then placed his hand on the upper part of his abdomen, just beneath his sternum.

Mark unbuttoned the front of the man's tan leisure suit and felt his abdomen. It was as hard as a board. "Involuntary guarding," he said to Mattie.

Mattie nodded.

He turned back to Mr. Askins. "Have you ever had an ulcer?"

"About a year ago. I stopped taking the medicine for it last month. I didn't think I needed it anymore."

"Has he been X-rayed yet?" Mark asked.

"When he came in," Mattie responded. "The film should be ready by now."

Mark left the examination room and walked across the Emergency Room to the radiology area. The X-ray film was in the view box where the technician had placed it. Mark studied the film for a moment. A thin black line of air under the left diaphragm identified the problem...a perforated ulcer. Mattie, as usual, had been right. The man needed surgery right away. Mark hurried back to room eleven and explained his diagnosis to Mr. Askins. Then he looked at the chart...Blue Cross/Blue Shield of Georgia.

"Who's on private surgery call?" he asked.

"Dr. Wilson was on last night and Dr. Jackson the day before, so it would be Dr. Haynes' turn today," Mattie replied.

"Get him down here right away," Mark instructed. He knew that Dr. Haynes would be pleased. Charity didn't get a large number of patients with sources of payment, although their numbers were increasing. Those who had it were a welcome sight for staff physicians with bonafide Georgia licenses. Although it meant more work, it also meant more income.

To help paying patients chose their doctors, the hospital furnished them a list of complication and death rates for staff surgeons, a policy Billingsworth initiated shortly after his arrival at Charity. Paying patients, like Rufus Askins, automatically went to whichever of the three surgeons with Georgia licenses...Jeremy Haynes, Todd Wilson, or Jack Jackson...was on private call.

Haynes and Wilson were relatively new additions to the staff, having come to Charity three years earlier. Dr. Jackson, on the other hand, had been at Charity prior to Billingsworth taking over the helm of the hospital. The other four staff surgeons, Drs. Sanchez, Salvatino, Ahmed, and Ajamian, were FMGs working on institutional licenses. Because they worked on institutional licenses, they, like Mark, were paid only sixty percent of what doctors with Georgia licenses were paid, and because they lacked a legitimate license they were not allowed to supplement their income from the care of private patients. All seven surgeons participated equally in the indigent patient rotation.

While waiting for Dr. Haynes to arrive, Mark went next door to check on another patient, a machine shop worker with a tiny fragment of metal in his eye. As he finished making an initial assessment, Mattie stuck her head in the door.

"Dr. Haynes is here," she said.

Mark walked back to room eleven and found Dr. Haynes bent over Mr. Askins examining his abdomen. When Dr. Haynes noticed Mark, he straightened up. Haynes wasn't much taller than Stottlemire, but he had a hell of a better disposition and the good looks to go with it. All the young, single nurses at Charity were crazy about his curly, blond hair and Paul Newman blue eyes. They considered him to be the hospital's most eligible bachelor.

"Did you see the X-ray?" Mark asked.

"Looked at it first," Haynes replied. "You were right. He has a perforated ulcer. What about lab work?"

"Electrolytes are okay. His hematocrit is down...28.2."

"Mattie, get him to the operating room right away," Haynes instructed. "Call the lab and tell them to type and match four units of packed cells. We've got to move fast before he goes into shock."

Mattie summoned an orderly who wheeled Mr. Askins out of the area, headed for the Surgery Suite.

The first half of the afternoon in the Emergency Room proceeded as usual...an elderly woman in congestive heart failure, a middle-aged man with a heart attack, a young woman with a gonorrhea infection of the pelvis, assorted pulled muscles and lacerations, a young man with asthma, an elderly man with pneumonia, and a teenage girl who, distraught over a breakup with her boyfriend, had attempted to commit suicide by taking a handful of her mother's sleeping pills.

At two-thirty, Sarah Jacobson, a frail-looking, young woman who worked part time in the business office to help support her pursuit of a degree in accounting at Georgia State University, came through the Emergency Room passing out paychecks to hospital staff, as was her custom every other week. Mark accepted his envelope, opened it, and glanced at his paycheck. He quickly looked at it again, this time more intently.

"What the hell! Half my pay is missing," he blurted out. "It must be a mistake. Mattie! Mattie!" he yelled across the Emergency Room. "Cover for me. I'll be right back."

He hurriedly made the trip back to the older part of the building. He needed every penny he could get. He had bills to pay, most of them past due. He would straighten the error out immediately, but he was sure it would take the hospital a few days to issue a new check. The bills would just have to wait a little longer.

He pushed the door open and charged into the Business Office waving his check in the air. "I want to see Mrs. Jones," he demanded of the middle-aged black woman eating a Snickers bar and drinking a Barqs root beer behind her desk. She tried to speak, but her mouth was full of candy and nothing came out. Pointing her index finger at her mouth, she chewed rapidly in an attempt to get the mass to a manageable state so she could swallow it.

"What seems to be the problem?" Mrs. Jones asked, standing in the doorway to his left under the **Payroll** sign. Her masculine-looking business suit accentuated her black, orthopedic shoes and horn-rimmed glasses.

"Something's wrong with my check. I've been shorted," Mark said loudly, handing her the check.

She glanced at it, then handed it back to him. "I'm sorry, Dr. Valentine, but that's the right amount," she said sternly, peering through her thick lenses.

"What do you mean, right amount? It's short!"

"Just a minute," she said. She retreated into her office and promptly returned with a business envelope in her hand. "You need to read this."

He took the envelope and pulled a one-page document from it. Through the legal jargon the meaning quickly became clear. Joanna had garnisheed a portion of his wages for back alimony payments.

He had a sinking feeling. What would he do now? He couldn't keep up with his debts before. He certainly wouldn't be able do it with what was left after the garnishment. Hell, he might have to choose between buying groceries or paying the rent.

"It's not fair," he said dejectedly as he handed the envelope and document back to Mrs. Jones. "My alimony payments are based on what I made as a plastic surgeon, which is a hell of a lot more than I get paid here. I've been sending Joanna what I can. I don't mind the child-support payments. I make them religiously, but there's no way I can keep up with the alimony payments. She doesn't need the money anyhow. She got almost everything in the divorce settlement."

"Dr. Valentine, I just work here," Mrs. Jones said. "I don't make the rules. If you have a problem, you need to talk to your ex-wife."

"You're right," he said. "That's exactly what I intend to do." He turned and left the Business Office. Joanna had a lot of explaining to do, and he was going to see to it that she did. He would go see her just as soon as his shift was over. He stormed back down the hallway to the Emergency Room. The rest of the day he could barely concentrate on taking care of patients. All he could think about was Joanna and what she had done to him. The more he thought about it, the madder he got.

———————

The sun was just beginning to set when Mark rang the doorbell of the large, brick house with the tall, white columns in Buckhead that once was his. No one answered. He waited. After what seemed to be a half-hour, but which in reality was no more than five minutes, he rang the doorbell again.

He knew she was in there. He intended to stand on the porch all night long if he had to. He banged hard on the door and rang the doorbell again. Finally the door opened and Joanna appeared in front of him wearing a flimsy, black nightgown and looking as gorgeous as ever. Her long, blond hair was in slight disarray, which was highly unusual for her. She could have sex for an hour and at the end of it look like she had just stepped out of the hairdresser's chair. When she recognized him, a scowl came over her face.

"Mark! What the hell do you mean coming over here without calling first?" She said angrily. "What do you want?"

Without a word, he pushed by her and walked through the foyer into the large family room. At the far side of the room, two double French doors overlooking the pool area occupied the wall to either side of a wide brick fireplace, which was outlined in white marble. On the opposite side of the room, two large, white bookshelves containing literary classics, small plants in brass planters, and figurines of angels and other objects framed a double French door leading from the foyer. The room was furnished with expensive European furniture, each item having been hand picked by Joanna without regard to cost. White marble columns surrounded the perimeter of the room and supported an open landing bordered by a white railing that looked down on the open area below. Joanna followed him into the room. He was going to have his say, and she was going to listen.

"You can't just barge in here like you own the place," Joanna said angrily. "I have a right to privacy."

He pulled the check out of his pocket and waved it at her. "How the hell do you expect me to live on what's left after you take your cut? I'm struggling just to get by and you're living here like the queen of England."

She took the check from his hand and briefly looked at it. Then she threw it at him. It floated in the air momentarily, then fell to the floor at his feet.

"Bitch," he yelled as he reached down and picked up the check.

She took a step toward him. "How you get by doesn't concern me. That's your problem. Now, if you don't mind, I'm busy. Good night!"

Her haughty attitude made him even angrier. "Damn you!" he said loudly, clinching his fist by his side. "I could kill you!"

"That's enough!" came the deep, masculine voice from the landing at the top of the staircase. "Joanna's right. You're out of line."

Barefooted and wearing a blue, striped robe, the man quickly walked down the stairs and approached him. Appearing to be about his age, the man was tall, maybe an inch taller than he. His face showed early wrinkling, from too much sun judging from his dark tan. His jaw was square and his eyes showed the self-confidence of a man who had faced danger and survived. He looked familiar. Mark had seen him before. But where?

Then it came to him. He was the stranger he had seen kissing Joanna on the balcony of the Starlight Motel a month before the divorce. Mark recognized the robe he was wearing too. It was one he had left behind when he moved out. "Who the hell are you?" he demanded.

"I'm Sam Kincaid, if it's any of your business. Joanna and I are engaged to be married."

"You're kidding," Mark said reflexively. He didn't know whether to be angry at him or feel sorry for him. Still, a part of him grieved the fact that Joanna loved someone else. He glanced at Kincaid's left hand. Where a wedding ring once had been, a pale band of skin now occupied its place. He wondered if Joanna had broken them up.

"It's time for you to leave," Kincaid said threateningly.

"I'm not going anywhere until I get some satisfaction." Mark replied angrily. Then he turned to Joanna. "I demand that you retract the garnishee order."

"Not a chance," she said. "I plan on getting all the money that's due me. Judge Clemmens told me that if you harass me about this, I can get a restraining order and have you put in jail."

"Joanna, why are you doing this? I know you don't need the money."

"Maybe I just like seeing you squirm. I got so damned tired of your all-important attitude when we were married. Everyone thought you were so wonderful...the great plastic surgeon. People fell all over you...the same people who treated me like a mindless bimbo. I just got fed up. Now it's your turn to pay for all those years, and I'm going to make you pay until it hurts."

"You really are cruel, just like your mother."

"Leave my mother out of this," she responded. "Mother was glad when I left you. She never did like you. She used to call you 'Doctor Asshole.'"

"The feeling's mutual. I never could stand her either. I don't know how your poor father has stood it all these years." He hesitated, trying to get his anger under control. It wasn't her mother he had come to discuss.

"Joanna, I demand that you drop the garnishee order," he said to her again, this time more forcefully.

Kincaid glared at him. "You're in no position to demand anything," he said with a threatening tone to his voice. "Now you'd better leave, and you had better do it now or I'll have you arrested for trespassing. I'm sure the police would be interested in the fact that you threatened Joanna." He walked to Joanna and put his arm around her waist.

Mark looked at Kincaid's arm around Joanna's waist with a fleeting jealousy, then he looked her squarely in the eye. "One of these days you're going to get what you deserve," he said sternly.

Joanna looked disgusted. "Mark, you don't have the guts to carry out a threat."

"Out!" Kincaid said loudly as he walked to the door and held it open.

Mark knew when he was licked. He gritted his teeth and stuck the check back in his pocket. "You two deserve each other," He said bitterly. Then he turned and left the house.

What would he do now? He couldn't get another job to pick up extra money. Charity was the only place he was allowed to work. His mother had done her work well. He felt the guilt setting in over the angry way he had handled the situation.

A few seconds later, the tires on his beat-up Porsche squealed loudly as it accelerated out of the driveway. One thing was sure...he needed a drink.

When he arrived at the curb in front of his apartment building, he was unusually tired. It had been a particularly stressful day in the Emergency Room, the traffic on the Interstate system had been worse than usual, and the experience with Joanna and Sam Kincaid had drained him. He could almost taste the beer in his refrigerator.

As he closed the car door and headed for the brick steps to the apartment entrance, a cheerful feminine voice from behind surprised him. He turned to see one of his neighbors, Susan Livingston, coming up the street toward him with a grocery bag in her hand.

Susan was a thirty three year old schoolteacher...fourth grade he thought he remembered her saying on another occasion. As usual, she wore glasses with big round lenses, her hair was bound tightly in a bun at the back of her head, and she had on very little makeup. She always wore clothes so loose that it was impossible to tell what kind of figure she had. The baggy, gray dress she had on today was no exception. Mark assumed her to be an old maid. She certainly looked like one.

"Hi Mark," she said with a smile that was surprisingly pretty for such a drab-looking person. "I haven't seen you for a while."

To be polite, he stopped and waited for her to catch up. "I see you've been shopping," he said as she arrived at his side. He thought about offering to carry the bag, but it didn't look very heavy, so he let it pass.

"Just a few things for one of the children's birthday party in my class tomorrow," she said. "Are you just getting home from work?"

He nodded his head. She didn't need to know about his detour to Joanna's house.

Suddenly, as they started up the steps, the curtains in the window to the left of the entrance moved ever so slightly.

"Did you see that?" he asked, stopping on the second step.

"See what?" Susan responded, stopping beside him.

"The curtains in that window just moved." He nodded his head in the direction of the window. "It's happened before."

"Oh, that's just Mrs. Grabosky. Don't worry about her. She doesn't mean any harm."

"What does she look like? I may have seen her the other day."

"She's a short, plump, little old lady with gray hair…about sixty five or so." Susan responded. "She wears glasses with real thick lenses, and lots of red rouge."

"That's her. She was sweeping the hallway when I came home from work. We spoke briefly, then I went on my way. Strange though, she knew my name and knew that I was a doctor at Charity."

"She makes it her business to know about everyone," Susan responded. "We refer to her as the resident snoop."

"We?"

"The other tenants and I."

"Sounds like a pretty strange old woman to me," he said as they walked up the remaining steps.

He gave a last glance at Mrs. Grabosky's window, then held the door open for Susan and followed her in. She stopped in front of her apartment door and, juggling the bag of groceries in one arm, opened her purse to search for her keys.

"See you," he said, continuing to walk toward his apartment.

"Mark," she said quickly.

He turned to see what she wanted.

"Would you like to come in and have a cup of coffee?" she asked, holding her apartment key up. "I could make some in just a few minutes."

"No thanks," he replied, shaking his head. "I'm too tired. I just want to get in my apartment and prop my feet up."

She had asked him in for coffee twice before. Fortunately, he had been able to come up with excuses to decline. Today, it wasn't coffee he wanted.

"Maybe some other time," she said dejectedly.

"Maybe," he responded, but he doubted it. He figured that having coffee with Susan had to be a pretty boring experience. Besides, she seemed too together to get her involved in his crappy life.

Entering the main room of his small apartment...a combination living room, dining room, and kitchen...he eyed the dirty dishes with food dried on them stacked in a haphazard pile on the counter near the sink. An empty pizza box sat on a cheap breakfast table that occupied the same side of the room. At the other end, a wooden coffee table cluttered with copies of Sports Illustrated and empty coffee mugs sat in front of a worn, gray couch. Days ago he had promised himself he would clean the place up first chance he got. It needed it now worse than ever.

He walked to the kitchen area, took a Bud Light out of the refrigerator, and quickly gulped down half of it. Then he walked to the coffee table, cleared out a spot, and sat the beer in it. There was still broken glass to clean up, but he would do that later.

He picked up the two-day-old newspaper from the overstuffed chair, still rolled up and bound tightly by a rubber band, and tossed it at the garbage can. It hit the rim with a thud, bounced a foot into the air, and landed on the floor next to the over-turned can.

"Damn," he muttered to himself. "That's the way things have gone all day."

Raymond and the children arrived in Audrey's hospital room. Wearing blue jeans and a white T-shirt, Raymond was short and stocky, not much taller than Audrey. His sandy hair was close-cropped, and he was handsome in a boyish kind of way. He sat in the chair by the side of Audrey's bed and took her hand in his. Betty Sue and Clinton sat quietly on the small sofa on the other side of the bed next to the wall, their eyes fixed on Audrey. Betty Sue was petite and blonde, with a trim adolescent figure. Clinton, on the other hand, was a miniature of his father.

Audrey had put on her best gown…a pink one with a little blue ribbon at the bodice, fixed her short brown hair, and put on makeup. She wanted to look her best for Raymond. He had called her earlier in the day with good news. He had been hired…a good job, paying almost as much as he had made at Winthrop Steel. She was ecstatic. They would go out and celebrate tomorrow evening.

"What did the doctor say?" Raymond asked, looking at her chest in the area of the left breast.

"It's good news," Audrey replied. "Dr. Wilson said that I don't have cancer. It was just a fatty tumor."

"Does that mean he didn't take your breast?"

She gave him a weak smile. "I'm still intact."

"I'm glad," he said without a lot of emotion in his voice. Then he bent over and gave her a quick peck on the cheek.

She wished he would be more demonstrative in showing his love for her, but she understood. That was just the way he was. She loved him and she knew he loved her. It didn't have to be said.

Betty Sue was so relieved that she almost cried. Clinton still didn't understand what was going on, but he was happy that his mother was okay.

"When can you come home, momma?" he asked. "I don't like it when you're not there."

"In the morning," she replied. "How did you all do today without me?"

"I cooked dinner tonight," Betty Sue said. "Daddy said it was real good."

Audrey smiled. "I'm sure it was. You're going to make some lucky man a good wife one of these days."

"Oh momma. Why do you say things like that?" Betty Sue said, blushing.

"Because it's the truth," Audrey responded proudly.

The four of them talked for an hour or so more, mostly about plans for the future.

"Time to go," Audrey said finally. "I love you all very much, but I'm very tired and I need to rest. Besides, Betty Sue you've got to practice your routines. With tryouts for the cheerleading team coming up Monday, you need all the practice you can get." Betty Sue had almost made the team last year. Audrey was positive that she would make it this time. "And Clinton, you have to work on your library project. You know it's due Monday." He had been working on the project for several days. Audrey had read what he had done so far and been impressed with how good it was. He was bound to get an A.

"Can't we stay just a little longer?" Raymond asked, not wanting to leave her alone again.

Audrey smiled and shook her head. As usual, he would do what she wanted. He kissed her good-bye and gently hugged her, being careful not to press against her sore breast.

"I'll come and get you in the morning right after breakfast," he said.

Betty Sue and Clinton stood and each in turn hugged their mother. Then they left the room with their father.

Audrey reached up and pulled the string that turned the light off over the head of the bed. Lying there in the dark she thought about going home in the morning. The children needed her. Betty Sue could pretty well take care of herself. She had learned to cook and to wash and iron clothes, but she was just beginning to date. She relied on Audrey for advice. Clinton, on the other hand, still depended on her a lot...more than he should, Raymond had said to her a hundred times. But he was her youngest and she enjoyed spoiling him.

For the first time, she noticed how quiet it was for a hospital. No one had been in her room for over an hour. She was thankful for the time to be alone. It had been a long day. She needed the peace and quiet. She thought about all the housework that would have to be done when she got home. Betty Sue would have to help her more than usual because she wouldn't be able to use her left arm for a while. Clinton could help to, doing small things like emptying the wastebaskets. She doubted that Raymond would be of much help. He detested housework. Besides, now he had his new job to think about.

Finally feeling sleepy, she closed her eyes and tried to relax. Just as she was about to doze off, she felt her heart flutter. It frightened her so badly she sat upright in the bed and pressed her hand to her chest.

The flutter disappeared as quickly as it had come. She felt relieved. Just my nerves, she reasoned. She lay back on the bed and again closed her eyes.

Then her heart stopped beating.

CHAPTER FOUR

"I want to thank you for coming in so early on Monday morning with such a short notice. We may have a problem," Billingsworth said, sitting at the head of the heavy, oak conference table. As usual, his attire was superb, perfectly color coordinated down to the red handkerchief in his breast pocket and his red tie. One by one he looked at the three other individuals seated around the table.

Marvin Lowenstein, in a gray business suit, was short, overweight, and chain-smoked. His direct approach tended to irritate people, but he was efficient and very cost conscious. As a result, he was a real asset to the hospital and, as Assistant Hospital Director, was next in line for Billingsworth's job. He could hardly wait to get it.

Kate Anderson, dressed in a starched white nursing uniform, was middle-aged, overweight, and suffered from a number of health problems...high blood pressure, stomach ulcers, and an irritable colon. Most of the people who knew her blamed her health problems on her job. As Director of Nursing Service, the stress of trying to staff a hospital that was almost impossible to staff kept her under a lot of pressure. Her major fault was talking too much. She never met a secret she didn't like, or kept.

Dr. Jack Jackson, who had been elected Chief of the Medical Staff because no one else wanted the job, was tall and thin as a rail, had a high opinion of himself, and lacked patience with anything that required a majority vote. Because of his physical appearance, the nurses, behind his back, referred to him as Icabod Crane. Having come straight from the Surgery Suite, he wore a green scrub suit, cap, and shoe covers. A green surgical mask hung from his neck by two of its four strings. He detested meetings like this one because they took him away from his surgery practice. He usually considered them a waste of time. Mrs. Anderson didn't make any attempt to hide the fact that she thought he was a pompous ass.

Billingsworth continued. "A patient in our hospital, an Audrey Touchstone, died of a cardiac arrest Friday night. She had had an excisional breast biopsy earlier in the day. The surgery went fine and there wasn't any problem with the anesthetic…she just up and died. There was absolutely no reason why this woman should have passed away. Her husband agreed to an autopsy. Maybe that will turn up something."

"Why did you get us all here this early in the morning to tell us that some patient died? Hell, they die all the time from something or other," Dr. Jackson said authoritatively. "I admit it's rare for a young, healthy patient to have a cardiac arrest and die. But it happens."

"It's not just this patient alone. I've had a feeling for some time that we've been having more than our share of cardiac arrests. I had Marvin come in yesterday and run off some data for us. The cardiac arrest rate for this past year was up fifteen percent over previous years."

"Why do you think the increased rate is a problem?" Dr. Jackson asked, impatiently looking at his watch.

"I don't know for a fact that it actually is a problem," Billingsworth answered. "It just seems odd that the number of cardiac arrests has increased so much after being stable for several years. I'm deeply trouble by what happened to the Touchstone woman. She was a mother of two. You can imagine how her family took it."

"Do you think they'll sue?" Dr. Jackson asked.

"I'm not concerned about that right now," Billingsworth replied. "I'm concerned about human life."

"Do you think someone is doing something to patients intentionally? Like euthanasia," Mrs. Anderson asked.

Billingsworth suddenly looked alarmed. "I certainly hope not," he said quickly. "That hadn't occurred to me."

"There's been a couple of cases of euthanasia reported in the news over the past few years," Mrs. Anderson continued. "You know what I mean…nurses who considered themselves angels of mercy going around hospitals killing terminally ill patients."

"Don't be ridiculous," Dr. Jackson said. "Who would want to do that at Charity?"

"You never know," Mrs. Anderson replied. "I doubt if any of the other hospitals expected anything like that to happen."

"Dr. Jackson's right," Billingsworth said. "You're jumping to conclusions. For one thing, the Touchstone lady was young…thirty nine years old, and she was hardly terminally ill."

Dr. Jackson brushed back a lock of salt-and-pepper hair that periodically fell down over his right eye. "Let's not make a bigger deal out of this woman's death than it actually is. One death doesn't prove anything."

"That's true," Billingsworth replied. "But there's still the problem of the increased cardiac arrest rate. How do you explain that?"

"It's probably just a chance occurrence," Dr. Jackson responded. "Hell, who knows, next year it may go back down."

"Or it could go up even more," Mrs. Anderson said quickly. Then she turned to Billingsworth. "What do you think we should do?"

"I don't know," Billingsworth answered. "That's why I called this meeting. Do any of you have any suggestions?"

After a few seconds of silence, Lowenstein spoke up. "I think we should try to pinpoint the problem better. We need more specific data."

Billingsworth shifted his weight in the chair. "What do you have in mind?"

"It might help to know which units the increase in cardiac arrests occurred on, and during which shifts. You know, to look for a pattern."

"Can you get that data for us?" Billingsworth asked.

Lowenstein leaned back in his chair. "No problem. We already have it. We just have to extract it from the main body of data. I'll put one of my people on it right away."

Billingsworth cleared his throat. "How long will it take?"

"We should have it in a day or so."

"Good," Billingsworth said. Then he paused. "Dr. Jackson, do you or Mrs. Anderson have anything to add?"

Neither responded.

"Okay then, let's meet back here when Marvin has the information ready for us. In the meantime, I suggest we keep this to ourselves."

———————

Mark was seeing his third patient of the morning, an elderly man with shoulder pain, when Mattie stuck her head in the door.

"Phil Overstreet is here to see you," she said discretely.

Mark took a deep breath and exhaled forcefully. "That's all I need, another interruption," he muttered disgustedly. He left the examination room and re-entered the central area. Overstreet stood by the Nurses' Station wearing a wrinkled, white lab coat that should have been put in the dirty-clothes hamper days ago. At sixty-five years of age, he had been director of Clinical Laboratory Services longer than most people could remember. He was scheduled to retire at the end of the year. Those who worked for him could hardly wait. Periodically, unannounced, he came to the Emergency Room looking for Mark.

As Mark approached him, Overstreet held out a small plastic container. "Time to pee in the bottle, doc," he said loudly.

At first, Overstreet's lack of tact had embarrassed him, but he had gotten use to it, since everyone who worked in the Emergency Room now was aware of why he came. Mark took the bottle and, as per routine, headed back to the Doctors' Office where he entered the small bathroom. Overstreet followed him and stood just outside the open door so that he could see in. Mark filled the bottle with urine, placed the cap on it, and handed it to him.

"Thanks doc. See you next time," Overstreet said as he left the office with the urine sample in his hand.

Mark breathed a sigh of relief. Thank God he hadn't drunk in the past twenty-four hours. If alcohol were to show up on his drug screen, he would be in deep shit. He would have to be more careful from now on.

———————————

As Mark re-entered the Emergency Room, motion suddenly drew his attention to the stretcher entrance.

"Hit the floor," a tall black man in a red ski mask yelled loudly as he stepped through the door. A second man, a shorter Caucasian wearing a blue ski mask, quickly entered the Emergency Room from the door that led from the main part of the hospital. Both waved their automatic weapons at the assortment of nurses, orderlies, and patients. The red-masked gunman pointed his AK-47 assault rifle at the ceiling and squeezed the trigger.

BAM-BAM-BAM

A patient to Mark's right screamed. A nurse in front of him fainted. "What the hell!" another nurse exclaimed. Then everyone hit the floor. Mark sprawled on the floor at the back of the room. The last thing he wanted to do was to argue with someone who had an assault rifle in his hand. He had both gunmen in clear view, and he could see Mattie lying about ten feet in front of him.

"Where's the head nurse?" the red-masked gunman demanded.

Mattie didn't move a muscle, and she didn't answer. Mark glanced nervously around the room, wondering where the hell hospital security was.

"Who's the head nurse?" red-mask demanded again, this time more loudly.

Mattie still didn't respond. The room was so quiet you could hear a pin drop.

"Now damn it, either you identify yourself, or I'm going to start shooting nurses one at a time until you do," red-mask growled angrily. He walked to the nurse on the floor nearest him, a young black girl named Ruby who had graduated from nursing school only a few months earlier. Nudging her with his foot, he pointed the AK-47 at her head. "Ready to die?" he asked.

Ruby whimpered softly and closed her eyes.

Taking a deep breath, Mattie meekly raised her hand. Mark watched her anxiously, powerless to intervene.

Red-mask turned in her direction. "Get up!" he demanded.

Mattie's knees looked weak as she struggled to her feet. Mark thought about rushing the gunman, but decided it would mean certain death for him if he did. He continued to watch, detesting the helpless feeling it gave him.

Red-mask approached Mattie menacingly and reached for the key that hung loosely on a cord around her neck. She took a step backward as he grabbed the key and ripped it off.

"Get the drugs," he instructed, tossing the key to the blue-masked gunman who caught it in midair with one hand.

Turning back to Mattie, red-mask motioned for her to lie back down. She quickly complied. Mark breathed a sigh of relief that the gunman hadn't hurt her

Blue-mask entered the Nurses' Station, inserted the key in the lock, and opened the narcotic cabinet. Then he pulled a white pillowcase from his back pocket and hurriedly emptied the cabinet of its assortment of vials, pills, capsules, and preloaded syringes.

"Got it," he yelled to red-mask when he had finished.

Suddenly, red-mask turned and approached Mark. "You! Get up!" he said loudly.

Mark felt the barrel of the AK-47 press against his ribs. He held his breath, hoping the man wouldn't pull the trigger.

"Get up or I'll kill you on the spot!" Red-mask yelled, pushing the barrel harder against his ribs.

A cold sweat broke out on Mark's brow. His heart pounded hard in chest. "I'm getting up! I'm getting up!" he said hastily as he got to his feet.

The gun-barrel suddenly disappeared from his ribs, only to reappear almost immediately at his right temple. He was terrified. Was this where his life was to end?

Red-mask grabbed Mark's wrist, jerked it behind his back, then pushed it upward toward his shoulder blades. A sharp pain shot through his shoulder.

"Ouch!" he yelled. "Take it easy."

Red-mask eased the pressure a little. "Let's go," he demanded, pushing Mark in the direction of the stretcher entrance.

"You don't need me," Mark pleaded. "You've got the drugs. Let me go. I don't need this."

The automatic doors opened.

"Shut up! Maybe we need a hostage," red-mask said loudly. Then he stopped and turned back toward the people on the floor. "Stay exactly where you are for the next thirty minutes. One of us will be watching you. If you move, you're dead." He pushed Mark roughly through the open door. Blue-mask followed.

Red-mask shoved Mark toward a late model, Mercury Grand Marquis, illegally parked in the ambulance space. He opened the door, pushed him into the back seat, and got in after him. Blue-mask got in on the other side, then both doors slammed loudly.

"Let's go!" red-mask yelled to the driver, a tall, white man who wore a gray chauffeur's uniform and a gray mask.

The tires squealed as the car roared off down the street. Blue-mask produced a folded cloth from the pocket in the back of the seat in front of him, placed it over Marks eyes, and tied it in the back. Mark wondered what the hell was going on. Why would these men need a hostage? They had the drugs. That was what they came for.

Blue-mask shoved him to the floor and pressed his foot hard against his back "Stay there and keep quiet," he ordered.

Mark grunted in pain as his head hit the floorboard. He would comply with everything they ordered him to do. He didn't want to make them mad. He had the feeling that they wouldn't hesitate to kill him if he did. He listened in the dark to the three of them laughing at the thought of all those people lying on the floor of the Emergency Room, their foreheads perspiring and their hearts pounding as they thought about the imaginary gunman watching them.

———————

Vito Maldini leaned back in the chair behind his richly stained, cherry desk on the second floor of his brick and marble mansion and waited. The thin, red stripes of his dark-blue robe matched those of his light-blue, silk pajamas. He ran his hand through his gray-streaked, black hair and studied the ashes on the end of his cigar. Finally, he took a deep drag and blew a thick cloud of heavy smoke toward the ceiling. Then he stared at the black, push-button telephone in the center of the desk in front of him. The call was twenty minutes late.

The phone finally rang. Maldini sat upright in his chair, reached for the telephone, and held it to his ear. "Maldini here," he said.

"We got him boss. It was a piece of cake," the voice on the other end of the line said through the background static of a cellular car telephone.

"What took you so long? I've been waiting almost half an hour."

"Boss, you wouldn't believe the road construction around here. It's everywhere."

"Did you get the drugs?"

"Yeah, all of them."

"Were you careful not to leave any prints?"

"No problem. We wore gloves."

"What about Dr. Valentine? Is he okay?"

"Valentine's fine. Not a scratch."

"Okay. Now listen carefully. I want you to stop at one of those construction sites and get some bricks or a concrete block."

"For what?"

Maldini leaned forward over the desk. "Just listen and I'll tell you. I want you to weight the drug sack down with whatever you can find and toss it in the nearest river."

"But boss, this stuff is worth thousands of dollars on the street."

"I don't care about that. The drugs can be traced. I don't want any of them showing up around here. Do you understand? It could ruin everything."

"Yeah. I understand, but I don't like it."

"You don't have to like it. Just do as you're told."

Mark was thoroughly confused. Who were these masked men and how did they know his name? Why would they go to all of the trouble of stealing drugs at gunpoint and then dump them into a river, or at least most of them. He wasn't sure. He had heard the three of them arguing in whispered tones about whether or not they would keep some of the drugs for future sale behind their boss' back. He wasn't clear on what their final decision was, but he really didn't care. He was more interested in who this boss was that they had been talking to on the telephone, and what he wanted with him.

After fifteen minutes or so, the car stopped. He heard the back door to his left open, only moments later to close again. Then the car resumed its journey. He assumed that the weights for the sack had been obtained. He estimated that another fifteen minutes or so passed, then the car stopped again. The same back door opened.

"Bombs away," the voice of blue-mask said from outside the car, followed almost immediately by a splash.

"The Chattahoochee River," Mark speculated. "We have to be to the West of town."

Blue mask reentered the car, and it resumed its journey.

Another ten minutes or so passed, then, over the road noise from his place on the floorboard, Mark heard the faint hum of a small airplane flying low overhead. For a few minutes, he listened carefully. No jets. It had to be a small airport. Hartsfield-Atlanta International was one of the busiest airports in the world. The roar of large jets would be nonstop if they were there. They had to be near Brown Field to the west of town.

The car slowed, turned right, then came to a stop. Mark heard a plane take off nearby, followed by one of the back doors of the car opening, then the other one. Moments later, hands gripped his upper arms firmly and led him out of the car.

"What now?" he asked himself silently. This escapade was getting to be more bizarre by the moment.

"Okay, let's go," the voice of red-mask instructed.

The hands again gripped his upper arms on either side. He heard the hum of the car engine, then briefly smelled the acrid odor of exhaust fumes as the car drove off. After what he judged to be no more than three or four minutes, he heard the voice of red-mask speak again.

"Steps ahead."

As they started up the steps, Mark sensed that one man had moved ahead of him and the other one behind him. Four steps later, he felt a hand on the top of head push down gently.

"Watch your head," the voice of blue-mask instructed.

A medium size plane, Mark concluded, lowering his head.

The hands led him down the aisle, pushed him into a seat, and fastened his seatbelt. His mind was racing. Who the hell were these men? What did they want with him? Where were they taking him?

"Okay, let's get this thing off the ground," the voice of red-mask snarled.

"Yes sir," replied a new voice from up ahead.

The plane taxied out to the runway, stopped briefly, then revved up its engines.

A jet. A small jet, Mark surmised from the sound of the engines.

The plane accelerated down the runway, took off, and disappeared into the late afternoon sky.

CHAPTER FIVE

"How many of them were they?" the police detective in a brown, wrinkled suit asked, adjusting his glasses on his crooked nose.

Mattie studied his face. She assumed the stubble on his chin and his blood-shot eyes meant that he had been up all night chasing down leads on an important case. "I only saw two," she answered.

"That would make three, then. They would have had someone driving the get-away vehicle. Did you see what they were driving?" He scratched his head above his right ear with the blunt end of his pen.

"No sir. They told us to stay on the floor. They said they would kill us if we got up."

"So you stayed on the floor?"

"You're damn right I did. I wasn't ready to die."

"Describe the men for me. Were they black or white?"

Mattie thought for a moment. "The tall one in the red mask was black. He seemed to be in charge. The other man, the one in the blue mask, was white and shorter…about your height."

"What color were their eyes?" the detective asked.

"Their eyes? You've got to be kidding. I was scared to death they were going to kill me any second and you wanted me to check out their eyes? They had the biggest guns I've ever seen. That's the main thing I remember."

"You're safe now. You can relax."

"Tell that to my knees," Mattie responded. "Those men scared poor Ruby so bad she wet her pants. She had to go home to change her uniform."

The detective continued to scribble in his pad. "Did they take anything?"

"You mean besides Dr. Valentine."

"Yeah. Besides Dr. Valentine."

"They emptied the narcotics cabinet. Took every single drug."

"Don't let anyone touch the narcotic cabinet," the detective instructed. "The fingerprint man is on his way."

"Won't do any good." Mattie said emphatically.

"What do you mean?"

"They wore gloves."

"Sounds like a professional job. I've never heard of anyone hitting an emergency room for drugs. I hope this isn't the start of a trend. Tell me about the doctor."

"Dr. Valentine has been working here for three months. He's a real nice guy and a good doctor. I think he has a lot of problems though."

"What do you mean, problems?"

"You know, personal problems. He can be real moody."

"What kind of personal problems?"

"I don't know for sure, but I think he drinks too much," Mattie said. "He's never come to work drunk or anything like that, but ever once in a while I get the impression he has a hangover."

"Do you think he might be in on this escapade? It's strange that they took him."

"Dr. Valentine? You've got to be kidding. He's as honest as the day is long. They said they needed a hostage."

"Okay. Okay. I had to ask," the detective said quickly. "Is he married?"

"No. Divorced. He doesn't talk about it much. It's obvious that he still carries a big torch for her. Nobody knows why. Rumor has it she's a real bitch."

"Any children?"

"He has a daughter. Lisa's her name. She's thirteen now. Joanna, the ex-wife, has custody of her. She stuck her in some fancy school in the southern part of the state…Valdosta, I think. She didn't want Lisa cramping her style, if you know what I mean. He talks about Lisa a lot. You can tell he's really crazy about her. He brought her by here on one of his days off once. She's a beautiful girl, and so polite. I think Mark wanted to show her off."

"Mark?"

"Dr. Valentine."

"Oh!" he said, scratching his right ear with his pen. "How long did it take hospital security to get here?"

"Zachary Dorfman, the head of security, arrived almost immediately, but by that time the men were gone. The whole thing didn't take over five or six minutes. The masked men were in and out in a flash." She looked at him quizzically. "You look tired. Have you been working on an important case?"

"No. I've been on vacation in Vegas. Had a hell of a good time. Didn't get back home until midnight last night. If you hear from Valentine, please let us know immediately. Here's my card."

Mattie took the card and without looking at it put it in her pocket. "Do you think they'll hurt him?"

"I don't know. There's no way of telling at this point what they might do. It's obvious that they're dangerous. I suggest you pray for your doctor."

After what seemed like an eternity, the plane's engines changed pitch, then it began to descend. The gunman in back of him stopped snoring and began to stir in his seat. The one in front of him stretched and yawned loudly. Mark was tired of the game, and he was weary of the mask that obscured his vision. He leaned back in the seat and listened intently for any conversation that might give him a clue as to where they were taking him, and why. None occurred.

Ten minutes later, the plane touched down. The landing was smooth. The plane taxied briefly, then came to a stop. Hands led him down the steps into a waiting automobile and placed him in the center of the back seat. Then both back doors slammed, followed by the driver's door closing. He couldn't feel anyone's presence in the seat on either side of him. For a moment he thought that he was alone in the back, then he heard the voice of blue-mask off to his right.

"Let's go," the voice said. "I'm ready to get this job over with and get home"

"Same here. I hate these out of state jobs," red-mask's voice said to his left.

Strange. It sounded to Mark as if they were sitting across from each other. Then he realized that the three of them were in a limousine. The hands immediately pushed him to the floorboard again, this time not quite as roughly. He stayed there, content to be quiet for now. It had been a long trip, one that he assumed must soon be coming to an end. The limo zigzagged in and out of traffic for what he estimated to be about twenty minutes, stopping frequently for what he assumed to be traffic lights.

After what seemed like another fifteen minutes, the stops began to occur less and less frequently, and the limo picked up speed. After another period of time, at least as long as the first, the limo slowed and turned right. The sound of the tires on asphalt abruptly changed to that of tires on brick, then the limo stopped. Mark heard the sound of an electric motor running, followed by a metallic clank.

Entrance gates, he concluded.

The limo began to roll again. The sound of the tires on brick continued for what he judged to be another three hundred feet or so, then stopped again. He was sure that it wouldn't be long now.

Firm hands helped him out of the limo, led him up a brick sidewalk, and guided him up a set of steps. As the hot sun burned down on the back of his neck, the sweet smell of azalea blossoms floated through the air and filled his nostrils.

Someone opened a door and the hands led him through it into a much cooler environment. The hands ushered him up a flight of stairs and through another door. Then the hands let go and he stood there in the dark. Seconds later, he heard the door that they had just come through close behind him. He sensed that the two men who had escorted him into the room had left. The room smelled of cigar smoke.

"Take the blindfold off," an unfamiliar, gravelly voice instructed.

Someone in back of him removed the blindfold. He stood there squinting, trying to get use to the light. He blinked several times, then the hazy figure with intense, dark eyes sitting at a desk in front of him began to clear.

Appearing to be in his mid-fifties, the man's black hair was streaked with gray. He had a thin black mustache, and a large jagged scar crossed his chin. He looked familiar. Mark had seen his sinister-looking face somewhere before, but where?

"Who the hell are you, and what do you want with me?" Mark snapped, half afraid and half pissed.

The man rose, smoothed the brushed-silk lapels of his Armani suit coat, then extended his hand. "Dr. Valentine, I'm Vito Maldini. Welcome to Miami. I trust your trip wasn't too unpleasant."

Mark let his hand hang by his side. Maldini could go to hell as far as he was concerned. The name, like the face, had a ring of familiarity, but he couldn't place it either.

Maldini lowered his hand and stared at Mark. Mark ignored him for a moment, then turned and looked around the room. The largest black man he had ever seen stood by the door behind him with his arms crossed, his fierce-looking eyes fixed on him. The short sleeves of the giant's white, knit shirt strained to contain his massive biceps. A shoulder holster was strapped to the left side of his huge, muscular chest.

Trying his best not to appear apprehensive, Mark walked to the window and surveyed the immediate area. He and Joanna had vacationed in Miami a number of times. He wanted to see if he could identify a familiar landmark. Palm trees dotted the landscape around the grounds, and flowering plants of seemingly every color…reds, pinks, blues, yellows, whites…were scattered in beds about the immaculately trimmed lawn. A tall, black, metal fence surrounded the estate. Beyond the fence, nothing was familiar. He turned and walked back in Maldini's direction.

"I demand to know what the hell's going on?" he said angrily as he approached him. "Three hours ago I was at work minding my own business. Then your thugs grabbed me and drug me off down here. What do you want with me?"

"I intend to explain that in due time, Dr. Valentine," Maldini answered calmly. "But first I'd like for you to be my guest for dinner."

"You didn't go to all this trouble to have someone to eat with. I demand to know what's going on. Why am I here?"

"There's no point in being unpleasant," Maldini said. "You're here on business. I told you I would explain in due time, and I will."

"What if I don't want to wait?" Mark said loudly, taking a step in Maldini's direction. With a soft-looking body and being no more than five-feet ten inches tall, he was sure he could take him easily.

Suddenly, Mark felt a heavy hand grasp his left shoulder from behind and squeeze it hard. Then he felt a blunt object press against his lower back. He instantly froze. He knew he couldn't take Maldini's huge bodyguard, not even in his best days.

"Put the gun away Willie," Maldini instructed. "Dr. Valentine is our guest. I'm sure he'll cooperate."

Mark swallowed hard. He was way in over his head. He didn't have any choice but to cooperate. Besides, he was hungry.

To his relief, the gun barrel moved away from his back. He smiled nervously at Maldini. "What time do we eat?" he quipped. Turning his head, he glanced behind him. Willie had returned to his position by the door and recrossed his massive arms. He looked even more menacing than before.

"That's more like it," Maldini said. "We eat in thirty minutes. That will give you plenty of time to change."

"What do you mean, change? This scrub suit is it. You didn't give me time to pack."

"We've taken care of that," Maldini said, punching a button on his telephone.

"Yeah boss," came the voice from the speaker.

"Dr. Valentine is ready. Would you please show him to his room."

Mark dropped his head and stared at the floor. God, he wished he had a drink.

———————————

The salads had been devoured, and the main course...veal parmegianna, capellini primavera, and angel-hair pasta...was being served by an older gentlemen wearing a black tuxedo. Maldini sat just to Mark's right at the head of the twelve-place table. The other ten places were vacant. To Maldini's right, however, sat unattended a single place setting with a salad.

Mark didn't know much about china, but it was obvious to him that the china in front of them was expensive. The silver, in a Grande Baroque pattern, was exquisite. He had seen silver like it before, at Joanna's parent's house. It had belonged her mother's family, and to her mother's family before that.

When the elderly gentleman in the tux finished setting the plates with the main course on them on the table, he poured the wine...a perfectly aged Cabernet Sauvignon. Mark stared at Maldini. He knew he had seen him somewhere before. If only he could remember where, it might help explain what he was doing there.

"We'll be having another guest for dinner shortly," Maldini said, glancing at the place setting with the salad. "I trust you like Italian food, Dr. Valentine?"

"I do. It's one of my favorites," Mark said. He had the strangest feeling that Maldini already knew that. "How did you know what size suit I wear?" he asked. He had looked in the mirror in his room prior to coming to dinner and been impressed with how elegant he looked in the expensive, pinstriped suit that Maldini had supplied him. He had never been able to buy anything off the rack. If he bought a suit big enough in the shoulders, he always had to have it taken up in the waist. He had been surprised by the perfect fit.

"I have my sources," Maldini responded. "I know a lot about you…probably not as much as your mother, but a lot."

"Why do you find it necessary to know so much about me?" Mark asked.

"We'll get to that in a little bit. I prefer to finish dinner before we talk business." He rolled some angel-hair pasta around his fork and put it in his mouth.

From Maldini's demeanor, it was obvious to Mark that it wouldn't do any good to push him, so he didn't.

"Okay, if you won't tell me why I'm here, answer one question for me," Mark said. "It's something I've wondered about ever since you ordered the blindfold taken off. You even introduced yourself and told me that I was in Miami. Why the blindfold?"

"Eat up, Dr. Valentine. We can talk as we eat. Angela is always late. The food will be cold if we wait for her. She doesn't expect us to wait."

"The blindfold," Mark persisted. He took a large sip of wine from the Waterford crystal and followed it with a bite of veal parmegianna. The veal was excellent. So was the wine. He took an even larger drink.

"Oh yes, the blindfold," Maldini responded. "I was wondering if you would ask about it. It wasn't to keep you from seeing where you were going. If you had asked, my men would have told you."

"Then, why?"

"Very simple. I'm sure that if you thought about it a little longer you could figure it out." Maldini took a bite of capellini primavera. "The men, Dr. Valentine, the men."

"You didn't want me to be able to recognize them."

Maldini leaned forward over the table. "Correct. Those are three of my best men. I rely on them for all my important dirty work."

"I still don't understand. Why is it so important that I not be able to recognize them?"

"It's simple. I might need them again someday. If we do business and then you double-cross me, it would be to my advantage for them to be just faces in the crowd."

"What do you mean by that?"

"They could be walking right behind you anywhere and you wouldn't know it. A quick thrust of a knife or a shot from a gun with a silencer and you would be history."

A chill ran up Mark's spine. He quickly took a large gulp of wine, then another. Who the hell was this guy? What did he want with him? He wanted to demand again that Maldini tell him what was going on, but he said that he would tell him in his own time, and it was clear to Mark that he meant it. He didn't have a choice. He would have to wait.

Suddenly the door swung open and a tall, striking woman wearing a tight, ankle-length, black cocktail dress entered the room. Appearing to be in her late twenties, her skin was smooth and lightly tanned and her shapely body was perfectly proportioned. Her dark, almost black hair was beautifully thick and had a silver luster. The central diamond in her platinum necklace had to be at least five karats. Matching diamond earrings dangled from her ears. She glided to the table and stood by Maldini, her arm draped around his shoulders.

"Angela, this is Dr. Valentine," Maldini said.

Her eyes met Mark's.

We should have waited, he thought. This woman is worth waiting for.

"Pleased to meet you Dr. Valentine," she said, extending her hand.

Mark stood and shook it. "Call me Mark," he stammered.

Maldini rose and pulled the chair out for her. She eased into it, then took a bite of salad.

"Is he going to do it?" she asked.

"We haven't discussed it yet. We're saving it until after dinner," Maldini answered. Then he sat back down.

Mark too took his seat.

"I wish you didn't have to do it," Angela said. "I'm worried."

"We've discussed that, and we're not going to go through it again. If it weren't necessary, I wouldn't do it," Maldini responded, a little irritated.

Mark's eyes were fixed on Angela. She was one of the most beautiful women he had ever seen. He was oblivious to the conversation.

After dinner, Maldini and Mark settled in the study to talk. To Mark's disappointment, Angela graciously excused herself. He lit a cigarette. Normally, he would have asked permission first, but he didn't think Maldini deserved the courtesy.

"Dr. Valentine, it's time to talk business," Maldini said.

"It's about time," Mark responded. "So why am I here?" He took a drag on his cigarette and blew a puff of smoke into the air.

"Well, you've probably seen me on TV, or read about me in the newspaper," Maldini replied. "If you have, you know I've got major, legal problems."

Then it came to him…this guy's a crook, the head of organized crime in south Florida. He had seen him on the evening news a week ago. Maldini had been coming out of a federal courthouse with a bunch of lawyers. The newscaster said that he'd just been indicted by a federal grand jury.

"Are you guilty?" Mark asked.

Maldini leaned back and crossed his legs. "That's beside the point. My legal counsel tells me that if my case goes to trial, I don't have a chance."

"What are you charged with?" Mark asked, trying unsuccessfully to remember what the newscaster had said.

"It's no secret…racketeering, money laundering, attempting to bribe a federal judge, you name it."

"Apparently you've been pretty hard to nail in the past. Why can't you beat this rap too?"

"It's not that easy. The feds have a witness…one of my most trusted men. I passed him over for a big promotion in the organization for someone he felt to be less qualified than him…my nephew Vinny. It really pissed him off. Now he wants revenge. He knows enough to put me away for life. The feds have him so well protected that an army couldn't get to him."

"So what does that have to do with me?"

"Everything. My only chance to stay out of prison is to change my identity and get out of the country. My face is too recognizable. I need a new one."

Now everything made sense. The drug heist was just a ploy. That's why his men dumped the drug sack in the river. He gave Maldini a stern look. "What if I refuse to cooperate?"

"I don't believe you will. I'm prepared to offer you $100,000 in cash for the job."

For a moment Mark was tempted. He badly needed money. Then he came to his senses. If he got messed up in Maldini's attempt to avoid prosecution, he would never get his license back. And besides, he could end up with legal problems of his own. He didn't know what the penalty was for helping someone like Maldini avoid prosecution, but he was sure it was substantial, and he didn't want any part of it.

"Well, Dr. Valentine, I need an answer. What's it going to be?"

Mark shook his head from side to side. "I don't think so. I've got problems of my own. Getting involved with you could only make them worse."

"Well then, I'm prepared to make you my back-up offer."

"What do you mean, backup offer?"

"By the way, how's Lisa doing in school?" Maldini asked, suddenly changing the subject. "My men tell me that she's an excellent student. I understand she's a good tennis player too…just like her mother."

"What does Lisa have to do with this?" Mark asked, startled that Maldini had brought her name up.

"My back-up offer, Dr. Valentine. If you do the surgery, I'll let your daughter live. One of my best men is just dying to meet her. He's never killed a pretty, young girl before."

Mark swallowed hard. "Keep Lisa out of this," he blurted out. "She's just a child. She doesn't know anything about you or your dirty dealings."

"That's up to you. I play rough, and I'll do anything to stay out of prison."

Mark didn't doubt it. Now that he knew who Maldini was, he was aware that his reputation for ruthlessness was legend. There was no way of knowing how many men he had killed personally, and how many more he had ordered killed. Mark knew he didn't have a choice. He would have to do the surgery.

"When do I do it?" he asked.

"Tomorrow. The sooner we get started, the sooner I can get out of the country and get on with my new life."

"Will Angela go with you?"

"Why do you ask?"

"Just curious."

"Gorgeous isn't she? I've known her since she was ten years old. She's the daughter of one of my old buddies. We've been going together ever since my wife died. Maybe I'll marry her someday, then maybe not."

For the life of him, Mark couldn't understand what someone as attractive as Angela saw in Maldini. Not only was he a lot older than she, and not particularly good looking, he was a snake. No ethics at all. His philosophy was to do whatever it took to get what he wanted…no consideration for others, no conscience. Getting in his way could be very hazardous to your health. Mark shifted in his chair. "I can't just operate," he said. "It's not that simple. Someone has to put you to sleep and monitor your vital signs to keep you alive from the anesthetic. That requires some pretty fancy equipment. Someone else has to assist me in surgery. I can't operate alone."

"No problem. I've thought of all that. My niece is a nurse anesthetist at Miami General. She will put me to sleep. She has a friend who is a surgical scrub nurse. She will assist you. They will be paid handsomely for their work. As for the equipment, we haven't spared a dime. You'll have the best equipment money can buy."

"It sounds like you've thought of everything."

"I have. This has been planned carefully. I can't afford any slip-ups. You operate on me in the morning, and we will have you back in Atlanta by tomorrow evening."

"What about the police? They're going to ask me where I've been."

Maldini uncrossed his legs and leaned forward. "That shouldn't be a problem. Why do you think we took the drugs?"

"I don't know. When it happened I thought it was just a drug heist."

"Precisely. It was supposed to look like a drug heist. That gave my men an excuse to abduct you as a hostage. When the police ask, you tell them that it was just that, a drug heist, and that your abductors decided to hold you for ransom until they discovered that you could hardly make your rent every month. Tell them that when your abductors found out you weren't worth a dime, they let you go. You couldn't identify the men who took you because they wore masks at first, then they kept you blindfolded after that. You have no idea what they look like, nor where they took you. The police can't prove otherwise. Cross me and you're dead."

When the conversation ended, Mark excused himself and retired to his room. The bed covers were turned back, and a maroon robe and pair of blue pajamas were folded neatly on a chair in the corner of the room.

He took a shower, put on the pajamas, and crawled into bed. Before his downfall he had been a damned good plastic surgeon. He had performed plastic surgery of one type or another on the wife of the wealthiest man in Georgia, a United States Congresswoman from Alabama, and a state Supreme Court justice from Louisiana. His reputation as a highly skilled plastic surgeon had spread, and people had come from all over the southeastern United States to see him, some from even further away. Tomorrow would be an interesting day. He looked forward to doing plastic surgery again, even if it was on a crook like Maldini.

CHAPTER SIX

"Adjust the light a little to the left," Mark instructed, his eyes peering from above the green surgical mask. Maldini had transformed the room into a first-rate operating room. Beverly, the scrub nurse, reached up a gloved hand and gently adjusted the surgical light. Maldini lay on the operating table covered up to his neck with green, surgical drapes. A plastic cap covered his head. Beverly had already shaved his face, including his mustache and temples, and swabbed the entire area with an antiseptic. For protection, she now carefully taped his eyes closed...first the right, then the left.

Leta, Maldini's nurse-anesthetist niece, sat on a stool at the head of the table. She had administered the anesthetic...an oxygen and fluorothane mixture...and removed the mask from Maldini's mouth and nose. She would periodically replace it during the operation to keep his blood-anesthetic level within a narrow range. Too low and he would begin to wake up and feel the lancinating pain of the scalpel cutting through the tissues of his face. Too high and he would quit breathing, or his heart would stop beating. She stared at the electronic monitors to her left, carefully watching Maldini's blood pressure, heart rate, respiratory rate, and an electrocardiogram tracing of his heart rhythm, ready to spring into action with a multitude of life-saving medications should any of his vital signs change precariously.

The three of them, Mark, Beverly, and Leta, wore surgical gowns over their matching scrub suits. Their uneasy eyes were visible between the surgical masks and caps. Because Mark hadn't met the two women before they dressed and entered the room, he couldn't tell much about what they looked like. Leta was the taller of the two and had Maldini's, piercing dark eyes. She stood across the operating table from Beverly who was shorter and somewhat heavier than Leta, and had sleepy-looking, gray eyes. He estimated that both women were in their early to mid-thirties. A tray with all the necessary surgical instruments sat on a stand to Beverly's right. They all stared at Maldini's expressionless face.

Mark reviewed in his mind the surgical procedures he would perform over the next six or seven hours. First, he would break Maldini's nose and straighten its Romanesque curve. He would also narrow the tip of the nose. The surgical instruments would be inserted through an incision on the inside of the nostrils so that a visible scar would not be left. Next, he would make an incision in each of the upper eyelids and remove the excess skin and fat that drooped slightly over the outer aspect of Maldini's eyes. He would then repeat the procedure beneath the eyes. Then he would make horizontal incisions in the wrinkle lines in his forehead just above his eyebrows and raise his sagging eyebrows. Next, using a Teflon graft, he would extend Maldini's chin about three-eight's of an inch. Then he would revise the large, jagged scar on his chin so that only a thin, almost invisible, line remained. Finally, he would make incisions in the temporal areas on each side, just above where the hair line had been before it was shaved, and pull the loose skin up tight, eliminating the major facial wrinkles and sagging neck skin. When he was through, even Maldini's mother would have trouble recognizing him.

"Scalpel," Mark said, holding out his hand, palm up.

Beverly reached to the surgical tray, picked up a scalpel, and placed it in his hand.

Billingsworth, Lowenstein, Mrs. Anderson, and Dr. Jackson took their seats around the same conference table in the seats they had occupied the previous day.

"I just got the preliminary autopsy report on Audrey Touchstone," Billingsworth said. "I had hoped that the autopsy would turn up an intrinsic heart defect to explain her death, like the accessory conduction pathway of Wolf-Parkinson-White syndrome. It didn't. Her heart was absolutely normal."

"Like I said before, it's unfortunate, but deaths do sometimes occur without an obvious cause," Dr. Jackson offered quickly.

"We all know that," Billingsworth responded. "This one case may not mean much by itself, but when the overall cardiac arrest rate increases by fifteen percent, we have to be concerned." He turned to Lowenstein who had a stack of papers scattered out on the table in front of him. "Marvin, what have you got for us?"

Lowenstein shuffled his papers. "I've got some real interesting information. But first, let me refresh your memories. You will recall that at our last meeting I reported that the cardiac arrest rate was up fifteen percent this past year. I arrived at that figure by comparing the rate for this past year to the three previous years, years in which the cardiac arrest rate was stable. Since our last meeting I have looked at the cardiac arrests for all three shifts for this past year...seven AM to three PM, three PM to eleven PM, and eleven PM to seven AM...and subtracted off the baseline cardiac arrests for each shift."

"Baseline cardiac arrests. What the hell are baseline cardiac arrests?" Dr. Jackson asked impatiently.

"I'm getting to that, if you will just give me time," Lowenstein responded, obviously irritated. "Baseline cardiac arrests are the averages of the cardiac arrests that occurred during each shift for the three years previous to this last one. The differences between the cardiac arrests for this past year and the average for the previous three years are the excess cardiac arrests for each shift...the ones that shouldn't have occurred.

The majority of the excess cardiac arrests occurred in the three PM to eleven PM and eleven PM to seven AM shifts, about equally distributed. Hardly any occurred during the seven AM to three PM shift."

"Isn't that kind of strange?" Mrs. Anderson asked. "Why wouldn't they be spread out over all three shifts?"

"It's real strange," Dr. Jackson replied. "If they were random occurrences, they should have been spread equally throughout all three shifts."

Billingsworth looked worried. "Do you think someone is doing something to patients to cause them to have cardiac arrests?"

"I didn't say that," Dr. Jackson replied. "I just said that I don't believe the pattern Mr. Lowenstein presented could have occurred by chance."

"How else would you explain the data other than someone purposefully causing the problem?" Billingsworth asked.

"I can't explain it," Dr. Jackson replied. "But surely there's a logical explanation. I can't believe someone would go around this hospital killing patients."

Billingsworth looked around the table. "Does anyone else have any thoughts about how this pattern could have occurred?" Everyone shook their heads.

"It might help to know what time during the shifts the cardiac arrests occurred," Mrs. Anderson offered.

"Why would we want to know that?" Dr. Jackson asked.

"Well, a shift on the floors is eight hours long," Mrs. Anderson replied. "Are the excess cardiac arrests distributed throughout the shift, or do they occur at some particular time, say at the beginning of the shift, in the middle of the shift, or at the end of it? The cardiac arrests could correlate with the times that people, other than nursing staff, are on the units, such as respiratory therapists or lab technicians."

Dr. Jackson rolled his eyes back in his head and looked disgusted. "It's obviously a nurse," he said sarcastically.

Mrs. Anderson narrowed her eyes, leaned forward, and started to respond.

Sensing the tension, Billingsworth cut her off. "Mrs. Anderson is absolutely right. The more information we look at the better chance we'll have of figuring out what's going on."

Dr. Jackson sat up straight in his chair. "Well, until we come up with another explanation, I think we're going to have to proceed under the assumption that we have a killer loose in the hospital, quite possibly a nurse."

Mrs. Anderson rolled her chair back from the table. "I resent that! Every time something bad happens around a hospital, everyone assumes that it's a nurse's fault. Your killer could just as well be an orderly, or for that matter a doctor."

"Come now Mrs. Anderson. Surely you don't believe a doctor would do such a thing," Dr. Jackson retorted.

"It wouldn't be the first time a doctor killed a patient, although I grant you most of the time, when it occurs, it's the result of negligence."

Billingsworth cleared his throat loudly. "Where do we go from here?" he asked quickly.

Lowenstein shuffled his papers again. "I can break the data down further if you wish."

"That's a good idea," Billingsworth replied. "We need to know how the excess cardiac arrests relate to staffing patterns…nurses, orderlies, and anyone else employed by the hospital."

"What about doctors?" Mrs. Anderson asked.

"Good question," Lowenstein replied. "What about doctors?"

"Marvin, you know very well we don't keep records on what time doctors make their rounds," Billingsworth responded. "The only way we could get that information would be to search all of the charts in medical records for the recorded times the doctors wrote progress notes or orders. That would be an enormous task. I think we should go with further analyzing the data we already have. We can always come back to doctors if we run into a dead end."

Everyone agreed.

Billingsworth looked more relaxed. "Good. Then I suggest we meet back here as soon as Marvin has the data for us."

As everyone stood to leave the room, Billingsworth quickly spoke up. "See you at the party Saturday afternoon."

As they left the room, each individual commented on how much they looked forward to it.

———————————

Six and a half hours after Mark began Maldini's surgery, it neared completion. Things had progressed as planned, without complications. Fatigue showed in Leta and Beverly's faces. Mark was getting pretty weary himself. He continued to place fine sutures close together in Maldini's skin to minimized scar formation. Suddenly, Leta jumped up.

"Ventricular tachycardia," she yelled.

The monitors had gone wild. Maldini's heart rate jumped to 200, his respiratory rate doubled, his blood pressure dropped sharply, and the normally narrow QRS complexes of the electrocardiogram became wide and bizarre. Mark instantly thought about Willie, the huge black man with the gun standing just outside the closed door, probably with his arms crossed. He was sure that Maldini had instructed Willie to kill him promptly if anything went wrong with the surgery. Beads of sweat burst out on his forehead. His heart skipped a beat.

Leta quickly drew a syringe full of Lidocaine and injected a bolus of it into the plastic tubing that led to the needle in the vein in the back of Maldini's hand. Mark held his breath as he watched the EKG tracing move across the screen of the monitor. The bizarre pattern didn't change.

"Damn," Leta said under her breath. She rapidly drew another syringe full of Lidocaine and injected it into the plastic tubing. A second passed, then two, then three. They all looked at Maldini, then at each other. The horror of moment showed in the eyes of the two women, and Mark assumed his as well. He looked back at the EKG tracing and followed the bizarre pattern as it again moved from left to right across the screen. Still no response to the Lidocaine.

"Normalize, damn it," he said loudly, beginning to feel that the situation might be hopeless.

Then abruptly, half way across the screen, the cardiac rhythm snapped back to a normal pattern. Mark took a deep breath and sighed in relief. Leta sat back down and wiped the sweat from her forehead with her sleeve. Beverly finished her silent prayer. Maldini would live. So would he.

Fifteen minutes later, Mark pulled his surgical gloves off and tossed them on the floor in the corner of the room. He could hardly wait to get out of the room and light a cigarette. Beverly cleaned the blood off Maldini's face, being careful around the fine sutures. Leta turned off the anesthetic mixture, but continued to monitor Maldini's vital signs. He would be awake in twenty minutes. One of his henchmen had obtained an ample supply of Dilaudid tablets from a street pusher so that the drug, normally tightly controlled by the Drug Enforcement Administration, couldn't be traced. Maldini would feel no pain. Mark expected soon to be blindfolded again, escorted back to the airport, and board the waiting jet for the flight back to Atlanta as Maldini had promised.

Mark awoke from a sound sleep as the Lear slowed and began its descent into Atlanta. The flight so far had been uneventful. The men who had abducted him were still somewhere in Miami. As a result, it hadn't been necessary for him to be blindfolded. The pilot had closed the cockpit door so that he was alone. It gave him time to reflect on his situation. No doubt about it, he was in big trouble. He had just gotten involved with an underworld figure who didn't put much value on human existence. His life was continuing its downhill spiral. He wondered where it would all end.

Leaning back in the seat, he thought about what he would tell Mattie and the others in the Emergency Room in the morning, and he felt nervous about his inevitable encounter with the police. He decided that he would do exactly as Maldini had instructed him to do...tell them that he had been taken hostage and that he couldn't identify any of his abductors because they wore masks at first, then they blindfolded him. No one who knew him would have any trouble believing that his abductors elected not to hold him for ransom because he didn't have any money. Maldini was right. They couldn't prove any different.

Mark was proud of the job he had done on Maldini's face. Maldini would look like an entirely different person when the incisions healed and the swelling abated. At the same time, he felt depressed because it reminded him of the profession he had loved and lost, possibly forever.

Strangely, he looked forward to returning to Miami in a week to remove Maldini's bandages and take out the sutures. He wasn't sure why. Maybe it was to inspect his handiwork, or maybe it was the possibility of seeing Angela again. He regretted that he hadn't been able to see her again before leaving. He wondered what she saw in Maldini. She could have most any man she wanted. It didn't make sense. He decided that both reasons for being excited about returning to Miami were good ones.

Through the window to his left, as the plan settled into its approach to Brown Field, the Georgia Dome, Six Flags Over Georgia, and Fulton County Stadium came into view. In the distance, through the window to his right, he could see the carved figures of Jefferson Davis, Stonewall Jackson, and Robert E. Lee in Stone Mountain. The beginnings of the Blue Ridge Mountains were visible further to the northeast. Ten minutes later, the plane touched down. He had never been so glad to get back home in all his life.

When he arrived at his apartment, he sat on the sofa and propped his feet up on the cluttered coffee table. Just as he reached for a copy of

Sports Illustrated, the telephone rang. He picked it up and held it to his ear. "Mark Valentine," he said.

"Mark, this is Daniel...Daniel Iverson."

Mark was pleasantly surprised. He hadn't talked with Daniel since the day after the licensure board took his license. Daniel had convinced him that he should follow the licensure board's recommendation and check into the Chemical Dependency Unit of Ridgeview Psychiatric Hospital. Daniel himself was an alumnus of the place, having gotten addicted to cocaine some ten years ago. It was a professional hazard of the trade for otolaryngologists because they used the drug in their practices to deaden and shrink the tissues of the nose for surgery. It was always around. Daniel had remained clean ever since. Mark had resumed drinking the day after being discharged from his twenty-eight-day stay at the hospital.

He and Daniel had been friends since college where they shared a dormitory room. Daniel had been the best man in his wedding. Daniel too was athletic, or had been in his earlier days. At six-foot-five, he had played forward on the college basketball team and was very good, but not outstanding. Unlike Mark, there were no professional offers when he graduated. He never expected any, so he wasn't disappointed.

Daniel continued. "I couldn't believe it when I saw on the news that you had been taken as a hostage from the Emergency Room. I've called your number every couple of hours all day long, praying that you would be back and unharmed. Are you okay?"

"I'm fine. My abductors let me go earlier today."

"Why do you think they took you? It seems strange that someone would take a hostage in a drug heist."

Mark hesitated. God he hated to lie to Daniel, but he didn't see that he had a choice. He recounted the story Maldini had instructed him to tell.

"How's Lisa?" Daniel asked, seemingly satisfied with his explanation.

"She's doing fine. I don't see her as often as I'd like to. She still goes to that private school Joanna stuck her in down in Valdosta."

"Is that bitch of an ex-wife still giving you a hard time?"

"Some things never change, I guess."

"Next time you see Lisa, tell her I said hello."

"I will. She was always very fond of you. I think she sort of thought of you as the uncle she never had."

"Let me tell you why I called," Daniel said, abruptly changing the subject. "I've been going to the local Caduceus meeting. You would be surprised at how many doctors around here have had alcohol or drug problems. We meet every Tuesday evening at seven o'clock in the conference room at Crawford Long Hospital. I don't think I could have made it without the support I get from this group. It's sort of like AA for doctors. We all seem to share common problems. A number of the doctors in the group have lost their licenses like you."

"I'm not surprised at that," Mark said. "When I was at Ridgeview there were twelve of us in the same boat."

"We talked about you last night," Daniel said. "I volunteered to call you and invite you to the meeting. Doctors who need advocacy with the licensure board can sign a five-year contract with the Caduceus Club for monitoring. The executive director of the club calls them regularly for drug screens, their Caduceus attendance is recorded, and the treatment management team follows their progress."

"Daniel, I don't know," Mark said. "I had a really bad experience with Caduceus meetings in treatment. Every time I went, I got real depressed. It reminded me of everything that I'd lost...Joanna, Lisa, my license, my career, my self-esteem, everything. Besides, the hospital monitors me with drug screens. Maybe I'll come someday, but not now. I'm just not up to it yet."

"I wish you would reconsider. The hospital doesn't carry near the weight with the licensure board that Caduceus does."

"Billingsworth has a tremendous amount of influence with the board. He knows a number of the board members personally. He's going to vouch for me at my hearing. At least I hope he is. My performance has been pretty poor of late, but I'm sure I can get my act together by then. I've got nearly eight months."

"Mark, I've heard doctor after doctor say that their lives were in shambles until they joined the Caduceus Club and got some direction from physicians who had experienced the same problems. You need to come to our meetings. How's AA going?"

"Not well. I haven't been in a while."

"How long is a while?"

"Two months."

"Two months! Are you drinking?"

"I wish you hadn't asked that."

"Well, are you?"

"I drink some. Maybe a little more than I should, but I can handle it. It's not a problem."

"Mark, you need to hear some of the doctors in Caduceus talk about their relapses. Most of them had attitudes just like yours…total denial. You have relapsed you know. Come to our meeting. You need Caduceus badly."

In his heart Mark suspected that Daniel might be right, but he just wasn't ready to do without the comfort alcohol provided when he needed it. He knew he couldn't go to Caduceus and continue drinking. "I'll think about it," he replied.

"Good. Let's keep in touch," Daniel said. "Good friends are hard to come by."

"Daniel, I can't tell you how much I appreciate hearing from you. You're still the best friend I've got."

He hung up the telephone and sat there for a moment reflecting on the first Caduceus meeting he had attended. It was during his first week at Ridgeview Psychiatric Hospital.

All twenty-two physicians sat in a large circle with the wall at their backs. Mark felt uneasy. He didn't know what to expect, but he had a sense of dread about the meeting.

"Welcome to the Tuesday night Caduceus meeting," the middle aged man in the brightly flowered shirt and Sigmund Freud beard said from across the room. "I'm Dr. Carl Barkley." His voice was high-pitched and had a nasal quality.

Mark had learned before the meeting that Dr. Barkley seemed to have a disdain for doctors with substance abuse problems. He referred to the non-physician patients as real people and implied that doctors had a God-like complex he called the M-Deity syndrome.

Dr. Barkley cleared his throat, then turned to the patient to his right, a tall man in a white shirt.

"And who are you?" he asked ritualistically.

"I'm Edward S, an alcoholic neurosurgeon from Atlanta," the man said. And so it went around the room.

"I'm Martha R, an alcoholic, drug-addict, family physician from New York," a skinny, older woman with a beaked nose said.

"I'm Joe M, a drug-addict pediatrician from Mobile," a short, stocky man in Bermuda shorts chimed in.

"I'm Charlie M, an alcoholic anesthesiologist from Birmingham," a sleepy looking man with unruly hair said.

Ten minutes later, everyone in the circle, including Mark, had introduced themselves.

"As is our custom, we use a portion of each meeting to get to know new members," Dr. Barkley said. "How many of you were admitted since our last meeting?"

Mark and two other fledgling patients meekly raised their hands.

Beginning immediately to his right, Dr. Barkley slowly looked around the circle, pausing just long enough at each new member for his intense, dark eyes to strike fear into their hearts.

"Please God, don't let him call on me," Mark prayed silently.

Dr. Barkley's eyes passed by him.

"Thank God," Mark said to himself.

When Dr. Barkley had finished scanning the entire circle, he quickly turned his eyes back to Mark.

"Dr. Valentine, tell us about yourself," he said sharply. "What brings you to Ridgeview?"

Mark swallowed hard. His heart leaped up into his throat. Barkley wasn't supposed to use his last name. It was against the rules.

"Dr. Valentine, we're waiting."

Mark cleared his throat. "Well, I've got a little alcohol problem."

The group broke out in spontaneous laughter.

Mark looked around the group in surprise. He hadn't expected anyone to laugh.

"A small alcohol problem! Come now Dr. Valentine. I understand you're a real lush. The licensure board didn't take your license and send you to a mental institution because you drink a little."

"I drink some, sometimes too much, but I'm not an alcoholic."

The group laughed again.

Mark was completely bewildered. He truly couldn't understand the group's response. Before he got out of Ridgeview, he would learn that the primary symptom of alcoholism is denial. Despite the fact that a drinker's life was in turmoil because of alcohol, he or she simply could not see the relationship between the drinking and the problems it caused. It wasn't unusual for alcoholics to view alcohol as the solution to their problems rather than the cause.

"Your ex-wife tells me that you have trouble with women too. I understand your divorce was a real nasty one, complete with photographs and all."

Mark sat up straight in his chair. "I was framed! I'm sure I was set up," he blurted out. "I don't remember exactly what happened."

"That's called an alcoholic blackout, Dr. Valentine," Dr. Barkley said with a cynical grin. "I thought you weren't an alcoholic."

Mark slid back down in his chair. It was obvious that Dr. Barkley was trying to make a fool of him in front of the group. He decided that he would do his best to prevent it from happening.

Mercifully, the Caduceus meeting ended an hour later. Dr. Barkley had succeeded. Despite Mark's efforts to the contrary, Dr. Barkley had made him look like an absolute idiot. He had been totally humiliated.

Prior to that meeting, the caduceus emblem, a shaft with twin snakes entwined around it, had been a symbol of all that was good about his life. He had prominently displayed it in polished brass on the brick wall by the door of his clinic. Every day, as he entered the building, he had looked at the emblem and thought about how good life had been to him. How quickly the Caduceus meeting had turned the emblem into an absolute, depressing symbol of all that was bad about his life. After the meeting, he vowed that if he ever got out of Ridgeview, he would never go to another Caduceus meeting as long as he lived.

CHAPTER SEVEN

It was five o'clock Saturday afternoon. The day was calm with hardly a breeze. The temperature had dropped overnight to a less stifling eighty-eight degrees. Four days had passed since Mark returned from Miami. The story he had told about his abduction had been on the TV news and in the paper the day after his return, and for the most part people had stopped asking him questions about it. He was glad. He was tired of lying. He parked a half a block away, the nearest parking place he could find, and walked to the only $900,000 house in the country owned and paid for by a charity hospital director. Those who weren't aware of Billingsworth's background as a general surgeon and avid investor in the stock market could only wonder how a man on such a relatively small salary could live in such rich surroundings.

Billingsworth threw a party once a year, the third Saturday in July, for the employees at Charity. They had been talking about it all week. Most of them looked forward to it. The less enthusiastic ones came because they knew it was expected of them. It was Mark's first time. He didn't bother to ring the doorbell. Mattie had told him it was an outdoor affair. She had also told him that no alcoholic beverages would be served. At first he had been reluctant to come. How could you have a party without beer? After fortifying himself with a few Bud Lights, he had decided to make a brief appearance so that Billingsworth would know he had been there. The party had started at four o'clock. He was an hour late.

Wearing faded blue jeans and a gray sweatshirt, he walked around the side of the house to the hum of a large number of people involved in partying in the back yard. When he turned the corner, the expansiveness of the area surprised him. It must have been at least three acres. A number of people splashed around in the full-sized swimming pool near the house. Four couples played doubles tennis on the two concrete courts behind the pool. A group of people played flag football in a large area free of shrubs and trees that spread out beyond the tennis courts. Dozens of others stood around talking. Children of various ages entertained themselves playing tag and other games. The smell of grilling hamburgers and hot-dog wieners filled the air.

Mark searched the crowd for familiar faces. Billingsworth was at the far left wearing a white chef's hat and apron and directing a number of men as they cooked the fair for the day on five home-barbecue grills. Marvin Lowenstein stood near the tennis court talking to a lady who appeared to be about his age…probably his wife. Despite effectively playing the role of number two in charge at Charity, it was common knowledge that he desperately wanted Billingsworth's job, and that he harbored some bitterness over the fact that he had been passed over when the hospital hired Billingsworth. Some suspected that his ambitions didn't arise out of loyalty to the hospital, but rather his desire to use Charity as a stepping-stone to the directorship of one of the more lucrative, private hospitals in the city.

A few feet to the right of the tennis courts, Mattie stood talking to three women…two older ones and an attractive younger one. Mark assumed that they also were nurses.

The heads of all the medical staff sections…surgery, pediatrics, internal medicine, family practice, obstetrics and gynecology, psychiatry, pathology, and radiology…were there. So were Mrs. Jones from the Business Office and most of the heads of the other ancillary departments.

The head of hospital security, Zachary Dorfman, leaned against one of the light poles watching four out-of-shape people play tennis. As usual, he wore khaki pants and a matching khaki shirt. His standard, gray T-shirt was visible at his open collar, his black shoes were spit-shined to perfection, and his sandy hair was close-cropped in military style. There was no denying that the look was quazi-military. A lot of people joked behind his back about the way he dressed, but he really didn't care what they thought. He was comfortable with who he was.

Dr. Overstreet was conspicuously absent. Mark assumed that with his impending retirement from the Clinical Laboratory he must have felt little pressure to attend this year's function. He wouldn't be missed. Mark recognized a number of other doctors, nurses, and administrative personnel whom he knew by name, several more that he knew by face only, and yet more that he didn't recall ever having seen before.

After surveying the area, he walked in Billingsworth's direction. He had great respect for the man. Prior to his heart problems, Billingsworth had been one of the most highly regarded surgeons in Atlanta. Because of his stature in the surgical community, Emory University School of Medicine had made him Clinical Professor of Surgery and allowed their general-surgery residents to rotate through his practice as part of their training. Mark had been fortunate enough to be one of those residents. It had been the best rotation of the year.

Approaching the gray clouds of smoke billowing up from the grills, Mark caught Billingsworth's eye. Billingsworth motioned for him to come over. He walked in Billingsworth's direction, speaking to various people along the way.

"Mark! I'm so glad you could make it," Billingsworth said as Mark approached him.

"I wouldn't miss it for the world," Mark replied, tongue in cheek. "People have been talking about your party for days." He stepped back to get out of the path of the smoke from the nearest grill. He wanted to ask Billingsworth if he had seen his cardiologist about his chest pain, but he didn't because he didn't want to put a damper on a day that Billingsworth seemed to be enjoying so much.

"I didn't see Mrs. Billingsworth anywhere," Mark said instead. "I hope she's well."

"She's fine. She just has a little headache. She's resting. She'll be out later if she feels up to it."

"If I miss her, please give her my regards."

"I will. She'll be glad to hear you were thinking about her."

"She probably won't remember me. It's been a long time."

"I'll bet she will. Martha seldom forgets anybody, and you were one of her favorite residents," Billingsworth looked around the yard. "I hope you enjoy the party. I do this every year. It's my small way of showing appreciation to the staff at Charity. I know it doesn't compensate for the low pay and bad working conditions, but I do want everyone to know that they're appreciated."

"I'm sure they do," Mark said, beginning to feel a little better about being there.

"Are you hungry?" Billingsworth asked.

He hadn't been until he smelled the food cooking. "Sure," Mark replied.

"What will it be, hamburger or hot-dog?"

Mark took a hot-dog bun and held it out. Billingsworth speared a steaming wiener on the grill and placed it on the bun.

"Mustard and ketchup are on the table at the end of the grills," Billingsworth said. "Soft drinks are in the coolers behind the table. Help yourself."

Mark walked to the table, stood behind a half-dozen adults with an equal number of small children, and waited.

"I'm surprised you made it," came a voice from behind him.

He turned to see Eric Stottlemire who had just joined the line. Stottlemire wore tan Bermuda shorts, dirty white tennis shoes without socks, and a white T-shirt with **Budweiser Beer** on the front in large orange letters that clashed with his reddish-brown hair.

"Why are you surprised?" Mark asked.

"I figured you had better things to do on Saturday afternoon."

"Well, I guess you figured wrong. I wouldn't miss Billingsworth's party for anything. I've been looking forward to it for weeks." He lied, but he felt Stottlemire deserved a lie.

"Here by yourself?"

"Yes. How about you?"

"I brought Betsy Barfield."

"I don't believe I know her."

"She's a nurse that works at the hospital. I date her sometimes. She's a cute little number. Not too smart though."

Mark decided he would let the remark pass.

Finally, it was Mark's turn at the table. He put a small line of mustard on the wiener and followed it with an equally small line of ketchup and a tablespoon of pickle relish. Then he walked around the table and took a diet coke from the cooler. Stottlemire followed him. Just as Mark took a bite of his hot-dog, a pretty, young woman with short, black hair walked up. She wore white shorts, a pink tank top, and light-blue deck shoes. Mark recognized her immediately. She was the one he had seen talking with Mattie and the other women when he arrived. He took a quick look at her pretty, tanned legs and her trim, athletic-looking figure.

"Eric, I wondered where you had gone," she said. "I'm sorry if I ignored you. I just got interested in what Mattie and the other nurses were talking about. Forgive me?"

Stottlemire ignored her request for forgiveness.

"I don't believe we've met," Mark said.

"This is Betsy," Stottlemire said nonchalantly.

"Hi Betsy," Mark responded, wondering what she saw in Stottlemire. "I'm Mark Valentine. Eric and I work in the Emergency Room together."

"Oh, you're the plastic surgeon that Eric talks about from time to time."

"Ex-plastic surgeon," Mark responded. "I'm sure he doesn't have anything good to say about me."

Before Betsy could answer, Stottlemire spoke up. "Mark, I still think you should take me up on the offer to go sky-diving with me. There's nothing like the adrenaline rush you get from it. My club's got a jump set for next weekend. What do you say?"

"I don't think so," Mark replied. He knew Stottlemire didn't have any real interest in him going, but instead was just trying to give him a hard time in front of Betsy. After all, why would he want him to go? He didn't even like him.

"I think you're scared," Stottlemire said in an obvious attempt to bait him.

"Now Eric," Betsy said. "Mark said he didn't want to go."

"Stay out of this," Stottlemire said sharply.

"Betsy, it was nice to meet you." Mark said quickly, having had enough of Stottlemire.

He took another bite of hot-dog and walked in Zachary Dorfman's direction. A retired marine military policeman, Dorfman, in his own way, was a lot like Billingsworth. He too demanded perfection when humanly possible. Billingsworth had hired him two months after he took over the helm at Charity. Of all the applicants for chief of security, he had been a standout, and had gotten the job hands down. It hadn't taken him long to discover that hospital security was almost as bad as medical care. He immediately set out to improve it. To cut down on the rampant theft of hospital property, he moved quickly to have security cameras placed in vital positions in the hospital. Employees carrying packages out of the building became subject to immediate search. Billingsworth supported his actions by firing anyone on the spot caught stealing from the hospital. Because of a rash of muggings, rapes, stolen car radios, and an occasional stolen car, Dorfman had floodlights installed in the parking lot and increased security patrols in the area. Although an occasional rash of thefts still occurred, primarily because of the part of town in which the facility was located, the hospital now was a

- 83 -

much safer place to work. An avid sports fan, Dorfman especially liked talking about the Braves' latest game whenever the opportunity arose.

"Stunk, didn't they," he said as Mark approached him.

Mark shook his head. "That's putting it mildly. They looked like a high school team." He pulled a cigarette from the pack in his shirt pocket, lit it, and took a deep drag.

"Five errors. Three in the seventh inning," Dorfman said disgustedly. "You can't get much worse than that. They just gave the game away."

"If I were Jamison, I would be pissed as hell. He pitched a pretty good game and deserved to win."

"I agree. He didn't get much support in the batter's box either. Three hits. That's pretty pitiful."

"And they were only singles at that."

Dorfman scratched his head. "The way the Braves played, it's hard to believe that they're only one game out of first place."

"I think the loses are the result of some kind of mental thing. Obviously, the Braves are a much better team than the Giants. Hell, the Giants are just two games from the basement. It doesn't make sense for them to have beaten the Braves two out of the last three games."

They continued discussing Atlanta Braves baseball for another ten minutes, then Mark ground the cigarette butt out in the grass with his foot, excused himself, and walked in Mattie's direction.

Mattie usually came to the party alone. Her husband left her a few years ago. Rumor had it that he ran off with a younger woman. The truth was that he just got tired of competing for her time with Charity. She had three grown children, but they had families and lives of their own.

As he approached her, Mattie turned to greet him. "Dr. Valentine. I hoped you would come. Are you having a nice weekend?"

"You don't want to hear about it," he responded.

She took him at his word and didn't inquire further. "Do you know these ladies?" she asked.

"I know Mrs. Anderson, the head of Nursing Service," Mark replied. Then he turned to the other two women. "I've seen you all around the hospital, but I don't believe we've ever met."

"This is Miss Fuller," Mattie said, glancing at a matronly-looking, white lady who appeared to be about her age. "She's the head nurse on the Pediatric Unit." Then she turned to a frail-looking, black woman who appeared to be a few years younger than Miss Fuller and Mattie. "And this is Mrs. Wormsly. She's the Assistant Director of Nursing Service."

He shook their hands and commented on being happy to meet them. Then he listened as they discussed their families, complained about the working conditions at Charity, and exchanged the latest hospital gossip.

"Bart Williamson, the head of purchasing, is leaving Charity," Mrs. Fuller said. "I just heard about it yesterday."

"You're kidding," Mattie responded. "I'm sorry to hear that. He seems like such a nice young man. Did he find a better job?"

"Hardly. He had been purchasing items for his personal use and charging them to the hospital. Apparently, the twenty-five inch color TV was the straw that broke the camel's back. A security guard caught him loading it into the back of his van last Thursday night."

Mark shifted his weight to the other foot. "Did Billingsworth fire him?"

"Anybody else would have. Because he had a wife and three small children, Dr. Billingsworth gave him a choice…return the items and resign, or have charges filed. Apparently Bart jumped at the opportunity to resign. He was seen cleaning out his desk yesterday morning."

"To bad," Mark said. "He'll have a tough time finding another job with that hanging over him."

"Did you hear the rumor about Dr. Jackson having an affair with some young nurse?" Mrs. Wormsly asked. "It's the hottest topic in the hospital."

"According to the rumor, he has a key to her apartment," Mrs. Fuller chimed in. "She even keeps beer in the refrigerator for him."

"You've got to be kidding. Who is she?" Mark asked.

"That's what makes it so intriguing," Mrs. Wormsly replied, "nobody seems to know."

"How does he get by with it?" Mark asked. "Surely his wife suspects something if the whole hospital knows about it."

"Apparently he just tells her that he has to work late a lot, and she falls for it hook, line, and sinker."

"I don't know why anyone would have an affair with him," Mrs. Anderson said with a disgusted look on her face. "Besides looking like Icabod Crane, he's a pompous ass. You would think he was the world's best surgeon. He can't even hold a candle to Todd Wilson and Jeremy Haynes. Everyone knows that they are much better surgeons than he is."

Mrs. Fuller spoke up quickly. "I understand he's extremely unhappy about Billingsworth's policy of furnishing complication and death rate data to paying patients to aid them in choosing their surgeons. It's costing him a lot of income."

"Given their track records, which of the three would you choose?" Mark asked.

Suddenly, he heard someone call his name. He looked up to see Stottlemire waving at him from the crowd watching the flag-football game. Betsy stood by his side. Mark knew Stottlemire wanted him to come over, but he wasn't interested. He gave Stottlemire a half-hearted wave and turned back to the group of women who had continued their discussion. A minute or so later, Stottlemire appeared at his side.

"Mark! They need two other players. Come on," he said.

"I don't think so," Mark responded. "I've gotten too old for that game."

"A has-been huh. I figured someone with your reputation as a great football player would jump at the chance to strut his stuff."

"Well, you guessed wrong again. I don't have anything to prove."

"That's not what the Board of Medical Licensure says."

Mark gritted his teeth and clenched his fist. His first impulse was to flatten Stottlemire. He was much bigger than Stottlemire and could do so easily, but he didn't want to make a scene. Instead, he took a deep breath and relaxed his fist. He wouldn't let Stottlemire provoke him. He turned back to Mattie. "Do you think you'll get the extra nurse you want in the Emergency Room?"

"I certainly hope so. With all the nurses that call in sick, we need another one desperately. Mrs. Anderson, what do you think?"

"It's not in the budget. You know what that means."

"Yes I know," Mattie said. "There won't be a new nurse unless we can talk Dr. Billingsworth into cutting the doctor's salaries so we can afford one."

Mrs. Anderson looked studious for a moment. "That's a good idea. Why don't we talk to him in the morning."

Concluding that he was being ignored, Stottlemire headed back toward the ballgame.

"Thanks," Mark said to the three women.

Mrs. Anderson smiled. "Do you think he knows we were putting him on?"

"I don't think so." Mattie answered.

"Who cares," Mark said, shrugging his shoulders.

———————

Three hours later, Mark left the party early to return home. As he headed up the steps of the apartment building, he hoped he wouldn't run into his plain-looking neighbor, Susan Livingston. Every time he did, she wanted to talk, like they were old friends or something. The bun at the back of her head, the large glasses, the scant makeup, and her baggy clothes turned him off. He didn't want to be delayed. There was a six-pack of cold beer in his refrigerator, and he was thirsty. He could hardly wait to get to it.

CHAPTER EIGHT

Tuesday morning Mark left his apartment and drove to Brown field. The Lear met him there and flew him back to Miami. A waiting limousine picked him up at the airport and delivered him to Maldini's estate. Sitting in Maldini's office, he puffed on a Marlboro and waited.

The door finally opened. Maldini entered the room wearing a dark-blue robe with thin, red stripes over lighter-blue, silk pajamas. His face was heavily bandaged. Willie, his huge black bodyguard, followed him into the room, glared at Mark, then took his customary stance by the door. Maldini extended his hand.

"Dr. Valentine. It's good to see you again," he said. "I trust you had a pleasant trip."

Mark put the cigarette out, rose, and reluctantly shook Maldini's hand. "A whole lot more pleasant than the first one," he said with a hint of sarcasm in his voice. He stared at the bandages on Maldini's face.

"It's time to see what you look like," he said. He unwrapped the bandages one layer at a time until the last bandage had been removed.

Maldini looked into his eyes expectantly. "Well, what do you think, doc?"

"Looks good for this stage of the healing process," Mark responded.

Maldini walked to a mirror on the wall and glanced at his image. His face was badly swollen. Large purple areas marked the areas above and below his eyes and around his nose, chin, and neck.

"Kill the bastard Willie! Kill him!" he yelled loudly.

Willie grunted, then reached for the gun in his shoulder holster and took a menacing step toward Mark. Mark quickly turned and looked in Willie's direction, then just as quickly back to Maldini.

"Wait! It's okay," he blurted out, taking a step backward away from Willie. "Let me explain."

Maldini held the palm of his hand out toward Willie. Willie grunted again, then stopped a few feet from Mark and replaced the gun in its holster. His hand remained on the handle.

"What do you mean, explain?" Maldini said. "You've ruined my face. It looks horrible."

"It's supposed to look that way at this point," Mark said quickly. "Tissues traumatized by surgery take a while to heal. In another week or so most of the swelling will be gone. The contusions will take longer, but your face will look fine."

"Contusions. What the hell are contusions?"

"Bruises. That's the medical term for bruises."

"Then why in the hell didn't you say bruises in the first place?" Maldini said angrily. "It's okay Willie. You don't have to kill him, at least not yet."

With a disappointed look on his face, Willie removed his hand from the revolver handle and moved back by the door.

"Doc, you'd better not be lying to me. If you are, my men will track you down and see to it that you suffer a long, agonizing death."

"You're going to have to trust me," Mark said reassuringly. "Your face will be fine, I promise." He studied his handiwork for a minute. He had done a damned good job. "You've got to lie down somewhere so I can remove the sutures...somewhere where the light's good."

"The operating room's still set up."

"Perfect. Let's go."

Mark and Maldini entered the makeshift operating room, followed by Willie who stopped just inside the door. Mark motioned to the operating table. Maldini walked to the table and sat on its side.

"Lie down on your back," Mark instructed.

Maldini swung his feet up on the table and lay down on his back. Mark took a suture removal kit from his pocket and opened it. Then he reached up and turned on the surgical light. Maldini squinted his eyes as the light struck his face. One by one Mark removed the sutures…all seventy-eight of them.

When the last suture had been removed, Maldini sat up, swung his legs over the side of the table, and motioned to Willie. Willie stepped out of the room.

Puzzled, Mark watched him leave, but remained silent. Momentarily, Willie returned with a leather briefcase in his hand. Approaching Mark, he stuck the briefcase out in his direction.

"What's this?" Mark asked.

"Open it and see," Maldini instructed.

Mark reached out, flipped the latches at the ends of the briefcase, and lifted the top. The green was staggering…twenties, fifties, hundreds, all neatly bound.

"What's this for?" Mark asked.

"I promised you $100,000."

"I assumed that when you threatened to kill Lisa, the money went out the window."

"Well, you assumed wrong. I'm a man of my word. There's the money. Take it."

Mark made a quick decision to take the money. He figured that he couldn't get into any more trouble than he was already in. Besides, how did you tell a man like Maldini no? He reached out, took the briefcase in his hands, and closed it.

"The limo is waiting for you. I trust you can let yourself out," Maldini said.

Mark nodded affirmatively, then left the room, briefcase firmly in hand. He hurried down the wide, marble staircase to the foyer. Just as he reached for the doorknob, a familiar female voice startled him.

"Mark! It's good to see you again. Vito said you would be back today. I've been looking forward to seeing you."

Mark turned around to see Angela standing by the wall wearing a pair of skimpy white shorts. Her nipples made small bulges in the thin cloth of her light-blue, cotton blouse. The blouse was tied at the midriff, revealing her naval.

"Angela! How are you?" Mark said, pleasantly surprised. God she looked good, he thought.

"I'm fine," she said, walking up to him. "How are you?"

"Wealthier," he said, patting the briefcase.

"How did the makeover turn out?"

"Really well. Maldini's face looks pretty bad right now, but that's to be expected. It will look better in a week or two." He paused. "What's really on your mind?"

"What do you mean?"

"You didn't wait on me just to ask how the surgery went. You could have asked your boyfriend that."

She smiled, obviously a little embarrassed at having been caught. "I just wanted to see you again. You can't blame me for that can you?"

He scanned her from head to toe, slowly undressing her with his eyes until her shapely body stood nude before him. He wondered if she had dressed so skimpily for his benefit.

"Are you okay?" she asked, in response to his non-response.

"Yes, I'm okay. I was just thinking about something."

"Me, I hope." She walked up close to him and touched his arm. "Let's go somewhere so we can be alone and talk."

The thought of being alone with her sent a spark of excitement through him. Just as he was about to agree to her request, the stark reality of the situation flickered through his mind, and he suddenly came to his senses.

"You're Maldini's property," he said, taking a step back. "I don't think he would like you talking to me like this."

She smiled coyly. "You sound like you think I'm trying to seduce you. All I want to do is get to know you better. Besides, what Vito doesn't know won't hurt him."

"It's not him I'm worried about. It's me," Mark responded. "I'll see you. My ride's waiting for me." He quickly headed for the door.

"Daniel, this is Mark. I just got back in town. I need to talk to you," Mark said into the telephone receiver.

"What's the matter? You sound upset."

"I can't talk about it on the telephone. Can I come over?"

"Sure. I'm just sitting here watching an old movie."

"Are you alone?"

"This really sounds mysterious. I can hardly wait to find out what's going on."

"Are you alone?" Mark asked again.

"I'm alone."

Daniel, like Mark had been divorced recently. His wife had just gotten tired of playing second fiddle to his career. The spark had gone out of their marriage years ago, and he had become tired of her constant complaining about his long working hours. The night after she filed for divorce, he had gone out and celebrated.

Twenty minutes later, Mark drove by the tennis courts and pulled into a parking space in front of a luxury apartment complex. He followed the sidewalk between two of the buildings, passed by the large pool, and climbed the stairs to apartment number B-27. He knocked on the door. Daniel quickly opened it.

He and Daniel had been friends since their college days. Daniel was a year older than he and, as a result, had graduated from Emory School of Medicine a year before him. At six-feet-five, his 250 pounds and slightly rotund face gave him a teddy bear appearance. A soft-spoken, gentle man, his disposition matched his looks. His white dress shirt was open at the collar, and he wore navy slacks. A matching jacket hung across the back of the upholstered chair to the right of the sofa. A red and white tie stuck out a few inches from beneath the jacket. A pair of black Rockports sat on the floor in front of the sofa. It was obvious that Daniel had come home from the hospital, gotten comfortable, and settled in to watch TV.

"Come on in," he said.

Mark entered the apartment. All the furniture appeared to be new. He was envious. New furniture was a luxury he couldn't afford. He walked to the sofa and took a seat. Then he flipped a cigarette out of the pack and lit it. Daniel slid into the chair next to the sofa and waited for Mark to speak.

"You're not going to believe what's happened to me," Mark said.

"Give me a try," Daniel responded impatiently.

"I'm not sure where to begin."

Daniel shifted his weight on the sofa. "How about at the beginning."

"I lied to the police and to you." Mark said after a brief pause. "I know who abducted me, and I know where they took me. It didn't have anything to do with drugs."

"You lied. Why?"

"I didn't have any choice. Maldini threatened to kill Lisa if I didn't cooperate."

"Vito Maldini?" Daniel asked quickly.

"You know who he is?"

"I know he's bad news. I heard the feds have got him dead to rights."

"They did, but he'll never stand trial."

"You sound like you have some inside information."

Mark leaned forward. "I do. I got it from Maldini himself. He's the one who had me abducted. When his henchman took the blindfold off, I was in his place in Miami."

"You've got to be kidding."

"I wish I were. The guy's eerie. All he had to do to have me killed on the spot was to nod his head."

"What on earth did he want with you?" Daniel asked.

"To make a long story short, I gave Vito Maldini a new face. He plans to skip the country."

"You what?"

Mark inhaled deeply, then blew a puff of smoke into the air. "I altered his appearance. He wanted to change his identity."

"Why did you do the surgery?"

"I already told you. He threatened Lisa. I would have done anything he wanted."

Daniel leaned back and crossed his legs. "So what's the problem?"

"If I go to the authorities, I put myself in danger. He threatened to have me killed if I double-cross him. There's no doubt in my mind that he meant it. Even if he didn't kill me, I'm not sure where I stand legally."

"What do you mean?"

"I could be charged as an accomplice."

"I don't see how. You did the surgery to protect your daughter. No jury on earth would convict you."

"I didn't tell you about the money."

"The money. What money?"

"The money Maldini gave me…$100,000."

"He gave you a $100,000 and you took it? Why didn't you refuse it?"

"You haven't met Maldini. It's not easy telling him no, especially when there's a huge, black guy standing behind you eager to pump slugs into you."

"Who knows you're involved?"

"Just Maldini's people."

"So what's the problem? I think it's a pretty safe bet that none of them will turn you in. Just keep the money and keep your mouth shut."

Mark rose from the sofa and began to pace. "But if I do, that monster will get away. He deserves to go to prison for life."

"It sounds to me like the only problem you've got is your conscience. You can't afford to have a conscience this time buddy. There's too much at stake. Maldini might carry through on his threat to kill you. Sounds like you'd better leave it alone and pretend it never happened."

"I know you're right. I really don't have a choice. I'll just have to try to put all this behind me."

"Good thinking. Where's the money?" Daniel asked.

Mark put the cigarette out in the ashtray on the end table by the sofa. "I hid it in my apartment. I couldn't just walk into a bank and deposit it. Banks have to report large deposits to the Internal Revenue Service as part of the war on drugs. I would have to explain where the money came from. If I keep it, I'll be guilty of income tax evasion."

"You always were a worrier. Most people wish they had that kind of money to worry about."

"On top of all this, it seems that the hospital may have a serial killer on the loose. It's supposed to be a secret, but the head of Nursing Service, Mrs. Anderson, couldn't stand knowing it and not telling someone, so she shared the information in strictest confidence in the head nurses' meeting."

"Do they have any idea who the killer is?"

Mark walked back to the sofa and flopped onto it. "Mattie Johnson, the head nurse in the Emergency Room, told me that at least one member of the administrative committee that's investigating the problem seems to think it's a nurse, but they don't have any evidence to back it up. Billingsworth's secretary, Edna, can't keep a secret either. She confided in Mrs. Anderson, who promptly told Mattie that Billingsworth suspects that a certain high-ranking hospital employee is behind the cardiac arrests."

"Who is it?"

"No one knows. Billingsworth doesn't have any solid proof, so he won't identify the person."

"Your life sounds worse than a soap opera. Maybe you'd better do what they taught us in AA," Daniel said.

"What's that?"

"Take things one day at a time."

Mark left Daniel's apartment feeling better. He would keep quiet, and he would keep the money, although he wasn't sure that he would ever have the nerve to spend any of it.

CHAPTER NINE

"Code nine, Administration. Code nine, Administration," a loud voice squawked with a sense of urgency from a speaker somewhere overhead.

"Let's go," Mark yelled at Mattie who stood just inside the Nurses' Station. He grabbed a stethoscope, stuck it in his pocket, and ran out the door. Mattie quickly followed.

"Out of the way," he shouted at a black orderly and a Filipino nurse who stood talking in the middle of the hallway up ahead. The pair looked up, hesitated, then quickly moved back against the wall. Long strides quickly carried him past them. He looked back at Mattie. She was beginning to lag far behind. Fear that the focus of the code might be Billingsworth kept him moving at a fast pace despite the fatigue that was beginning to set in his legs.

Minutes later, he arrived at Administration. He pushed the door open and rushed in. Edna stood next to the wall looking scared to death.

"It's Dr. Billingsworth," she said hysterically. "He was talking to me, then he grabbed his chest and slumped over on his desk. I called the code. I think he's dead."

Mark hurried into Billingsworth's office and found him as Edna had described…slumped over his desk and motionless.

"Help me with him," Mark instructed Edna who had followed him in.

She hesitated, then moved quickly to his side. They sat Billingsworth upright in the chair and rolled him around to the open space in front of the desk. As they lifted him out of the chair, Mattie arrived, gasping for air, and helped them position him flat on his back on the floor. Kneeling beside Billingsworth's apparent lifeless body, Mark placed the earpieces of his stethoscope in his ears, then held the diaphragm to Billingsworth's chest.

"No heart beat," he said aloud.

Mattie knelt at Billingsworth's head, pinched his nose closed, then blew two quick breaths into his mouth. His chest rose and fell with each breath. Edna huddled in the corner and began to whimper. Mark could hear the excited voices of a number of people as a crowd began to gather outside the door. He quickly loosened Billingsworth's tie and collar, then placed one of his hands palm down on Billingsworth's chest and the other one on top of the first.

"One one-thousand, two one-thousand, three one-thousand," he said to himself as he compressed Billingsworth's chest with each count. After the fifth chest compression, Mattie bent over and again blew a puff of air into his lungs.

As they began the third CPR cycle, a short black nurse arrived with the crash cart and a portable IV pole. She pulled out a drawer on the crash cart and withdrew an endotracheal tube. Mark quickly took it in his hand and replaced Mattie at Billingsworth's head. The nurse took Mark's place compressing Billingsworth's chest. Mark tilted Billingsworth's head back and expertly slipped the endotracheal tube into his mouth and down his airway. Mattie hurriedly started an intravenous line and connected it to the bag of lactated Ringers solution that she had hung on the IV pole. Mark connected an Ambu bag to the end of the endotracheal tube and squeezed it forcefully after every fifth chest compression, forcing precious air into Billingsworth's lungs.

"I'll take over," a young thin respiratory therapist said to Mark as he burst into the room. He quickly knelt at Billingsworth's head, connected an oxygen line to the Ambu bag, and began squeezing the bag as Mark had done. Mark repositioned himself on his knees at Billingsworth's side and ripped open the front of his shirt. Buttons flew everywhere. He quickly reached for the paddles of the charged defibrillator and placed them on Billingsworth's bare chest. Then he glanced at the electrocardiogram tracing on the small screen of the defibrillator. A wiggly line made its way across the screen.

"Ventricular fibrillation," Mark said loudly. "The heart's not pumping any blood. Stand back!"

Everyone stopped what they were doing and immediately took a step backward. Mark simultaneously pushed the buttons on the two paddles. Billingsworth's body jerked violently. Mark looked back at the tracing. The same wiggly line continued its movement across the screen.

"Damn," he said. "Give him five cc of one in five-thousand epinephrine."

The respiratory therapist and the young, black nurse resumed CPR. Mattie took a vial from the crash cart and snapped its top off. Then she drew its contents into a syringe and injected it into the IV in Billingsworth's hand.

"Stand back," Mark said again.

Everyone cleared. He pushed the buttons on the paddles. Billingsworth's body again jerked violently. Mark quickly looked at the electrocardiogram tracing and prayed for a heartbeat. "Come on damn it, beat," he said aloud. He anxiously watched the wiggly tracing as it again made it's way across the screen unchanged. "Give him two amps of sodium bicarbonate," he ordered. "He has to be acidotic by now."

The nurse and the respiratory therapist again resumed CPR. Mattie snapped the top off the two vials of sodium bicarbonate and drew their contents into a syringe. She quickly injected the solution into the IV tubing.

"Clear!" Mark said loudly.

Everyone again drew back. He pushed the buttons on the paddles and for a third time Billingsworth's body jerked violently.

"Please God, let him respond," Mark prayed silently.

The wiggly line continued uneventfully about half way across the screen, then suddenly a single QRS complex occurred, then another, then another, and finally the tracing reverted to a normal pattern.

Everyone breathed a sigh of relief. Mark wiped the sweat from his forehead with sleeve and silently thanked God for answering his prayer. Billingsworth had escaped death, at least for now.

"Get him to the Coronary Care Unit," Mark commanded. "Call cardiology and tell them to get someone up there stat."

———————————

Mark slumped on the sofa in his apartment, popped the top on a can of diet coke, then lit a cigarette. He had called the Coronary Care Unit an hour after the episode with Billingsworth and spoken with one of the nurses about his status. She had informed him that Billingsworth indeed had suffered another major heart attack, and that he had not yet regained consciousness. A ventilator breathed for him. Mark's concern for Billingsworth went way beyond the fact that he was the only one with the potential of testifying favorably at his up-coming licensure board hearing. Mark truly cared for him. He was a decent man. He had done so much for others, including him. He didn't deserve to die.

Mark wanted a drink to soothe his jangled nerves, but he was determined to make it through the night without alcohol. Somehow he felt he owed it to Billingsworth. He picked up the remote control, pointed it at the TV, and flicked through channel after channel until he had come full circle. There wasn't a damn thing on worth watching. With forty channels you would think that there would be at least one with something interesting on it. He tossed the remote control to the other end of the couch. Then he picked up the latest copy of Sports Illustrated from the coffee table and flipped through it's pages for a couple of minutes before tossing it back on the table. Just as he slid down on the couch, the telephone rang. He picked it up and put it to his ear.

"Mark Valentine," he said.

"Hi Mark. This is Susan. I'm cooking dinner and thought about you. There's plenty for two. Would you like to come over and eat with me?"

The image of Susan passed through his mind…the hair in a bun at the back of her head, the oversized glasses, the skimpy makeup, and those awful, loose-fitting clothes. He started to say no but caught himself. He was hungry, and he didn't think he could face another frozen TV dinner. Besides, with Billingsworth and all, it had been a tough day. He could use some company. "Sure, why not," he answered.

"You will? That's great," she replied, happiness obvious in her voice. "It will be ready in about thirty minutes."

"Good. That will give me time to take a shower and change my clothes." He hoped that Susan wasn't as boring as she looked.

Mark knocked on Susan's door. He had decided that spending a couple of hours with her couldn't be any worse than sitting home alone worrying about Billingsworth. He could always excuse himself and leave right after they ate.

"Come on in," the cheerful voice said from somewhere inside. "I left the door unlocked for you."

He opened the door and entered the room. Unlike his apartment, Susan's looked great…nice furniture, rugs that looked new, and tasteful pictures on the wall. Her apartment was laid out just like his…a main room and a slightly cracked door at the far side that he assumed led to a single bedroom. The main room was vacant. Whatever was cooking in the oven smelled great.

"Where are you?" he asked, his voice slightly raised.

"I'm in the bedroom. Make yourself at home. There's coffee in the kitchen. I'll be right out."

He walked to the kitchen area, lifted the coffee pot from the coffee maker, and poured a cup. As he turned around he noticed the pictures on the front of the refrigerator…line drawings of an elephant, a flower, and a cat. For the most part, the crayon coloring stayed within the lines.

He paused and scratched his head. The pictures didn't fit with his concept of Susan. Did she have children? If so, where were they? He walked to the other side of the room and looked around. Susan's taste in furnishings was excellent. As he took a sip of coffee, a photograph sitting on a bookshelf of a distinguished looking, older couple caught his eye. Her parents, he surmised.

Continuing to sip on the coffee, he looked at several other photographs that he assumed were nieces, nephews, uncles, and aunts. Finally, his eyes settled on a photograph of a young couple. The man wore a black tuxedo, the woman a white bridal gown. They made an attractive couple. The girl looked a little like Susan, but a lot prettier. He decided that it must be her sister.

Finally, the bedroom door opened and a gorgeous creature glided into the room. Her auburn hair fell softly about her face, and her short black cocktail dress accented her ample breasts, perfect waist, and attractive knees. A jangling gold bracelet looped her left wrist. Her emerald-green eyes literally twinkled in the artificial light. He set the coffee cup on the end table and stood in the middle of the floor with his mouth open.

"Susan? Is that you?" he asked in disbelief.

"Who were you expecting?" she asked with the beautiful smile he had seen once before.

"I was expecting you, but I've never seen you like this before," he stammered.

"Well, that's your fault. I've been trying to get you over here for a month."

He smiled. "You should have given me a hint. If I'd known you looked like this, I would have clawed your door down. You look great," he said. "Why do you dress the way you do?"

"I usually look awful, don't I?"

"Awful might be putting it mildly."

"Come sit down and I'll tell you." She walked to the sofa and sat down.

He walked to the bookshelf, picked up the wedding picture, and joined her on the sofa.

"It's you isn't it?" he said, holding up the picture.

"Yes. It's me twelve years ago," she replied, sadness showing in her eyes.

He thought he saw a hint of a tear. "Who's the guy?"

"That's Tim. We were married for eleven years."

"What happened?" he asked, expecting her to tell him about the divorce.

She stared at the floor and didn't say a word. Her chin quivered ever so slightly.

"It's none of my business," he said. "I shouldn't have asked."

"No, I want to tell you about it. It's just that it's hard for me."

He wanted to put his arm around her to comfort her, but he wasn't sure he should. "I have plenty of time," he said. "Tell me about it when you're ready."

She nodded, then leaned forward and looked into his eyes. He could tell that she wanted him to kiss her, so he did.

"Ummm. I needed that," she said.

Suddenly the timer on the oven went off, startling them both. Susan got to her feet and headed for the stove.

"That's all?" he asked, like a little boy who had just lost his favorite toy.

"Don't worry. The night's young. We have plenty of time."

He leaned back on the sofa and watched her cross the room. He couldn't believe how beautiful she was. She opened the oven door, took out the pot, and sat it on one of the cook top eyes.

"Are you ready to eat?" she asked.

"I'm starving. What's for dinner?"

"My mother's recipe for pot roast. My father's crazy about it, so I thought you might like it too."

He watched her as she filled his plate with roast, potatoes, carrots, and onions, all in their own gravy.

"You started cooking that before you called me," he said. "How did you know I'd come?"

She put much smaller portions on her plate. "I didn't. I just took a chance. The worst thing that could happen would be that I'd have to eat pot roast all week." She carried the two plates across the room and sat them on the table. He pulled the chair out for her. Once she was seated he took his seat.

"I hope this tastes as good as it looks," he said.

"I think you'll like it. I have some wine. Would you like some?"

"No thanks. I promised myself I wouldn't drink tonight."

"Why tonight? What's the occasion?"

"A friend of mine had a heart attack today. He's in the Coronary Care Unit on a ventilator. He doesn't like it when I drink. I really ought to quit. I ought to quit smoking too. One day I'll do both." He took a bite of roast. "Your father's right. This is fantastic."

"I'm really sorry about your friend. I hope he'll be all right."

"Me too. I didn't realize how much I cared about him until today."

She stared at him for a moment. "Tell me about yourself. I know you're a doctor and that you work at Charity. I know you played football at the University. My father said you were the greatest quarterback in the history of Georgia football. He has a framed picture of you in your uniform hanging in his study, along with some other players he was fond of. Mom says he's a football fanatic."

"I know the type. Georgia has a lot of football fans like that. We could use some more."

"Dad was a close friend of the coach when you played at the University, so he got to watch the team practice a lot. He never missed a game when you were playing. He talked about you all the time." She took a bite of carrots.

"Where do your folks live?" he asked, trying to change the subject.

"In Columbus. Dad's in the insurance business. He took me to see you play a couple of times. You were great. I used to look at your picture and pretend that you were my boyfriend. I was a cheerleader in the ninth grade at the time. When you moved in here, I felt like I had known you for years. Then after we talked in the hallway that first day, I knew I had to get to know you better."

"I'm sorry I didn't cooperate."

She finished chewing a morsel of roast and swallowed it. "Me too. Dad said that a lot of people were upset when you turned down an offer to play professional football." She took another small bite of roast.

"It was a matter of priorities. The Miami Dolphins drafted me high in the first round. They offered me a lot of money, but I wanted to go to medical school. I had wanted to be a doctor for as long as I could remember."

She nodded understandingly.

"I was facing four years in medical school, three years of general surgery residency, and two more years of plastic surgery fellowship. I would have been thirty-one years old before I could go into practice. I didn't see anyway to play ten or twelve years of pro football and then go to medical school, so I made a choice. I still think it was the right one." He speared a piece of potato with his fork.

"What made you want to be a plastic surgeon?"

"It was an easy decision. So much of medicine deals with death and dying. I wanted to do something that made people happy."

"Do you practice plastic surgery at Charity?"

Mark dropped his head. "No. I wish I did. I work in the Emergency Room."

"What happened to the plastic surgery career?"

"That's a long story. I try not to think about it. I'll tell you about it someday, but not tonight. I've had enough bad things happen today."

After dinner they adjourned to the sofa. He felt content. A good meal...the best he had had since his life began falling apart...and a beautiful woman. He felt better than he had in a long time.

"You were going to tell me about Tim," he said. "Do you feel up to it yet?"

She nodded. "We loved each other very much. We had just made arrangements to adopt a child when he was killed…a beautiful little girl named Catherine."

"What happened?"

"Tim was killed in an automobile accident on his way to work. A drunk driver going the wrong way on a one-way street hit him head on. The doctors said the impact tore his heart away from the aorta. He died instantly. I miss him so much." Thin streams of tears ran down her cheeks.

He put his arm around her. She laid her head on his shoulder.

"When did it happen?" he asked.

She wiped the tears away with the back of her hand. "A little over a year ago. After Tim died, I was so distraught that the adoption agency thought I was too unstable to raise an infant by myself, so they canceled the approval they had already given to the two of us. Another couple adopted Catherine. The woman at the agency wouldn't tell me their names. She said it was against the rules."

He wanted to ask her why they hadn't had children of their own, but decided against it. He would ask her some other time. Maybe when he knew her better.

"But why the masquerade?" he asked instead.

"I dress like that to avoid men. Up to now, I just haven't been ready to get involved in another relationship."

"Well, it worked," he said. "You've been a well kept secret." He gave a little chuckle in an attempt to cheer her up.

She stood, walked to the recorder, and inserted a tape. He dimmed the lights and followed her. They stood there in the middle of the floor holding each other close. He could feel her firm breasts pressing against his chest, rising and falling with each breath. Her perfume was intoxicating.

"Mona Lisa, Mona Lisa, men have named you. You're so like the lady with the mystic smile," Nat King Cole sang softly.

She slipped her shoes off, then they began dancing slowly in rhythm with the music. She caressed the back of his neck. He slipped his hand down to the small of her back and pulled her closer. Their bodies moved as one.

"I hope you like music from the sixties," she whispered softly. "I don't care much for this modern music, with lyrics you can't understand."

He mumbled his agreement. Holding her soft warm body close, he could care less what the music was.

When the last song on the tape had been sung, they stood still for a moment, not wanting to end the embrace. They kissed, then he took her hand and led her into the bedroom where they hugged and kissed some more. He unzipped the back of her dress. She slid it down over her hips, let it fall to the floor, then stepped out of it.

As she stood there in her black lace panties, he kissed her moist lips and gently caressed her round, firm breasts until her nipples were hard and erect. She passionately kissed him back, then stepped to the bed and lay down on her side. He stripped to his shorts and joined her.

For a while they lay on their sides kissing, their nearly nude bodies pressing against each other's. Then he rolled over on his back and pulled her on top of him, her legs straddling one of his. As the passion of their kissing intensified, their breathing got heavier and heavier. He reached down and slipped her panties over her hips and down around her thighs. She bent one leg and slipped her foot out of them. Then she repeated the maneuver with the other leg. He slid his hand down her firm belly...first to her naval, then to her pubic hair, and finally to the warm, wet place where no man had been in over a year. Gasping in little breaths, she tugged at his shorts. He withdrew his hand and took his shorts off. She adjusted her body, then reached down between his legs and gently caressed him until he was fully erect and pulsating. He responded by kissing her breasts and running the tip of his tongue around her hard nipples.

Gasping for breath, she arched her back and moaned softly. His heart pounded hard inside his chest. He rolled over on top of her. She immediately spread her legs. Then he kissed her as he hadn't kissed anyone in years. Their passion grew and grew until he thought he was going to explode. Finally, he adjusted his body and started to enter her.

Suddenly, she stiffened and tried to roll over. His body gave way to the pressure and she moved quickly out from under him. She turned on her side with her back to him and pulled her knees tightly up against her chest.

"I'm sorry. I'm sorry," she said, crying as if her heart would break. "I didn't mean for it to go this far. Please don't hate me."

"What's wrong?" he asked, confused by the sudden turn of events.

"Just as we were about to do it, I suddenly thought of Tim, and I felt so guilty. He was the only man I ever slept with. Please give me some more time. I'll make it up to you. I promise."

In the past year and a half, one thing he had come to understand was pain, so he snuggled up to her back and put his arm around her. He caressed her head and gently kissed her on the temple. "It's okay," he said. "Please don't cry. I understand."

An hour later, he quietly closed the door to her apartment. Despite the fact that their lovemaking hadn't culminated in the sexual act itself, he had enjoyed Susan's company immensely. Unlike Joanna, she was a warm and caring person. He looked forward to seeing her again. He would give her time, all the time she needed.

They had made a date for Saturday evening…dinner and a movie. It would be the first real date he had had since before he and Joanna were married. It would be Susan's first date in over twelve years. It would be fun dating again, especially with Susan. Maybe the downhill course of his life had taken a turn for the better. God, he hoped so.

Just as he exited Susan's apartment, he had the distinct impression that Mrs. Grabosky's door had just closed.

CHAPTER TEN

Thursday was a routine day in the Emergency Room. At the end of his shift, Mark said good-bye to Mattie and the rest of the staff. As he opened the door to the Doctor's Office, he was surprised to find a pretty, young nurse with short, black hair sitting in Stottlemire's lap behind the desk. She immediately jumped to her feet, pulled her uniform skirt down, and began fidgeting with the buttons on her white blouse, which was open to the waist. Mark stared briefly at her bare breasts, then looked at Stottlemire. Stottlemire casually leaned back in the chair and put his feet up on the desk, seemingly unconcerned about her plight.

"I'm sorry. I didn't know you were here," Mark said, somewhat embarrassed. The woman looked down at the floor and continued to button her blouse

"That's okay," Stottlemire said. "No problem."

Mark returned his eyes to the woman. She raised her head and nervously looked at Stottlemire.

"You remember Betsy Barfield," he said. "You met her at Billingsworth's party."

Mark nodded affirmatively.

"Hi Mark," Betsy said meekly as she buttoned the last button on her blouse.

"Betsy was just leaving," Stottlemire said.

She looked shocked, as if she didn't know she was just leaving. She hesitated, then walked to the door and looked back at Stottlemire. "Call me?" she said.

"Sure," Stottlemire replied.

With a dejected look on her face she turned and left the room.

Mark talked with Stottlemire for a few minutes about problems in the Emergency Room that needed addressing, then he excused himself and left the Doctors' Office. He took the elevator to the fourth floor, wondering the whole way what an attractive woman like Betsy Barfield could possibly see in someone as obnoxious as Stottlemire.

Exiting the elevator, he entered a drab hallway. A half-dozen tired-looking men and women sat around talking to each other in a waiting room to his left. He walked toward the set of double doors at the end of the hallway. Plain white paper obscured the view through the small windows. The sign on the wall next to the doors stated **Coronary Care Unit**. A small speaker with a single push button occupied the wall next to the sign. He pushed the button and waited. Several seconds passed.

"Yes?" said a female voice from the speaker.

"This is Dr. Valentine."

"Who?"

"Dr. Mark Valentine from the Emergency Room."

"Okay, come on in."

The lock on the door clicked. He pushed the door open and entered. Ten hospital rooms with large glass windows faced a central nurses' station. A young, black nurse sat at the desk staring at a rack of ten small video screens, each displaying the electrical activity of the heart of an individual patient. Number three belonged to Ed Billingsworth.

"How's Dr. Billingsworth doing?" Mark asked.

She reached for a red notebook on the desk in front of her. Opening the notebook, she pointed at a page of electrocardiogram rhythm-strips. "He had a series of irregular heartbeats earlier today. Dr. Agarwall, his cardiologist, ordered a stat potassium. It came back low, so he ordered some intravenous potassium chloride. It apparently worked. His cardiac rhythm is stable now."

Mark thanked her, walked to room number three, entered it, and stood at the side of Billingsworth's bed. Billingsworth lay there motionless, his eyes closed. A clear, plastic bag of intravenous fluid hung at the head of the bed, supplying fluid to a pump through a segment of plastic tubing. The pump then delivered the fluid at a constant rate through another segment of tubing to a vein in the back of his hand. A ventilator, connected to the end of an endotracheal tube protruding from his nose, made a hissing sound as it intermittently pumped life-sustaining air into his lungs.

"How's he doing?" Mark asked the tall, male nurse who had followed him into the room.

"About the same. He still hasn't woke up. His blood pressure has been a problem. It fell pretty low this morning. Dr. Agarwall had to start him on a dopamine infusion. It seems to be maintaining his pressure fairly well."

"What about his breathing?"

"He fought the ventilator for a while this afternoon, trying to breathe on his own. Dr. Agarwall thought that it was a good sign. He reduced the IMV to eight, but Dr. Billingsworth's blood gases deteriorated, so he had to bump it back up to twelve."

"What does Dr. Agarwall say about his prognosis?"

"Not good. He gives him a fifty-fifty chance of making it. Are you a friend?"

"I would like to think so. I owe him a great deal. I hope I'll get a chance to show him my appreciation."

The male nurse turned and left. Mark sat by Billingsworth's bed for an hour, then said a silent prayer for him and departed the Unit. As he walked by the waiting room, someone called his name.

"Mark. Mark Valentine. Is that you?"

He turned to see an attractive, older woman walking toward him. She wore an expensive-looking, blue, two-piece outfit. Her graying hair was in slight disarray, and she looked tired.

"Do you remember me?" she asked. "I'm Martha Billingsworth, Ed's wife. I'm so glad to see you. How have you been?" She put her arms around him and gave him a motherly hug.

"Of course I remember you. You were so nice to me when I rotated through Ed's practice. I missed you at the party Saturday. How are you doing?"

"Not well. Ed and I celebrated our thirty-third wedding anniversary last week. If he dies, I don't know what I'll do." Tears swelled up in her eyes.

"I'm sure he's going to be okay," Mark said. "Dr. Agarwall said he tried to breathe on his own earlier today." He had been taught in medical school not to give false assurance, but somehow he felt that Mrs. Billingsworth needed it. Besides, what he said about Billingsworth trying to breathe on his own was almost true.

"Where are your boys?" he asked.

She wiped a tear from her cheek with a tissue. "Brad flew in from California yesterday. He stayed here with Ed all night so I could get some rest. He went home this morning when I returned. He'll be back after while. Jim is in Honduras working on an oil deal. He can't get a plane out until late tonight. We expect him sometime in the morning."

"If I can do anything, please call me."

"Thank you Mark. That means a lot to me." She gave him another motherly hug.

"As you all know, Ed Billingsworth is in the Coronary Care Unit fighting for his life," Lowenstein said, sitting in Billingsworth's place at the head of the conference table. "He still hasn't regained consciousness, and he may never do so. In Ed's absence, I've taken it upon myself as Acting Hospital Director to call this meeting tonight. There was another cardiac arrest yesterday afternoon. The patient, a forty-three-year-old, white female admitted for appendicitis, didn't make it."

Dr. Jackson and Mrs. Anderson sat silently and shook their heads.

Finally, Dr. Jackson broke the silence. "This is getting out of hand. We have to do something."

Mrs. Anderson looked at him contemptuously. "We can't do anything until we know what we're dealing with. That ought to be obvious."

Lowenstein quickly spoke up. "It's worse than we thought. We've analyzed the data for the first quarter of this year. The cardiac arrest rate is up another five percent. It seems to be increasing with time".

Mrs. Anderson gasped.

Lowenstein passed out several sheets of paper. "As you can see from the graph on the first page, the excess cardiac arrests, the ones that shouldn't have occurred, cluster around two distinct time periods, with peaks at six AM and nine PM."

"Well, that rules out doctors," Dr. Jackson interjected. "Most of us don't come in until after seven, and it's rare to find one of us around here after five."

"Most doctors?" Mrs. Anderson said quickly. "That means that a few do round early in the morning and others late at night. We can't rule out a doctor no matter what you say."

Dr. Jackson squirmed in his chair and brushed back the troublesome lock of hair from his eye. "I still think the most likely candidate is a nurse."

Lowenstein hastily interceded. "We don't even know if there's anything to be a candidate for yet. You're both jumping to conclusions. The fact that the cardiac arrest rate is up, and apparently seems to be increasing, doesn't prove for a fact that someone is purposefully causing the problem. Let me present the data before we attempt to come to a conclusion."

Mrs. Anderson and Dr. Jackson stared at each other for a moment, then looked at Lowenstein. Both nodded affirmatively.

"Now take a look at the second page," Lowenstein said.

Mrs. Anderson and Dr. Jackson put down the first page and stared at the second one.

"As you can see by the bar graph, I've grouped patients according to their ages…thirty to thirty-nine years, forty to forty-nine years, fifty to fifty-nine years, and so forth. The red bars are for the past year. The black bars beside each red bar are the averages for the same age ranges for the previous three years. When we subtracted the black bars from the red ones we found something very interesting."

"Get to the point," Dr. Jackson said impatiently.

Lowenstein continued. "The differences between the red bars and the black bars are the excess cardiac arrests at specific ages. As you can see, the differences between the two become greater as we move from the older age ranges to the younger ones."

"Were still waiting to find out what all that means," Dr. Jackson said even more impatiently.

"In a nutshell, it means that the average age of patients in the excess cardiac-arrest group is much younger than the average age of the group as a whole. In fact, the average age of patients in the excess cardiac-arrest group is forty-seven. The average age in the group as a whole is sixty-three. This is highly statistically significant…at the 0.01 level to be exact."

"So what the hell does that mean?" Dr. Jackson asked, beginning to fidget in his chair.

"It means that the increase in cardiac arrests occurred in a younger group of patients than would have been expected for the group as a whole."

"Maybe we just admitted a much sicker bunch of younger patients this past year," Mrs. Anderson said.

"I wish that were the case," Lowenstein replied. "I've compiled a list of admitting diagnoses for the excess group. Take a look at page three."

Dr. Jackson and Mrs. Anderson located page three.

"As you can see, the most common diagnosis in this group was breast mass, the second most common diagnosis was intestinal adhesions, the third was cholecystitis. You can read the rest for yourselves. None of these illnesses should have been fatal"

"Well, I don't think there's any doubt about it," Dr. Jackson said. "We definitely have a problem. Someone in our hospital is killing patients. But why, and how? It doesn't make any sense."

"It certainly rules out euthanasia," Mrs. Anderson said.

"How's that?" Lowenstein asked.

Mrs. Anderson continued. "Mercy killings involve terminally ill patients who are expected to die, or patients in prolonged vegetative states. None of the patients fit that description. Something else has to be going on."

"What about the exact cause of death? What did the autopsies show?" Dr. Jackson asked.

"That's another confusing point," Lowenstein answered. "The autopsies, in all cases, failed to reveal a specific cause of death. Just like Audrey Touchstone, their hearts were perfectly normal."

"What are we going to do?" Mrs. Anderson asked. "This problem is obviously bigger than we're capable of handling. We have to report it to the police."

Lowenstein thought for a moment. "I don't believe that would be a good idea."

"Why not?" Mrs. Anderson asked with a perplexed look on her face.

"Yeah, why not?" Dr. Jackson chimed in.

"For two reasons," Lowenstein continued. "First, despite our statistics, we don't have any hard evidence that a crime has been committed. All of this evidence is circumstantial at best."

"What's the second reason?" Dr. Jackson asked.

"Our budget hearing is in four weeks. Can you imagine the fuel this kind of thing would furnish the city councilmen who oppose Charity? They would use this to cut our budget to the bone. They might even use it to close the hospital down. Lord knows they would love that. As it stands now, the opposition only needs one or two more votes to put us out of existence. Before we go off half-cocked, we need to have some better evidence."

"If we can't call the police, what are we going to do?" Mrs. Anderson asked.

"I'll ask Zachary Dorfman to get his security people to keep an eye out for anything suspicious."

"Good idea," Dr. Jackson said. "That way if we get criticized for not calling the police, we can say that we had our own security force working on the problem."

"That's not why I said I would get Dorfman on the case," Lowenstein replied. "I think it's the prudent thing to do at this time."

"You said we needed better evidence," Mrs. Anderson said. "What do you have in mind?"

"My staff worked hard to get the information I presented today. However, we still don't have any data related to staffing patterns. If we could identify one person who was in the vicinity of all, or at least most, of the excess cardiac arrests when they occurred, we might have a better handle on the problem."

"How long will it take you to get the additional data?" Dr. Jackson asked.

"Let me summarize our situation before I answer that," Lowenstein said. "Correct me if I'm wrong. It seems that we may have a person or persons in our hospital randomly doing something to cause relatively young, healthy patients admitted for non-life threatening illnesses to have cardiac arrests, with a significant percentage of them dying."

Dr. Jackson and Mrs. Anderson looked at each other with bewilderment on their faces.

"So how long will it take to get the additional data?" Dr. Jackson asked again.

"Just a few days," Lowenstein responded. "Why don't I have my secretary call you and schedule another meeting when it's ready."

Saturday evening finally arrived. Mark stood in front of Susan's door wearing his best sport coat, a navy one that he had paid $400 for when he could afford to pay $400 for a sport coat. His gray slacks had come back from the cleaners and were wrinkle free. He wore a white shirt with a button down collar. His tie was maroon and navy striped. He had dug his dress shoes out of the closet and spit-shined them until he could see himself in them. He felt like a college freshman about to enter the lobby of the girls' dormitory to pick up a date. He was irritated at himself for being so nervous. He was a grown man. It wasn't as if this was his first date, although he felt like it. He knocked, then waited.

Seconds later, Susan opened the door wearing a black, knit tunic over a red-and-black, chiffon, ankle-length skirt that was split up both sides to just above the knees. A long, gold chain dangled around her neck. Small, round, gold earrings and a wrist bracelet matched the chain. He told her how beautiful she looked and she countered with how handsome he looked.

"Let me get my purse," she said. Then she stepped back into the apartment only to reappear almost immediately.

He took her hand and they left the apartment building. The evening air was still hot and thick despite the fact that the temperature had dropped a few degrees since sun down. In the distance, the full moon illuminated the trees reaching above the buildings.

Fifteen minutes later, Mark pulled into the crowded parking lot at Gallaria Mall. He had made dinner reservations at Winfields. After dinner they would take in a movie at the theater complex in the mall.

Driving up one row after another, he finally found a parking place. They left the car and entered the restaurant. Passing by the crowd of people in the waiting area who had not had the foresight to make reservations, they checked in with the tuxedoed, young man at the podium, which stood just outside the dining room entrance.

"Reservations for two...Dr. Mark Valentine," Mark said.

The man looked down his list. "Ah, here it is," he said after a few seconds. "Someone will be right with you."

They stepped back and waited.

A few minutes later, another young man in a tuxedo appeared from the dining room. "Dr. Valentine?" he asked, looking around the crowd.

"That's us," Mark said, holding his hand in the air.

"Follow me."

They followed him to the rear of the crowded restaurant where he seated them at a table faintly illuminated by candlelight. A piano played softly somewhere in the background. They studied the menu for a while as their eyes adjusted to the light level, then they ordered...New York strip, medium well, for him, shrimp scampi for her. She ordered iced tea. He ordered a Bud Light.

A few minutes later, the waiter delivered the drinks. They each took a sip and stared into the other's eyes.

"How do you like teaching?" he asked, eager to know more about her.

"It's wonderful. I've been teaching for ten years. I taught in junior high for a while, but I had wanted to teach in elementary school ever since I graduated from Columbus College. When an opening became available, I applied for it and got it."

"You really like teaching fourth graders?"

"I love it. Ten year olds are at such a wonderful age. They're so cute and so eager to learn. I never know what to expect when I get to school. They bring me apples, make me valentines, and color pictures just for me."

"I saw the pictures on your refrigerator the other night. At first I thought your children must have done them. Later that evening you said that you and Tim couldn't have any. I was confused about the pictures, but now I understand."

She started to reply, but hesitated as the waiter returned and placed their salads in front of then. When he was gone, she continued. "Tim couldn't father children. He had mumps when he was twelve." She hesitated. "It left him with a problem with his sperm count."

Sensing that the topic was making her uncomfortable, Mark changed the subject. "You said you grew up in Columbus. What about brothers and sisters?"

"None. Mom was thirty-five when I was born. She had an extremely difficult labor. The doctor told her that she couldn't have any more children, that it would be too dangerous. So I'm it. What about you?"

"Same here."

She smiled. "Your mother had a difficult labor?"

"No, smart aleck. I'm an only child. My parents were too busy to spend much time raising children. My father was a design engineer for Marion-Marietta. My mother was a nurse. When they weren't working, they traveled...London, Paris, Rome, Australia. They even went to the Soviet Union once. I think I spent most of my early childhood with a baby-sitter."

"They didn't take you with them?"

"Not when I was young. They felt like I would slow them down. When I was older and less trouble they did."

"Where are they now?"

"In heaven, I hope. They died during my first year of general surgery residency."

Sadness crossed her face. "Oh, I'm so sorry. What happened?"

"A plane crash on one of their trips. I still miss them, mostly on holidays. But for the most part, though, I've dealt with it pretty well."

"I'll be glad when I can say that about Tim. It's still hard, but it's getting easier."

"I hope I can help."

"You've already helped. I'm so glad we finally met."

He reached across the table and squeezed her hand. "Me too."

The waiter brought the main course, then refilled Susan's tea glass. Mark ordered another Bud Light. He wanted to tell her about Maldini, but his better judgment told him not to get her involved.

"What do you like to do in your spare time?" he asked.

"I read a lot. I'm just finishing *The Runaway Jury* by John Grisham."

"Do you like Grisham?"

"His plots are great, but sometimes it's a little hard to keep track of his characters."

"Who else do you like?" He took a drink of beer and followed it with a bite of steak.

"Before *The Runaway Jury*, I read *Disclosure* by Michael Crichton."

"The author of *Andromeda Strain*?"

"I'm impressed. Do you read much?"

"Not as much as I used to. Medical journals…that's about all I read now."

"Well rounded, huh?" She took a bite of shrimp scampi.

"Things change so fast in medicine, I don't have time for much else."

"I was just kidding." She looked studious for a moment. "Mrs. Grabosky said you're divorced."

"How would she know that?" he asked.

"She makes it her business to know about everyone."

"She's right. It's been a year and a half now. I'm having a real struggle accepting it. I miss Lisa, my daughter, a lot. She's thirteen now."

"Tell me about her," Susan said. "I bet she's pretty."

"She's very pretty. She looks a lot like her mother. She doesn't have her mother's nasty disposition though. She's very sweet, very caring, aware of other people's feelings."

"A lot like you."

He hadn't thought about it, but he guessed that she was right. He did care about other people. He would never go out of his way to intentionally hurt someone as Joanna had done on a number of occasions.

"Lisa's an excellent student," he said. "Makes almost straight As. I'm very proud of her. She's done well despite her handicap."

"Handicap?"

"She was born with a hearing problem. Actually, she's severely deaf."

"How does she do so well in school if she's deaf?"

"For one thing, she hears a little with her hearing aids. She wears two. She says two help her tell which direction sounds come from. You can't tell she has them on. She wears her hair down over her ears. She's had speech and language training since she was eighteen months old. That's helped tremendously. In the early days, a lot of the work had to be done at home. I have to give Joanna credit. She worked with Lisa for hours on end, helping her to learn how to pronounce difficult words correctly."

"Lisa must be very smart."

"She is. She works hard too. The biggest problem she has is talking on the telephone. The one in her dorm room has an amplifier that makes voices louder. That helps a lot."

"Thirteen-year-old girls certainly need to talk on the telephone. It's good that she can do it. I remember when I was her age. I lived on the telephone. Does she have a boyfriend?"

"No, not really. I think she's still a little too young for that. She has some friends that are boys, but they mostly study together and things like that. She likes boys, but right now she's more interested in her studies."

"Does she want to be a doctor?"

"Far from it. She doesn't like all that blood and guts stuff. I think she's more interested in designing things. Maybe she'll be an architect some day."

"I can hardly wait to meet her." She paused. "The divorce must have been hard on her."

"It was hard on both of us. I don't think I'll ever get over the way it happened."

"What do you mean?"

"At the hearing, Joanna's lawyer produced some pictures of me in bed with a buxom brunette. We were both stark naked. I remembered the woman from about a month before. She had come up to my table at

Alfredo's Bar and asked if she could join me. I was feeling sorry for myself because Joanna had refused to sleep with me for the hundredth time, so I invited her to sit down. We chatted for a while, then I went to the cigarette machine to get a pack of Marlboros. When I returned to the table, I finished my drink. Five minutes later my head became fuzzy and my speech began to slur. The next morning I remembered the warm body next to mine, the smell of cheap perfume, and the flashing lights, but I thought it had been a dream."

"Do you think she drugged you?"

"I'm sure of it. Unfortunately, I couldn't prove it at the divorce hearing." He paused for a moment. "Can we change the subject? Talking about the divorce makes me depressed."

Susan nodded. "I understand. Do you play golf?"

"No. Never have. Why do you ask?"

"I thought all doctors played golf."

He smiled. "You mean like all blondes are dumb."

"And all red-heads have bad tempers," she countered. Then she got a serious look on her face. "How's your friend?"

"Billingsworth?"

She nodded her head. "Is he okay?"

"I didn't see him today. Mattie, the head nurse in the Emergency Room, said he was about the same. I'm going to check on him tomorrow after work."

"I thought he might be better."

"Why is that?"

"You're drinking."

He didn't respond.

They finished the steak and the scampi. Susan declined dessert. He did the same. Then they made a vow not to talk about anything else unpleasant the rest of the evening. This was to be a happy night. He paid the bill. Then, holding hands, they headed for the movie complex.

CHAPTER ELEVEN

Mark had been trying to take things one day at a time as Daniel had suggested, and it seemed to be working. He felt better. After work he drove to Alfredo's Bar. Alfredo's was an old establishment that catered to a loyal clientele. With its linoleum floor, plain booths, and checkered tablecloths, it was small and unassuming. He ordered a drink, chatted with some friends for a while, then got involved in a pool game. He was proud of himself. He had made a decision to do a better job of controlling his drinking. Despite the fact that such attempts had been short-lived in the past, he knew this time would be different.

Three hours later he left the bar, pulled away from the curb, and headed home. The temperature continued to drop and, although it would be considered sweltering by northern standards, the temperature was a grateful eighty-two degrees. A gentle but erratic wind blew out of the west. He lit a cigarette, then made a left turn. After two blocks, he stopped at a signal light and reached to turn the radio on. Suddenly, a jolt from behind threw his head back against the headrest. His aging Porsche catapulted forward.

He quickly looked in the rearview mirror. A Spanish-looking man with a black goatee got out of a late-model, blue Pontiac Bonneville and stood looking at the front of his car.

"Damn! If it's not one thing it's another," Mark said to himself in disgust. "Who is this jerk?"

He put his cigarette out in the dashboard ashtray, got out of his car, and waited for a red Chevy pickup, driven by a gawking driver, to pass.

Then he walked to the back of his car. The man with the goatee wore black pants and a black, long-sleeved shirt. His greasy, black hair was slicked back across the temples with too much gel. A rubber band bound a six-inch tuft of hair at the back of his neck. The upper buttons on his shirt were open, revealing thick, black chest hair and two gold chains. A diamond earring in his left earlobe sparkled in the Pontiac's headlights. His dark eyes had a sinister look that sent a chill through Mark.

Mark studied the front of the man's car. The grill had suffered some minor damage, but he didn't see any other consequences of the accident.

"Gee, man. Why did you stop so suddenly?" the man asked, his eyes darting between the front of his car and Mark's face.

"I stopped because the light was red, and I didn't stop suddenly," Mark replied.

"Are you calling me a liar, man?" the man said hostily. His eyes narrowed menacingly and the right side of his face began to twitch.

"What difference does it make whether I stopped suddenly or not. You hit me from behind. That automatically makes it your fault. One of us needs to call the police," Mark said, irritated. He turned his back to the man to inspect the damage to the Porsche. "Shit! This is all I need," he said bitterly. The bumper was badly dented and a taillight was smashed.

Suddenly, the man's shadow, cast by the Pontiac's headlights on the back of the Porsche, made a quick movement. Mark immediately turned to see the man lunging at him with a wicked-looking knife in his hand, aimed directly at his heart.

"I'll kill you, you son of a bitch," the man yelled wildly.

Using all the athletic ability he possessed, enhanced by a sudden rush of adrenaline, Mark deftly sidestepped him and delivered a sharp blow to the back of his neck. The man looked surprised at how easily Mark had made the maneuver, then promptly lost his balance and fell forward on his hands and knees.

"What the hell's wrong with you? Are you crazy?" Mark screamed. The knife in the man's hand was huge. Mark knew that his next move might be the difference between life or death.

As the man attempted to get up, Mark quickly stepped forward and, with all the energy he could muster, kicked him hard in the ribs. The man grunted in pain as the force of Mark's blow knocked him back against the grill of the Pontiac. The knife flew from his hand, clattered harmlessly on the pavement, then bounced underneath the car.

Mark quickly turned and made a dash for the door of the Porsche. When he reached it, he jumped into the front seat, turned the key in the ignition, and sped away.

As he neared the next intersection, he looked in the rearview mirror. The blue Pontiac followed closely behind him. He quickly looked both ways, then sped through the signal light just as it turned red. Then he looked in the rearview mirror again. A gray sedan screeched to a halt as the blue Pontiac ran the red light.

"Damn," Mark said aloud. "What the hell's wrong with that guy. The damage to his car wasn't that bad."

The Porsche's tires squealed loudly as Mark made a sharp right turn onto Peachtree Place. The blue Pontiac made the same turn and stayed right behind him. Two more sharp turns failed to elude it. Traffic got thinner and thinner as they sped further away from the main streets. Suddenly, the side mirror on the driver's side of the Porsche exploded.

"What the hell?" Mark muttered, quickly looking in the rearview mirror.

The man held a pistol out the window of his car, ready to fire again. Mark slammed on the brakes, spun the steering wheel clockwise, and stepped hard on the accelerator pedal.

As the Porsche skidded sideways, another shot rang out, ripping a hole in the passenger-side windshield. Mark dodged the spray of glass splinters as the Porsche barreled into the opening of a narrow alleyway. He checked to see if the bullet had hit him. Thankfully, it hadn't.

Careening down the alleyway, Mark barely made it through an open-ing narrowed by metal garbage cans and picked up speed. The blue Pontiac slowed, then turned and accelerated into the alleyway right behind him. As it rapidly approached the narrowed section, its right fender struck the garbage cans, causing then to clang loudly as they bounced off the brick wall of the building. The Pontiac veered sharply to the left and made contact with the wall. Sparks flew everywhere. The man regained control of his car, pulled back to the center of the alley-way, and picked up speed again. He continued in hot pursuit. Mark began to sweat. How the hell was he going to lose this guy?

He exited the alleyway, barely missed a white Ford mustang, and turned left. Two blocks later, he made another sharp left turn and gunned the accelerator, rapidly passing the few cars and trucks in the nearly deserted area of town. Veering to the left at the next intersection, he entered Jones Street and bounced across the railroad tracks. The blue Pontiac stayed right on his tail.

"Shit!" he muttered. "This is getting ridiculous."

A block later he made a right turn, then quickly turned left onto Simpson Street. Almost sideswiping a black pick-up truck, he picked up speed again,. The driver of the truck yelled at him angrily and blew his horn. Mark ignored him. The blue Pontiac flew by the pick-up and stayed close behind him. Traffic began to get heavier again.

Mark decided that his only chance was to beat the man to the inter-state highway. He was sure he could outrun him if he did. His Porsche was old, but it could still run rings around a Pontiac. He roared through three more intersections, running all three red lights as cars screeched to a halt and sounded their horns. Then he saw the sign…Interstate 20 West, 1/2 Mile…and he breathed a sigh of relief. He stepped on the accelerator pedal and picked up speed. Finally reaching the on-ramp, he roared up it without slowing down. As he approached the top of the ramp, he looked back. The Pontiac bolted onto the ramp just behind him.

Timing his speed, he pulled into the rapidly moving traffic on the Interstate at high speed. Then he pushed his foot down on the accelerator pedal even more, moved to his left, and worked his way toward the fast lane. He looked at his speedometer…70 mph, 80 mph, 90 mph.

As he weaved in and out of the heavy traffic, the Porsche's engine hummed like the precision instrument it was. He looked in the rearview mirror. The Pontiac began to fall behind. He pushed the accelerator pedal further to the floor…90 mph, 100 mph. He looked in the rearview mirror again. The Pontiac was nowhere in sight.

"Thank God," he said under his breath. "I thought I'd never shake him." He had seen the last of the blue Pontiac, for now.

———————————

His mind was still on the attempt on his life when he arrived back at his apartment building and knocked on Susan's door. No answer. He knocked again. Still no answer. Hearing a door open behind him, he turned to see Mrs. Grabosky standing just outside her apartment door wearing a well-worn chenille robe. Her hair was up in pink curlers.

"It won't do you any good to knock," she said. "She's not in there. Her mother took ill. She's gone home to Columbus."

"What time did she leave?"

"I just got back from a prayer meeting a few minutes ago, so I don't know the exact time she left. When she got in from work earlier, she told me that she was going to leave sometime after dinner. I think she was waiting on you to get home. I guess she got tired of waiting."

"Did she say when she'd be back?"

"Not exactly."

"What did she say?"

"She said that if she didn't see you tonight to tell you that she hoped to be back by the weekend. The doctor expected her mother to recover fairly quickly. I wondered how long it was going to take for the two of you to get together."

He ignored her last statement and turned to walk toward his apartment door. Abruptly, he stopped and turned back. "What's wrong with her mother?"

"Pneumonia. Came down with it last night. It was pretty sudden. She had a temperature of 102 degrees. Antibiotics brought it right down."

He decided to test her…to see just how nosy she really was. "How's her father taking it?"

"He was really worried at first. Susan said he always spends the night with her mother when she's in the hospital."

Pretty damn nosy, he concluded. He turned and walked toward his apartment door, disappointed that Susan wasn't home. He would see her this weekend when she got back from Columbus. He opened the door, entered his apartment, and flipped the light on. He couldn't believe his eyes. The place was a wreck. Every drawer in the kitchen had been pulled out and every cabinet door was open. Their contents…pots, pans, skillets, plates, cups, bowls, glasses…were strewn about the floor. He stared at the mess for a moment, then carefully picked his way through it and entered the bedroom where a similar sight greeted him. Even the mattress on his bed had been turned upside down and ripped open. Who the hell would have done such a thing, he wondered. And why? What did he have that was worth steeling?

"The money!" he blurted out. He rushed to the closet and opened the door. All the clothes had been ripped off their hangers and lay in a tangled heap on the floor. He quickly reached to the shelf at the top of the closet and shoved aside the pile of clothes.

"Damn," he said loudly. The briefcase with the money was gone.

He immediately thought of Daniel Iverson. He was the only one he had told about the money. Then he felt guilty for even thinking such a thing. Daniel had a lucrative otolaryngolgy practice. He certainly didn't need the money. Besides, he was an honest person and a good friend.

He wouldn't do such a thing. Mark reached into his shirt pocket, pulled out the Marlboro pack, and took the last cigarette from it. He placed the cigarette between his lips, then wadded up the empty pack and tossed it at the wastebasket in the corner of the room. It missed wide to the left. He stared at the basket for a moment, then lit the cigarette and headed out the door.

————————

"Daniel, open up. It's me, Mark. I've got to talk to you," Mark yelled, knocking loudly on the door.

Daniel opened the door wearing a pair of blue pajamas and a sleepy look on his face. "What's the matter?" he asked, rubbing his eyes.

Mark quickly entered the apartment. Daniel closed the door behind him.

"Things have gotten crazy." Mark said. Then he paused. "Did I wake you?"

"Yes, but it's okay. I had just gone to sleep. I had a busy day and I was really tired. You sound frantic. What's up?"

Daniel sat down on the sofa. Mark sat in the chair next to it.

"Someone broke into my apartment and took the money," he said.

"All of it?"

"Yes, all of it. Maldini gave it to me in a briefcase. I didn't take it out. When I got back from Miami, I put the briefcase under some clothes on the shelf in my bedroom closet. I never expected anyone to steal it. No one knew it was there."

"What about your gangster pal? He knew you had it. He gave it to you."

"Maldini's no pal of mine," Mark said emphatically. "Besides, he didn't just give me the money, he insisted I take it. Why would he do that if he were going to steal it back? It doesn't make sense."

"I guess you're right. You're sure no one else knew about it?"

"No one except you. I told you, remember?"

"You don't think I took it?"

"Of course not," Mark said quickly. "You asked me who else knew about it. I just answered your question."

"Did you report the break-in to the police?"

"Are you kidding? The only thing that was taken was the money. I couldn't report that."

"Sounds to me like the thief solved one of your problems."

"What do you mean?"

"Well, you were worried about being guilty of income tax evasion because you couldn't report the money to the Internal Revenue Service. Now you don't have that problem any more."

"Good point," Mark replied. "I'd almost convinced myself I could spend it. I had a shiny, new, red Porsche picked out in my mind. I guess I should be grateful to the thief. He probably saved me from myself."

"You said things had gotten crazy. What else happened?"

Mark leaned back in the chair and crossed his legs. "Someone tried to kill me." he said calmly.

"They did what?"

"You heard me. Someone tried to kill me. I was involved in an automobile accident. A guy hit me from behind at a signal light, then he tried to stab me."

Daniel leaned forward. "Are you okay? Did you get hurt?"

"No. We fought briefly, then I managed to get in my car and out run him. I lost him on the Interstate."

"Where did it happen?"

"A few blocks from Alfredo's Bar. The guy just came up and hit me from behind. Then he tried to act like it was my fault. We exchanged some words, then he pulled the knife on me. It wasn't a regular sized knife, like a hunting knife. It was much bigger. He had it stuck in his belt behind his back."

"Maybe it was a robbery attempt. You know how bad the crime rate is around there, and it's getting worse. I don't know why you go to

Alfredo's. That part of town is really dangerous. It has the highest crime rate in the city."

"I like the people who go to there. Besides, I've never had any trouble before."

"You've just been lucky," Daniel said.

"Maybe. But you are right about the crime rate. We've been seeing more and more injuries at Charity. A lot of them are the result of muggings. The number of DOAs has picked up too. Most of them are from robberies. It's gotten to be a dangerous world out there."

"Well, at least no one can accuse you of leading a dull life."

Mark slumped in the chair "Listen, I'm ready to give up the excitement for a while. It's getting to be too much for me."

"How is Billingsworth?" Daniel asked.

Mark shook his head. "I went to see him earlier this evening. He's not any better. I talked to his wife. She's taking it awfully hard. I hope he makes it for her sake. He's a good man. The world needs more like him."

The hour was late when Mark finished talking to Daniel and arrived back at his apartment. He stepped over the contents of drawers and cabinets, still scattered on the floor, and climbed into the tub to take a shower. Afterwards, he put on his shorts and, with considerable difficulty, turned the damaged mattress over so that the ripped side faced downward. He replaced the ruined bed linens with new ones and got into the bed.

An hour later, he was still awake. The events of the past several days...his abduction, Maldini's surgery, Billingsworth's heart attack, the attempt on his life, the ransacking of his apartment, the missing money...wouldn't stop running through his mind. Finally, he got up, flicked on the light, and went back into the kitchen area. With some difficulty, he located a package of instant Cocoa on the floor, mixed it with a cup of water, and put it in the microwave.

Two minutes later, the Cocoa was ready. He took the cup out of the microwave, walked across the room, and slumped into the over-stuffed chair. He located the remote control and turned the TV on to Jay Leno who was just beginning to interview his last guest on the Tonight Show...an author Mark had never heard of, talking about a book he also had never heard of. He sipped the hot drink slowly, trying not to burn his mouth.

Just as the Tonight Show concluded, he finished the Cocoa. Then, feeling drowsy, he walked back to his bed, climbed in it, and turned off the light. He was asleep in ten minutes.

CHAPTER TWELVE

The apartment on South Cobb Drive was pitch black and dead silent. The fluorescent hands of the clock on the bedside table indicated the time to be two-thirty in the morning. Suddenly, the doorknob on the door leading from the outer hallway began to turn, then it stopped. The door was locked. After a minute or so, the credit card made a slight, scratching sound as it slid up, then down in the lock. The lock clicked, then the doorknob turned again. This time, hardly making a sound, the door opened. A shadowy figure entered the main room from the out-side hallway. In its hand it held a small flashlight that cast a narrow beam of light around the floor. The beam focused on one object after another, then it explored the remainder of the room…the kitchen table, the TV against the wall, the sofa and overstuffed chair, the untidy coffee table…and settled on the bedroom door.

Guided by the light beam, the intruder carefully picked its way through the mess on the floor until it arrived at the bedroom door. Quietly opening the door, it crept silently across the floor, continuing to avoid objects in its path. When it reached the side of the bed, it stopped and stood there in the dark, hovering over the sleeping form. The light beam flashed briefly across the sleeper's face. Satisfied that it had found the person it was looking for, the figure bent over the motionless body and reached out a hand toward its chest.

Awakened by the light beam, Mark suddenly bolted upright and lunged at the figure hovering over him, tackling it around the waist.

They fell to the floor with a loud crash. Mark rolled over, straddled the intruder, and drew his fist back, ready to deliver a forceful blow to its face.

"Stop! Don't hit me," a female voice yelled out.

He loosened his grip on the intruder's clothes, then quickly stood and turned on the lamp on the bedside table. The intruder lay on the floor flat on her back, looking good in a pair of white slacks and a tight-fitting, pink blouse.

"Angela. How did you get in here?" he asked. "The door was locked."

She sat up and faced him. "With a credit card. My father taught me how to open locks with one when I was thirteen years old. It comes in handy ever once in a while."

"Why didn't you just knock on the door?"

"I didn't want to wake up any of your neighbors. I'd just as soon they not know I'm here."

He extended his hand. She took it. Then he helped her to her feet. Realizing that he wore only his shorts, he immediately reached for his blue jeans and slipped them on. Angela laughed a little laugh, tickled at his modesty. Then they sat on the side of the bed. Her smile quickly turned into a dead-serious look.

"Vito's gone berserk," she said. "After you left, he became obsessed with protecting his new identity. Except for a few trusted henchmen, he's given orders for everyone to be killed who can identify him."

"How do you know that?"

"Do you remember his niece, a nurse anesthetist named Leta, and her friend Beverly…the ones who assisted you with Vito's surgery?"

"Sure. They seemed like a couple of nice people. They were good at what they did."

"Were is right. Their bodies turned up in a Dumpster in downtown Miami yesterday morning. Their throats had been cut from ear to ear."

Mark swallowed hard. "How do you know Maldini's responsible?"

"He has a hit man he uses for special jobs…a mean little guy who likes to cut people up. You can bet it was his handiwork."

"Is he a Spanish-looking guy with a black goatee and a tic?"

"A tic?"

"You know, a facial twitch. It's a nervous habit."

"Jesus is Cuban, or at least half Cuban. The other half is Italian. His full name is Jesus Dimaria. How do you know what he looks like? Have you seen him?"

"I've more than seen him. He tried to kill me yesterday...pulled a knife on me. I thought it was a robbery attempt. You said he was half Italian and half Cuban. That's a strange combination. What else do you know about him?"

"I know a fair amount. Most of it I learned from my father, and from Vito. I met Jesus a few times. I didn't like the way he looked at me. He gave me the creeps."

"Go on." Mark instructed. "If he's after me, the more I know about him the better."

"Let's see. His father was a low-level Mafia member. His mother was the father's second wife. She was the daughter of Cuban immigrants. He had two older half-brothers who were full Italian from his father's previous marriage. The story goes that they gave Jesus the nickname, Little Castro, and taunted him unmercifully. When he was fourteen, he retaliated. I guess he just got tired of the constant hazing. He stabbed his older half-brother in the stomach with a butcher knife."

"Did he die?"

"No. But he almost did. After a stormy course, he pulled through. Vito said that the stabbing gave Jesus a powerful feeling, a feeling he liked. Jesus spent a couple of years in the state reform school for the incident."

"It doesn't sound like it did him much good."

"It didn't. When he returned home, he became fascinated with knives and began collecting them. When several neighborhood dogs turned up with their throats cut, everyone suspected Jesus, but no one ever proved that he did it. When he saw the movie, Crocodile Dundee, he knew he had to have a big knife like Dundee's."

"I've seen the knife up close," Mark said. "It's scary. I hope I don't have to see it again. Jesus is a strange kind of hit man. I never heard of one who uses a knife."

"Oh, he'll use a gun if he has to. He keeps one in the glove compartment of his car. He's even been know to rig a car with plastic explosives from time to time."

"I'll never understand what drives a guy like that…to kill people without giving it a second thought."

"Vito said that Jesus carries a big chip on his shoulder. Because he's of mixed blood he can never become a full member of the Mafia. That's why his angry outbursts occur so unpredictably."

"Why does Maldini keep someone like him around?"

"Despite his ugly disposition, Jesus is good at what he does. Potential victims seldom escape him."

"I did."

"I think you may be the exception. He's probably somewhere right now steaming over the fact that you got away."

The thought sent a cold chill up Mark's spine.

"Do you think Jesus made this mess of your apartment?" Angela asked, looking around the room.

"Oh my God! He's been here!" Mark blurted out. "Jesus took the money."

"What money?"

"The money Maldini gave me to do his surgery. I hid it in the closet when I got back from Miami. When I came home last night, my apartment had been ransacked and the money was gone. Maldini must have decided he wanted it back."

"That doesn't make any sense. Vito's worth millions. I've seen him gamble away more than a $100,000 in a single night and not miss a wink's sleep over it. My guess is that Jesus decided to take the money for himself. With you dead, who's to know?"

Mark shifted his weight on the bed. "You still haven't told me what you're doing here."

"I came to warn you. Vito has gone berserk. He's put out a hit list on almost everyone who can recognize him with his new face. He's only sparing a few of his most trusted men. You're at the top of the list. I'm positive I'm on his list too. If he would kill his own niece, I know he wouldn't hesitate to do the same to me."

"God, he really is a monster. What are we going to do?"

"Well, we can't stay here," Angela replied. "We're sitting ducks. We'll have to get out of here tonight."

"I know just the place," Mark responded. "We can check in just as soon as we get there."

He reached into the closet behind the pile of clothes on the floor, and took out a small suitcase. Then he quickly packed some essential items…razor, toothbrush, toothpaste, deodorant, shaving cream, shaving lotion, and a change of clothes. Suitcase in hand, they left the apartment and walked toward his car.

"What about my car?" Angela asked.

"You'd better follow me. We're going to have to ditch it somewhere. We need to delay Maldini finding out that you're in Atlanta as long as we can."

He got into his beat-up Porsche. She got into her shiny, red Mercedes that she said Maldini had given her earlier in the year for her twenty-eighth birthday. They drove for almost twenty minutes, finally coming to a river. The bank sloped steeply down to the water. He parked at the top of the bank. She pulled up beside him. Then they got out. He joined her by her car. The bright moon illuminated the murky water below.

"What are we doing here?" she asked.

"We've got to get rid of your car. It can't be seen in Atlanta."

"Oh no! You're not going to put my car in there," she said, looking down at the water.

"Well, what do you suggest? It's a rolling advertisement that you're here."

She hesitated, then frowned. "I guess you're right, but I sure do love my car."

He opened the driver-side door of the Mercedes, put the car in neutral, and let off the emergency brake.

"Give me a hand," he said as he walked to the rear of the car.

She followed him. "What do you want me to do?"

"Push," he answered.

Spreading his feet, he planted them firmly on the ground. Then he placed his hands on the back of the car and began to push.

"Wait!" she yelled. "My suitcase."

He took his hands off the car. She opened the back door on the driver's side and took a suitcase, considerably larger than his, from the floorboard.

"Now we can push," she said.

She sat her suitcase on the ground and joined him at the back of the car. Together, they pushed harder and harder until the Mercedes began to roll. Finally, it reached the incline and careened wildly through the pine trees toward the water below. It hit the water with a large splash. Its momentum carried it at least thirty feet out into the river. They watched as it slowly sank further and further into the water. Finally, it went tail up and disappeared beneath the surface.

"Do you know how much that car cost?" Angela asked sadly.

"I have a pretty good idea. Believe it or not, I used to own a new Mercedes."

"I want you to know we just sank two year's salary for most people."

"Well, my mother used to say 'Never cry over sunk Mercedes,'" he said with a smile.

She frowned. "That's a terrible joke. What do we do now?"

"Let's get out of here."

A short time later, they pulled in front of the office of a shabby motel. The neon sign on top of the pole by the street read **Starlight Motel, Rooms 24 Dollars.** Angela stayed in the car while he went inside to get a room. A few minutes later, he returned with a room key. He parked the Porsche around back, carried their suitcases up the steps, and entered room number twenty-two. It was a familiar room. He had seen his ex-wife and her lover, Sam Kincaid, come out of it and hug and kiss on the balcony two years earlier.

Mark awoke, as was his custom, at six o'clock in the morning. Angela was sound asleep in the other bed. She had been worn out from driving most of the day yesterday and a major part of the night.

Mattie would be at work in an hour. He would call her then and tell her not to expect him at Charity for some time. He didn't know when he would be back…maybe days, maybe weeks, maybe never. He looked around the room, studying it carefully. He could have had a number of other rooms. He had chosen this one intentionally.

Lying there in the early morning light, he thought about Joanna and Sam Kincaid, and wondered how may times they had made love in the very bed he was lying in. It still hurt, but time was beginning to numb the pain. He hoped that staying in this room, a process in medicine called desensitization, would serve to ease the pain even more.

He turned the TV on to CNN, as was also his custom in the morning. He kept the volume low so as not to disturb Angela. A world congress on human rights abuses, more drug-related killings in a New York ghetto, another earthquake in California…nothing about Maldini.

A few minutes after seven, he dialed the number of Charity Emergency Room and asked to speak with Mattie. Almost immediately, she came to the telephone.

"Mattie, this is Mark," he said.

"Dr. Valentine, where are you? You're late. Dr. Stottlemire's really upset this time."

"Tell him I won't be in today. I don't know when I'll be back."

"You what?"

"You heard me. I won't be in today. Stottlemire will have to do the best he can. He can get the residents at Emory to fill in for me until I get back, if I ever do. They're always looking for moonlighting opportunities to supplement their meager pay."

"Mark, what's wrong? What's going on?" Mattie asked quickly.

"It's a long story. Someone's out to kill me. He's already killed two people and made an attempt on my life. It's not safe for me to come to work."

"Someone's trying to kill you? Who?"

"I can't tell you that. If I did, it would put your life in danger too. Tell Stottlemire I'm sorry. I'd be there if I could. How's Billingsworth doing?"

"About the same. He tries to breathe on his own ever once in a while, but then he quits. He's not had anymore cardiac arrhythmia problems, and his vital signs have remained stable the last couple of days, but he's still in a coma."

"I'm sorry to hear that. I had hoped he would be much better. Give me your home telephone number so I can call you every once in a while to check on his progress."

She gave him the number. He wrote it down on a piece of paper and put it in his billfold.

Half an hour later, he left a note on his bed for Angela…**Gone To Get Us Some Food, Be Right Back**…and went to a deli down the street to get two take-out breakfasts, complete with coffee. The Starlight didn't have a restaurant. When he returned, Angela was awake and sitting on the side of the bed. She had been alarmed at first when she awakened and realized that he wasn't there, but then she spotted the note, read it, and been relieved.

He handed her a Styrofoam container containing her food and set both Styrofoam cups of coffee on the bedside table. Then he sat down on the bed opposite her. They ate the scrambled eggs, bacon, and grits in silence. The hot coffee was especially good.

"What do you think we should do?" she asked when they had finished eating. "We can't live here forever."

"I think we should get out of the state until Maldini's captured. How much money do you have?"

She reached for her purse, opened it, and took out her billfold. Then she pulled several bills from the billfold and handed them to him.

He counted them. The total was $175. Then he pulled his billfold out of his back pocket and counted...$75. He held Angela's money out toward her. She held up her hand with her palm toward him.

"Keep it," she said. "We're in this together."

He nodded, then put the money in his billfold and replaced the billfold in his pocket. "We can't get very far on $250," he said dejectedly.

"I've got a credit card," she said. "We can get lots of money on it."

"Let me see it."

She handed him the card. He looked at it...**Visa Gold**. The name on the card startled him...**Vito Maldini.**

"This is Maldini's card. How did you get it?" he asked, handing it back to her.

"No it's not. It's my card. He just pays the bill."

"We can't use it."

"Why not?"

"He could trace its use directly to Atlanta."

"What about your card? You do have one don't you?"

"Yes, I've got one, but it's over the limit."

She smiled. "Just my luck. I picked a poor doctor."

He didn't smile back. "We've got to come up with some money, but from where?" He thought for a moment. "Joanna! She's got loads of money. She'll have to lend us some."

"Who's Joanna?"

"My ex-wife. Unfortunately, we're not on very good terms."

"Do you think she'll give you the money?"

"I hope so. Even Joanna can understand a life or death situation. After we get the money, we'll go to the police. I can give them a perfect description of Maldini's new face."

———————————

Mark parked the Porsche in front of Joanna's house and reached for the car door handle.

"Should I come with you?" Angela asked.

"Sure," he responded. "She might be more apt to believe me if you corroborate my story."

They left the car, walked to the porch, climbed the steps, and crossed the porch to the front door. He rang the doorbell and waited.

No one came to the door.

"She's probably asleep," he said. "She usually stays in bed until ten o'clock." He rang the doorbell again.

Still no response.

"Come on," he said, taking Angela by the hand. He led her around to the back of the house where he put his face up to the window in the door and peered in.

"Is she in there?" Angela asked.

"I'm sure she is. It's too early for her to go anywhere." He tried the doorknob, expecting the door to be locked. To his surprise, the door opened. "It's not like Joanna to leave the door unlocked," he said. "She usually keeps this place locked up tight as a drum."

He pushed the door open and entered the hallway that led to the kitchen on the right and the family room on the left. Angela followed him.

"Why are all the lights on?" she asked.

"Joanna leaves them on when she's home alone. She feels safer that way. She worries about crime a lot."

They looked around the downstairs part of the house. Joanna was nowhere to be seen.

"Come on," he instructed, again taking Angela by the hand.

He led her up the spiral stairway to the second floor. They walked to the end of the landing, pushed the door of the master bedroom open, and walked in. Joanna was not there either.

He turned and led Angela out of the bedroom back along the landing to the guest room Joanna had slept in the last six months of their marriage. He opened the door and looked in. Joanna lay on the bed on her back with the covers up around her neck. A book lay beside her. She appeared to be sound asleep.

"She must be back on sleeping pills," he said. "I used to get on to her about taking them. The house could burn down and she would never know it." He walked to the bed and shook her gently. "Joanna, wake up," he said softly. "I've got to talk to you."

She didn't move.

Angela came up from behind and stood by his side. "What's wrong with her? Is she okay?"

He shook her again. "Joanna, wake up," he said a little louder.

Still no response.

He shook her harder. "Joanna! Wake up," he yelled, frightened that she might have accidentally overdosed on sleeping pills.

She continued to lie motionless. He reached down and placed his fingers on the side of her neck...no carotid pulse. Now he was sure of it. She had taken too many sleeping pills, and probably drank on top of them. He quickly took the covers in his hand and pulled them down around her waist, ready to begin CPR

Angela gasped. He stopped in his tracks. Fresh blood covered the entire front of Joanna's gown and pooled around her in a large circular area on the bed linens. A two-inch gash was clearly evident in the gown over her heart. He quickly pulled the covers back up. With a heart that had been ripped open and the resulting massive blood loss, CPR would be worthless.

"Jesus?" he asked, already knowing the answer.

Angela nodded her head. "Jesus," she said. "How long do you think she's been dead?"

"Judging by the looks of the blood, at least fifteen to twenty minutes. Jesus couldn't have been gone long."

Angela quickly looked around the room as if she expected to see Jesus lurking in a corner. Mark took his handkerchief from his pocket and picked up the telephone. Then he pulled a pen from his shirt pocket and dialed a number.

"What are you doing?" Angela asked nervously. "Let's get out of here. Jesus could still be in here somewhere."

"I'm dialing 911. We can't just leave her here like this."

The 911 operator answered.

"Someone's been murdered," he said. Then he gave her the address.

"Who is this?" the operator asked.

He hung up the telephone. Then he and Angela rushed out of the house the way they had come in, carefully wiping his prints off the bedroom and back doors.

As they got into his car, the thought flickered through his mind that he wouldn't have to pay any more alimony payments. He immediately felt guilty and forced the thought from his mind.

———————

Mark and Angela sat silently at the small table in their room at the Starlight Motel and stared at each other. Joanna's death had left a hollow spot in his heart. Despite their differences, she had been an integral part of his life for a long time. He would miss her. Finally, he broke the silence.

"I don't understand why Jesus killed Joanna. She didn't have anything to do with Maldini's surgery. I doubt if she even knew who he was."

"Maybe Jesus thought she knew where you were and wouldn't tell him."

"I haven't seen her or talked to her since well before Maldini's surgery. She didn't have the slightest idea what I'd been up to."

"Jesus didn't know that. When she denied knowing your whereabouts, he probably thought she was lying and lost his temper. He killed a man once just because he didn't like the way he looked at him."

"He sounds crazy."

"A lot of people would agree with you. If he's on your trail, he can be your worst nightmare."

"Well, he is on our trail, at least mine, and I don't mind telling you, I'm scared."

"You have a right to be. I'm pretty damn scared myself. When do we go to the police?"

"In the morning. I'm not up to it now. I'll give them a description of Maldini's new face and explain to them that I did the surgery under threat to my daughter's life, and that now Maldini wants to kill me. I'll tell them that Jesus murdered Joanna. You can corroborate my story. They'll understand and, with any luck at all, Maldini and Jesus will be apprehended quickly and we can get on with our lives."

CHAPTER THIRTEEN

Mark dozed off and on during the night. He could hear Angela tossing and turning in the other bed. He was sure he could have her any time he wanted, but this morning his mind wasn't on sex. It was on Joanna and Maldini and Jesus. He hated Jesus for what he had done to Joanna. Even she didn't deserve such a horrible fate. He tried not to think about the details of her death, but most of all he tried to push the thoughts of how she must have suffered at the end to the furthest recesses of his mind. What kind of man would commit such a heinous crime...to brutally murder someone simply because she couldn't give him the information he wanted, with no guilt over his deeds, no compassion for his victims or their families?

As much as he hated Jesus, he hated Maldini even more. After all, Maldini was the one who had sent this vicious animal after him. How could Maldini justify to himself the pain and suffering he inflicted on others?

Mark thought about the people Jesus had killed...first Leta and Beverly, then Joanna. He knew Jesus was out there somewhere looking for him. He wondered where he was now and what he was up to. Did he know where they were? He could be just around the corner and they wouldn't know it. They would have to stay on the go, stay one step ahead of him. Mark knew he had been lucky in their first confrontation. He feared a second. He was no match for a professional killer, especially one as vicious as Jesus. He wondered how many more murders there would be. He hoped he wouldn't be the next.

He dressed…the usual worn blue jeans and T-shirt, watched the news, smoked a cigarette, then awakened Angela. As she dressed, they discussed Maldini's obsession with keeping his new face secretive, Joanna's death, and Jesus' relentless pursuit of his victims.

"When do we go to the police?" Angela asked.

"We're on our way. Surely, with the information I'll supply them, they'll be able to find Maldini quickly. Once Maldini is captured, Jesus won't have any reason to continue pursuing me."

They left the room, got into the Porsche, and pulled out from behind the motel. Mark could hardly wait to get to the police station. With the information he had, he was sure they would be happy to see him. He turned into the drive in front of the motel office and parked near the entrance.

"Why are you stopping here?" Angela asked.

"To get a newspaper. I want to see if there's anything in it about Joanna's death."

"Good idea."

He left the car and disappeared into the motel office. A few minutes later he returned with the morning edition of the Atlanta Constitution folded in his hand. Getting into the car, he handed the newspaper to Angela.

"See what you can find." he instructed.

As Angela unfolded the paper, he pulled out into the heavy traffic on the street in front of the motel. The police station was located downtown. They would take the Interstate to the downtown area, get off on the Peachtree Street exit, then weave their way along a series of one-way streets that seemed to lead in no particular direction, but instead followed the natural flow of the landscape. Once there, he would simply tell them that, under threat to his daughter's life, he had done Maldini's surgery. They didn't need to know about the money. He didn't have it anymore anyway.

Suddenly Angela made a commotion on her side of the car. "Mark! Stop! We can't go to the police," she said excitedly.

He eased off on the accelerator and glanced over at her. "Why not? What's wrong?" He quickly pulled into the right-hand lane.

"Find a place to stop and I'll tell you."

He immediately turned right into the parking lot of a Starvin Marvin's food store and parked in a space by the building. It was obvious from the expression on her face that something bad was wrong.

She handed him the newspaper. He read the headline in disbelief...**Doctor Prime Suspect In Ex-wife's Vicious Murder**. He read the copy. It described the murder scene just as he and Angela had seen it...all the lights on, no evidence of burglary, Joanna's body in the bed, and the pool of blood. A neighbor had seen him and an unidentified female sneaking around Joanna's house the morning of the murder. The description of Angela was pretty accurate except for the height, which was given as five feet five inches...two inches shorter than her actual height. His six foot two frame often made women appear shorter beside him than they actually were. The article went on to say that an eyewitness, Sam Kincaid, reported that Mark had threatened Joanna two weeks prior to the murder. The District Attorney, who had political aspirations, was quoted as practically guaranteeing a conviction.

"What are we going to do?" Angela asked

"You already said it. We can't go to the police. Let me think."

"The District Attorney is going to charge Mark Valentine with murder one and ask for the death penalty if he is convicted," Detective Smith said as he walked into Lieutenant Carmichael's cluttered office in the Atlanta police station. "Did your hear?"

Carmichael, a tall angular man in his late forties, looked up from his desk. "It was just on the radio. What makes him think that it's going to be so easy? We have to find Valentine first. Right now we don't have a clue as to his where-abouts."

Shorter, heavier, and a little younger than Carmichael, Smith eased into the chair in front of the desk. "The D. A. needs a big one. Something to spout off about in his campaign. You know he's planning on running for Governor in the next election."

"Is there anyone in the state who doesn't know it by now? You have to admit that getting a conviction of a doctor gone bad for the murder of his wealthy socialite wife would be a hell of a feather in his cap. What have you got for me?"

"We found prints of three individuals in the house. One set belonged to the victim. We don't have positive identifications on the other two yet." Smith took a sip of coffee from a blue mug with a gold, police-badge replica on it. "The prints of one of the other individuals were in a number of places in the house, the kind of pattern you would expect for someone living there. They were smaller than most men's prints. We think they belong to the daughter, Lisa. She goes to a private school in Valdosta. Although she lives in the dorm, she comes home fairly often."

"What about the other set?" Smith asked.

We don't know who they belong to yet. They're men's prints. Hopefully they belong to the killer."

"Do you think they're Dr. Valentine's?"

"I don't know. He's never been charged with a serious crime before, so his prints aren't on file."

"What about prints from the door of the bedroom where the victim was killed?"

Carmichael leaned back and crossed his legs. "There weren't any prints on the bedroom door. We feel certain that the killer entered and left the house by the back door. There weren't any prints on it either."

"Think the prints were wiped off?" Smith asked.

"Without a doubt. Even if the killer wore gloves, there would still be some remnants of prints on the door. You know, from whoever used the door before him."

"You'd better give this information to Captain Kincaid right away," Smith said. "Seems he has a personal interest in this case. He wants Valentine in the worst way. Word has it that he and the victim were kind of sweet on each other."

"I heard they were engaged to be married. If it's true, I'd hate to be in Valentine's shoes. The Captain can be a real bad ass when he wants to. I wouldn't put anything past him."

———————————

Mark and Angela sat across from each other on the sides of their beds with bewildered looks on their faces. Neither spoke. What would they do now? Everything had seemed so simple when they left to go to the police station. Now the police were after Mark, as was Jesus. Angela finally broke the silence.

"Vito told me you had a daughter," she said. "How old is she?"

Mark suddenly sat upright. "Oh my God!" he blurted out. "Lisa! I should have called her by now."

"How awful. I'll bet she's already learned about her mother's death from someone else," Angela said with concern in her voice.

"No! You don't understand. If Jesus went after Joanna to get to me, he'll go after Lisa too. We've got to do something." He picked up the telephone and dialed a number.

"Who are you calling?" Angela asked.

"Lisa's dorm room."

He let the telephone ring ten times. No one answered.

"Damn! She must have already gone to class," he said dejectedly. He hung up the telephone and quickly dialed another number.

"Briarwood Academy. This is Mrs. Edwards, Administrative Secretary to Mr. Callaway," the voice on the other end of the line said after the second ring.

"Mrs. Edwards, how are you? This is Dr. Valentine. We met once when I was down there visiting my daughter, Lisa. I need to talk with Mr. Callaway." He held his breath, hoping she hadn't heard about Joanna's death.

"I'm sorry, Mr. Callaway is out of town. I expect him back after lunch. Can I have him call you?"

Thank God, he thought. Apparently she hadn't heard. "That will be too late. I believe Lisa's life is in danger. She has to be taken somewhere and hidden until I can get there. I'm leaving now. I should be there in a little over three hours. Can you do that?"

"Let me get this straight. You want me to take Lisa out of class and hide her somewhere until you get here."

"Yes, it's very important. It's a matter of life and death."

"Dr. Valentine, I can't do that without Mrs. Valentine's permission. She told us when she enrolled Lisa here that we were not to honor any requests from you."

"Mrs. Edwards, you didn't listen to me. Lisa's life is in danger. Joanna can't give her permission."

"Mrs. Valentine said you would try anything to usurp her authority."

"Damn it! Joanna's dead!" he blurted out without thinking. "Haven't you read the newspaper?"

"Yes. I read the Valdosta Gazette every morning. The paper didn't say anything about Lisa's mother dying."

Since he had let the cat out of the bag he pressed on. "The Atlanta paper! It was on the front page."

"I don't take the Atlanta paper."

"Mrs. Edwards, I'm getting very frustrated. Can't you just take my word for it?"

"Dr. Valentine, I don't have the authority to pull Lisa out of class without her mother's approval. You'll just have to wait until Mr. Callaway gets back and discuss it with him."

"Are you retarded? I just told you that my daughter's life is in danger and you act like it's of no significance. What's wrong with you?"

"There's no call for that kind of attitude. Have you been drinking? Mrs. Valentine said you had a drinking problem."

"No, I haven't been drinking. Have you?" he asked sarcastically. Then he slammed the telephone down.

"Come on. Let's go," he said to Angela. Hand in hand they rushed out of the room.

He thought about calling the police and telling them to get to Briarwood Academy as fast as they could, but decided that it wouldn't do any good. After all, they had already come to the conclusion that he had murdered Joanna. He doubted that they would take him seriously if he told them the real killer was going after Lisa. Besides, they probably had never heard of Jesus since he was from out of state. Then there was the possibility that Mrs. Edwards would call the police when Joanna's death made the local news and she discovered that he was the prime suspect. He feared that the focus of the police would be on capturing him, rather than protecting Lisa. They might even prevent him from getting to her in time. As much as he didn't want it to be, it was up to him.

"Where are we going?" Angela asked.

"To Lisa's school," he replied. "Pray that we get there in time."

———————————

They reached Interstate 75 and headed south. They would pass through two towns...Macon and Tilton...spaced along the highway between Atlanta and Valdosta, the site of Briarwood Academy. The speed limit all the way was seventy miles per hour. The Porsche wouldn't see that speed again until they reached Valdosta, 220 miles away, at least not if he could help it.

Once outside Atlanta, the traffic thinned out and the Porsche picked up speed. He couldn't shake the vision in his head of Jesus and Lisa and that big knife. He had to beat him to Briarwood Academy. The alternative was too gruesome to think about.

He glanced at Angela. She sat in the passenger-side seat against the door, turned slightly in his direction. Her attractive legs protruded from a blue miniskirt that came down to mid-thigh. Her pink sweater accentuated her full breasts. He was glad she had left Maldini and come to Atlanta. He needed the company…someone to take his mind off all the bad stuff that was going on. She was so much different than Susan. Susan had grown up in a small town with middle-class, family values. Angela, on the other hand, had grown up virtually within the Mafia. He wondered what her values were.

He pulled up behind an elderly couple in a white Buick Century doing exactly sixty-five miles per hour. He assumed that they had the cruise control set so that they wouldn't exceed the speed limit. He slowed briefly, then switched lanes and easily passed them. Easing down on the accelerator pedal, he picked up speed again and tried to relax. The Buick slowly fell far behind in the rear-view mirror.

CHAPTER FOURTEEN

The blue Pontiac passed through Macon at ten o'clock, slowed slightly as cars entered the highway, then passed them and sped onward toward Valdosta. "The kid is bound to know where her father is," Jesus mumbled. "She'll talk or else." He was tired of fooling around. He had a job to do and he was ready to get on with it. He had plans for the future...$100,000 worth of plans. With Mark Valentine out of the way, Maldini would never know he took the money.

At ten fifteen, Mark and Angela crossed the Sabbath River and reached Macon. Tilton and Valdosta were still ahead, miles down the highway. Unknown to them, Jesus was fifteen minutes up ahead.

After eighty miles and two telephone calls along the way, Mark still hadn't been able to reach Lisa. He was beginning to feel frantic. He pressed his foot harder on the accelerator pedal, and the Porsche raced up the highway faster and faster. Concern increasingly showed on Angela's face. He was aware that she felt his fear about not getting to Valdosta in time. Angela continued talking to him in an attempt to calm him down.

"Tell me about Lisa," she said.

"She's the light of my life. I know every parent feels that way, but she really is special. I think her hearing loss has been more of a problem to me than it has to her. She's always handled it well."

"Was she born deaf, or did she have an infection of some sort?"

"She was born deaf. She's never known any difference."

"When I was growing up, one of our black maids had a deaf son," Angela said. "I think he must have been eighteen or nineteen years old at the time. He couldn't talk at all. He grunted a lot and signed. I could never talk to him because I didn't know sign language. His mother used to sign to him all the time. She was about the only one I knew of who could communicate with him. His father refused to learn sign language. He always relied on the mother to do the communication."

"That's really sad," Mark said. "You'd think he would have cared enough to learn." He settled back in the seat and was silent for a moment. "Tell me about yourself. How did you get mixed up with someone like Maldini?"

"It wasn't by design. It just sort of happened. My father worked for the organization. When I was small, I used to think that he was a legitimate businessman. He always wore a suit and tie and had very flexible working hours. I didn't find out until I was twelve that he was a member of the Mafia. My father was a businessman all right, but not a legitimate one. He was in charge of loan-sharking for the mob. It was a real shock to me. I was so embarrassed I could hardly face my friends at school. Turned out they all already knew about it. I felt really dumb when they told me."

"That's how you met Maldini?"

"Yes. When I was growing up, he was in and out of our house all the time. I could tell that he was real important. He always had lots of money, and a chauffeured limousine drove him everywhere he went. He was sort of like an uncle to me. After I graduated from high school, he started asking me out."

"You said his wife died. When was that?"

"About three years after I graduated."

Mark glanced in her direction. "He asked you out while he was still married?"

"Yes."

"Did you go?"

"A few times. I didn't feel comfortable about it though, knowing his wife so well. I finally told him that I wasn't going to see him any more. He was real persistent, but he finally gave up."

"What did his wife die of?"

Angela frowned. "He didn't kill her if that's what you're thinking. She died of breast cancer."

"Well, I have to admit the thought crossed my mind. So you got back together after her death?"

"Yes, but not immediately. I think it was about a year or so later."

"But why? He's a terrible man."

"He's not all bad. He can be very kind and loving at times, and he is very generous. He lavished me with presents…diamonds, furs, anything I wanted. I felt like a queen. I guess I just got caught up in it all."

"I can see where that could happen," Mark said.

"I'm glad it's over. My relationship with him was going nowhere. He used to talk about how bad his marriage was. When his wife died, he said that he would never get married again. I expected our relationship to end some day, but in my wildest dreams I never expected it to be like this. I don't think I can ever get use to not having money."

He certainly could understand that. He still hadn't gotten use to it himself.

Crossing the Tobesokee River, they put Macon behind them and headed for Tilton.

———————

At eleven o'clock, the blue Pontiac roared through Tilton. Valdosta was forty-three miles away. Jesus was gaining confidence. He would be at Briarwood Academy soon. Once there, he would stop and ask directions to the girls' dormitory. He had never been to Valdosta before, and he had never seen Lisa. He hadn't even seen a picture of her, but he knew what she looked like. She was tall for her age, blonde, and good looking. He wouldn't have any trouble finding her. After all, how many girls with a description like that had a hearing problem?

Five minutes later, Mark and Angela passed through Tilton and headed toward Valdosta.

"Tell me more about Maldini," Mark instructed.

"What else do you want to know about him?" Angela asked.

"Everything. How old is he for one? He looks a hell of a lot older than you."

"He is. He's fifty six."

"How did he get to be such a crook?"

"I think it came to him naturally. He grew up in the tough, water-front district of Miami. He still brags about beginning his crime career at the age of seven by stealing apples from a local supermarket. By the time he was eighteen, he was specializing in strong-arm work, and had developed a pretty bad reputation. If there was a real dirty job to be done by the Mafia, he almost always got the assignment. By the time he was twenty-five he had already killed a few men, at least that's what my father told me. A lot of what I know about Vito I learned from him. The Galante family rewarded Vito for his good work by officially inducting him into the Mafia as a soldier. After that, he rose up rapidly through the ranks. By the time he was in his early forties he had become a cap-tain in charge of illegal gambling and loan-sharking in the western sec-tion of Miami. There's one really bad thing he's supposed to have done. I'm embarrassed to tell you about it."

"It's too late to stop now. You've perked my curiosity."

She hesitated, then proceeded with her story. "Once, when he caught an associate skimming money off the top, to make a point, he had him bound and gagged and a lit cherry bomb stuffed up his rectum."

"You've got to be kidding."

"No. I swear I'm telling the truth."

"Did the man survive?"

"I was told that he did, but that he would have to live the rest of his life with a colostomy bag."

"That's really awful. What else?" Mark asked.

"Because of the large profits Vito supplied to the upper echelon of the Mafia, Frank Galante, the head of the family, eventually appointed him under boss, responsible only to him. His job was to supervise all illegal operations. You know, narcotics, extortion, gambling, racketeering. I don't know what else."

"What about legal operations? I've heard the Mafia operates a number of these as fronts."

"You're right. They do," Angela responded. "Things like garbage collection, vending machines, trucking, construction, restaurants, and restaurant supply houses. Vito was involved only marginally in these activities. To promote the facade of being a legitimate businessman, Galante himself personally supervised those operations. Vito got involved only when his special talents were needed."

"What did you mean, special talents?"

"I'll give you an example that my father thought was ingenious. Occasionally, Vito used the services of the family's legally operated funeral homes to dispose of bodies of men who had crossed the family in one way or another. They were placed in caskets along with the naturally deceased and buried. Apparently, not a single body disposed of in this manner ever turned up to cause the family a problem."

"Your father was right. That is pretty ingenious. How did Maldini get Galante's job? Did he kill him?"

"No. Somebody else did…a rival mob boss. Vito seized the opportunity and became the head of the family. He rapidly built the operation into one of the top money-making ventures in the national organization."

"How does he stay out of prison?"

"It's not because the FBI hasn't tried to put him there. They've pursued him relentlessly, but they haven't been able to pin anything on him. Cases that were prepared against him always collapsed before they made it to trial. Seems that it was impossible to find a witness with sufficient suicidal tendency to testify against him."

Suddenly, movement in the rearview mirror caught Mark's attention. Despite the Porsche's high speed, a black Lincoln Town Car rapidly approached them from the rear.

"Maldini," he said aloud. His palms suddenly felt cold and clammy and beads of sweat burst out on his forehead. Angela quickly turned and looked out the rear window.

"I wish I had my Smith and Wesson with me," Mark said. Unfortunately it was still in the drawer of the bedside table in his apartment. He berated myself for not thinking to get it when they fled. Things had just happened too fast.

The Lincoln Town Car pulled up right on their bumper, hesitated, then veered out to the left and pulled up beside them. Mark nervously peered through its windows, expecting to see one of Maldini's henchmen pointing a gun right at him. Instead, an elderly man with a paunch was slouched down behind the steering wheel. An equally elderly woman in the passenger seat was reading a magazine. The Town Car pulled out ahead of them and disappeared at rapid speed over a hill in the distance. It was only then that he realized how jumpy he was.

———

The blue Pontiac roared past the **Welcome To Valdosta** sign. Unknown to Jesus, Mark and Angela were only minutes behind, and gaining. As he came to Exit 5, surrounded by numerous motels, he slowed and exited the highway onto St. Augustine Street. Then, almost immediately, he turned right into an Exxon station and parked by the building. He left the car and entered the food shop. Rows of shelves full of snacks, canned goods, and other assorted items occupied the central part of the store. A glass-enclosed cooler containing soft drinks, juices, and beer lined the entire back wall. The store was empty except for two young, black men standing by the cooler and a bored-looking, female clerk behind the counter. Jesus walked to the cooler, took out an Old Milwaukee beer, and returned to the front of the store. He stood in line behind the two black men while they paid for a six-pack of beer and attempted to joke with the clerk. When she failed to find them funny, they took their beer and left.

Jesus stepped up to the counter, plopped down a ten-dollar bill, and waited while the clerk counted out his change. "How do I get to Briarwood Academy from here?" he asked as the last penny was placed in his hand.

The clerk scratched her head for a moment. "Get back on the highway and go to Exit 4. You can't miss it. It's surrounded by another group of motels. Get off there onto Hill Avenue going east. Two blocks after you pass the Lowndes County Historical Museum on the left, take a right on Patterson Street. Keep going until you come to a fork in the road. Patterson Street continues on to the right as U.S. Highway 41. Take the left leg of the fork, which is Statenville Highway. Briarwood Academy is located five miles down the highway on the right. You can't miss it."

"Thanks," Jesus said, handing a five-dollar bill back to the clerk.

Before the clerk could thank him, Jesus turned and left the store. He got back into his car and, as instructed, headed back to Interstate 75.

A short time later, he came to Exit 4 and got off the highway onto Hill Street. As the buildings of the downtown area began to appear off to his left, he passed the Historical Museum, went two blocks and took a right onto Patterson Street. He continued down Patterson Street until he came to the fork and swung left onto Statenville Highway. He watched the odometer on his dashboard. As it indicated that he had come five miles, the complex of red brick buildings up ahead came into view. Approaching the buildings, the sign at the entrance identified the complex…**Briarwood Academy.**

As Jesus slowed to turn into the entrance, his heart began to beat rapidly. He felt good, almost euphoric. He recognized the feeling. It was one he liked. He always experienced it just before closing in on his prey. With any luck at all he would soon have the information he came for. Either that or he would see to it that Valentine's daughter wouldn't live to tell about their encounter. The right side of his face began to twitch uncontrollably.

Mark estimated that they had to be within a mile or two of Valdosta's city limits. He was beginning to feel better. Maybe they would beat Jesus to Briarwood Academy after all. He hoped that news of the fact that the police were looking for him hadn't made it to Valdosta yet. If it had, the police might try to prevent him from getting to Lisa, a possibility that worried him a great deal. He pushed the accelerator pedal further to the floorboard and picked up speed, anxious to cover the last few miles as fast as he could.

Suddenly he noticed the flashing, red and blue lights in his rearview mirror. He looked down at the speedometer…eighty-five miles per hour.

"Shit!" he said, half under his breath. A highway patrol car was right on his bumper.

"What are we going to do?" Angela asked.

"I don't know. If he asks for my driver's license, we're dead. He's bound to know that I'm wanted for murder." He took his foot off the accelerator and gently applied pressure to the brake pedal. The Porsche slowed to fifty miles per hour, then thirty, then fifteen. The patrol car stayed right on its bumper. Finally, Mark pulled off the pavement onto the shoulder and the Porsche came to a stop. The patrol car pulled up and stopped right behind it.

"Damn!" Mark said aloud. "We don't have time for this. There's no telling where Jesus is right now. He could already be at Briarwood Academy for all we know." He rolled the window down on his side and waited while the heavy-set, uniformed, highway patrolman sauntered up to the car. His belt strained to contain his bulging stomach.

Finally reaching the window, the patrolman bent over and looked in. He slowly took off his dark, Airforce-style sunglasses, folded the earpieces, and put the glasses in his shirt pocket.

"Going kinda fast weren't you buddy?" he asked in an unfriendly voice. "Do you know what the speed limit is around here?" He took his ticket book out of his pocket.

"Yes sir," Mark replied, trying to act as humble as he could. "It's seventy." His eyes were fixed on the ticket book.

"I clocked you at eighty five. What's your hurry?" the patrolman asked. He took a quick look at Angela's legs. She caught his eye and smiled. He immediately looked down at his ticket book and cleared his throat.

What's my hurry? A crazy man may kill my daughter any minute...that's the hurry, Mark wanted to say, but he knew the truth would cause more trouble than a lie. "I just wasn't paying attention to how fast I was going," he responded. "If you let us go, I promise to drive under the speed limit the rest of the way."

The patrolman opened the ticket book and took a pen from his shirt pocket.

"Oh shit!" Mark thought. "He's going to ask for my license." He held his breath.

"Where are you going?" the patrolman asked.

Mark cleared his throat. "To Valdosta. My daughter's in school at Briarwood Academy. I'm real worried about her. She was admitted to the hospital there this morning. Her doctor called me nearly three hours ago and told me that she has double pneumonia. She's on the critical list. He said that she's in the intensive care unit on a ventilator." He glanced at Angela. "Her mother is real upset. Lisa is our only child." He nervously looked at his watch...five precious minutes had elapsed.

Angela gave the patrolman her best worried look. "My husband was just in a hurry to get by our daughter's side. You can understand that, can't you?" She managed to shed an actual tear. "I'll see to it that he stays within the speed limit the rest of the way."

The patrolman's gruffness suddenly changed to an understanding tone. "Gosh mam, I'm really sorry to hear that. I got three kids of my own. I guess I would be breaking the speed limit too if one of mine was that sick." He looked at his ticket book, hesitated, then put it back in his pocket.

Mark wiped the sweat from his brow. Angela looked relieved.

"Okay, I'm going to let you off this time, but stay within the speed limit," the patrolman said. "At the rate you were going you would have ended up in the hospital too, or worse yet, dead." He turned and walked back toward his car.

Mark looked at Angela. "Thank God," he said, just barely audible within the car.

The patrolman suddenly stopped and turned back in Mark's direction.

"Now what?" Mark mumbled.

"By the way, did you know you have a busted tail light?" the patrolman said as he approached the window again.

"Yes. I got tail-ended at a red light this morning on the way here. I plan on getting it fixed right after I check on our daughter."

"Well, you better get it fixed before you come back through here or I'll have to give you a citation. I hope your little girl gets okay. You all drive carefully now, you hear."

They watched him get into his car, pull out around them, and head down the highway.

Mark looked at his watch again. "Damn!" he said disgustedly. "We've lost ten minutes."

Angela nodded sympathetically. She knew he was a bundle of nerves on the inside.

They stayed a few hundred feet behind the patrol car for about a half-mile. The speedometer never varied from seventy miles per hour.

"Don't tell me this guy is going to stay in front of us all the way to Valdosta," Mark said angrily. "Maybe I should pass him and try to out-run him."

"Don't do that," Angela said quickly. "We might both end up in jail. That wouldn't do Lisa any good. Give him a little more time."

Reluctantly, Mark agreed.

Finally, the patrol car came to an area between the two slabs of concrete that was worn bare of foliage from cars making U-turns. It crossed the area and headed back in the other direction. Mark watched the car in the rearview mirror until it was safely out of sight. Then he rapidly picked up speed. It would take a roadblock to stop him now.

They finally made it to the entrance of Briarwood Academy. Mark nervously looked around for signs of police surveillance. Seeing nothing unusual, he turned into the drive. Could luck be with them? he wondered. Was it possible that news of Joanna's death hadn't reached Valdosta yet?" His guess was that it would be reported in the afternoon newspaper.

He drove past the Administration building on the right and the main classroom building on the left, still half expecting a hoard of heavily armed policemen to jump out from behind the trees. Instead, all he saw were scattered pockets of blue-uniformed students.

They passed the gymnasium with the indoor pool on the right and the boys' dormitory on the left, then made a left turn. Coming out of the turn, Mark spotted a small crowd of students up ahead in front of the girls' dormitory. He pulled up behind the group, parked by the curb, and glanced around the area again. Still no sign of the police. Mark and Angela quickly got out of the car and walked up to the crowd. He tapped a male student on the back. The student, like all the others, wore a blue uniform. He appeared to be about Lisa's age.

"What's going on?" Mark asked anxiously.

The boy turned toward him. "I don't know for sure," he said. "As we were walking back from class, this blue car pulled up. A man jumped out, grabbed one of the girls, and drove off. It happened so fast, no one had time to do anything about it. She didn't even have time to scream."

Mark's heart sank. He knew Jesus had Lisa. "What's the girl's name?" he asked quickly.

"I don't know. I'm new here. I don't know very many people."

"What did she look like?"

"She was taller than most of the other girls. Blonde hair. Real cute."

Mark looked at Angela, the pain was obvious in his face. Angela put her arm around his waist in an attempt to comfort him.

"Maybe we can catch them," she said sympathetically. Then she looked at the boy. "How long have they been gone?"

"At least fifteen minutes."

"Damn," Mark said. "That's too much of a head start."

Dejected, they walked back to the car. Angela got in on her side and sat down. Mark took one more look in the direction the blue Pontiac had driven off in, then opened the car door on his side. Just as he was about to get in, a female voice with a slight speech impediment broke the silence.

"Daddy! What are you doing here?"

He turned in the direction of the voice, and his spirit lifted immediately. "Lisa!" he said excitedly. "Thank God you're safe. I thought you had been kidnapped. I was worried sick." He put his arms around her and hugged her tightly.

"You thought I'd been kidnapped. You're kidding?"

"No, I'm dead serious. A man just kidnapped a girl from right here in front of your dorm. From her description, I thought it was you."

"That must be Tiffany. We're in the same class. People say we look a lot alike. She came ahead with everyone else. I stayed behind for a few minutes to talk to my chemistry teacher. I didn't understand one of our homework problems. I can't believe Tiffany's been kidnapped. I didn't think her parents were worth that much money."

He suddenly remembered Angela. "Lisa, this is Angela," he said. "She's a friend of mine."

Angela walked around the car and extended her hand. Lisa shook it as she had been taught to do at Briarwood Academy. Then she looked Angela up and down. Mark wondered what she was thinking. She would tell him later that she was admiring the beautiful woman in the tacky outfit who was with her dad.

Mark took a deep breath, then slowly let it out. "Have you heard about your mother?" he asked nervously.

"What about mom? Has something happened to mom?"

"We need to talk, but not here," he said. "Jesus may come back when he discovers he made a mistake."

"Jesus. Who is Jesus? Will you please tell me what's going on?"

"I'll explain it all to you, but first we've got to get out of here."

CHAPTER FIFTEEN

Mark parked the Porsche in a wooded area ten miles outside of Valdosta. Lisa sat in the front seat with him. Angela had taken a low profile in the back. He was about to do the hardest thing he had ever done in his life...tell his thirteen-year-old daughter that her mother had been brutally murdered. He decided that the best thing to do would be to keep it short and simple. He would, of course, leave out the gory details...no Maldini, no Jesus, no big knife. He would tell her about all that in due time.

"Lisa, I have something to tell you. It's bad news. I'd give anything if I didn't have to tell you this."

"Don't tell me something else has happened to you."

"It's not about me. It's about your mother."

"What about mom?"

"She's dead," he said in a voice so weak that it surprised him.

The blood suddenly drained from Lisa's face. "You're kidding, right?"

"I wish I were. Angela and I found her at home in the bed."

"Mom didn't say anything about being sick. I talked to her on the phone two days ago."

"She wasn't ill. She was murdered," he said in a voice now stronger.

"Murdered? Who would want to kill mom?" Tears formed in her eyes.

"The police think I did it. Lisa, you know I didn't kill your mother."

"Daddy, you don't have to tell me that. I know you didn't. You loved her despite the terrible things she did to you."

He leaned over and hugged her. "I love you," he said.

"I love you too daddy," she said, crying softly.

He was on the verge of crying himself, but he forced the tears back.

He and Lisa sat in the car holding each other for several minutes. He told her about going to Joanna's house to borrow money, finding the back door unlocked, and finding Joanna already dead. She buried her head in his chest. Tears streamed down her face.

He had learned about the grief process in medical school…denial progressing to bargaining, followed by anger progressing to depression, then finally acceptance. The progression from denial to acceptance usually took months for some and years for others. A few never completed the sequence and lived the rest of their lives hung up in the grief process. Because it wouldn't be safe for Lisa to attend her mother's funeral, and thereby achieve normal closure, initial progress for her would be difficult. If he ever got out of this mess he was in, he would get her counseling. She would need it. Who knows, maybe they all would.

Finally, Angela spoke up from the back seat. "What do we do now?"

He turned his head in her direction, his arm still around Lisa. " Our first priority is to get Lisa to a safe place. Any ideas?"

"Not me," Angela replied. "I'm a long way from home."

"It's got to be someplace Maldini won't think of," he said.

"Who's Maldini? What's going on?" Lisa asked. "Why do you have to get me to a safe place?"

"Maldini's the man responsible for your mother's death. I'll tell you all about him later."

Lisa rubbed the tears from her face with the back of her hand.

"Mark, what about your parents?" Angela asked.

"I don't have any."

"What do you mean, you don't have parents? Everyone has parents."

"Not everyone. Mine died fifteen years ago. Besides, if my parents were still alive, that's the first place Maldini's men would look."

"Then what about friends? You do have friends don't you?"

"Not many. I used to have a lot of friends. Somehow, most of them disappeared when things started going downhill. Daniel Iverson is my best friend, but he's a bachelor. I don't think he would relish the thought of taking care of a teenage girl."

"What about the head nurse you're always talking to on the telephone?"

"Mattie?"

"Yeah, Mattie."

"I'm sure Maldini knows about her."

"What about the school teacher you wrote me about?" Lisa asked. "The one you've been dating?"

Suddenly, Angela sat upright in the seat. "You've been dating someone? You didn't tell me that," she said sharply.

"Susan! That's it," he said excitedly. "She's visiting her parents in Columbus. Her mother's been ill." He turned to Lisa. "If her parents would keep you for a little while, it would be perfect, completely out of Atlanta."

"Do you know her parents?" Lisa asked.

"Sort of."

"Daddy, what do you mean sort of? Either you know them or you don't."

"Well, I know them indirectly."

"Indirectly?"

"It's too complicated to explain right now. Susan can get them to let you stay, I'm sure of it."

"Well, I guess we're off to Columbus to see your sweetie," Angela said sarcastically.

He gave her a disapproving look. This was no time for petty jealousy. She quickly apologized. He turned the car around and headed back to the highway.

Twenty miles outside of Columbus, Mark stopped at a Chevron station and filled the Porsche's tank with gasoline. Then he counted the money in his billfold...$124. The gas was an even $16. Their funds were getting desperately low. They would have to find a way to get some money soon. The little they had left wouldn't last long.

Mark entered the building and, in an attempt to conserve money, paid the clerk, a hefty middle-aged woman with red hair, with his Chevron card. He was sure that Maldini couldn't trace a gasoline credit card.

Returning to the car, he plopped in the seat, cranked the engine, and backed out of the parking space. Just as the ancient Porsche rattled back on the highway, Angela spoke.

"Don't you think we ought to call Susan and get her to ask her parents about keeping Lisa instead of just showing up on their doorstep?"

He glanced back at her. "I can't."

"Why not?"

"I don't know their telephone number."

"That's not a problem. You can get the number from directory assistance. What's their names?"

He eased his foot down on the accelerator pedal. "Damned if I know."

"You don't know their names? How do you expect to find them if you don't know their names?"

"Don't worry. I've got it all figured out. We'll find them." He was sure that Mrs. Grabosky could give him their names, but calling her would be too risky. Maldini's men might question her. He doubted that she could keep a secret.

———————————

Three days after their previous meeting, Lowenstein's secretary called Dr. Jackson and Mrs. Anderson to schedule an emergency meeting. The three of them assembled around the usual conference table. Lowenstein spoke first.

"There was another cardiac arrest this morning…a 38 year old black male who was in the hospital for an acute flare-up of a pseudocyst related to his chronic pancreatitis. Surgery was avoided because medical management was successful. He was doing so well that he was scheduled for discharge later this morning."

"Did he survive?" Dr. Jackson asked quickly.

"The code team, lead by Dr. Eric Stottlemire from the Emergency Room, got there pretty fast. I was told that Stottlemire did a hell of a good job. We can probably thank him for the man's survival."

"Thank God the man didn't die," Mrs. Anderson. said. "When's it going to stop?"

"I do have some good news," Lowenstein said. "We've identified an individual who was working on virtually every unit when the excess cardiac arrests occurred. She was working on the unit this morning when the latest one happened."

"Fantastic," Dr. Jackson blurted out. "Who is it? I lay odds it's a nurse."

Mrs. Anderson exhaled deeply and gave him a disgusted look.

"Well, it is a nurse," Lowenstein replied.

Dr. Jackson glared at Mrs. Anderson. He didn't have to say a word. The smug look on his face said it all.

Lowenstein continued. "She has an exemplary record. She's not someone you'd suspect of killing patients."

Dr. Jackson straightened his bow tie. "Well, it wouldn't be the first time a serial killer had been described as a nice person prior to being discovered. Don't keep us in suspense. Who is she?"

"I see no reason to keep her identity from you any longer," Lowenstein said. "Her name is Betsy Barfield."

"Betsy Barfield!" Mrs. Anderson said in disbelief. "Not Betsy. She's one of our better nurses."

Dr. Jackson looked irritated. "Who the hell is Betsy Barfield?"

"She's a PRN nurse…works on any unit she's needed," Mrs. Anderson said. "She's five feet four or so. Short, black hair. A real cute girl. Surely you remember her. Dr. Stottlemire brought her to Dr. Billingsworth's party."

Dr. Jackson shook his head. "How the hell do you expect me to know every nurse that works in this hospital? They come and go all the time. Poor pay and bad working conditions, I say."

Mrs. Anderson leaned back in her chair. "She's been working here for five years."

"Well, I still don't know her."

Lowenstein cleared his throat. "I want to remind you that, at this point, we don't have any proof that she's killed anyone. I talked to the head nurses on some of the units where she's worked. They remembered several of the cardiac arrests. They swear that Betsy was nowhere near the patients' rooms when the arrests occurred. In fact, a couple of times she was in the cafeteria on her coffee break. One time, she had even clocked out and left the building."

"That doesn't make sense," Dr. Jackson exclaimed. "How could she be killing patients if she's nowhere near them?"

"That's the problem," Lowenstein said. "The missing piece of the puzzle."

Dr. Jackson and Mrs. Anderson shook their heads and looked perplexed.

"It has to be more than just coincidence that she was working on virtually every unit when the cardiac arrests occurred," Dr. Jackson said. "Where was she when the latest one took place?"

"She was in a new patient's room at the other end of the hall doing a nursing assessment. She had been there for at least an hour."

"What does Zachary Dorfman say? Have any of his people noticed anything unusual in her behavior?" Dr. Jackson asked.

"He hasn't been told about her yet. We just identified her late yesterday afternoon. I did speak to him earlier about his general surveillance. None of his people have picked up anything that would be of help to us. I'm going to talk to him about Miss Barfield as soon as this meeting is over."

"This situation gets more and more confusing," Dr. Jackson said, scratching his head. "Why don't we just lay this Betsy person off and see if the cardiac arrest rate goes down?"

"Lowenstein responded promptly. "It's not that simple. You can't just lay someone off without just cause, at least not in this day and time. That would open us up to a major lawsuit."

"Mr. Lowenstein's right," Mrs. Anderson said. "We tried that once with a nurse who was clearly incompetent. It cost the hospital almost a half million dollars. Seems that we didn't have enough documentation, according to the jury, despite a file full of incompetent acts she had committed."

"We can't just let her keep on working here and killing patients," Dr. Jackson exclaimed.

"I'm afraid we don't have a choice about her continuing to work here," Lowenstein said. "Again, let me point out that we don't have any concrete evidence that she's killed anyone."

"Do you think Mark Valentine from the Emergency Room might be involved in this somehow?" Dr. Jackson asked. "He's accused of murdering his wife. If he would do that, there's no telling what else he might do. Maybe we're making a mistake fixating on one suspect at this stage of the investigation."

"I hadn't thought of that," Lowenstein responded.

Mrs. Anderson quickly spoke up. "Why would Dr. Valentine kill patients in our hospital?"

"Why would anyone kill patients in our hospital?" Dr. Jackson responded.

Mrs. Anderson shook her head. "Now that we know about Betsy, can't we call the police in?"

"I don't think so," Lowenstein responded. "We still don't have any evidence strong enough to warrant a police investigation. We only suspect Betsy Barfield, based on evidence that they would consider pretty flimsy. Besides, there's still the problem of the budget hearing. I'm not willing to risk our budget, and possibly the future of the hospital, on what little evidence we have."

"Well, what do we do next?" Mrs. Anderson asked.

Dr. Jackson spoke quickly. "Let's get all the other nurses to watch her and report anything suspicious to us."

Mrs. Anderson rolled her eyes back in her head and gave him her best disgusted look. "That's the dumbest thing I've heard yet. What if she's innocent? She could sue us for slander. Besides, you can't turn the nursing staff into spies. That's a ridiculous suggestion."

Dr. Jackson ignored her and looked at Lowenstein. "Well, you're in charge. What do we do now?"

"Now that we have a suspect, I'll get Dorfman to focus his surveillance on her. I want to get his input on Dr. Valentine as a possible suspect as well. Dorfman seems to know him pretty well. In the meantime, I expect each of you to continue keeping what we discuss here in strictest confidence, especially about Betsy Barfield. It's extremely important that she not know she's a suspect."

CHAPTER SIXTEEN

Welcome To Columbus Georgia, Population 240,000, the sign by the side of the highway read. Lisa hadn't said a word since they left the wooded area outside of Valdosta. Mark was worried about her. It wasn't like her to be so quiet. Usually she talked your head off. He knew that it would be unrealistic to expect her to behave any other way, given the fact that only a few hours earlier she had been told that her mother had been murdered. He was thankful that she hadn't pressed him about details. He knew the questions would come as soon as the initial shock wore off. In the meantime, he had a task to do…finding out the names of Susan's parents.

They passed through the interchange at North Bypass. The sign above the right-hand lane of the interstate indicated that Fort Benning Army Base was located to the southeast of town. They continued straight ahead toward the downtown area. A mile past the interchange, they exited Interstate 85 onto Manchester Bealwood Connector. Crossing Manchester Expressway near Saint Francis Hospital, they followed the Connector to the downtown area. Pemberton House, the former home of the inventor of Coca Cola, and Springer Opera House, a national historic landmark, contrasted sharply with the multi-story, arched, modernistic building of the consolidated city and county governments.

"Now what?" Angela asked from her front seat position as they exited the Connector onto Fifteenth Street. She had swapped places with Lisa at the last rest stop Lisa appeared to be asleep in the back seat.

"We find the high school in town with the best football record," Mark responded.

"Have you lost your mind? Surely we didn't come all this way to watch a football game."

"No, we didn't. We came to locate a football coach who can tell us the name of Susan's father. Besides, it's baseball season."

"Oh," she said. Then she paused, appearing to be in deep thought. "I don't get it. What does a high school football coach have to do with all this? Who is this coach anyway?"

"I don't know yet. That's why we're looking for a winning football team."

"I still don't get it."

"It's simple. Susan's father is a football fanatic. Susan told me so. I've known a hundred people like him. It doesn't matter what level the football is...high school, college, professional...they're all nuts about the game. I'm laying odds that the coach knows her father by his first name."

"What if he doesn't?"

"Then we try another high school. If that doesn't work, we keep on trying high schools until we run out, then we start checking insurance agents."

"Insurance agents?"

"Her father's an insurance agent." He stopped behind a METRA bus at a signal light. It's acrid exhaust fumes filtered into the car and burned his eyes.

"I get your point. There's a lot more insurance agents than high schools, so we start with the coaches."

"You've got it."

The light turned green. When the traffic cleared, the bus turned right. As the exhaust fumes faded, he proceeded straight ahead to the east bank of the Chatahoochee River. Turning left on Broadway, he passed a branch of Southtrust Bank and pulled up by a pay phone on the following block.

"Who are you going to call?" Angela asked.

"A sporting goods store."

Looking a little bewildered, Angela slumped down in the seat. He knew she wanted to ask why, but she didn't. He would explain it to her when he got back. He walked to the telephone, studied the telephone book for a couple of minutes, then placed a call.

A few minutes later, he returned to the car. "I've got it," he said. "I called the sporting good store with the largest advertisement in the phone book and spoke to the manager. Hardaway High is the largest high school in the city, and the one with the winningest football record. They haven't had a losing season in ten years. They won their conference the last five years and finished in the top five in the state the last three. The coaches name is Bubba Jarvics."

"Bubba?" Angela asked.

"Bubba," Mark replied.

"What do we do now?" Angela asked.

He looked at his watch...four o'clock. "I'll bet Bubba's still at school."

Angela looked confused. "I don't know about Columbus, but in Miami the schools are vacant this time of day. Everyone's gone home."

"Not everyone. I'll bet the football team is still there."

"You confuse me too much. If it's baseball season, why would the football team be there?"

"I played high school football in Georgia. I know how it works. Schools with winning traditions practice year round. They don't call it football practice, but they're there just the same. They do aerobic exercise of some sort to stay in shape and lift weights to build muscle mass."

"You played football? Were you any good?" Angela asked.

"A few people thought so," he replied with a wry grin.

Fifteen minutes later, he pulled into the parking lot of Hardaway High. It was empty except for a dozen or so cars, mostly shiny, new sports models.

"When I was a student, I used to have to walk to school. Now look at what the kids drive," he said, parking by a red Corvette.

Lisa reached forward and tapped Angela on the shoulder. "What did he say?" she asked.

He was relieved. He had begun to worry that she had withdrawn deeply within herself out of grief over her mother's death. She indeed had been asleep.

Angela turned and faced her. "He said that he used to have to walk to school."

"And the snow was knee deep," Lisa replied. "Mom told me he had a Mustang."

"That wasn't until my junior year. I had to have one to get to football practice and back. Besides, it was a used one."

Angela repeated his words. Lisa read her lips.

"I rest my case," Lisa said, sitting back in the seat.

They got out of the car and headed up the steps to the four glass entrance doors of the school. Mark pulled on one of the handles. The door was locked.

"Damn!" he said to himself. He tried another door, then another one. They were all locked.

"What do we do now?" Angela asked.

"We go around back. The door to the gym has to be open."

Following the sidewalk, they walked around the side of the school to the back where they came to a single door. He walked up the steps and tried the latch. The door was unlocked. "Come on," he said.

Angela and Lisa followed him into the building and down a hallway. The sound of a basketball bouncing on the floor, the screeching of tennis shoes, and a male voice yelling commands got louder and louder as they approached the door at the end of the hallway.

When he opened the door, the sounds got even louder. Ten athletic looking boys in red and green pullovers were playing basketball. A middle-aged man with red hair and wearing gray sweats stood at the side of the court yelling instructions. He was a couple of inches shorter than Mark and a good twenty pounds heavier, all muscle. It was obvious that he had spent a lot of time in the weight room over the years. A whistle hung loosely on a cord around his neck.

"Hustle, damn it, hustle," he yelled at one of the players who lagged behind the others on a fast break.

Two other men, who appeared to be somewhat younger than the coach, sat in the stands with ten equally athletic-looking boys, waiting their turns to play.

"Now I'm really confused," Angela said. "What season did you say it was?"

"It's still baseball season. The football players play basketball among themselves in the off-season to stay in shape. At least the skilled players do. My guess is that the rest of the team, the linemen and linebackers, are working out in the weight room."

She nodded her head. He got the feeling that she finally understood.

"Why don't you and Lisa wait in the stands and watch the game," he said. "I'm going to talk to the coach."

He approached the man with the whistle from behind and tapped him on the shoulder. "Excuse me. I'm looking for Bubba Jarvics," he said, his voice raised above the noise of the game.

The man turned in his direction. "I'm coach Jarvics," the man said. "What can I do for you?"

"I need to talk to you. It's very important," Mark responded.

Jarvics looked at him for a moment, then turned toward the two men in the stands who were obviously assistant coaches. "Take over for me," he said. He took the whistle from around his neck and tossed it to one of the men. Then he turned his attention back to Mark. "We can go to my office. It's so noisy out here you can hardly hear yourself think." He turned and walked toward the door that Mark, Angela, and Lisa had just come through.

Mark glanced in the stands. Lisa was watching the boys in shorts run up and down the court. The ten boys in the stands stared at her. The two assistant coaches eyed Angela.

Mark followed Jarvics into the office. Jarvics took a seat behind the desk. Mark sat in a chair directly in front of him. A maroon banner with white letters on the wall over Jarvic's head proudly declared **Georgia State Football Champions, 1987.**

"What can I do for you?" Jarvics asked.

"I'm looking for someone. I don't know his name. He's a real football fan. I'm guessing that he attends all of Hardaway High's games and comes to practice a lot. He has daughter named Susan Livingston. She's a schoolteacher in Atlanta."

Jarvics interrupted. "You look awfully familiar. Do I know you?"

Mark's heart leaped up into his throat. Had Jarvics seen a picture of him on the news related to Joanna's murder? He took a deep breath and tried to calm himself.

"I'm sorry, I forgot to introduce myself," he said quickly. "I'm Joe Williams from Atlanta. I'm a friend of Susan's. She's home visiting her sick mother. I need to contact her real badly, but I don't know where her parents live. I figured you might know her father. He's in the insurance business here in Columbus."

"What's his name?"

"That's the problem. I don't know."

"I'm sorry. I'm afraid I can't be of any help." Jarvics looked at him quizzically. "Did you play football? You look like a football player."

Mark wished he could tell him who he was. He could use the emotional lift. Good Georgia football fans never forget, especially an All America quarterback who led the Bulldogs to their only national championship. The fact that it happened nineteen years ago hadn't seemed to dull their memories any.

"No, never did." Mark said instead. "The games too rough for me. I was in the band...played the tuba." As long as he was lying, he figured he might as well go all the way. "How many other high schools are there in this town?" he asked.

"Six all together," Jarvics responded.

Mark felt dejected. Their search could take several days. They didn't have the money or the time for it.

He shook Jarvics' hand, then left the office and headed back to the gym to give Angela and Lisa the bad news. It was too late to try another high school today. They would have to find a place to spend the night...more of their precious money spent...and try again in the morning.

As he reached the gym door, Jarvics yelled at him from just outside his office. "Mr. Williams. Wait a minute. You might try Curly Richardson. He was the coach here before me. He retired last year and I replaced him. He was the coach here for thirty years. If anybody knows the person you're looking for, it would be him."

Mark turned and walked back toward the office. Maybe luck would be with him for a change. "You wouldn't happen to have his phone number would you?" he asked as he followed Jarvics back through the door.

"Sure do. I talk to him regularly," Jarvics said. "Talked to him yesterday in fact. Great football coach. He could have coached in college if he wanted too. He had lots of offers, but he preferred working with the young kids." Jarvics wrote Curly Richardson's telephone number down on a note pad, pulled off the sheet, and handed it to Mark.

"Mind if I use your phone?" Mark asked.

"Be my guest," Jarvics replied. "Just pull the door to behind you when you're through. Are you sure you never played football? I can't shake the feeling that I've seen you before. You look awfully familiar, and you sure don't look like a tuba player."

"I'm sure," Mark said with a broad smile.

Jarvics turned and left the office. Mark dialed the number. Three rings later, a frail female voice answered.

"Richardson residence," she said.

"Could I speak to coach Richardson please?"

"Who may I say is calling?"

"Joe Williams."

"Just a minute. Curly's out in the back yard working in the flowerbeds. I'll go get him."

A few minutes later, Curly Richardson came to the telephone. "This is coach Richardson," he said. "Do I know you Mr. Williams?"

"No you don't," Mark replied. "Bubba Jarvics gave me your name and number. I'm looking for a friend. She's here from Atlanta visiting her family. I thought you might know her father. He's a real football fan. Probably goes to all of Hardaway High's ball games and comes to watch practice a lot."

"What's his name?"

"That's the problem. I don't know his name. He's in the insurance business here in Columbus."

"That may be Jimmy Singletary. What's his daughter's name?"

"Susan Livingston."

"Yep, Jimmy's your man. He used to bring Susan to some of our games when she was a child. Jimmy loves football almost as much as I do. It's a shame about Tim's terrible accident. It really devastated Susan."

"Yes I know. She told me about it. Do you know how I can contact Mr. Singletary?"

"Sure do. He lives in the old Adam's place on Elm Street, but at this time of day he would still be at his office."

"Thanks coach. I appreciate this more than you'll ever know." Mark hung up the telephone and searched the desk for a directory. Finding one in the upper-right drawer, he looked up Jimmy Singletary's number. Two were listed...a home number and an office number. He put the book back in the drawer and dialed the home number. It was Susan he really wanted to talk to. The telephone rang several times. Just as he was about to get discouraged, a familiar voice answered.

"Singletary residence," she said.

"Susan, is that you? This is Mark."

"Mark! I've been worried to death about you. Are you okay?"

"I'm fine. Have you heard about Joanna?"

"Yes. It was in the afternoon paper."

"I didn't kill her, but I know who did," he said quickly. "You've got to believe me."

Susan hesitated. He wondered if she were trying to make up her mind whether to believe him or not.

"Where are you?" she asked finally.

"I'm in Columbus."

"You're in Columbus? Where?"

"At Hardaway High. Coach Richardson gave me your father's name. I looked up the number."

"Coach is a nice man. He and my father have been friends for a long time."

"I've got to talk to you. It's a matter of life and death. Can you meet me some place? It will have to be discrete. The police are looking for me."

"Why don't I come and pick you up? I can be there in fifteen minutes."

He felt relieved. Maybe she did believe him. Why would she come and pick him up if she didn't?

"That would be great," he replied. "I'll wait for you in front of the school. It's pretty deserted. I'm sure it will be safe." He was about to hang up when he caught himself. "I'm not alone. My daughter, Lisa, is with me, and a friend."

"A friend of Lisa's?"

"No. A friend of mine."

Suddenly he felt awkward and guilty. How would he explain Angela to Susan? Nothing had happened between the two of them. What he had said was true. Angela was just a friend, unfortunately a very sexy-looking one. Besides, Susan didn't have any hold on him. They had only dated twice, if you counted the night she invited him to dinner in her apartment. He didn't have anything to feel awkward and guilty about, so why did he?

CHAPTER SEVENTEEN

At FBI headquarters in Washington D.C., Walter North paced back and forth in front of the standard-issue, wooden desk and American flag. His white shirtsleeves were rolled almost up to his elbows, and his tie was loosened at the collar. A picture of the President of the United States adorned the wall behind the desk.

Just under six feet tall, North was beginning to gray at the temples, and in recent years had developed a small paunch as a result of too many years at a desk job. He had been head of the organized crime division of the FBI for seven years, promoted to the position for the work he had done in helping get the illusive crime boss, John Giovani, convicted. Vito Maldini, a similar crime figure, would go to prison too if he had his way. He had pursued Maldini relentlessly for the past five years, and finally had him where he wanted. He had gotten a grand jury indictment, and finally had a witness that was willing to testify against Maldini in court. Now Maldini had disappeared. That didn't worry him too much. Maldini was an easily recognizable figure. His face had been in the newspaper and on TV for weeks. Normally he would be tracked down and captured without a lot of difficulty, but what he had just heard worried him.

"Say that again," he instructed Special Agent Daryl Barnes.

Daryl Barnes stood just inside the door. Ten years younger than North and a couple of inches taller, he had the lean muscular look of an active law enforcement officer. He wore his navy suit, white shirt, and red tie like a uniform, having at least five identical sets in a closet at home. His brown hair was close-cropped, and his face had a perpetual dead-serious look.

"Rumor has it that Maldini got his face changed so he couldn't be recognized," Barnes said.

"Plastic surgery?"

"Yeah."

"Damn! Do we know who did it?" North asked.

"Not exactly, but we do have some information."

"Well, let's hear it."

Barnes leaned back against the doorframe. "If you can believe what you hear on the street, some down-and-out plastic surgeon did the job."

"What do you mean down and out?"

"Lost his license. Drug abuse or something."

"Do we have any confirmation of the rumor?"

"No. But it has to be more than coincidence that Maldini's niece and a friend of hers were found in Miami last week with their throats cut."

"How does that tie into the case?"

"The niece was a nurse anesthetist. The friend was a scrub nurse."

North stopped pacing and sat on the corner of his desk. "Sounds like the rumor might be true," he said. "Do we know the plastic surgeon's name?"

"No. He's supposedly somebody from the southeastern United States," Barnes responded.

"What else?"

"There's not any more. That's it."

"What do you mean, that's it? Where in the southeast?"

"Nobody seems to know."

"That isn't much to go on," North said, starting to pace again. "Any other leads?"

"Wait a minute." Barnes said quickly. "Let's not give up on this one too soon. I've thought it through. It might lead to something."

"Okay, go on."

"I checked with the Chief of Staff at George Washington University Hospital. There's a thing called the National Practitioner's Data Bank. It's a registry of some sort that keeps track of doctors who have had problems with their licenses. You know, restricted or revoked for things like drug abuse, malpractice, sexual involvement with patients, or just plain incompetence. Hospitals use the data bank to check on doctors when they apply for admission to their medical staffs. It's part of the credentialing process."

North walked behind his desk and sat in the chair. "I'm beginning to get the idea. We could access this data bank, find out the names of plastic surgeons who have had their licenses revoked, then track each of them down for questioning."

"Right! Hopefully it will lead us to our doctor."

"How far back in the data bank should we go? Five years? Ten years?"

Barnes straightened his tie. "I vote for five. I sure wouldn't want to have my face carved on by somebody who hadn't been in an operating room for ten years."

"Okay, five it is. Which states? The southeastern United States covers a lot of territory."

Barnes walked over and sat down in a chair by the desk. "I suggest that instead of looking at states, we look at an area within an arc with Miami at its center."

"Good idea. What radius do you want to use? Five hundred miles? One thousand miles? Fifteen hundred miles?"

"Lets go with a thousand. If we don't find our doctor within a thousand miles of Miami, we can extend the arc."

"Where is this data bank?" North asked.

"Some place called Camarillo, California," Barnes responded.

"Where the hell is Camarillo, California?"

"It's in southern California, north of Los Angeles."

"Do you know how to access the data bank?"

"Hospitals just write letters. Then their credentials committees sit back and wait two or three weeks for the information to come in."

North cleared his throat. "We can't wait that long. Why can't we just get our office in Los Angeles to obtain an order from the local federal judge there? The order could require that the information be turned over immediately. With any luck at all they should be able to fax the information to us by tomorrow afternoon."

"Good idea. I think we need to locate this doctor as fast as we can."

"What's the hurry?"

"If Maldini had his own niece and her friend killed, he could be systematically eliminating people who can identify him. We may have to save our doctor's life before we can question him."

"What are you going to tell the press about Maldini's disappearance?" North asked.

"I don't know yet," Barnes responded. "I'll have to talk to Director Armstrong. This could be a sensitive matter for the President."

"Why's that?"

"He campaigned heavily on the law and order issue...promised sweeping changes in how we fight crime. Unfortunately, he hasn't been able to get any of his programs through congress. The opposition party blocks every effort he makes. With the election coming up next year, he's depending on Maldini's conviction to overshadow his failure to get his anti-crime programs passed."

Mark and Lisa sat on the front steps of Hardaway High and waited. Angela stood. She didn't want to get her blue, mini-skirt dirty. At Lisa's insistence, Mark had filled her in on the details of her mother's death. She had continued to handle it well, at least on the surface.

Fifteen minutes later, Susan's yellow Camry pulled into the lot and stopped directly in front of them. Mark got into the front seat. Angela and Lisa got into the back. Susan looked great in her navy shorts, pink halter-top, and white tennis shoes, no socks. He couldn't get over how beautiful her emerald-green eyes were. He leaned over and gave her a peck on the cheek.

"I'm so glad to see you," he said. "I was real disappointed when I discovered that you had gone out of town. How's your mother?"

"She's fine now. She came home from the hospital yesterday. She feels a little weak, but other than that she's okay."

Angela cleared her throat. She hadn't taken her eyes off Susan since her Camry pulled up.

Mark turned toward the back seat. "Susan, this is Lisa."

"Hi Lisa," Susan said. "Mark's told me a lot about you. You've got a great dad."

"I know," Lisa replied. "I'll be glad when he gets out of this mess."

Angela cleared her throat again, this time a little louder

"And this is Angela. She's a friend," Mark said nervously.

"Angela, it's good to meet you too," Susan said. Then she looked at him with a hurt look on her face. "Mark, you didn't tell me your friend was so attractive. Have you known each other long?"

"Just a couple of weeks," he replied. "We have something in common. Someone's trying to kill both of us." He looked around the area. "We need to get out of here. Where can we go to talk?"

"My folk's house would be fine. I told dad I was coming to meet you. At first, he wanted to call the police, but he agreed to wait and hear your side of the story."

"I think I'd better stash my car somewhere out of sight. Where do you suggest?"

"There's an abandoned warehouse on the way to the house. You can park behind it."

"Why not put it in a river?" Angela said sarcastically.

Ignoring Angela's remark, Mark got out of Susan's car and headed for his Porsche. Angela followed him. He turned and held up his hand.

"You go with Susan and Lisa," he said. "I'll meet you at the warehouse."

Angela stopped, hesitated, then got in the front seat with Susan. Susan made a wide turn out of the parking lot back onto the street. He followed her Camry through the downtown area to the abandoned warehouse. She pulled around back and stopped next to the building. He parked the Porsche beside the Camry. Then, spreading his legs wide to fit in the cramped space, he climbed into the back seat with Lisa.

"What did you all talk about behind my back?" he asked.

"Angela told me about Maldini and the surgery," Susan said. "She told me about Jesus too. It's horrible. What are you going to do?"

"We plan on getting out of the state until the police resolve this mess," he answered.

"We?" Susan asked quickly.

"Angela and I. Maldini's out to kill her too."

"Oh. Where are the two of you going?"

"Charleston, South Carolina, I think. In the meantime I need some place for Lisa to stay. I don't think it's safe for her to be with us. I was hoping you could get your parents to keep her for a while, at least until we get settled somewhere. She won't be any trouble. She's a good kid."

Lisa gave him a hard look. She had chastised him in the past for calling her a kid.

"What do you think?" he asked.

"About you and Angela going to Charleston?" Susan replied.

"No. About Lisa staying with your parents."

"Oh. I'm sure they wouldn't mind. They love children, even teenagers."

Susan pulled out from behind the warehouse and headed home. She passed Columbus College on the left, then turned right at Columbus Museum. A short time later they arrived at the house on Elm Street. It looked like you would expect a house on Elm Street to look…two story red brick with a large porch all the way across the front. Two white rockers sat on one end of the porch and a white swing on the other. Three enormous elm trees filled the front yard. The four of them crossed the porch, opened the front door and entered the foyer. Almost immediately, a high-pitched, shrill bark emanated from inside the house.

"That's Ellie, mother's miniature schnauzer," Susan said. "She's just letting you know that you're in her territory."

Suddenly, a small salt-and-pepper dog appeared in front of them and ran up to Mark's feet.

"Yap, yap, yap."

He reached down and rubbed her head. She stopped barking and licked his hand.

"That's amazing," Susan said. "She usually doesn't take to strangers very fast."

He laughed. "I guess she's a good judge of character."

They entered the main part of the house where Susan introduced them to her parents. Her father appeared to be about sixty-five. His white hair, combed back neatly above his ears, was slightly balding at the crown. He was a little overweight and had a small paunch. Half glasses perched precariously on his nose. Wearing a casual, flowered housedress, her mother was an attractive, motherly looking woman who appeared to be a few years younger than her father. Susan had obviously inherited her emerald-green eyes from her.

Mark told Mr. And Mrs. Singletary the whole story…Maldini's surgery, Joanna's death, Jesus' attempt on his life, and Angela's fear that Maldini was out to eliminate most of those who could identify him, including her. Angela verified his story. Lisa told them about Jesus coming to her school and kidnapping the wrong girl. Believing their story, the Singletarys agreed to let Lisa stay with them. That decision made, Mrs. Singletary stood up and faced them.

"Are you folks hungry?" she asked.

They were all quick to say yes. In the excitement of the day, the three of them had forgotten to eat lunch.

"Good!" Mrs. Singletary said. "When I came home from the hospital, the neighbors brought us enough food to feed an army. I've been wondering what I was going to do with it all."

They followed her into the kitchen and took their seats at the table. Mr. Singletary said the blessing, then they dug in. The food was delicious…fried chicken, potato salad, baked beans, tossed salad, and apple pie with vanilla ice cream. Mark was dying for a beer, but he knew better than to ask. Susan had told him that alcohol wasn't allowed in the house. Neither was smoking.

After dinner, Mark turned to Mrs. Singletary. "I can't tell you how much I appreciate you letting Lisa stay with you. It's a tremendous weight off my mind." He glanced at Angela, then back at Susan. "Now that Lisa's taken care of, I guess Angela and I had better get going."

"You're leaving?" Susan asked quickly. "Where are you going?"

"To a motel. We've imposed on your parents enough tonight."

"Not on your life!" she blurted out. "I mean, there's plenty of room here. You have to stay. I insist."

"Susan's right," Mrs. Singletary said. "You have to stay."

"We won't take no for an answer," Mr. Singletary chimed in.

Mark glanced at Angela, then back to Mrs. Singletary. "I guess it's settled then. We stay."

"Good," Susan said.

Mark had gone about as long as he could without a cigarette. "If you all would excuse me, I need to go outside for a little while."

The Singletarys nodded. They seemed to know why he felt it necessary to leave their company. He was sure that Susan had told them about his smoking habit. As he started to leave the dining room, Angela jumped up to follow him.

"Angela. That's such a pretty name," Mrs. Singletary said quickly. "It means angel you know. You're so pretty. You could be an angel. Have you and Mark known each other long?"

While Mrs. Singletary occupied Angela, Susan quickly rose from her chair and followed Mark. Angela watched them leave the room, trapped by Mrs. Singletary who continued asking her questions.

He exited the front door, walked to the swing on the front porch, sat down, and lit a cigarette. Susan joined him. As a gentle wind rustled the leaves of the huge elm tree, they slowly swung back and forth. The moon faintly illuminated the houses across the street. Lights in their windows gave evidence of families having dinner, talking, watching TV, and looking forward to tomorrow. He was envious. They had no Maldini, no Jesus, no nightmare to haunt them. He didn't even know if he would be alive tomorrow.

"Why so silent?" Susan asked.

"Just thinking."

"Care to share your thoughts?"

"Feeling sorry for myself, I guess. When Joanna divorced me, I thought that was the worst thing that ever happened to me. Then the licensure board revoked my license. Plastic surgery was my life. It was who I was. The board stripped me of my identity. I was completely devastated. I thought my life was over. I even thought about killing myself."

"But you didn't."

He slipped his arm around her and gave her a hug. "No, I didn't. I'm too much of a survivor to give up that easy."

"Mark, is that you?" Angela asked, coming out the front door.

Still wearing her white nurse's uniform, Betsy Barfield sat in the living room of her apartment with the shades drawn and stared nervously at the telephone in front of her on the coffee table. After a few minutes, she picked it up and dialed a number from memory. A male voice answered.

"Hello," it said.

"I was just thinking about you," she said timidly. "I haven't heard from you in four days. Are you still angry with me?"

"That depends."

"On what?"

"Whether you've changed your mind or not."

She hesitated. "I heard a rumor today that Administration is investigating the cardiac arrests. They're talking about a serial killer being loose in the hospital. I know they suspect me."

"It's all in your mind. Why would they suspect you?"

"I don't know. I feel like everyone is watching me. Security has been showing up more often on the units where I've been working. Yesterday, one of them followed me down the hall into a patient's room. He said he wanted to ask me about one of the other nurses. He acted like he had a crush on her."

"You're just imagining things. He probably did have a crush on her. It happens."

"Maybe you're right. I just feel so guilty."

"They'll never figure it out. I'm too smart for them. You've got nothing to worry about. Trust me. What we're doing is fool proof."

"Please tell me you're not angry with me," she said, with a slight quiver in her voice.

"You do your part, and I'll keep my part of the bargain. Then you won't have to worry about me being angry."

"When can I see you?"

"Soon."

"How soon?"

"I'll call you."

"I love you," she said meekly.

She waited for him to reply. He didn't. She hung up the telephone. Then she bent over, placed her face in her hands, and sobbed uncontrollably.

Chapter Eighteen

When the others had excused themselves and gone to bed, Mark and Mr. Singletary stayed up late to talk. Neither of them was sleepy. They were both in the mood for conversation about football, a shared passion. Mr. Singletary spoke first.

"How do you think Georgia will fare in the Southeastern Conference this fall?" he asked.

"It all depends," Mark replied. "The offensive line will return intact. That's a real plus. A couple of defensive backs, an outside linebacker, and both tackles graduated from the defensive unit. That could be a problem."

"Their backups for the most part were pretty good last year, and we did have a good recruiting year," Mr. Singletary countered. "I think the coaching staff can fill those positions adequately, don't you?"

"You're probably right. I think that overall the defensive unit will be strong. The big question in my mind is the quarterback position. Jerry Raines' early departure for the pros took us all by surprise, especially after he practically guaranteed everyone that he was going to stay for his senior year."

"It was more than a surprise to some fans. It made a lot of them downright angry. They took him at his word."

"He had every right to change his mind."

"I know, but I don't blame him in the least. The pros waved a heck of a lot of money in front of him. Who wouldn't have been tempted?"

Mark want to say that he hadn't been, but he didn't.

For the next hour and a half they discussed the strengths and weaknesses of each and every team in the Southeastern Conference. Then Mark leaned back in the chair, crossed his legs, and changed the subject.

"I'm sure glad I met Susan," he said. "She's one of the nicest people I know."

A slight smile crossed Mr. Singletary's face. "She's always been a pleasure to be around, even as a child, at least most of the time."

"That doesn't surprise me."

"Don't get me wrong. She can be real headstrong if she believes in something. Once when she was nine years old, she decided that a neighbor was mistreating his dog...a real mangy animal. She worried me to death about it until I marched over there with her and confronted the man. Sure enough, she was right. He kept the dog chained in the back yard, most of the time without adequate food or water. She wouldn't be satisfied until we filed a cruelty to animal complaint."

"What happened?"

"The authorities confiscated the dog and fined the neighbor."

"I'll bet that made her happy."

"You would have thought so. When she found out that the dog was going to the pound, nothing would do but for us to adopt it. She wouldn't take no for an answer, so we did. She nursed it back to health. It turned out to be a real cute mutt. We had it for ten years, until it finally died of old age."

"You said she was a pleasure most of the time. What did you mean?"

"She had a spell as a teenager where she was pretty rebellious. Nothing serious. She violated her curfew a number of times and dated a boy we didn't like...a real tough guy who rode a motorcycle and wore his hair down to his shoulders. She even smoked for a while, but I don't think she ever drank."

"Sounds like the usual stuff to me."

"That's what we finally decided."

"Where's the boy now?"

"He turned out real well. He's a successful lawyer for a big firm in Atlanta."

Mark smiled. "A lawyer, huh. I'm not so sure I'd say he turned out well."

The next morning, Mrs. Singletary felt much stronger and, with Susan's help, was cooking breakfast. Angela slept later than the rest of them, but was there by the time the food was on the table. They all took their seats. Mr. Singletary said the blessing, then they began eating. Ellie sat on the floor looking back and forth from Susan to Mr. Singletary as they took bites of food. Finally, Mr. Singletary took a small piece of bacon in his hand and, without looking, lowered it to his side and dropped it to the floor. Ellie gobbled it up and waited for more.

"I saw that Jimmy," Mrs. Singletary said. "You know that upsets her stomach."

"Oh mother, it was just a small piece," he said. "It won't hurt her."

Angela stared at Mark. "Did you forget to shave this morning?"

"No. I figured that with my picture plastered everywhere, I'd better do something to change the way I look."

"Good idea. I like men with beards. It makes them look sexy."

"Mark is sexy enough without a beard," Susan countered.

Mark shifted in his chair. "I need to get rid of my license plate and get another one," Mark said to Mr. Singletary, quickly changing the subject. "I don't think we'll get very far with the old one. Every policeman in this part of the country must be looking for a Porsche with an Atlanta tag. Any ideas?"

"Where is your car now?"

"I left it behind the abandoned warehouse downtown."

"I think you're going to have to do more than change the tag. You're either going to have to get another car or have yours painted another color."

"You're probably right, but I don't have the money to do either."

"I have a friend in town who owns a body shop. I'll bet he would paint your car on credit. He owes me a favor."

"I'd sure feel a lot better if he would. What about the tag?"

"He buys wrecked cars to get the undamaged fenders, hoods, and trunk lids. There's bound to be some unexpired tags on them."

"Jimmy, do you think we ought to get involved in this?" Mrs. Singletary asked, concern obvious on her face.

"From what we've heard, it's clear that Mark is innocent. Besides, he hasn't been charged with anything. He's only a suspect, and he has got a paid assassin after him. As Christians, what else could we do?"

"You're right, I guess," she responded.

Mr. Singletary rose, walked to the telephone on the wall, dialed a number and chatted for a few minutes.

"What did your friend say?" Mark asked when he returned.

"He said to bring the car over first thing in the morning. He'll replace the broken taillight, fix the dent in the fender, and replace the broken windshield. That amount of work usually takes a couple of days. I told him that the owner of the car wouldn't be in town that long. Because things were a little slow right now, he said he would put some extra men on it, and that he might be able to get it back to you at the end of the day."

After breakfast the next morning Mark decided to take a walk. He had been cooped up in the car nearly all day the day before, and he needed some time in the open spaces, not to mention a cigarette. His beard was showing signs of progress. He thought it would be safe to go outside, especially if he wore sunglasses.

While Susan was occupied helping her mother with the dishes, Angela donned her sunglasses and joined him. The sky was slightly overcast. Rain was predicted, but the roar of thunder was still far away. As they strolled along the sidewalk, he pulled a cigarette from the Marlboro pack in his shirt pocket, lit it, inhaled deeply, then coughed briskly.

"That's a terrible cough," Angela said. "You really ought to quit."

"I'm going to one of these days. With everything that's been going on lately, this just isn't a good time."

"All of you smokers are just alike," she responded. "There's never a good time." She hesitated for a moment. "Susan seems like a nice girl."

"She is. She's been having a hard time of it ever since her husband died a year ago."

"What happened?"

"MVA."

"MVA?"

"Sorry. Motor vehicle accident. He was killed in a car wreck."

"That must have been terrible for her. I can't imagine having a policeman come to your door and tell you that your husband has just been killed. How's she doing?"

"Better, but she's got a ways to go."

"Do you love her?"

"What do you mean, do I love her? We've only had one date."

"Just one?"

"Well two, I guess."

"You didn't answer my question. Are you in love with her?"

"I don't know. It's too early to tell."

She smiled at him and took his hand in hers. "Good, then there's still a chance for me."

He squeezed her hand, then took the cigarette butt from his mouth, tossed it on the sidewalk, and put it out with his foot.

Twenty minutes later, they turned the corner and headed back to the house. Suddenly, Mark stopped in his tracks.

"What is it? What's wrong?" Angela asked.

"Look up ahead."

Half way up the block, a black and white patrol car sat in front of the Singletary's house. The car was empty. The driver was obviously in the house.

"What do we do?" Angela asked.

Pulling Angela by the hand, Mark turned and walked rapidly back around the corner until the patrol car was no longer in view.

"Do you think he's looking for us?" Angela asked.

"I expect he's looking for me. I'm the one wanted for murder. Why else would he be here?"

"Maybe he's selling tickets to the policeman's ball," she said, trying to defuse the tension in the situation.

Mark didn't appreciate her attempt at humor. Letting go of her hand, he walked a few feet back toward the corner until he could barely see the car through the shrubbery. A very long five-minutes later, a young, uniformed policeman came out of the house, got in the car, and drove off.

Once the car was safely out of sight, Mark took Angela by the hand. "Come on," he whispered.

They hurried back to the house, almost in a run, and ducked in the front door. As they entered the foyer, he heard Susan and her parents chatting in the den. Lisa giggled at something they said.

"What's going on?" he said to Angela. "The laws breathing down my neck and they sound like nothing's happened."

As he and Angela entered the den, everyone stopped talking and looked up.

"What did the cop want?" Mark asked.

"Oh, that was just Eddy," Mr. Singletary said. "He stops by ever once in a while for a cup of coffee. We've known him since he was in grade school. He used to mow our yard."

"He wasn't asking about me?"

"Lord no. Eddy's a good cop, but I don't think it would ever occur to him that someone wanted by the police might be hiding out under our roof."

Mark breathed a sigh of relief, then sat down in the chair opposite Susan. Angela took a seat on the arm of the chair. A few minutes later, she caught Susan's eye. They sat there staring at each other while the rest of them talked.

The rest of the day passed quickly. That night Mark noticed that Lisa had a concerned look on her face. He assumed it was because of her mother's death.

"Lisa, are you okay?" he asked. "You've hardly said a word? That's not like you."

"Daddy, I'm really worried about Tiffany. Do you think that awful man hurt her?"

"I don't know. He's capable of anything, even killing a child."

"Oh no! I hope he didn't kill her," Lisa responded quickly. "Can we call the school and find out if she's okay?"

"I don't know. I'm worried that the call might be traced."

"That's highly unlikely," Mr. Singletary said. "Only the police can tap a phone, and they would do so only if they expected you to call. Is there any reason why they would expect you to call the school?"

"None."

"Then I think it would be safe."

Mark looked at his watch. "It's too late to call today," he said. "I'll call in the morning."

Lisa nodded her approval.

Early the next morning, Mr. Singletary took Mark back to the warehouse to get his car. After picking it up, they delivered it to the body shop. Mark had decided to have it painted black, figuring a dull color might attract less attention

Finished at the body shop, they returned to the house. As Mark had promised Lisa, he called Briarwood Academy. Mrs. Edwards answered the telephone.

"Mrs. Edwards, this is Mark Valentine," he said. "I wanted to find out how the young girl, Tiffany, is that the man abducted yesterday."

"Dr. Valentine, the police were here looking for you," she said excitedly. "When you called yesterday morning, you told me that Mrs. Valentine had been murdered. You didn't tell me that you were the one who did it."

"I didn't kill Joanna, but that's not why I called. Tell me about Tiffany. Lisa's worried sick about her. I promised her I would call you."

"I don't know if I should be talking to you or not."

"It's okay Mrs. Edwards. You won't get in any trouble," he said calmly. "Just tell me about Tiffany. I won't tell anyone I talked to you."

Mrs. Edwards hesitated...to think it over, he assumed. "The police came and interviewed her," she said finally. "Tiffany told them that the man had insisted that she was Lisa. She of course denied it. She even showed him that she wasn't wearing hearing aids. He made her repeat things he whispered to her with his mouth hidden. When she repeated everything correctly, he got upset and pushed her out of his moving car. An elderly couple driving behind them saw the whole thing. They picked her up and took her to the local hospital"

"Mrs. Edwards, is she okay?"

"She had some pretty bad bruises and scrapes, but no broken bones. Fortunately, the shoulder along that stretch of road was soft."

"What did she tell the police about the man who abducted her?"

"Dr. Valentine, don't you think you ought to turn yourself in? I'm sure you would get a fair trial."

"Maybe," he said. "What did she tell the police?"

"Not a lot. She said that he was about average height and had a beard. She said that he had an accent of some sort, but she couldn't identify it. They asked her about the car. She said it was pretty cluttered with beer cans and empty cigarette packs, but appeared to be fairly new. She said that it was a blue American-made car, but she couldn't identify the make or the model."

"Anything else?"

"No, that was about it. To tell you the truth, the police were more interested in you than Tiffany's kidnapper. When they discovered that you had been here and taken Lisa, they got real excited and called somebody in Atlanta, a Captain Sam Kincaid."

"He's been spotted in Valdosta," Kincaid said to Detective Carmichael as he leaned back in his chair behind the desk. "There was a kidnapping at Briarwood Academy...a young girl named Tiffany Bumgartner. Right afterwards, Valentine shows up and abducts his own daughter. He had called earlier in the day, claiming that his daughter was in danger. Mrs. Edwards, the Headmaster's Administrative Secretary, said that he had been drinking."

"What's the connection?" Detective Carmichael asked, standing in front of the desk sipping coffee from a Styrofoam cup.

"I don't know. Tiffany told the police that her kidnapper had mistaken her for Valentine's daughter. Something really strange is going on there."

"What do you think it is?"

"I don't know. There's something else. Valentine had a lady-friend with him, a good-looking chick in her late twenties."

Kincaid propped his feet up on the desk. "Any idea who she is?'

"None. My men asked around about her at Charity and at Valentine's apartment building. No one had the slightest idea who she was."

"Do we have any idea where the three of them might have gone?"

"No, but they won't get very far," Carmichael said. "Every cop in Georgia is on the lookout for two adults and a kid in a beat-up, green Porsche with an Atlanta tag. It's just a matter of time. Then I'm going to see to it that that son-of-a-bitch gets what he deserves."

Carmichael finished the coffee and crumpled the cup in his hand. "I'm sorry about the finger-print thing Captain. It never occurred to me that the prints in Joanna's house that we attributed to the killer belonged to you. If I had known it, I certainly wouldn't have made such a big deal out of them."

With Lisa taken care of, it was time to locate some money. Mark leaned back in the chair and reached for the telephone. Ellie hesitated, then jumped up in his lap and nuzzled his hand. He petted her on the head, then dialed a number that he had called often as of late.

CHAPTER NINETEEN

"Daniel, I need your help," Mark said into the telephone.

"What's up?" Daniel responded.

"You remember I told you about Vito Maldini and how I altered his facial appearance?"

"How could I forget something like that?"

"Well, he's trying to kill me. The guy who tried to stab me at the stoplight is a Mafia hit-man named Jesus Dimaria."

"You've got to be kidding."

"This is too serious to kid about."

"How did you find out the name of the hit-man?"

"Angela, Maldini's girlfriend, told me. She's with me now."

"You stole his girlfriend? No wonder he wants to kill you."

"No, I didn't steal his girlfriend. He wants her dead too. She came to warn me. Maldini's gone berserk. He's ordered nearly everyone killed who can identify him."

"The guy sounds crazy. Where are you now?"

"In Columbus. Jesus went after Lisa at Briarwood Academy."

"He didn't hurt her did he? Is she okay?"

"She's fine, but it was a close call."

"What are you doing in Columbus?"

"Susan's parents live here. They're going to keep Lisa until this mess blows over."

"I don't believe I know Susan. Should I?"

"I guess I haven't told you about her. I've dated her a couple of times. She's really nice. The kind of girl you'd like to take home to momma."

"Great! I wondered when you were going to get over that witch you were married to."

"Well, I'm not over her yet, but I'm working on it."

"You said you needed a favor. What can I do for you?"

"You can loan me some money. We've got to get out of Georgia if we're going to stay alive."

"You and Susan?"

"No, me and Angela."

"Sounds to me like you're taking the wrong woman."

"Angela's really nice too. Great body."

"Sounds like she's the kind of girl you'd like to take home to daddy."

"How much money do you need?"

"Can you spare $1500?"

"Is that all? I'll loan you as much as you want. All you have to do is ask."

"Fifteen hundred should be enough to last us until I can find a job."

"Do you want me to wire you the money?"

"No, it might be traced. I don't want to take a chance on anyone finding out where Lisa is. Besides, we plan on going to Charleston, South Carolina. If I use a false name, maybe I can get a job at the University of South Carolina School of Medicine as a research assistant."

"A research assistant? Do you know how little those guys make?"

"I've got a pretty good idea. I'm afraid this is a case of beggars can't be choosy. I'll be grateful for anything I can find."

"What do you want me to do about the money?"

"Angela and I will come and get it. Atlanta's on the way to Charleston. We can breeze in and out of there so fast that Jesus will never know we passed through."

"When are you coming?"

"If we leave late this afternoon, we can be there before dark."

"I'll be looking for you. Be careful."

The time to leave for Atlanta arrived. In the brief time they had been together, Lisa and the Singletarys had bonded well. Mark was thankful for that. It made leaving her easier. He hugged her and told her that he loved her. Then he and Susan hugged and said good-bye. Angela looked on disapprovingly. It was obvious that Susan hated to see him go, especially with Angela, but she understood the seriousness of the situation.

"Keep in touch," Susan whispered in his ear.

"I'll call you periodically to check on Lisa," he responded.

He felt secure with the new paint job, the repairs to the Porsche, and the different license plate. He had never cared for black, but somehow it looked good on the old car. Without the broken windshield and the dented front fender, the Porsche looked almost new...a far cry from the green wreck he had driven into Columbus. He would still have to be careful though, and he would have to obey the speed limit. He couldn't afford to be stopped by the police, not even for a minor traffic violation.

As they pulled onto I-185 headed northeast, dark clouds hung low over the horizon. The weather alert on the car radio predicted heavy rain, with the possibility of thunderstorms and winds gusting up to thirty miles per hour.

The fax arrived at FBI headquarters. Over the past five years, twenty-nine plastic surgeons in the southeastern United States had been disciplined by their state licensing boards. Eighteen had had their licenses restricted in one way or another, and eleven had had their licenses revoked. Six of the eleven had practiced within 1000 miles of Miami.

On the wall, an arc with a 1000-mile radius from Miami had been drawn in black ink on a map of the southeastern United States. Six pins with round, red heads identified the location of each of the six plastic surgeons with revoked licenses...Orlando, Tallahassee, Chattanooga, Memphis, Little Rock, and Atlanta.

"I've prepared summaries of each of the six doctors," Special Agent Barnes said to Walter North as he handed him six sheets off paper. North took the sheets and studied them.

Carl F. Pinkerton, M.D.
48-year-old Caucasian male
Convicted of Medicare fraud - billing for services not rendered
License revoked in 1996
Address - 231 Amherst Drive
Orlando, Florida

Arthur M. Jones, M.D.
62-year-old Caucasian male
Repeated bouts of alcoholism and malpractice
License revoked in 1995
Address - 873 Sprucewood Street
Tallahassee, Florida

William Q. Dickinson, M.D.
48-year-old African-American male
Convicted of cocaine trafficking
License revoked in 1997
Address - 932 48th Court
Chattanooga, Tennessee

Archibald R. Wood, M.D
57-year-old Caucasian male
Sexual misconduct with female patients
License revoked in 1998
Address - 67 Brookshire Boulevard
Memphis, Tennessee

Caldwell L. Witherspoon, M.D.
59-year-old Caucasian male
Malpractice - negligence resulting in multiple disastrous outcomes
License revoked in 1997
Address - 756 Aerosmith Lane
Little Rock, Arkansas

Mark A. Valentine, M.D.
42-year-old Caucasian male
Alcohol dependence - under the influence in the operating room
License revoked in 1999
Address - 337 Avondale Avenue
Atlanta, Georgia

North finished reading the summaries, then looked up at Barnes. "Are these their current places of residence?"

"No, they're their addresses at the time their licenses were revoked," Barnes said. "We don't have their current addresses. We'll have to track them down. The ages are correct. We calculated them from the birth dates given in the data-bank information."

North put the papers down on his desk. "I spoke with Director Armstrong this morning. He met with the President immediately after our last talk. The President wants to keep Maldini's disappearance quiet as long as we can. Seems he's worried about what the appearance of a botched job might do to his ratings. As a result, the Director has given this case top priority. He moved Maldini to the top of the Ten-Most-Wanted list. The full resources of the agency are at our disposal."

"Then we'd better get to work," Barnes said. "I'll contact the local offices and get them on it right away."

"I don't want the local offices involved, at least not yet," North responded. "This case is too important. I want our own men to handle it."

"Good idea. I'll disperse a man to each of the six locations immediately."

"Better send two. Be sure it's your twelve best men. I want this matter expedited as rapidly as possible. This may be the most important case they ever work on."

"Consider it done."

"I expect you to report directly to me," North said. "I want to hear from you just as soon as you've located the six doctors."

"What do we do when we find the doctor who did Maldini's surgery?" Barnes asked.

"Pick him up. He'll be charged with conspiracy to obstruct justice."

Twenty miles outside Atlanta, the sky darkened and the wind picked up. Only a sliver of blue sky was left in the east, and it was fading fast. Mark glanced at Angela. She smiled at him and placed her hand on his thigh. He reached down and slid his hand into hers. They were two people bound by a common bond...fear for their lives. He would miss Susan. There was a good chance he might never see her again.

Just outside the city limits, scattered drops of rain began cascading off the windshield. As he reached to turn the windshield wipers on to the lowest speed, a bright flash of lightening suddenly lit the horizon. A loud crack of thunder quickly followed. He squeezed her hand, then let it go and gripped the steering wheel with both hands.

As usual, traffic got heavier and heavier as they approached Atlanta. Thin clouds of steam rose a few feet into the air and hovered like ghosts above the hot pavement. Traffic in the outgoing lanes to their left moved along bumper-to-bumper as hoards of Atlanta's workers headed for the suburbs. He slowed, changed lanes, and blended in with the multitude of cars and trucks headed toward the downtown area.

Daniel lived near Baptist Memorial Hospital where he did most of his surgery cases. Mark was familiar with the hospital. It was where he had practiced before his downfall. To get there they would have to take I-285 East to I-75 north, then follow it through Spaghetti Junction to Highway 210. From there, the hospital was located two blocks north on Boulevard Road. Daniel's apartment was five blocks further north near the Atlanta Civic center. Traffic would be heavy all the way, slowed considerably by the bad weather and the inevitable accidents that occur on Atlanta's highways when it rains.

"Tell me about your friend. How long have you known him?" Angela asked.

Mark glanced at her, then focused his eyes back on the wet pavement ahead. "We met in college. Daniel was a sophomore when I was a freshman. We lived in the same dorm and even roomed together one year."

"Did you go to medical school together?"

"Yes. He enrolled at Emory a year before I did. My first year there was really hard. He helped me a lot...told me what to expect from the various professors and loaned me some of his notes. He knew from the time he entered pre-med that he wanted to be a surgeon, but he didn't settle on otolaryngology until his senior year in medical school."

"Oto-what?"

"Otolaryngology. You know. Ear, nose, and throat surgery."

"Oh! Why didn't you say so?"

"Sometimes I forget that everyone isn't familiar with medical terminology." She smiled coquettishly. "I guess I'll forgive you this time."

The rain now came down steadily. Flashes of lightening continued to light the horizon, and seemed to be getting closer. He let go of the steering wheel with his left hand and adjusted the windshield wipers to a faster speed. Then he braked as the car in front of him slowed, then changed lanes. The spray from its tires temporarily clouded the Porsche's windshield. When the wipers had cleared away the spray, he picked up speed, being careful to stay just within the speed limit. Cars passed on either side of them at a rapid speed.

"What happened to your plastic surgery career?" Angela asked. "Working in that emergency room you told me about doesn't sound too pleasant."

"The Emergency Room's the pits. I can tolerate it a lot better now than I could when I first went to work there. One good thing about it, the people who work there are great, at least most of them are."

"The plastic surgery career?"

"That's a long story. I'd just as soon not go into it."

"Well, we've got lots of time."

"It depresses me."

"Maybe talking about it is what you need."

"When did you become a psychiatrist?" Mark asked.

"You don't have to be a psychiatrist to know that talking about a problem helps. Don't you ever watch the talk shows on TV?"

"No. They come on in the afternoon. I'm always at work."

"Well?"

"Well, what?"

"You know what I mean."

"You're right. I learned about talk therapy on the psychiatry rotation in my junior year of medical school. It's the basis of group therapy."

"I'm listening."

"Well, I guess since we're in this mess together you might as well know what got me here."

"Go on."

"Alcohol."

"Now that's a real surprise," Angela said sarcastically.

"It helped my depression."

"What were you depressed about?"

"The divorce. I tried so hard to make the marriage work, but Joanna wanted more than I had to give…more time, more money, more everything. Finally, she got it all."

Angela looked at him sympathetically, then leaned over and gently kissed him on the cheek.

———————

The rain slacked off a little as they pulled into the apartment-complex parking lot. Mark's heart immediately skipped a beat. Two Atlanta police cars with their red and blue lights flashing were parked straight ahead near the building. He let off on the accelerator. Then, noticing that both cars were empty, he breathed a sigh of relief and made a hard left turn. He continued down the parking lot to its furthermost end where he parked in one of the few available parking spaces, separated from the police cars by at least thirty cars.

He looked at Angela. Her eyes were wide. It was obvious that she had been as startled as he by the unexpected presence of the police.

"What are we going to do?" she asked.

"I don't know, but we've got to get to Daniel and get the money."

"Why do you think the police are here?"

He shook his head. "I don't know that either," he said. "Domestic violence occurs at a high rate in apartment buildings. Someone could have beaten up his wife, or his girlfriend. Or the police could be investigating a burglary, or arresting someone that's wanted for a crime. They could be here for any number of reasons."

"How are we going to get to your friend's apartment?"

"I can't go. It's too risky. Even with my beard someone still might recognize me."

"But you said we had to get to the money."

"We do, or at least one of us does. The police aren't looking for you. You'll have to go."

"In this rain? I'll get my hair wet."

He reached behind the seat, took out a black umbrella, and handed it to her. "This ought to solve that problem."

She stared at the umbrella for a moment, then took it in her hand. "Okay, I'll go. What's your friend's apartment number?"

"B-27"

She took the umbrella, pushed the car door open, and let the umbrella up. Then, giving him one last look, she left the car and headed toward the opening between the buildings.

He watched the rain bounce off of the umbrella as she made her way down the parking lot, carefully avoiding puddles on the glistening, black pavement. Moments later, she disappeared between the buildings. He reached for the radio, turned it on to a local station, and waited for Angela to return.

"No news yet on the where-abouts of Mark Valentine, the doctor accused of brutally murdering his ex-wife," the announcer said. "The local Police Chief believes that he may have escaped to another state. He was last seen at Briarwood Academy in Valdosta following a bizarre, double kidnapping which occurred only minutes apart. The police have no significant clues in the first kidnapping, that of Tiffany Bumgartner, other than the fact that the abduction was committed by a bearded man of average height with an accent of some sort. The police have accused Dr. Valentine of kidnapping his own daughter. However, an eye witness told a representative of this station that she went with him of her own free will."

Mark turned the radio off, then stared in the direction of the opening between the two buildings where Angela had disappeared...and waited. A few minutes later, two uniformed policemen appeared from between the apartment buildings and got into one of the police cars. Mark slumped down in the seat and watched the patrol car as it exited the parking lot.

Moments later, Angela appeared and, avoiding the puddles in her path as carefully as she had when she departed, walked in Mark's direction. When she reached the car, he leaned over and opened the door for her. She slid into the seat beside him and placed the wet umbrella on the floorboard in front by her feet.

"Did you get the money?" he asked. Then he saw the terror in her eyes. "What is it? What's wrong?"

She swallowed hard. "It's Daniel. When I got to his apartment, a policeman was standing outside the door. I wanted to run, but I got hold of myself. I walked up to him as calmly as I could and told him that Daniel was a friend of mine. He was very nice, kind of young. I asked him what was wrong." Then she paused.

"Yes. Go on. Don't stop now," Mark said quickly.

"He told me that Daniel's daughter had come to visit him and found him sitting in a chair with his hands tied behind his back. He was dead. His throat had been cut, and he had been tortured. The policeman said that his nose was broken and both eyes were blackened. He had cigarette burns on his forearms and his thighs. His daughter was hysterical but she managed to dial 911."

"Jesus, that son-of-a-bitch," Mark said loudly. "Daniel never did anything to hurt anyone. He was a good man."

"What do we do now?" Angela asked. "We're almost broke."

Suddenly, his mouth felt dry. He wanted a drink in the worst way. "We get the hell out of here."

CHAPTER TWENTY

The sign painted on the plate-glass window said **Make Every Day A Party Day...Alcoholic Beverages.** Shelf after shelf of liquors, whiskeys, and wines were evident through the window. Mark hadn't spoken a word since leaving Daniel's apartment complex. He was numb on the inside. The only true friend he had left in the world was dead because of him. If he hadn't gotten him involved, Daniel would still be alive. He wondered if his life would ever turn around, or would things just keep getting worse? He feared it would be the latter.

He and Angela sat in the car and waited in silence until the rain slackened into a fine drizzle. Then he left the car and entered the package store, only to return a few minutes later with a brown, paper bag in his hand

"Where are we going now?" Angela asked as he got back into the car.

He placed the package on the seat beside him. "To find a place to stay tonight. We'll make some definitive plans in the morning." He started the engine.

A half-hour later, they checked into another low-budget room. This time the Budget King Motel. The walls needed painting and the gray carpet was dirty and badly worn. The bedspreads were in need of washing. He went to the ice machine for a bucket of cubes, then settled into a chair for a night of drinking. Angela watched him as he mixed drink after drink and quickly disposed of each in an attempt to dull the pain of Daniel's death. Finally, she spoke up.

"Mark you've had enough. You're going to regret this in the morning."

"I'll worry about that tomorrow," he said. Then he poured himself another drink.

"Okay. You can drink yourself to death if you want to. I'm going to take a shower." She entered the small bathroom and pulled the door to behind her.

For a few minutes he listened to the water running in the shower. Then he put his drink down on the table and thought about how Angela must look with the water bouncing off her naked body. He pictured her firm round breasts, smoothly curved hips, and shapely buttocks.

Angela and Susan were both attractive, and both had good bodies. Susan was warm and affectionate and nice, the kind of woman you dream about being a mother to your children and sharing the rest of your life with. It wasn't that Susan wasn't exciting, because she was. Angela, however, was the kind of woman that most men would give their right arm to spend just one night with. Few were ever lucky enough to experience the reality of such a dream, and here he was, alone in a motel room with her. The alcohol was having an affect on him. He felt aroused.

He finished his drink, picked the brown paper bag the bottle had come in up from the table, and wadded it up in his hand. Then he tossed it at the wastebasket next to the wall. It fell short and landed in front of the can.

"Shit," he said aloud. He blamed the miss on the fuzziness in his head from the alcohol.

When Angela finished her shower, she returned to the bedroom with a white towel wrapped loosely around her body. He glanced up at her and thought how sexy she looked. She slowly walked in his direction, almost cat like, until she stood directly in front of him. Bending over, she placed her hand on the back of his neck and kissed him hard on the lips. Then she looked into his eyes and dropped the towel to the floor. Daniel's death temporarily passed from his mind.

The next morning, Mark awoke before Angela. Feeling guilty about the night before, he reminded himself that Susan didn't have any hold on him. After all, they had had only one real date, if you didn't count that night in her apartment. He blamed his sexual encounter with Angela on the alcohol. It wasn't the first time he had done something under the influence that he might not have done sober.

Trying to shake the guilt feeling, he looked in the mirror and admired his short beard. It was coming in nicely. He wondered if he should dye his hair, but decided against it. He figured he looked different enough with the new beard.

Sitting in the chair he had done his drinking in the night before, images of Daniel's torture and death kept creeping back into his mind. He tried to push them into the furthermost recesses of his subconscious, but they wouldn't go away. He stared at the vodka bottle sitting on the table where he had left it the night before, still half full. He knew how to suppress the unpleasant thoughts. A few drinks would do it, but he knew better than to start drinking this early in the morning. He would be drunk by noon if he did. He took the bottle in his hand and placed it in the bottom drawer of the dresser. Then he sat back down in the chair and focused on Angela. She had the kind of beauty that required no makeup. Even with her hair messed up from their passion of the night before, she was beautiful. He was sure that she had initiated the love making to stop him from drinking. She had to know that he would need a clear head this morning to make a decision about their next move. He leaned back in the chair and closed his eyes. Where would they go? What would they do? The money was running low and they would be out soon. Where would they get more? He knew he could have asked the Singletarys for money when he and Angela were in Columbus, but they were doing enough just keeping Lisa. Besides, until two days ago they had been total strangers.

He turned the ancient TV on to CNN, keeping the volume low as had become his custom so as not to disturb Angela. Nothing much drew his interest until about half way through **The World Report.**

"No new clues on the were-abouts of Dr. Mark Valentine, according to the Atlanta police spokesman," Bernard Shaw said. "From the home of Mr. And Mrs. Robert Ellison, the victims parents, we bring you this exclusive interview."

A news clip of Joanna's parents appeared on the screen. A middle-aged man wearing a green jacket and yellow tie sat in a wingback chair facing an older couple who sat side by side on a Victorian sofa.

"With us today are Mr. and Mrs. Robert Ellison, parents of wealthy socialite, Joanna Valentine, who was recently murdered here in Atlanta," the interviewer said. "Her ex-husband, Dr. Mark Valentine, who is suspected of brutally killing her, is still on the loose. Robert Ellison is well known to Georgians, having just completed his third term as a state senator. Mr. Ellison, I understand that you're somewhat skeptical that Dr. Valentine actually committed this crime."

Joanna's father leaned forward and cleared his throat. "Mark and Joanna had their problems, but I just can't believe he would do anything to hurt her, especially anything as violent as the brutal act that killed her. He loved her too much. As far as I know, he never physically abused her during their fifteen years of marriage."

The interviewer turned to Joanna's mother. "Mrs. Ellison, I understand that you haven't been as kind in your statements about your ex-son in law."

"I hate to disagree with my husband on national TV, but I never did feel comfortable about his relationship with Joanna. For one thing, he drank too much, and he did threaten to kill her. I hope they catch him soon so that he can be brought to justice for the murder of my precious daughter."

The interview lasted a couple of minutes more, then Bernard Shaw appeared on the screen again.

"According to Vince Goodwin, the District Attorney charged with the case, he expects Dr. Valentine to be apprehended soon. He stated emphatically that the full force of his office has been brought to bear on the case, and he assured the public that he would give his undivided attention to the prosecution of Dr. Valentine once the matter comes to trial. Some who know Mr. Goodwin suspect that his interest in this case may be more than seeing that justice is done, since it is common knowledge that he plans to run in the upcoming Governor's race. A conviction of Dr. Valentine would certainly be a feather in his cap."

The station moved on to the weather report…another storm front was expected to move through, but not for a couple of days. Light showers off and on between now and then were predicted.

Tired of the TV, Mark rose and walked to the window to study the area around the motel and to check the weather. Because of the early morning hour, the streets were almost deserted. Despite the fact that the rain had stopped during the night, the pavement was still wet and glistening. Suddenly, a blue Pontiac a block away caught his eye as it turned the corner and headed in the direction of the motel.

"Jesus," he mumbled under his breath. He quickly moved away from the window, being careful to keep the car barely in view. How had Jesus found them? Did he know which room they were in? Should they stay where they were and see what he was up to, or should they bolt and run for it?

The blue Pontiac moved slowly down the wet street toward the motel entrance. Mark stood frozen by the window. The car slowed even more, then turned into the motel drive. He strained to get a look at the driver, but the glare on the windshield made it impossible.

The Pontiac made a right turn in front of the office and proceeded down the drive in the direction of their room. He held his breath as he leaned forward in an attempt to keep the car just in sight. The view of the driver was still obscured. Finally, as the Pontiac passed directly in front of their window, he looked at the grill…no damage. There should have been damage. Jesus had hit him from behind. He had seen the damaged grill with his own eyes. Jesus must have gotten it fixed, he reasoned. After all, he had gotten the damage to the Porsche repaired.

He leaned forward in an attempt to get a better look. Suddenly the driver came into view...an elderly, black woman wearing a yellow, maid's uniform. The car proceeded past the window and parked at the end of the row of cars. Only then did he notice his sweaty palms, his shirt sticking to his back, and the knot in the pit of his stomach.

Daryl Barnes handed Walter North the report. The twelve agents had worked quickly and effectively in tracking down the six ex-plastic surgeons. Sitting behind his desk, North thumbed through the pages, then handed the report back to Barnes.

"Give it to me in a nutshell," North said.

Barnes opened the report. "Dr. Carl Pinkerton of Orlando, Florida. Convicted of Medicare fraud. He's still in the federal penitentiary at Talladega serving eight to twelve."

"Well, I guess that rules him out. Who's next?"

"Doctor Arthur Jones of Tallahassee, Florida. Lost his license because of alcoholism and malpractice. He couldn't handle the shame and depression, especially after his wife left him. He committed suicide six months ago."

"That's another one eliminated. Keep going," North instructed.

Barnes eased into the chair in front of the desk. "William Dickinson. Black physician from Chattanooga, Tennessee. Convicted of cocaine trafficking. He never served a day in prison. The conviction was thrown out because the defense claimed that the jury was guilty of racial discrimination. Sure enough, one of the jurors had written a letter to the editor in a local newspaper some twenty years ago claiming that whites were intellectually superior to blacks. He had later apologized and become a vigorous proponent of equal rights, but the clipping was there, and the judge was ultra-liberal. The prosecutor was so frustrated by the decision that he elected not to retry the case, especially since the same judge would preside. Dickinson was difficult to track down, but our agents finally located him in San Francisco, living like a king. He grinned slyly when asked how he came by all the money. He vacationed on the French Riviera all summer and returned to this country only a few days ago"

"How do we know he was out of the country the whole time?" North asked.

Barnes leaned back in the chair and stretched. "We checked with Customs. His passport wasn't used in the interim. Besides, this guy sure doesn't need money from Maldini."

"What about blackmail? Maldini could have something on him."

"We checked. No prior relationship with Maldini. I doubt he's our man."

"Who's next?"

"Dr. Archibald Wood of Memphis, Tennessee. Lost his license because of sexual misconduct with his female patients. He's seriously ill with AIDS. Seems he liked men too. He contacted the virus from a male lover."

"Well, I think that rules him out. Not even Maldini would want to be operated on by somebody with AIDS. Who's next?"

"Dr. Caldwell Witherspoon of Little Rock, Arkansas. Lost his license because of malpractice resulting in a number of disastrous outcomes. He's teaching surgery at a fly-by-night medical school in the Caribbean. He's been out of the country for two years."

"He hasn't been back at all?"

"He's been back several times. He still has family here. Comes home regularly for Christmas and a few other holidays."

"What about recently?"

"Negative. He's been lecturing at the school everyday for at least a month."

"What about weekends?"

"He's made surgery rounds every weekend. The other faculty surgeon has been out sick."

North pushed his chair back, stood up, and began to pace behind his desk. "Okay, keep going. Who's next?"

"Dr. Mark Valentine of Atlanta, Georgia. Lost his license because of alcoholism. He still lives in Atlanta and has been working in the Emergency Room at Greater Atlanta Charity Hospital since he got out of Ridgeview Psychiatric Hospital three and a half months ago. He underwent treatment for his alcohol problem there. Present whereabouts unknown."

A perplexed look came over North's face. "Our agents couldn't find him? How could that be?"

"He's wanted for the murder of his ex-wife. He took off and just disappeared. No one knows where he is."

"This case is getting more bizarre by the minute. Why do the police suspect him?"

"He threatened her in front of an Atlanta police captain a couple of weeks before her death."

"You've got to be kidding…in front of a police captain? Makes you wonder about the seriousness of the threat doesn't it."

"What do you mean?"

"If you were serious about killing your ex-wife, would you threaten her in front of the police, especially a captain?"

"I see your point."

North stopped pacing and sat back down. "What's the police captain's name?" he asked.

"Sam Kincaid," Barnes replied.

"How's he involved in this?"

"He and Valentine's ex-wife were lovers. Planned on getting married. He's assigned himself to the case. Apparently there's vengeance in his motive. We looked into his record. He's a real bad-ass."

"What do we have on him?"

"He's forty-five years old. He's been a member of the Atlanta police force for twenty-two years, and for the past ten he's been a captain. He's a college graduate…masters degree in criminology from Georgetown University. Apparently his special knowledge of the criminal mind has served him well."

"How's that?"

"Over the years, he's cracked a number of particularly difficult cases, some of them deemed unsolvable by his peers. As a result, the most difficult cases are now routinely assigned to him."

"You said he was a real bad ass. What did you mean?"

"Our source says that some of his fellow officers consider him to border on being an egomaniac. Some of them question his tactics. To him, the end apparently justifies the means. If it takes a broken jaw or a few fractured ribs to get information from someone who is reluctant to talk, then so be it. He's been called before the ethics committee a number of times for use of excessive force, but he's always managed to squeeze by. Apparently the committee goes easy on him, sort of looks the other way, because of his reputation for delivering the goods."

"Any other background?"

Barnes crossed his legs. "He's divorced. Seems he hasn't been nearly as successful in his personal life as in his career. His wife, the second one, left him for the same reason the first one did…verbal and physical abuse. The court papers quoted her as saying that she had suffered too many black eyes and broken noses at his hand to stick it out any longer. The fact that he was hardly ever home, always working on one case or another, didn't help matters much."

"Makes you wonder what Mrs. Valentine saw in him doesn't it?"

"Apparently she found his aggressive demeanor exciting. One of her friends said she liked living on the edge."

"Do you think Kincaid poses a real danger to Valentine?"

"The feeling among his fellow officers is that if he gets to Valentine first, Valentine's as good as dead. I'd say its fifty-fifty who kills him first, Maldini or Kincaid."

"Put all the men you need on this case," North instructed. "We've got to find Valentine fast, that is if he's still alive."

CHAPTER TWENTY-ONE

"We've got her," Lowenstein said excitedly. "I didn't want to wait until in the morning to break the news to you, so I asked you all to meet after work today. I apologize for the inconvenience."

"You caught Betsy Barfield killing a patient?" Dr. Jackson responded.

"No. But it's almost as good. This afternoon she showed up on her unit with slurred speech and pinpoint pupils. A security guard noticed her acting strange right after she clocked in. He immediately called Zachary Dorfman. A drug screen's pending, but I think it's just a formality. She had twenty-three pills in her pocket. The head nurse looked them up in the PDR."

"What were they?" Dr. Jackson asked.

"Mepergan."

"Mepergan?" Mrs. Anderson repeated quizzically.

"Yes, a combination of Demerol and Phenergan".

"We know what Mepergan is," Dr. Jackson said sarcastically. "Where did she get it?"

"We don't know for sure. At first she refused to say. Then she said she bought it on the street outside the hospital."

"Do you believe her?" Mrs. Anderson asked

"I don't know. She could be protecting someone, but then again you can buy almost anything you want on the streets around here."

"What about the hospital?" Dr. Jackson asked. "She could have stolen it from a narcotic cabinet."

"None's been reported missing," Lowenstein answered.

Mrs. Anderson leaned forward. "It's a prescription drug. She could be getting it from a doctor."

Dr. Jackson quickly responded. "That's a possibility. Maybe she had a legitimate reason for taking it. Mepergan is a commonly prescribed medication for pain."

"I'm afraid not," Lowenstein said. "She cried when we questioned her, but she finally admitted she was addicted to narcotics. She said she started taking Mepergan because it made her feel good, but eventually she got to the point where she had to have it to prevent withdrawal symptoms. She tried to stop two or three times, but every time she did she got extremely anxious and developed terrible stomach cramps and diarrhea. She swore that even her bones hurt."

Mrs. Anderson suddenly looked concerned. "Where is she now?"

"She's on the Chemical Dependency Unit getting detoxed. That will take about five days, I'm told. She'll be there another twenty-three days for rehab."

"Good," Mrs. Anderson said. "She really is a nice girl."

"Nice girl?" Dr. Jackson blurted out. "Nice girls don't go around killing people."

"So far she's only been found guilty of substance abuse." Lowenstein said. "There's still no hard evidence that she's involved in the cardiac arrests. Hell, she hasn't even been near most of the patients when they arrested. I remind you that one time she had even clocked out and gone home, and two other times she was in the cafeteria on her coffee break."

"Well, did you interrogate her about the cardiac arrests?"

"No. The last thing I want to do is accuse someone of murder without justification. I've got the hospital attorney working on the best way to approach the matter without putting the hospital at risk."

"What did Dorfman say about his surveillance of her prior to this morning...any unusual behavior?" Dr. Jackson asked.

"I asked him to join us today. He's waiting outside," Lowenstein responded. "Why don't I let him answer your question?"

Lowenstein stood, walked to the door, and opened it. Dorfman entered the room wearing his usual quazi-military garb and took a seat next to Dr. Jackson.

"Had you turned up anything unusual in Betsy Barfield's behavior prior to this afternoon?" Dr. Jackson asked.

"No. Before this afternoon's episode her behavior wasn't any different than the other nurses's in the hospital. I spoke to some of the head nurses about her. They all said that she was a good nurse."

"Have you had time to look into her background?" Dr. Jackson asked, brushing back the troublesome lock of hair from his eye.

"I did a quick check. I reviewed her personnel file and obtained some additional information using my connections downtown. Neither one turned up anything significant. Her police records show only an occasional speeding ticket. She did get caught once with some of her friends smoking marijuana as a teenager. There's no evidence that she's been anything but clean since."

Dr. Jackson quickly corrected him. "You mean until this afternoon."

"Of course I meant until this afternoon," Dorfman said, somewhat irritated.

"What about mental illness? Any history of that?" Mrs. Anderson asked.

"Her personnel record showed that she had a minor episode of depression when she was in nursing school. Her boyfriend dumped her. She saw a psychiatrist a few times, and apparently got over it fairly quickly."

"Any family history of mental illness?" Dr. Jackson asked.

"She's adopted. Never knew her real parents."

Dr. Jackson scratched his head. "So we still don't have any idea how she's been causing the cardiac arrests?"

Lowenstein corrected him. "If she's the one responsible."

"Well, I think she is," Dr. Jackson countered. "I just don't know how and why she's doing it."

"Well, at least we got what we wanted," Mrs. Anderson said.

"How's that?" Dr. Jackson asked.

"She's off the floor for at least a month. We'll see what happens to the cardiac arrest rate while she's gone."

"What do you mean, off the floor for a month?" Dr. Jackson blurted out. He turned in Lowenstein's direction. "Surely you're going to fire her?"

"If we fired every employee who's had a drug problem, we wouldn't be able to keep the hospital doors open. It's the hospital policy to take employees back after they complete a rehab program. They're monitored, of course, with random, observed drug screens for two years. The Board of Nursing will be notified in compliance with state law, but the board's usual policy is to put nurses on probation the first time they're found to have a drug problem. We have a number of them working in the hospital now. We can't treat Betsy any different."

Dr. Jackson leaned forward. "Damn it. All I've got to say is that it's a hell of a way to run a hospital. In the old days we would have fired her and asked questions later. She wouldn't have had any of these newfangled ideas like rehabilitation. Once a drug addict always a drug addict, I say."

Lowenstein turned back to Dorfman. "The committee wanted to ask you some questions about Dr. Mark Valentine," he said. "You seem to know him pretty well. Do you think he might be involved in our cardiac arrest problem? After all, he killed his ex-wife."

Dorfman uncrossed his legs and leaned forward. "He's accused of killing her," he said sternly. "There's a big difference. A lot of us have our doubts. I think that trying to link him to the hospital murders is pretty far fetched. For one thing, he's never even mentioned Betsy Barfield. I'm not sure he even knows her. She and Dr. Eric Stottlemire, the head of the Emergency Room, seem to have some sort of relationship going on. You might want to talk to him about her."

"Do you think Betsy told the truth about where she got the drugs?" Lowenstein asked.

"I doubt it," Dorfman replied. "She acted awfully suspicious when I questioned her…like she was hiding something. I'm going to talk to her again, and turn up the pressure."

———————————

"Mattie, this is Mark. Is it safe to talk?"

"Mark! How are you? I've been worried to death about you."

"I'm okay. Is it safe to talk?"

"Yes. My grandchildren spent the night with me, but my daughter picked them up a few minutes ago to take them to school."

"I was hoping I could catch you before you went to work. I guess you've heard about Joanna's death?"

"Yes, the police were all over the place at Charity. A police captain named Sam Kincaid was especially obnoxious. He acted like he was on a personal vendetta."

"I expect he is. He was Joanna's lover, the one who broke us up."

"I knew something was wrong with him. Did you kill her?"

"No, of course not."

"I didn't think so. I told that police captain he was looking for the wrong man. Where are you?"

"I'm back in Atlanta."

"Back in Atlanta? Where have you been?"

"To Columbus. Jesus went after Lisa. I took her to Columbus for safe keeping."

"Who is Jesus?" Mattie asked.

"It's all too complicated to go into now. I'll explain everything to you in time."

"You're being too mysterious. You can trust me you know."

"I know I can," Mark responded. "Please be patient for now. How's Dr. Billingsworth?"

"He's doing better. His blood pressure is holding up well without medication. He's not had any more cardiac arrhythmias and his heart is getting stronger. He's still on a ventilator and not fully alert, but it looks like he has a good chance of making it. Dr. Agarwall moved him to a private room on the step-down unit yesterday afternoon. His cardiac and respiratory statuses are being monitored by telemetry."

"Great! That's the best news I've had in days. In fact, it's the only good news I've had. Any progress on Charity's serial killer problem?"

"The administrative committee met last night. Mrs. Anderson called me immediately afterwards. She couldn't wait until this morning to tell someone. They caught the suspect nurse high on drugs. She had a pocket full of Mepergan. She said she bought it on the'street. Dorfman doesn't believe her. He thinks that some doctor may have been supplying her with it."

"What's her name? Anybody I know?"

"I'm not sure. Do you know Betsy Barfield?"

"Betsy Barfield. The name's familiar."

"She's a PRN nurse. Works any shift she's needed on. She dates Stottlemire some."

"Now I remember her," he said quickly. "I caught Stottlemire making out with her in the doctors' office one evening. He had introduced her to me earlier at Billingsworth's party."

"I just can't believe that she would kill someone," Mattie said. "She's the nicest young lady. Always very polite."

"What times did you tell me the peaks occurred in the excess cardiac arrest data?"

"The three-to-eleven and the eleven-to-seven shifts."

"No, not the shifts, the times," he said quickly.

"Oh! Six in the morning and nine in the evening," Mattie responded. "Why? What are you thinking?"

"Betsy isn't the only one who is at work at those times."

"What do you mean? Who else?" Mattie asked.

"Stottlemire. He works the seven P.M. to seven A.M. shift. Both peak time periods fall within his shift."

"Do you think he's involved?"

"I don't know. He might be. You said that Billingsworth's secretary, Edna, told you that Billingsworth suspected a certain high level hospital employee, and Stottlemire is head of Emergency Services. I'll bet you anything that the only doctor in Betsy's life is Stottlemire. What if he were supplying her with narcotics to do something to the patients to cause them to have cardiac arrests?"

"Why would he do that?"

"For the high it produces. As head of the code team he would have to rush up and attempt to save the patients' lives? You know how crazy he is about skydiving. He's even tried bungee jumping a time or two. He works the night shift because that's when the heavy trauma comes in. It's more exciting then."

"I still don't get it."

"In a life and death situation, the adrenal glands secrete adrenaline. Adrenaline is a stimulant, sort of like the body's own amphetamine or cocaine."

"How awful. I can't believe anyone would put someone's life in danger for kicks."

"Oh my God!" Mark exclaimed suddenly.

"What's the matter? What is it?" Mattie asked.

"Stottlemire! He'll go after Billingsworth. Billingsworth's the only one who can identify him, other than Betsy, and it sounds like she's too intimidated to talk. Billingsworth's a sitting duck."

"Surely you don't think Stottlemire would kill Dr. Billingsworth. He's been really good to him since he came to work at Charity."

"If Stottlemire is behind the cardiac arrests, I wouldn't put anything past him. He must be a real sick person."

"What are we going to do?"

"I don't know. I've got to think. I'll call you back." He hung up the telephone, then reached over and gently shook Angela. "Angela, Angela wake up," he said softly.

Angela turned over in his direction, then glanced at the clock. "Mark. What are you doing up so early?" she asked, rubbing her eyes.

He sat down on the side of the bed, put his arm around her, and kissed her on the cheek. "I called Mattie before she went to work. We've got a problem."

"Another one. What now?" Angela asked.

"I think Dr. Billingsworth is in danger. Do you remember that arrogant doctor in the Emergency Room I told you about…Eric Stottlemire?"

"Yes. What about him?"

"I think he may try to kill Billingsworth."

"Why would he do that?"

He sat on the side of the bed. "He may be the one causing the cardiac arrests at Charity."

"I thought they suspected a nurse."

"They do. He and the nurse may be in it together."

"I still don't understand what it has to do with Billingsworth?"

"Billingsworth suspects Stottlemire. I'm sure Stottlemire knows it."

She sat up in the bed. "Why would he think Stottlemire was involved?"

He shook his head. "I don't know. He must have had some information that made him suspicious."

"What kind of information?"

"Billingsworth was compulsively organized. You can bet that if he had information it's filed away in his office somewhere. He kept records on all the doctors that worked for him. He liked to add things from time to time, sort of personal notes to remind him of something good, or bad, that a doctor had done…things he didn't want the Personnel Department to know about. I bet if we searched his office we could find whatever it was that made him suspicious."

"Then let's do it," Angela said enthusiastically.

"We'll do it after dark," Mark responded. "When no one's around."

––––––––––––––

Special agent Daryl Barnes rushed into Walter North's office. "We've got some more information on Valentine," he said excitedly.

"Let's have it," North said, looking up from his desk.

Barnes sat down in the chair in front of the desk. "Get this. Two weeks before Maldini disappeared, Valentine was abducted at gunpoint from the Emergency Room at the hospital where he works. He was gone for two days. The local police investigated the incident and concluded that the abduction was part of a drug heist."

"Why would a doctor be abducted in a drug heist?"

"Valentine told some tale about being taken hostage and then being held over-night, apparently because the abductors considered holding him for ransom."

"Why did they let him go?" North asked.

"Because he was financially bankrupt. We checked it out. He was four months behind on his alimony payments, drives a beat-up old Porsche, and lives in a cheap apartment in northwest Atlanta."

"Do you think he did Maldini's surgery during that two day period?"

"It's a good possibility. The timing sure is right."

"Anything else?"

Barnes crossed his legs and leaned back in the chair. "Prescription drugs form the hospital where Valentine works showed up on the street in Miami last week. Not many. Just a portion of what was taken."

"How do we know the drugs came from his hospital?" North asked.

"A handful of them had a batch number on them. We traced the number through the manufacturer. They were shipped to Greater Atlanta Charity Hospital a month ago."

"Why would someone as wealthy as Maldini sell the drugs on the street? Besides just bringing in pocket change, he had to know they could be traced to Charity."

"My guess is that some of his men did it behind his back. You can't trust a crook, even if he works for you."

"You're probably right. Any progress on locating Valentine?" North asked.

"None. He's just disappeared."

"When was he seen last?"

"Four days ago," Barnes replied. "There was a double kidnapping at Briarwood Academy, a private school in Valdosta, Georgia where his daughter goes to school. He had a woman with him, a real looker who fit the description of Maldini's girlfriend, Angela Petrino."

"Why would Maldini's girlfriend be running around the country with Valentine?"

"I don't know. None of this makes any sense."

"Was Valentine involved in the kidnappings?"

"One of them. He kidnapped his daughter."

North scratched his head. "Why would he do that?"

"Damned if I know," Barnes replied.

"You said there was a double kidnapping."

"The other girl was about the same age as Valentine's daughter. Funny thing, her description is almost identical to that of his daughter…long, blonde hair and all. The kidnapper dumped the girl out of the car ten minutes later." Barnes stood up, walked to the door, and leaned against the facing.

"Do you think he got the wrong girl?" North asked.

"I wouldn't be surprised. Valentine nabbed his daughter right after that."

"Any identification on the kidnapper?"

"There were at least fifteen eye-witnesses, all school kids. It happened so fast that none of them got a good look at him except the kidnapped girl, and her description was pretty nondescript…short stature, goatee, accent of some kind. You wouldn't believe the different descriptions we got from the others…tall, short, black, white."

North leaned forward over the desk. "What about the car?"

"Late-model, American-made…Oldsmobile, Pontiac, Chevrolet. Take your pick. The only thing they could agree on was that it was blue. The police are looking for the guy, but they don't have much to go on."

It was nine o'clock in the evening. Mark and Angela had waited all day for the administrative offices at Charity to empty. He hoped the receptionist in the lobby wouldn't recognize him. Because he had worked there for only three months and now had a light beard, there was a good chance she wouldn't. He would have to take the chance. There was too much at stake not to. They decided that while Angela occupied the receptionists, he would walk through the lobby as if he were on his way to visit a relative in the hospital. Angela would then meet him in the hallway that led to Administration. This time of night, the area around Administration should be deserted. Hopefully, they could get into the office quickly, find what they wanted, and get out before the security guard made his hourly rounds.

They left the motel and made the brief trip to Charity. The sky now was temporarily clear, but the evening was still gray and damp. He parked in the center of the large parking lot by the side of the building so that the renovated Porsche would be as inconspicuous as possible, lost among the mass of cars and trucks. Then, holding hands, he and Angela walked toward the building. He stared for a moment at the side entrance which he normally entered when coming to work, thinking how much easier it would be if they could open the door and walk in.

"Just a moment," he said, letting go of Angela's hand. He walked to the side entrance and tried the door. Sure enough, it was locked.

"I just had to try it," he said, returning to her side. "Who knows? Security could have screwed up and left it unlocked for once."

"Sounds like wishful thinking to me," she said, taking his hand again.

"I've been guilty of that a lot in the last few months," he responded.

They walked around the building to the front entrance. Pockets of people stood around smoking on the front steps. By federal law, the hospital had become a smoke-free facility well over four years ago. Despite the fact that the hospital furnished ashtray stands for the convenience of smokers, they seldom used them. Cigarette butts littered the steps and the sidewalk.

For a moment, he and Angela stood on the large, brick porch and looked through the glass of one of the entrance doors. The receptionist sat at a desk to the right of the lobby, across from the double set of elevators. A half-dozen people stood around in the lobby talking. As planned, he stayed outside the door while Angela entered the lobby. As she approached the receptionist at the desk, he opened the door and entered the building. He walked across the open space as casually as he could. When he reached the middle of the lobby, he glanced in Angela's direction, just a brief diversion of his eyes. If anyone were watching, they wouldn't have noticed. The receptionist was looking through her file for the name of the patient Angela had given her. She never looked up.

Completing his walk through the lobby, he entered the hallway on the other side. The familiar green sign hanging from the ceiling directly in front of him indicated that hospital rooms were straight ahead and Administration was to the left. He turned left and located the door to Billingsworth's outer office. Waiting on Angela, he thought about having been there only a few days earlier when Billingsworth had his heart attack. He visualized him slumped over the desk, and Edna standing against the wall almost paralyzed with fear. He said a silent prayer for him. Charity needed Billingsworth to recover. So did he. Without Billingsworth he didn't have a hope in hell of getting his license reinstated.

Mark had never been in that part of the building at night before. It was quiet, very quiet, almost eerie. He wished Angela would hurry. He wondered what was keeping her? Finally she turned the corner and walked in his direction.

"What took you so long?" he asked as she approached him.

"The receptionist insisted on double checking her files. She said that she was almost positive she remembered someone being in the hospital by the name I gave her."

"What name did you give her?"

"John Smith."

"Very original."

"It was all I could think of."

He put his arm around her shoulders. "Okay, it's time for you to do your stuff."

CHAPTER TWENTY-TWO

Angela took a credit card from her purse and slid it between the door and the door facing. A few seconds later, the outer door to Billingsworth's office complex was open. They entered the blackness of the outer office that belonged to his secretary, Edna. Angela closed the door behind them, then he felt her move away from him.

"What are you doing?" he asked.

"I'm searching for a light switch. You can't see a thing in here."

"Don't turn the light on," he instructed quickly.

"Why not?"

"I don't want anyone to see the light shining under the door."

"How are we going to find what were looking for in the dark?"

"I thought of that," he said. He reached into his pocket, pulled out two penlights. Then, locating Angela's hand, he placed one of the penlights in it. Then he pressed the switch on his. The penlight cast a narrow beam of light straight ahead onto the door of Billingsworth's office.

Angela flipped the switch on her penlight. "Neat," she said, focusing the beam on the back of Mark's head.

He tried the doorknob. The door opened.

"Come on," he said softly.

She followed him into Billingsworth's office where they focused their attention on the eight file cabinets sitting against the wall to their left. Mark had seen them there many times before.

"What do we do now?" Angela asked.

"You start on that end and I'll start on this one."

"What are we looking for?"

"A file with Stottlemire's name on it. It will be with the files of a lot of other doctors."

"You know what we're doing is illegal."

"Listen, I'm wanted for murder. What's a little breaking and entering?"

They continued looking through drawer after drawer. Finally Angela broke the silence.

"I've got it," she said excitedly.

He approached her and looked over her shoulder at the manila folder, illuminated by her penlight. **Eric Stottlemire, M.D.** was hand printed on the tab. She opened the folder. Together they studied its contents...a standard application for employment, copies of a medical license, a medical school diploma, a residency training certificate, and a Drug Enforcement Association certificate which allowed him to write prescriptions for controlled substances like narcotics. Then they came to a document that raised Mark's excitement level...the report of psychological testing. He read the date...October 22, 1980.

"Why would Billingsworth be interested in something that was done so long ago?" Angela asked.

"I don't know," Mark replied. "But if Billingsworth kept it in his file, he must have considered it important."

He scanned the report. The Shipley Institute of Living Scale indicated that Stottlemire had an IQ of 165. He pointed to the IQ on the page.

"That's in the genius range," he said. "I knew Stottlemire was intelligent, but I had no idea his IQ was that high."

He continued reading the report. The Minnesota Multiphasic Personality Inventory was reported as normal except for very high peaks in the four and the nine scales. The Rorshack, inkblot test was in agreement with the finding. Based on these two tests, the report ended with a diagnosis of sociopathic personality disorder.

"I'll be damned," Mark said aloud.

"What does that mean?" Angela asked.

"It means that Stottlemire has a tendency to feel no remorse what-so-ever for harm he causes others. He basically lacks a conscience."

"Then he could be the one behind the cardiac arrests."

"His psychological profile is certainly compatible with the possibility. He could be responsible for the cardiac arrests, and despite the fact that people have died, feel absolutely no remorse about it."

The last item in the file was a letter attached by a paper clip to the back of the psychological-testing report. They quickly read it.

Ed Billingsworth, M.D., Hospital Director
Greater Atlanta Charity Hospital
2500 Magnolia Avenue
Atlanta, Georgia 30349

Dear Ed:

At your request, as a close personal friend I am supplying you with the enclosed material. I'm doing this in strictest confidence. Normally, I wouldn't share part of a patient's file without that person's consent, but in this case I feel that the information is of the utmost importance in your pursuit of hiring Eric Stottlemire to run your emergency room. I do want to emphasize that the testing was done when he was fifteen years old. Youth Court Judge, William P. Marshal, ordered the testing as part of an investigation into the untimely death of Eric's stepfather. The stepfather was a strict disciplinarian. He and Eric had a history of frequent arguments. When Eric's fingerprints were found on the gun used to shoot the man, Eric confessed to the crime. His lawyer, paid for by his well-to-do mother, claimed that years of physical abuse had left Eric with the inability to tell right from wrong when it came to the stepfather's death. The jury fell for it hook line and sinker. Instead of first-degree murder, as the prosecution wanted, he was convicted of manslaughter. Because he was a juvenile, he got off with a year in the state reform school and two years probation. The allegations of abuse by the stepfather were never verified. When Eric turned eighteen, his court record, as is the custom with juveniles, was wiped clean. To my knowledge, he has been a model citizen ever since he was released from reform school. However, if there is anything to the old adage "Leopards never change their spots," Eric Stottlemire, under the right circumstances, could be a very dangerous man.

Best wishes, your friend

Thomas Schnyder, Ph.D.
Consulting Psychologist

"If Billingsworth knew all of this, why would he hire him?" Angela asked.

"Apparently he needed someone in the worst way to run the Emergency Room, and Stottlemire was good. There's no denying that. Billingsworth told me one time that he was one of the best emergency medicine doctors Emory had ever turned out. And he apparently had a clean record after his stepfather's death, or Billingsworth would have additional information in his file. I guess Billingsworth felt he was worth taking a chance on."

Mark closed the folder and replaced it in the file. Just as he was about to close the drawer, Angela pulled out another manila folder.

"What's that?" he asked.

"Take a look," she said, handing him the folder.

Written on the tab was **Mark Valentine, M.D.**

Mark opened the folder. It too contained the usual things…job application form, medical school diploma, residency training certificate, and a copy of his institutional license which gave him permission from the licensure board to work at Charity. No Drug Enforcement Association certificate. He lost the privilege of prescribing controlled substances when he lost his medical license. Stottlemire had to sign charts after him when he wrote orders for narcotic pain medication. It was a source of embarrassment to him. Stottlemire gloated over the authority it gave him.

In addition, the file contained six drug-screen reports, one for every two weeks Mark had worked at Charity. Fortunately, they were all negative. A positive one would have resulted in his immediate termination, the loss of his institutional license, and return to an alcohol rehabilitation program. It would dash any hopes he had of ever getting his license back. A separate sheet of paper noted the three times in the last month that he had been late to work. A notation was penciled in the margin…**Drinking?** He suddenly felt very small. He had no idea Billingsworth suspected.

The last item in the folder was a letter from Dr. Allen, Chairman of the Board of Medical Licensure, assigning him to Dr. Billingsworth for a period of one year. It was dated a little over three months ago. Dr. Billingsworth was to file a formal report at the end of the year detailing his progress at Charity, and testify to the contents of the report in front of the licensure board at his follow-up hearing, now only seven and a half months away.

"Heavy stuff," Angela said, shaking her head.

He replaced the folder in the drawer and closed the file. At the sound of whistling, he froze. Someone was coming down the hallway. The whistling got louder and louder until it stopped just outside the door.

Mark looked at Angela in the dim light furnished by the penlights. "Did you lock the door behind you when you came in?" he whispered anxiously.

"I think so," she whispered back.

They both held their breath. The doorknob turned a couple of times, but the door didn't open.

"Thank God, it's locked," Mark said silently to himself.

The whistling resumed and faded away as the security guard continued his rounds down the hallway, trying door after door to be sure they were locked. Mark and Angela began to breathe easier again.

"Do you want to look at any more files?" Angela asked.

He looked at her like he thought she had lost her mind. "You've got to be kidding."

"I was. Do you think I'm crazy? Let's get out of here."

Located two blocks from the Atlanta police station, O'Leary's was a favorite hangout of off-duty, police officers. Sam Kincaid eased into a booth at the back of the bar and took a sip on a draft beer. He came to O'Leary's often, drank a couple of beers, usually by himself, and then left. Time was too precious to waste on idle chitchat. There were murderers, burglars, and dope dealers to catch.

As usual, the bar was crowded, and loud. Kincaid preferred to sit in the back where there was less commotion. Tonight he was frustrated. Despite the best efforts of the Atlanta police force and the state highway patrol, not to mention a multitude of county sheriffs and their deputies, Mark Valentine still remained at large. He lit a cigarette and stared into his beer.

"What's up?" Grady Sullivan said, approaching the booth. He slid into the side opposite Kincaid and tossed his wrinkled blue jacket on the seat beside him.

Despite being a few years younger than Kincaid, Grady's baldhead and coarse features made him look much older. Kincaid considered Grady to be a friend, or at least as close as he came to having one. He and Kincaid had worked together for nearly five years. Sometimes they relaxed over a beer and discussed cases that had them baffled.

Kincaid looked up. "This damn murder case has got me stymied."

"Joanna's?"

"Yeah. How could Valentine simply disappear?"

Grady hesitated. "How are you handling her death? I've been concerned about you."

"I'm doing okay. I did love her you know, at least in my own way. God, she had a hell of a body. Great in bed too. The thing I'm pissed about the most is the money."

"What do you mean?"

"I'm so damned tired of working for the peanuts the city pays us. We risk our butts every day for almost nothing. Hell, a plumber makes more than we do. A couple of years ago I got to thinking about retirement, not right away, but someday. I took a look at my pension plan. Shit! I'd have to live in poverty if I ever retired, or work until I dropped dead chasing some half-assed crook. I decided that there had to be a better way."

"Did you find one?"

"You're damned right I did, and she was gorgeous."

"Joanna?"

"Yeah, Joanna. I met her at a charity affair. She was one of the sponsors. The Mayor asked me to go with him. He thought someone was out to get him because of an unpopular stand he had taken on a crime issue. I think he just wanted an unofficial bodyguard. Joanna just sort of swooped into the room...made a hell of an entrance. You could tell by looking at her that she was loaded. That's when I thought of it."

"Thought of what?"

"A way out. It was a piece of cake. She was bored to death in her marriage. I called her on the phone a few times. At first we just made small talk. Then one day I suggested that she meet me at a motel. She got so excited at the thought of sneaking around behind her husband's back that I thought she was going to cum in her pants, right on the telephone. We met at the Starlight Motel regularly after that."

"Was that when Juanita divorced you?"

"Yes, but not because of Joanna. She didn't even know about her. She had been threatening to divorce me for years. I turned the pressure up. She couldn't stand the heat and finally filed the papers."

Grady waved at the waiter. "How did you get Joanna to divorce her rich doctor?"

"It wasn't hard. I put her in touch with a sleazy, private detective who introduced her to a good-looking hooker. They framed him. It worked like a charm."

"Do you think you'll get Valentine?"

Kincaid took a sip of beer. "Sure. Sooner or later. The bastard won't get away."

The waiter, a young man in a white apron, came to the booth and stood over Grady. "What'll you have?" he asked.

Grady pointed at Kincaid's drink. "Same as him."

The waiter nodded, then turned and left.

"Do you really think Valentine did it?" Grady asked.

Kincaid leaned forward. A snarl crossed his lips. "He's guilty as hell. I heard him threaten to kill her."

"A lot of men threaten their wives," Grady responded. "They rarely carry through on it."

"He has to be guilty. Why else would he run? Besides, he was seen outside her house the day she was murdered."

"Good point."

Kincaid pushed his beer away. "Damn, I was that close," he said, holding his hands six inches apart.

"To catching Valentine?"

"No. To having it made."

CHAPTER TWENTY-THREE

Mark awoke the next morning at a quarter to seven. Angela, as usual, was still asleep. He rolled out of bed and walked across the room where he sat at the table in his shorts. He picked up the telephone and dialed Mattie's home number. He wanted to tell her what they had found in Billingsworth's office. It rang six times…no answer.

"Damn," he mumbled under his breath. "She's already left for work." He hung up the telephone and lit a cigarette. He would call her at Charity Emergency Room in thirty minutes. He leaned back in the chair and wondered how he had gotten into such a mess, and how he was going to get out of it. Most importantly right now, he wondered how he was going to save Billingsworth's life. He knew he could call the police and give them an anonymous tip, but he doubted that they would believe him. Why should they? The story did sound pretty far-fetched. He sat and waited for Mattie to arrive at work.

Wearing only black, lace panties and no bra, Angela finally awakened and sat on the side of the bed as he dialed the number of Charity Emergency Room. "Who are you calling?" she asked.

"Mattie. I tried to get her at home this morning but she wasn't there. I hope she's at work."

Angela looked him up and down. It was obvious to him that she was admiring his athletic-looking body. She had told him after their love-making episode that he looked much better without clothes than Maldini. He didn't consider that to be much of a compliment.

Pearl, the unit clerk, answered the telephone.

"Could I speak with Mattie please?" Mark said in a deep voice, his speech slowed slightly to keep from being recognized. "It's an emergency."

"Who's calling?" Pearl asked.

"Her son-in-law. One of her grandchildren has been in an accident."

A few seconds later, Mattie came to the telephone. "Willie, what's wrong? Who's hurt?"

Mark felt bad about alarming her. He had blurted out the statement about her grandchild without thinking. "Your grandchildren are okay," he said. "This is Mark."

"Mark! Thank goodness it's you. Pearl scared me to death when she told me that someone had been hurt. Willie bought Andrieko a three-wheeler last week. I thought certain something bad had happened to him."

"I'm sorry. I didn't mean to scare you."

"I've got some bad news," Mattie said with a concerned tone in her voice. "At first Betsy Barfield claimed that she had gotten the Mepergan on the street."

"It's possible. There's a drug dealer on every corner around the hospital."

"Dorfman didn't believe her, so he questioned her again later. He really put pressure on her. He was adamant that she had gotten the drugs from a doctor. He told her that her story didn't make any sense. Medical people don't buy drugs on the street. They either forge prescriptions, or get a doctor to write them. People on drugs in this business always know who the easy touches are. She finally admitted that she had gotten the prescriptions from a doctor."

"I'm not surprised," Mark said. "Some doctors make a mint supplying addicts with drugs. It's completely unethical, not to mention illegal. Who's the doctor?"

"Are you sitting down?"

"Yes. Why so mysterious?"

"Mark, she said she got the prescriptions from you."

"She what?"

"You heard me. She said she got them from you."

"That's ridiculous. Why would I furnish her with drugs?"

"She said it was a simple trade...sex for drugs. I guess she felt that since you were already wanted for murder, her claim would be believable."

"Surely Dorfman didn't believe her. Hell, I've never even been alone with her."

"He thinks she's protecting someone. The members of the administrative committee looking into the cardiac arrests aren't as sure."

Mark slammed his hand down on the table. "Shit! Things keep getting worse. Falsely accused of Joanna's death, now this."

"Why didn't you call me last night?" Mattie asked. "I waited up until midnight to tell you what Betsy told Dorfman."

"It was real late when I got back. I didn't want to wake you."

"Got back from where?"

"Billingsworth's office. You wouldn't believe what he had in his files. Stottlemire killed his stepfather when he was a teenager. Psychological testing showed that he had a sociopathic personality."

"I never dreamed he would have done anything that awful," she said.

"I think he's our man, but we need more evidence than what we have...something to tie him directly to Betsy Barfield's drug habit."

"What do you have in mind?"

"Proof that he's the one who's been supplying her with drugs, instead of me."

"How are you going to get that?"

"I don't know," he responded. Then it came to him. Prescriptions come in bottles, and prescription bottles have the doctor's name on them. But how could he get his hands on one of Betsy Barfield's prescription bottles? The answer was obvious...search her place of residence.

"Do you have any idea where Betsy lives?" he asked.

"I know she lives in Delray Apartments. Dr. Stottlemire mentioned it once. But I don't know the apartment number."

"Do you know where Delray apartments is located?"

"Not exactly. I know its two or three miles north of here."

"No problem," he responded. "I can look the address up in the phone book. How are things going at Charity?"

"We have a new crime wave. When Mr. Lowenstein worked late last night, someone stole his Park Avenue. Apparently they hot-wired it. That's the third car this month that's been stolen. Dorfman's increased the parking lot patrols. I hope it helps. If its not one thing around here it's another."

"Sorry to hear that," Mark said. "Listen, I've got to go."

"Call me later today and let me know what you find."

"I will."

"You promise?"

"I promise. I really am sorry about not calling you last night."

"Be careful," Mattie said.

"We will," he replied.

"We? You didn't tell me you were with someone. Anyone I know?"

"No. Just a sexy lady who's good at breaking and entering."

At ten o'clock in the morning Mark and Angela pulled into the parking lot of Delray Apartments. The building was located in the middle of a commercial area, mostly small shops and stores and an occasional service station. After looking the address up in the telephone book, he had located the complex without difficulty. The brick structure consisted of ten apartments, five above and five below. A metal-railed landing ran the length of the upper floor, bordered on each end by a set of stairs. The building was old but appeared to have been maintained in a good state of repair. Ten mailboxes imbedded in the brick of the apartment-complex wall were located in a single area at the center of the lower level. Except for a fishing boat, which occupied one parking space at the far end, the small lot was empty. He parked just to the right of the mailboxes, got out of the car, and read the name and number on each box.

There it was, fourth mailbox from the left on the top row. A small, hand-written square of paper behind a plastic cover identified B. Barfield's apartment as number 204. He went back to the car and stuck his head in the window.

"I've got it," he said. "Number 204. Come on."

Angela got out of the car and followed him down the sidewalk and up the steps at the end of the building.

"Slow down," she said as he took the steps two at a time. "I can't keep up with you."

He slowed and reached back for her hand. "Sorry," he said. "I guess I'm just overly anxious to get into Betsy's apartment and see what we can find."

"Her apartment's not going anywhere and neither is she, at least not for awhile. You did check with Mattie to see if Betsy has a roommate didn't you? We don't want to barge in on anyone."

"I checked. She lives alone."

They reached the door with 204 on it. He knocked.

"What are you doing? You know no one is home."

"I just want to be sure."

They waited a couple of minutes. As expected, no one came to the door.

"Satisfied?" Angela asked.

"Yes," he replied. "Now it's time for you to do your stuff."

She reached into her purse and pulled out her trusty credit card. Then, inserting it into the crack between the door and the frame at lock level, she moved it up, then down.

Nothing happened.

"Damn," she said disgustedly.

"What is it?" he asked quickly.

"The deadbolt is on."

"Can't you unlock it?"

"Not with a credit card. A locksmith could do it. It takes tools spe-cially designed for unlocking deadbolts. What are we going to do?"

"I guess we could call a locksmith," he answered.

"Get serious."

"Well, it's either that or get the apartment manager to unlock the door for us."

"I didn't see an office when we drove up."

"These small apartment buildings seldom have resident managers. They're usually owned by someone looking to supplement his regular paycheck with some extra money. Between the monthly mortgage pay-ment, the cost of keeping the place up, and the rent they collect, they're lucky to make enough money to make the aggravation worthwhile. You have to own a bunch of these to make any real money."

"How do you know so much about it?"

"I used to own a dozen apartment buildings scattered around Atlanta. A bunch of houses too. I hired a manager to take care of the whole bunch."

"What happened to them?"

"The judge at the divorce hearing ordered them sold. Joanna got most of the money from them, along with about everything else."

"Do you think we can get by with calling a locksmith?"

"Why not. You don't think every locksmith in the city knows Betsy Barfield personally do you?"

"No, I guess not."

"Then Betsy, all you have to do is call a locksmith and then meet him at the door."

"What about the people who live in the other apartments? What will they think if they see us standing out here while a locksmith breaks into Betsy's apartment?"

"They're probably all at work. You didn't see any cars in the lot did you? These aren't the kind of apartments you raise a family in, so there shouldn't be any spouses and children around."

"You must be right. I haven't seen a single tricycle."

They returned to the car, located a telephone booth a few blocks away, and found the name of a local locksmith in the yellow pages. Angela placed the call. Mark listened with her.

"Ask him how much it will cost," he instructed.

A man answered. "Triple A Locksmith," he said in a bored voice.

"Hi. This is Betsy Barfield," Angela said. "I walked around the corner from my apartment to the grocery store to buy a few things. When I got back, I discovered that I had lost my keys. I went back to the grocery store, but they hadn't seen them. I'm so upset I don't know what I'm going to do."

"Who referred you to me?"

She hesitated, obviously not expecting the question. "I saw the sign on your building a few days ago. Can you help me?"

"Sure," the man replied. "Give me fifteen minutes to get there. There hasn't been a lock yet that I can't open."

Mark nudged her with his elbow.

"Oh, how much will it cost?" she asked.

He told her twenty dollars. She gave him the address. Then they got into the car and headed back to the apartment building. A block away, Mark pulled into a BP food store.

"Why are we stopping here?" Angela asked.

"You told the locksmith that you had gone to the grocery store. You need some groceries."

They bought a loaf of bread, a box of crackers, a two-liter diet coke, and a can of sardines, then drove back to the parking lot and got out of the car. He handed Angela the bag of groceries.

"What happened to chivalry?" she asked.

"I'm not going with you. Take the bag to Betsy's door and wait for the locksmith. Smile at him a lot and act helpless."

She took the bag. "I think I can manage that."

"You'll need this," he said, pulling a twenty-dollar bill from his billfold and handing it to her.

She headed toward the stairs. He reparked the car near the boat, no more than forty feet away from the door to Betsy's apartment. He waited as Angela climbed the stairs and set the bag of groceries by Betsy's door. He had a clear view of her and was close enough so that if he listened carefully he would be able to hear her conversation with the locksmith.

Several minutes later, a white Datson pickup truck with **AAA Locksmith** on the door, along with the telephone number Angela had called, pulled into the lot and parked in the space Mark had vacated a few minutes earlier. A burly man in his mid-forties wearing gray work clothes got out of the pick-up and ascended the stairs. Mark slid down in the seat and watched from the Porsche.

"Good afternoon mam," the man said as he approached Angela. "I'm Bobby Lee Jones. Lost your keys, did you?"

"Yes, can you help me?" Angela replied.

"No problem. I opened the door to 105 last week. A Mrs. Elkins. Do you know her?"

"No. I really don't. I've seen a woman come in and out of that apartment a time or two, but I don't know her name. I haven't lived here long."

He looked at the lock. "Piece of cake," he said. "I'll need some identification. How do I know you live here?"

She took a deep breath. Mark could tell she was thinking fast.

"You do have some identification, don't you?" Bobbie Lee asked.

She smiled coyly. "Of course I do, but I lost it with my keys. My billfold and my keys were together. I thought I put them in my purse at the store, but when I got home they were gone. I can't imagine what happened to them. I'm expecting company for dinner. I don't know what I'll do if I can't get inside," she said, looking worried. "It's the first date I've had in two months, and I was really looking forward to it, if you know what I mean." She smiled at him again, flirting to the hilt.

Bobby Lee looked her up and down, probably wondering how someone who looked like her could go for any length of time without a date. "Sorry lady. Without identification, I can't let you in."

She gave him a dejected look. "I'm a nurse. I work in the Emergency Room at Charity. You can call there and ask them." She placed her hand on his arm softly and blinked her eyes.

"Yeah, I guess I could do that," Bobby Lee said quickly. "I've got a cellular phone in my truck. Give me your name again."

"Betsy Barfield," she said, still smiling. "Just ask for Mattie. She's the head nurse."

"Oh hell!" Mark thought. "I hope she knows what she's doing. Mattie's sharp. Maybe she'll figure it out."

Bobby Lee turned to leave, then stopped. "What's the number?"

Angela looked as if she were about to panic, but quickly got control of herself. She had watched Mark dial the number several times. He prayed she would remember it.

"Well, you do know the number don't you?" Bobby Lee said impatiently.

"Of course I do," she said. Then she blurted out a telephone number.

"Damn," Mark said under his breath. "She missed it."

"Okay. I'll be right back," Bobby Lee said.

They watched him as he made his way to his truck.

A few minutes later he returned. "You gave me the wrong number," he said, approaching Angela.

She again got the panicky look on her face.

"You missed it by one digit," Bobby Lee said. "I figured it was because you were upset about losing your keys and worried about your date tonight. I called information and got the right number."

She instantly appeared more relaxed and smiled at him. "Sorry."

"No problem. Mattie had some good things to say about you. You must be a good nurse." He looked her up and down again.

Mark had a pretty good idea what he was thinking.

"I try to be," she said.

Bobbie Lee unlocked the door. She handed him the twenty-dollar bill. He again looked her up and down, hesitated, then turned, walked down the stairs, and got in his truck.

As the Datson pulled out of the parking lot, Mark left the Porsche and joined Angela on the landing. Together they entered Betsy's apartment. It consisted of a combination living room and dining room, small kitchen, single bedroom, and one bath. It was nicer than his, but a little smaller and in much better condition.

He closed the door behind them. "You start in the kitchen. I'll take the bathroom," he said.

"What are we looking for?"

"Pill bottles. Any kind."

He walked into the bathroom, opened the door to the medicine cabinet, and inspected its contents…a bottle of Mercurochrome, a bottle of aspirin, a package of birth control pills, a bottle with two penicillin tablets in it. No Mepergan.

He closed the cabinet door and glanced around the room. Nothing unusual. He could hear Angela opening cabinet door after cabinet door and closing them behind her in the kitchen. He finished in the bathroom and headed for the kitchen.

"Find anything?" he asked as he approached her.

"Not yet. Why don't you start on the drawers," she responded.

When he opened drawer number three, he immediately spotted a bunch of pill bottles. "Got something," he said excitedly.

Angela quickly rushed to his side. Together they stared into the drawer at a half-dozen pill bottles. He took the bottles out one at a time and read the labels…Benadryl, Actifed, Carafate, Sudafed, Motrin, Humabid LA, Tessalon Pearls.

"Find what we're looking for?" Angela asked.

"No, not a controlled substance in the bunch," he said dejectedly.

They finished searching the kitchen, then searched the living room and dining room area…nothing.

Beginning to get discouraged, they adjourned to the bedroom. Angela looked through the dresser. He searched the chest-of-drawers. Again no controlled substances. He walked to the bedside table and opened the top drawer.

Bingo…it was full of pill bottles.

He tried to control his excitement, hoping that it wasn't another false alarm. He picked up a bottle at random. It was empty. He looked at the label…**Meperidine 50/Promethazine 25.**

"I've got it," he called out.

Angela hurried to his side and stared into the drawer. He handed her the pill bottle.

"What is it?" she asked, looking at the bottle.

"Meperidine is the generic name for Demerol, and promethazine is the generic name for Phenergan. The promethazine potentiates the anti-pain action of the meperidine and reduces the tendency meperidine has to make people nauseated. In a combination of fifty milligrams of meperidine and twenty-five milligrams of promethazine, its major manufacturer sells it by the trade name Mepergan. It's cheaper in the generic form."

"I repeat, what is it?"

"Oh! It's a narcotic pain medication. It's what Betsy had in her pocket when she was caught under the influence at Charity. It's a popular drug of abuse in the health professions."

She smiled. "Thanks."

He smiled back. "You're welcome." Then he read the doctor's name…**Eric Stottlemire, MD.** "We've got him," he said, unable to contain his excitement.

He inspected the other bottles…fifteen or twenty of them he estimated, all the same, and all empty. He reached out and hugged Angela tightly.

"What do we do now?" she asked.

"We go get some lunch."

"Great. I'm starving. How much money do we have left?"

"Eighty nine dollars," he replied with a worried look on his face. "We'd better eat at McDonalds."

"You've got to be kidding?"

"Welcome to poverty."

———————————

Arriving back at the motel a little before one o'clock, Mark sat in the chair and dialed the number of Charity Emergency Room, again disguising his voice. Pearl answered the telephone. He asked to speak to Mattie. She came to the telephone.

"I was right," he said. "Stottlemire is behind the cardiac arrests. Betsy Barfield had a drawer full of empty prescription bottles with his name on them, all for Mepergan."

"I can't believe all this is happening," Mattie said. "First, all that commotion in the Emergency Room with the guns and your abduction, then we find out someone's been killing patients, Lowenstein's car got stolen, Betsy claimed she got her drugs from you, now Dr. Stottlemire's going to try to kill Billingsworth. I've been a nervous wreck waiting for you to call me back."

"What's wrong?" he asked. "Has something else happened?"

"If Dr. Stottlemire is going to strike, he'll have to do it tonight," Mattie said with an urgent tone to her voice.

"Tonight. Why tonight?"

"Dr. Agarwall is going to transfer Dr. Billingsworth to the Cardiac Rehabilitation Unit at Emory first thing in the morning."

"Shit," he said aloud. He had to do something to prevent Stottlemire from killing Billingsworth, but what? "Can you work a double shift tonight?" he asked.

"A double shift? That would mean I'd have to work twenty four hours straight."

"I know. I wouldn't ask you to do it if it weren't extremely important."

"What do you have in mind?"

"If Stottlemire goes after Billingsworth tonight, I want to be there."

"What does that have to do with me working a double shift?"

"I want you to watch Stottlemire, and if he leaves the Emergency Room, call me. The Doctor's Lounge will be deserted that time of night. I'll be there. Can you pull a double?"

"Lena called in sick again. So far I haven't been able to find anyone to replace her. I'll stay tonight and fill the slot myself."

"Great. I'll go to the lounge when Stottlemire comes on duty tonight at seven and wait for you to call. What room is Billingsworth in?"

"402."

He hung up the telephone.

"What's going on?" Angela asked, having heard only his side of the conversation.

He explained his plan to her.

"This is just like the cops and robbers game we played when I was growing up," she said.

"Yes, but this time it's for real," he replied.

CHAPTER TWENTY-FOUR

Special Agent Daryl Barnes entered Walter North's office and sat in the chair in front of his desk. "Did your secretary give you my message?" he asked.

"About Valentine's daughter?" North responded.

"Yes. We've located her. She's in Columbus, Georgia staying with a Mr. and Mrs. Singletary."

"How do they fit into the picture?"

"They're the parents of a Susan Livingston, a friend of Valentine's."

"A girlfriend?"

"That's unclear at this time. We think so."

"How did you locate the daughter?" North asked.

"Valentine used his gasoline credit card twenty miles outside of Columbus. From that, we knew he was either going to Columbus or passing through it. Hoping we would get lucky, we focused on Columbus. We checked on everyone that he worked with in the Emergency Room, the few friends he has, and his neighbors. The only match was Susan Livingston. She was born and raised in Columbus."

"How did you find out that Valentine's daughter was staying with her parents?"

"Stroke of luck. We placed a call to the local police chief and gave him the kid's description...thirteen years old, tall girl for her age, attractive, long blonde hair, and a hearing problem. He passed the information on to the people on his force, and bingo. One of the younger policemen, an

Eddy Clark, had actually been in the Singletary home and spoken with the girl."

"What made him sure it was her? Surely she didn't volunteer her real name."

"She didn't, but she did fit the description perfectly. At first the officer thought she had an accent, but when he noticed that she couldn't understand very well what he was saying without looking at his face, he came to the conclusion that she was lip reading."

"Any doubt that it's her?"

Barnes shook his head. "Absolutely none."

"Get a man down there immediately," North instructed. "Is anything else new?"

"A Unit Clerk in the Emergency Room at Charity, a Pearl Cook, reported that she thought Valentine has been making calls to a nurse there...a Mattie Johnson."

"Is she a girlfriend?"

"Hardly. She's an older, black woman. Apparently they're good friends. The clerk said he confides in her a lot."

"Does the clerk know Valentine?"

"Yes, she's worked with him for the past three months."

"He just called there and said 'Let me speak with Mattie Johnson?'"

Barnes leaned back in the chair and cracked his knuckles. "Not exactly. He tried to disguise his voice. Said he was Mrs. Johnson's son-in-law."

"How did the clerk know it wasn't the son-in-law?"

"The son-in-law's called there before. She knows his voice. She said the caller didn't sound anything at all like him."

"What made her think it was Valentine?"

"She was pretty sure that she heard Mattie Johnson say Mark."

North leaned forward. "Let's get the phone in the Emergency Room tapped as soon as possible."

"It's already done. One of our men, disguised as a telephone repairman, put the bug in the phone earlier this afternoon, around two o'clock."

"Any results yet?"

"No, but if were lucky it won't be long."

"It looks like things are finally beginning to open up. Between locating Valentine's daughter and tapping the telephone in the Emergency Room, we should have the elusive Dr. Valentine in custody soon."

"There's something else."

"What's that?"

"The hospital turned Valentine in to the Drug Enforcement Administration for possible narcotics violation. They think he's been writing a drug-addict nurse prescriptions for narcotics."

"Without a license?"

"They suspect he's been using his old DEA number, and the pharmacy didn't pick up on the fact that it had been canceled. Each prescription is a felony."

"So what?"

"What do you mean, so what?" Barnes asked.

"When you're wanted for first-degree murder, what's a few felonies?"

At six thirty, Mark left the motel and headed for the Doctors' Lounge on the second floor at Charity. Angela had wanted to come with him, but he insisted that she stay at the motel. He felt that he would be less conspicuous moving around on his own. She had been concerned about his welfare because she was sure Jesus was still in Atlanta.

"Atlanta's a big place. Don't worry, I'll be fine," he had said. Still, he couldn't help but worry. He had the uncomfortable feeling that Jesus was closing in on him.

As usual, traffic on the interstate highway leading to downtown Atlanta was heavy, but moving along at a brisk pace. Outgoing traffic, due to a multi-vehicle accident involving a jack-knifed eighteen-wheeler, had slowed to a crawl.

A half hour later, he exited the Interstate onto Magnolia Avenue. Stopping at the first traffic light, he glanced at his watch...seven o'clock. He had to hurry. Stottlemire would be arriving at the Emergency Room about now.

Out of habit, he looked in the rearview mirror. Cars lined up behind him bumper to bumper. Then he glanced to his right, and his heart skipped a beat. A uniformed, Atlanta policeman in a black and white squad car stared right at him. Shaken, he quickly turned his head and fixed his eyes on the traffic light.

"Please Lord, don't let him recognize me," he said silently. "Billingsworth's life depends on me getting to Charity." A vision of the policeman getting out of the car and asking him for his driver's license passed through his mind, followed immediately by a vision of him standing on the pavement by his car in handcuffs. Stottlemire was going to make an attempt on the life of someone he cared for very much, and who would be a major factor in whether or not he got his license back, and he stood a good chance of being physically restrained, helpless to do anything about it. He wanted to look at the policeman again to see if he were still staring at him, but he didn't dare. He was too nervous. He was afraid the policeman would see the fear in his face. He closed his eyes and said a silent prayer.

"Turn green, damn it. Turn green," he said under his breath. His heart pounded hard in his chest. "How long is this damn light going to stay red?"

Finally, the light changed to green. He deliberately delayed pulling out, waiting to see if the squad car would pull out ahead of him.

Suddenly, the cycling red and blue lights on top of the car came to life, followed by a short blast of the car's siren that caused him to jump in the seat. He instinctively looked in the direction of the siren.

The squad car's tires squealed loudly as it pulled out, turned right, and sped off down the street. He took a deep breath, then let it out slowly. He was sure that the new paint job and license plate was all that had prevented the policeman from recognizing him. The beard probably hadn't hurt any either.

Suddenly, a car horn sounded behind him. Then he realized that he still sat in the same spot. The traffic on both sides of him already moved ahead at a rapid pace. He gave a quick wave of his hand to the driver behind him, muttered "sorry" under his breath, and moved straight ahead.

Arriving at the parking lot at the side of Charity, Mark again parked near its center and walked to the front of the building where he peered into the lobby through the glass in one of the front doors. As usual, the receptionist sat at a desk to the right across from the double set of elevators. A number of people stood around in the lobby talking. This time he would have to get past the receptionist without Angela's help. He stood at the top of the steps and waited.

Within ten minutes, a group of seven black people, who appeared to range in age from three or four to their seventies, came down the street and started up the steps. An elderly man with a cane and a pronounced limp struggled with the steps and lagged behind the others. A bearded, younger man stayed behind, holding the older man's arm as he ascended each step with difficulty. The remainder of the group waited on the porch at the top of the steps. A small child reached up and tugged unsuccessfully on the handle of the heavy door.

When the elderly man finally reached the top of the steps, the younger one who had helped him up the steps held the door open while the group entered the lobby. Mark watched through the glass as they approached the receptionist.

With the receptionist occupied, he calmly walked across the lobby. When he reached the hallway on the other side, he glanced up at the familiar sign hanging from the ceiling...Administration offices to the left, hospital rooms straight ahead. He continued straight ahead. When he reached the newer part of the building, he took the stairs to the second floor. Charity doctors always made their afternoon rounds early so that they could get out of the hospital as soon as possible and beat the Atlanta, rush-hour traffic. It was a rare doctor who was still in the hospital after five o'clock. He expected to wait for Mattie's telephone call undisturbed in The Doctors' Lounge.

Carefully opening the door at the top of the stairs, he ascertained that the hallway was empty, then he passed through the door and closed it behind him. He walked to the door down the hall on the right with the words **Doctors Lounge** inscribed on it and entered the room. A wooden coffee table sat in front of a Naugahyde-covered sofa and matching chair against the wall to the right. A ceiling-to-floor bookcase filled with out-of-date medical texts and journals occupied the opposite wall. In front of the bookcase, the electrical and cable cords of a nineteen-inch TV disappeared between the books. A small refrigerator and a microwave oven sat on a counter at the far end of the room. Just to their right, a coffee maker contained what appeared to be an inch or so of day-old coffee. A door next to the counter led to a small bathroom.

He settled in on the sofa, propped his feet up on the coffee table, and stared at the telephone on the wall by the refrigerator. The clock, high on the wall over the coffee maker, indicated the time to be twelve minutes after seven. He pulled a cigarette from the pack and lit it.

An hour and several cigarettes later, Mattie still hadn't called. He wondered when Stottlemire would make his move. He hoped it would be soon. Boredom was beginning to set in. He hated the thought of spending the night in the lounge with little to do.

He rose, walked to the coffee maker, and emptied the stale coffee into the sink. Then he ran some tap water into the pot, swished it around, and poured it out. After refilling the pot with water, he placed it back in the coffee maker, took a packet of coffee from a drawer under the counter top, and started a new pot of coffee.

Attempting to entertain himself while he waited for the coffee to brew, he walked to the bookcase and, one at a time, inspected the books. Some of them were so old that they must have been purchased at the time the original hospital was built. He wondered why Administration hadn't thrown them away.

He located a textbook entitled Facial Reconstruction by Jeremy Aldridge, MD and flipped the cover open. It was published by Macmillan and Company in 1953. With the book in his hand, he walked back to the couch and sat down, again propping his feet up on the coffee table. As he turned the pages, he was amazed that a few of the procedures described in the book were still in use today, in modified forms. Most, however, appeared archaic and had long since been replaced by more modern techniques. He placed the book on the coffee table, walked to the coffee maker, poured a cup of coffee, and took a sip. Then he walked back to the sofa, sat down, and resumed browsing through the book.

An hour, three cups of coffee, and several more cigarettes later, he finished looking at Facial Reconstruction, replaced it on the shelf, and looked around for something else to occupy his time. Boredom had arrived in full force. Finding nothing of interest, he walked to the TV, turned it on to CNN with the volume turned all the way down, and settled back on the sofa.

At nine thirty the sound of footsteps coming down the hall awakened him from a light sleep. He bolted upright, turned the TV off, and looked around the room for a place to hide. Finding none, his eyes fixed on the bathroom door. The steps got closer and closer, finally stopping in the hallway just outside the lounge door.

He hurried into the small bathroom. It contained only a lavatory, urinal, and a commode in a stall. The person, whoever he was, now moved around inside the lounge. Mark wanted to open the bathroom door a crack to see who it was, but he was afraid he would be seen.

Concerned that the person might come into the bathroom, he opened the door to the stall, entered the small compartment, and fastened the latch behind him. Sitting on the commode, he dropped his pants down around his ankles so that it would appear from under the stall door that he was using the commode. Seconds later, he heard the bathroom door open, then the footsteps entered the bathroom. He listened intently as they stopped just outside the stall. Then the person tried the door. Fortunately Mark had locked it.

"Hey man. How much longer are you going to be in there?" a man's voice said with a slight accent.

Oh shit, Mark thought. The voice belonged to Jesus Dimaria.

Mark's pulse began to pound hard in his temples, and sweat beaded up on his brow. He took a deep breath and exhaled slowly in an attempt to regain his composure. What would he do? He had to answer Jesus. He would be suspicious if he didn't.

Mark cleared his throat. "It's going to be a while," he said, using the same voice he had used when he called Mattie in the Emergency Room. "My bowels are torn up something fierce. Must have been the enchiladas I ate for dinner."

"I gotta use the bathroom, man. You've got to get out of there right now," Jesus said in a threatening voice.

Mark thought quickly. "There's another one down the hall to the left. It should be empty. I'm going to be here a while."

Jesus hesitated for a moment. Mark wondered if he would elect to go to the other bathroom, or have a conflict over that one.

"Thanks man," Jesus said after a pause.

Mark wiped the sweat from his brow with his sleeve. Apparently Jesus had to go to the bathroom so bad that he wasn't prepared to argue about the location. He listened as the footsteps carried Jesus out the lounge door and down the hallway.

Jesus had to be looking for him, he assumed. Why else would he be at Charity? He must have ventured into the lounge by chance, looking for a bathroom. He thanked God for Jesus' more immediate problem. He pulled his pants up and opened the stall door. Then it happened.

The telephone rang.

He hurried back into to the lounge and picked it up. "Hello," he said excitedly.

"Stottlemire just left the Emergency Room," Mattie said with an urgent sound to her voice.

"Great," Mark replied, thankful that the waiting was over. "Call Dorfman and tell him to get to Billingsworth's room as fast as he can. Tell him that with any luck at all I'll have Charity's serial killer for him."

He hurried out the door, nervously looked in the direction that Jesus' footsteps had carried him in search of a bathroom, then trotted to the elevator. He pushed the up button, looked up then down the hallway, and waited. The wait was short. The elevator door opened and he quickly stepped inside.

The Coronary Care Unit was located on the fourth floor on the same end of the building as the Doctors' Lounge. The Step-down Unit, located adjacent to the Coronary Care Unit, consisted of twelve regular hospital rooms, differing only in the fact that a rack of cardiac monitors sat on a counter top in the Nurses' Station. Each monitor displayed an electrocardiogram tracing from a single patient. A trained cardiac nurse carefully watched the tracings, ready to push a button on the monitor to record any unusual electrical activity or spring into action if a life-threatening arrhythmia appeared.

Mark was familiar with the hospital numbering system for rooms. Number 402 was located on the same side of the building as the Coronary Care Unit, two rooms down the hallway on the right, and just across from the elevator. The Nurses' Station was located further down the hallway. He figured that it would be easy for him to take the elevator to the fourth floor, then quickly walk, undetected, across the hallway to Billingsworth's room.

Standing in the elevator, he watched the bright floor-indicator lights...two, three, four. The elevator stopped with a jerk, then the door opened. Looking to his right and then to his left, he briskly walked across the vacant hallway and entered Billingsworth's room. The room was filled with flowers, potted plants, and get-well cards. Billingsworth lay in the bed beneath the window at the far side of the room. The ventilator sitting against the wall at the head of the bed hissed intermittently as it pumped life-sustaining air into his lungs.

Quick steps carried him to the bed where he gently shook Billingsworth and called his name. Sedated to keep him from fighting the ventilator, Billingsworth barely managed to open his heavy eyelids. When he saw it was Mark, a hint of a smile crossed his lips. He tried to speak, but nothing came out.

Mark sat down in the chair by the bed and told Billingsworth everything that he and Angela had discovered about Stottlemire. Billingsworth opened his eyes ever so slightly a couple of times during the recitation, but gave no indication that he comprehended anything that was said to him. It didn't really matter. Mark talked mostly to calm his nerves while he waited for Stottlemire to make his appearance. He knew it wouldn't be long. At the most, it was a ten-minute trip from the Emergency Room.

He placed his hand on Billingsworth's shoulder and gently squeezed it. Then he heard footsteps coming down the hallway. He quickly stood up, walked across the room, and ducked into the bathroom, leaving the door cracked just enough to see the head of Billingsworth's bed. Hiding in bathrooms was getting to be a habit he didn't care for.

The footsteps stopped outside Billingsworth's room. Then Mark heard the door open. A man of short stature wearing a white, lab coat and with a gray stethoscope draped around his neck walked across the floor and sat down in the chair by Billingsworth's bed. From Mark's position in the bathroom, he strained to see the man's face, but without success. Never the less, he knew it was Stottlemire. He could tell by the height, the unruly reddish-brown hair, and the habit of wearing his stethoscope around his neck.

Stottlemire reached out and put his hand on Billingsworth's arm. Mark watched him closely, ready to spring into action if he made a threatening move. Mark couldn't believe Stottlemire's calmness. He didn't appear the least bit nervous. But then Stottlemire always had been a cool one. Anyone who could sky dive and bungee jump had to have nerves of steel, he reasoned.

"Ed, it's Eric," Stottlemire said. "How are you doing today?"

Mark couldn't tell from his position in the bathroom if Billingsworth responded or not, but based on the experience he had just had with him he doubted it. Then Stottlemire lowered his head and sat there in silence.

"What's he doing?" Mark wondered. Then it came to him. He couldn't believe it...Stottlemire was praying.

Finally, Stottlemire raised his head and stared at Billingsworth. "You've got to make it," he said with compassion in his voice. Then he paused for a minute before continuing. "Emory has a first-rate Cardiac Rehabilitation Unit. They're doing great things. I spoke with the head of the unit today, a Dr. Carlisle. He said that you've got an excellent chance of making a full recovery, but it will take time, lots of it." He reached out and touched Billingsworth's arm again. "I wish I could stay longer, but I've got to go. The Emergency Room's a nightmare tonight. They're stacked up all the way out to the waiting room." Stottlemire stood up, stared at Billingsworth for a moment, then turned and left the room.

Mark had the distinct impression that he saw a tear running down Stottlemire's face as he passed by the crack in the bathroom door. He was dumbfounded. What he had just witnessed didn't make any sense. Stottlemire obviously cared a great deal for Billingsworth. His action certainly wasn't that of a sociopath. Could the report they had seen in Billingsworth's office be wrong? After all, the psychological testing was done twenty years ago. Stottlemire was just a kid at the time, and he must have been under a hell of a lot of stress, judging by the letter from Billingsworth's psychologist friend. The stress could have affected the results.

Mark left the bathroom and returned to the chair by Billingsworth's bed, still trying to figure out what he had just witnessed. If Stottlemire wasn't Charity's serial killer, who was? Was Billingsworth's life really in danger? If so, would the killer strike tonight? How did Betsy Barfield and her narcotic addiction fit into all this, if at all? His perfectly clear picture had become terribly murky.

Billingsworth again opened his heavy eyelids and mumbled something with a thick tongue. Mark leaned closer.

"What did you say, Ed?" he asked. "I couldn't understand you."

Billingsworth mumbled what sounded like the same thing. Mark shook his head. He didn't have the slightest idea what Billingsworth was trying to tell him, but he felt sure it was the name of the killer. He leaned back in the chair and wondered what his next move would be. Then he froze.

Footsteps again came down the hallway toward the room.

CHAPTER TWENTY-FIVE

Startled by the footsteps, Mark quickly ducked back into the bathroom, again leaving the door open just a crack. Almost immediately, the door to the hospital room opened and a man of ordinary stature wearing a pair of dark slacks and a white dress shirt entered the room. Mark strained to see the man's face as he had done with Stottlemire, but again from his position in the bathroom it was impossible.

Unlike Stottlemire, from behind, the man didn't have any identifying characteristics. He could be any one of fifty or sixty Charity employees. He walked to Billingsworth's bed and stood over him for a moment. Then he walked to the head of the bed, bent at the waist, and pulled an electrical cord from the wall. Immediately the intermittent hissing of Billingsworth's ventilator stopped.

Mark knew he had to act fast. Billingsworth wouldn't last long without the precious air that the machine delivered to his lungs. He threw the bathroom door open and lunged across the room at the man at full speed.

Hearing the commotion, the man turned just in time to see Mark barreling out of the bathroom. "What the hell!" he exclaimed.

Mark grabbed him by his shirt and spun him around. The man threw his arm up in front of his face in an attempt to protect himself, but to no avail. Mark landed a right cross solidly on his jaw. The man sprawled awkwardly to the floor with a loud thud. He immediately made an attempt to get up, but staggered back against the wall and collapsed in a pile. Mark stood over him, waiting for him to try to get up again. The man lay dead still.

"Oh my God! I've killed him." Mark said aloud. He quickly bent over and placed his fingers along side the man's neck. The carotid pulse was strong. Mark thanked God. The last thing he needed was to be wanted for a murder he did commit. He glanced at Billingsworth. Billingsworth had taken on a dangerous-looking blue hue and was gasping for breath.

Mark rushed to the head of the bed and plugged the ventilator cord back in. The machine immediately resumed its intermittent hissing. Billingsworth's chest again moved up and down in rhythm with the hissing. Within a couple of minutes his normally pink color returned almost to normal.

Mark returned his attention to Billingsworth's assailant. He had to tie him up to keep him secure until Dorfman got here, but with what? Looking around the room, he settled on a lamp on the bedside table. He quickly unplugged it and, using the cord as a rope, tied the man's hands together. Then he tied his hands to the heavy, metal bed-frame.

He obtained a paper towel from the bathroom and wrote a note to Dorfman…**Marvin Lowenstein tried to kill Dr. Billingsworth. He may be the hospital's serial killer. Damned if I know why.** He signed his name to the note and placed it on the floor in front of Lowenstein.

"What's going on in here?" a heavy-set, black nurse demanded, bursting into the room. She looked at Mark, then she froze.

"Lowenstein tried to kill Billingsworth," Mark blurted out in an attempt at an explanation.

The nurse stared at Lowenstein on the floor for a moment, then returned her eyes to Mark. "I know you," she said excitedly. "You're Dr. Valentine. You're wanted for murder. I'm going to call security."

"Don't bother," he said. "I've already taken care of that."

The nurse rushed out of the room and hurried back down the hallway toward the Nurses' Station.

He followed her out of the room and crossed the hallway to the elevator where he pushed the down button, then nervously waited. Two young nurses in white uniforms came out of the Nurses' Station and gawked at him.

"Come on, damn it," he muttered to himself as he stared at the floor numbers above the elevator door. He could hear the elevator slowly making its way from the basement. He nervously looked down at the floor, then he looked down the hallway in the direction opposite the Nurses' Station. That end of the hallway was unoccupied. Finally he returned his eyes to the numbers above the elevator door. The elevator had stopped on the third floor. He looked back in the direction of the Nurses' Station. The number of gawkers had turned into four. He again returned his eyes to the numbers above the elevator door.

Finally, the elevator door opened. He paused impatiently while an elderly woman and a younger one got off. He assumed that the older woman's husband was in the hospital with heart trouble and that the younger woman probably was a daughter. He smiled nervously at them and nodded. They smiled back. Then a male voice yelled at him from the direction of the Nurses' Station.

"Stop! FBI!"

He quickly looked around to see two men in dark-blue suits walking rapidly in his direction. The gawking nurses quickly stepped back out of the way as the men broke into a trot. The man in the lead reached inside his jacket and pulled out a gun. The one behind him did the same.

What now? Mark wondered. Why would the FBI be after him? He assumed that it had to do with Joanna's death, but he couldn't figure out why her death would be a federal offense.

The doors opened. He jumped into the elevator. The doors hesitated, then closed just as the two FBI agents reached the spot where he had been standing. The elevator jerked, then began its descent. Like a lot of other things lately, the FBI pursuing him didn't make sense. Maybe they were some of Maldini's men pretending to be FBI agents.

He got off the elevator on the second floor, ran down a flight of stairs, and headed at a fast pace back toward the hospital entrance. As he passed by the side door that security promptly locks at five thirty he stopped and quickly returned to it. He pushed on the horizontal bar. To his surprise the door sprung open. He rushed through it, crossed the small area of grass between the hospital and the parking lot, and hurried through row after row of cars until he spotted the Porsche up ahead.

Something was wrong. A young black man stood by the car. The driver-side door was open and another man was inside the car.

"Get away from there," Mark yelled loudly as he quickened his pace.

The explosion was enormous. A huge ball of fire rose high into the air from where the Porsche had been and lit the entire parking lot. His ears rang painfully, and every bone in his body vibrated from the blast. A thick cloud of smoke billowed upward toward the sky.

"Christ!" he said loudly. He covered his head with his arms as debris began falling all around him.

Suddenly, he heard the squeal of tires. He looked up just in time to see a familiar blue Pontiac speed out of the parking lot.

"Jesus, that son of a bitch," he muttered. "He's going to get me yet."

The taxi dropped Mark off in front of Joanna's large, brick house with the white columns in Buckhead. He walked briskly up the driveway to the back of the house and tried the back door. As expected, it was locked. He took a step back, raised his leg, and delivered a forceful blow to the door with his foot. The door flew open with a loud crash. Glass and splinters of wood flew everywhere.

He entered the house and walked to the wet bar where he opened a drawer. Searching around among its contents, he found what he was looking for…the keys to Joanna's Jaguar. Keys in hand, he left the house, walked by the pool, and entered the garage. He opened the door of the

Jaguar, sat in the driver's seat, and turned the key in the ignition. The car roared to life.

"God I hate this car," he mumbled as he pulled the lever at the front of the seat by the floorboard and slid the seat back to its furthest position. Then he reached up and pushed the button on the automatic control fastened to the sun visor. The garage door clanked and ground as it rose to the ceiling. He backed the Jaguar out of the garage, put the transmission in drive, and roared out of the driveway.

On the way back to the motel something kept bothering him. He could understand why Lowenstein would want to kill Billingsworth. That wasn't the problem. It was common knowledge that he wanted the Hospital Director's job as a stepping-stone to the directorship of one of the more lucrative, private hospitals in the city. He was still bitter because the hospital board had passed him over when it hired Billingsworth. If Billingsworth survived, there was no telling how much longer he would hold down the job, and Lowenstein was an impatient man. But why would he want to kill patients? It would be to his detriment. He had to know that the city council only lacked a vote or two to close Charity down. The bad publicity might do the hospital in. It would be like shooting himself in the foot. Besides, why would he change his modus operandum? Patients were dying of cardiac arrests, not unplugged ventilators.

If neither Stottlemire nor Lowenstein were the serial killer, then who was? One thing he had learned over the years…if it doesn't make sense, look elsewhere. Who in the hospital stood to benefit from patients having cardiac arrests, with many of them dying?

Suddenly, the answer came to him. He had been so focused on Stottlemire that he had over looked it. He had to hurry. The killer might still make an attempt on Billingsworth's life before the night was over.

Fifteen minutes later, he came to a screeching halt in the motel parking lot, got out of the car, and hurriedly entered the room. Angela lay on the bed watching TV

"Thank goodness you're back," she said as he closed the door. "I've really been worried about you. Did you stop Dr. Stottlemire?"

He walked across the room and slumped in the chair by the table. "He came to Billingsworth's room, but he didn't try to kill him. Marvin Lowenstein, the Assistant Hospital Director, showed up after Stottlemire left and unplugged Billingsworth's ventilator. I stopped him just in time. Hospital security has him under arrest." Mark reached for the telephone.

"But you were so sure that Dr. Stottlemire was the serial killer," Angela said.

"All the evidence pointed to him, but I was wrong. I don't have time to explain. I've got to get in touch with Dorfman."

He dialed the number of the Charity switchboard and, disguising his voice again, asked the operator to page Dorfman. He was sure he would still be in the hospital. A few seconds later, Dorfman picked up on the line.

"We've got a problem," Mark said. "Marvin Lowenstein's not the hospital's serial killer. Can you get the hospital's computer people to take a look at the data Lowenstein was studying?" Mark asked.

"Sure. No problem," Dorfman responded. "What do you think it will turn up?"

"Ask them to pay particular attention to the doctors of the patients in the excess cardiac arrest group. The name of the killer should become obvious. Oh, and another thing. You need to post a guard at Billingsworth's door until he's transferred to Emory in the morning."

Before Dorfman could respond, Mark hung up the telephone. Then he turned to face Angela.

"Jesus and the police aren't the only ones after me," he said. "The FBI's gotten into the act. Two agents tried to stop me at Charity. They even pulled their guns. And that's not all. When I got to the parking lot, some young thugs were trying to steal my car."

"Did they get it?"

"They got it all right. The Porsche exploded into a million pieces."

"What happened to the men who were trying to steal it?"

"There's not enough of them left to bury."

"How awful. Why would your car explode?"

"Dynamite, plastic explosives, who knows. Jesus did it."

"How do you know it was Jesus?"

"I saw his car speeding out of the parking lot immediately after the explosion. Besides, he came into the Doctors' Lounge while I was at Charity. I hid in the bathroom until he left."

"I told you he's relentless. He just won't give up. What are we going to do now?"

"I don't know about you, but I'm going to have a drink." He walked to the dresser, opened the drawer, and took out the half-full bottle of vodka, and poured a glass full.

———————

The next morning Mark felt someone shaking him roughly. He opened his eyes to see Angela standing over him, already dressed. He still sat with his clothes on in the chair he had done his drinking in the night before. On the table in front of him was the empty vodka bottle. God, his head hurt.

Angela made a cup of coffee from the instant coffee supplied each room by the management in an attempt to partially compensate for the lack of a restaurant. Then she sat the coffee in front of him.

"Drink it," she commanded.

He looked at her through bloodshot eyes. "Do I have to?"

"You have to."

He lit a cigarette, then took a sip of coffee. "Where did you get this stuff?"

"Never mind. Just drink it."

He finished off the first cup, then she made him another, and another. After the third cup of coffee and his fourth cigarette, he began to feel better. He thought he might actually live.

"I need some aspirin," he said. "My head is killing me."

She walked to her purse, took out a small tin, and dumped a couple of aspirin in her palm. Then she walked back to him and placed the aspirin tablets in his hand. He swallowed them with a gulp of coffee, then screwed up his face.

"God, that was awful," he said.

"What do you expect? Nobody takes aspirin with coffee."

"They do if their head hurts bad enough."

"We were that close," Daryl Barnes said as he walked into Walter North's office. "Valentine barely got away."

"I've already heard," North replied from his usual position behind the desk. "How did our agents know that he would be at the hospital?"

"The phone tap."

"He called?"

"Not exactly. The head nurse in the Emergency Room, Mattie Johnson, called him last night around nine thirty."

"I assumed you questioned her. What did she have to say about the call?"

Barnes walked up and stood in front of the desk. "She denied making it. Not only that, she denied talking to Valentine. She said someone had called the Emergency Room and asked to speak with a Dr. Eric Stottlemire. She said that she told the caller that he had just left the Emergency Room."

North rolled his chair back from the desk. "Maybe that's what happened."

"Not a chance. The bug clearly shows that she made the call."

"Did our agent ask her who had called this Eric Stottlemire as she claimed?"

"She said the person didn't identify himself."

"How convenient. Did we get a trace on the call?" North asked.

"No. It didn't last long enough," Barnes responded. "We checked the hospital telephone computer. Guess what? The call was made to an extension within the hospital...the Doctors' Lounge."

Black scratched his head. "Why would Valentine be inside the hospital in the Doctors' Lounge?"

"I have absolutely no idea. There's a lot of things about this case I don't understand."

"What happened after the call?" North asked.

"We got some local agents over there right away, ten of them. The Doctors' Lounge was empty, but someone had been there. The coffee pot was still hot and an ashtray had a bunch of fresh cigarette butts in it. Our men fanned out over the hospital. Two of them spotted Valentine getting on an elevator on the fourth floor. They recognized him despite a new beard. They yelled at him to stop, but the elevator door closed and he got away. The agents searched the hospital, but he had vanished into thin air. Not a trace. It's a big place."

"Any clues to his where-abouts?"

"None. We hope he'll call the Emergency Room again."

"Any reason to think he will?"

"No, but you never know. That hospital's a strange place. Anything could happen."

North rolled his chair back up to the desk "I think our agents need to talk to Mattie Johnson again. She's obviously concealing something. You said weird things were going on. What did you mean?"

"For one thing, there was a commotion on the fourth floor where Valentine was spotted. Seems that the Assistant Hospital Director, a Mr. Marvin Lowenstein, tried to kill a patient there, a guy named Ed Billingsworth who just happens to be the Hospital Director."

"Do you think that Mr. Lowenstein is tied into this case somehow?"

"Could be," Barnes replied. "By the time our men got to the fourth floor, the Chief of Hospital Security, a Zachary Dorfman, had placed him under arrest and was waiting for the police to arrive. He said that Valentine had sent him a message to get to Billingsworth's room as fast as he could."

"Does Zachary Dorfman know Valentine personally?"

"Yes. He said that they talked about sports from time to time before Valentine split. He said he hadn't seen him in several days."

North cleared his throat. "Anything else strange happen?"

"A car exploded and burned in the parking lot. Two young hoods were killed, apparently trying to steal the car. The Atlanta police investigated...plastic explosives. They traced the license-plate number to Columbus. It belonged to a William Kellerman."

"Did you question Mr. Kellerman?"

"It wasn't possible. He died in a head on collision two months ago."

"Sounds like someone switched plates. Who did the exploded car belong to, or do I need to ask?"

"If you're thinking Valentine, you're right. The police traced the serial number on the block. The car was definitely his Porsche. He had had it repainted black."

"Do we know how he got away from the hospital?"

"No. I assume it was on foot, but we can't rule out someone picking him up."

"Or him flagging down a taxi."

"We thought of that. We're checking out every taxi company on that side of Atlanta. If a driver did pick him up, he should remember him. He's tall, six-feet two, athletic build, dark hair, and now has a short beard. He was wearing blue jeans and a gray T-shirt when he was spotted getting on the elevator. I doubt taxi drivers in that part of town get very many fares that fit his description."

North tapped his fingers on the desk. "When will you know about the taxi?"

"Our men are working on it around the clock. If a taxi did pick him up, we should know it by tomorrow afternoon. Hopefully, the driver will be able to tell us where he took him."

"Do you think Maldini is responsible for the explosion?"

"I think it's a damn good bet," Barnes replied.

"Daryl, it's time for you to head south. I think you would be a lot more effective directing this operation from Atlanta."

CHAPTER TWENTY-SIX

Feeling better, Mark took a shower, dressed, and rejoined Angela in the bedroom area. "I guess it's time to check in with Susan," he said, sitting down in the chair by the telephone.

Angela gave him a pouting look. "Susan?"

"To check on Lisa," he added quickly. He picked up the telephone and dialed the Singletary's number. Mrs. Singletary answered. He asked to speak with Susan. She came to the telephone almost immediately.

"Mark! I thought you would never call," she said with a distressed sound to her voice. "Something awful has happened."

"What is it? What's happened?" he asked quickly.

"It's Lisa. She's disappeared."

"What do you mean disappeared? People don't just disappear. When did it happen?"

"This morning. About an hour ago. She went out in the back yard to play with Ellie. When I called her to come in for breakfast, she didn't answer. Dad went to check on her and found the gate open. Ellie was wondering around in a neighbor's yard."

"Do you think Lisa just went for a walk?"

"I don't think she would have done that without telling us. Besides, she certainly wouldn't have left the gate open for Ellie to get out."

"I guess you're right. Did you call the police?"

"Yes. They came immediately and checked around the neighborhood. No sign of her. Mrs. Jenkins, who lives down the street, told them that she had seen two strange men in the neighborhood last night and again this morning."

"What did they look like?"

"According to Mrs. Jenkins, one was a tall, black man. The other was a shorter, white man. Both appeared to be in their early forties."

The empty feeling in the pit of his stomach told him that Maldini had Lisa. The two men had to be blue-mask and red-mask. They certainly fit their descriptions. Trying to find something positive to hang on to, he was thankful that Jesus hadn't been the one who abducted her. Blue-mask and red-mask hadn't hurt him. Maybe they wouldn't hurt her. When it became clear to them that Lisa didn't know where he was, surely they would let her go.

"The police have unofficially put out a missing person's watch for her as a favor to my father," Susan continued. "They can't do it officially for twenty four hours. Do you think the two men had anything to do with her disappearance?"

"They sound like two of Maldini's men. The two that abducted me from the Emergency Room."

"There's more," Susan said. "Not thirty minutes after we discovered that Lisa was missing, an FBI agent showed up at the door. He flashed his badge and asked questions about you. He seemed to think that Lisa might know where you were."

"What did you tell him?"

"Don't worry. We told him that we didn't know anything. He asked if Angela were still with you. I don't know how he knew about her, but he did. We said that we didn't know. I'm pretty sure he knew we were lying. Funny thing though, he knew that you were in Atlanta. He said that two of their agents had seen you there, at the hospital, but that you had gotten away from them."

Mark told Susan about Daniel's death, their break-ins of Billingsworth's office and Betsy Barfield's apartment, Stottlemire turning out not to be the killer, Marvin Lowenstein showing up in

Billingsworth's room, his narrow escape from the FBI, his car blowing up, and taking Joanna's Jaguar. He went on to tell her that Charity's computer people were analyzing Lowenstein's data, and that he felt certain the results would identify the hospital's serial killer. He didn't tell her about having sex with Angela. No matter how hard he tried to convince himself that Susan didn't have any hold on him, he couldn't shake the guilt feeling.

"Where can I reach you if we hear anything?" Susan asked.

"At the Budget King Motel," he responded. He gave her the telephone number, then lowered his head and stared at the floor. God how he hated Maldini.

"I'm sure the police will find Lisa," Angela said, trying her best to comfort him.

He appreciated her effort, even though he didn't believe her.

———————————

A half hour later, the telephone rang. Mark leaped to his feet and answered it. "This is Mark," he said.

"We got a note from Maldini," Susan replied. "It just came in the mail."

"Read it to me," he instructed.

"Dr. Valentine. I'm sure you know by now that I have Lisa. If you want to see her alive again, you will have to come and get her. Come alone. You have forty-eight hours to show up. If you're not here by then, or if you get the police or FBI involved, I personally will see to it that she suffers a slow, agonizing death. The clock starts ticking at twelve noon the day you receive this letter."

"He kidnapped Lisa to get at me," Mark said anxiously. "He's using her as bait. Is there a postmark on the envelope?"

"Yes, it was mailed from Miami yesterday."

"He mailed the note before he kidnapped her?"

"It looks that way. What are you going to do? You're no match for Maldini and his men," Susan said. "You've got to let the police handle it."

"You saw what the letter said...no police. He'll kill her if the police get involved. You didn't tell the police about the letter did you?"

"No, I wanted to talk to you first."

"Good. Keep it that way."

"I'm coming back to Atlanta this afternoon," Susan said. "If you need to call me, I'll be at my apartment. Be careful."

His mother had been wrong. Reasonable discussion wasn't always an option. Sometimes you did have to confront your enemy in a hostile manner. He was fed up. Kidnapping Lisa was the last straw. The police and the FBI could fool around looking for Maldini as long as they wanted to. He was the one Maldini wanted, and he would be the one Maldini got. He was going to go get Lisa, and if Maldini got in his way it would be too bad for him. But first, he had some unfinished business to attend to.

———————

"Welcome to the noon REBOS meeting of Alcoholics Anonymous," the middle-aged man standing behind the podium at the front of the room said. "I'm Oscar G." The sleeves of his white, dress shirt were rolled up to his elbows and his tie was loosened at the collar. "For new members in the group, REBOS is sober spelled backward."

Rows of tables, occupied by men and women in various stages of recovery from alcoholism, lined the concrete floor. One table at the far right was designated as a non-smoking table. It was empty. Two large coffee urns, one with regular and the other with decaff, sat on a table at the back of the room.

Mark took a seat at a table near the center of the room, across from a younger man who wore blue jeans and a T-shirt with the sleeves cut off at the shoulders. A tattoo of an eagle with the words God bless America under it decorated the deltoid area of his right arm. An elderly man with a toothless smile and thinning, gray hair sat to his right, and a redheaded woman in wire-rimmed glasses, who appeared to be in her mid-thirties, sat to his left. A small metal ashtray and a mug of coffee sat in front of nearly every person in the room. He watched the man at the podium, the meeting chairman for the week, through the thick, bluish-gray smoke that hung in the air.

"Could we have a moment of silence," Oscar G said from his podium.

Everyone in the room obliged. Some bowed their heads and said silent prayers. Others simply sat quietly.

A few seconds later, Oscar G spoke again. "Ernie M, would you lead us in the Serenity Prayer."

All eyes focused on a fortyish looking man in a plaid shirt who stood up. Then, in unison, the group recited the Serenity Prayer.

"God, grant me the serenity to accept the things I cannot change, the courage to change the things I can, and the wisdom to know the difference."

Ernie M sat back down and took a sip of coffee. Mark took a drag on his cigarette. It felt good to be back at an AA meeting, a feeling that surprised him. He had never cared much for AA meetings in the past. They weren't for him, he had thought. After all, he wasn't an alcoholic, or so he had thought at the time. He tried not to think about Lisa. The thought of her in Maldini's hands caused him extreme emotional pain. He wanted to focus on the meeting for now. He would give Lisa his full attention as soon as the meeting was over.

Oscar G continued. "Martha R, would you read 'What AA is and is not.'"

A woman in her mid-forties, her face wrinkled beyond her age by too many years of alcohol and nicotine abuse, stood and read from a small card. "Alcoholics Anonymous is a fellowship of men and women who share their experience, strength, and hope with each other that they may solve their common problem and help others to recover from alcoholism."

Mark leaned back in his metal folding chair and took another drag on his cigarette. Someone on the other side of the room coughed briskly. Martha R continued.

"The only requirement for membership is a desire to stop drinking. There are no dues or fees for AA membership; we are self supporting through our own contributions. AA is not allied with any sect, denomination, politics, organization, or institution; does not wish to engage in any controversy; neither endorses or opposes any causes. Our primary purpose is to stay sober and help other alcoholics achieve sobriety."

Her reading finished, Martha R sat back down.

"Wilbur J, would you read How it Works," the chairman said from behind the podium.

An older man with graying hair and wearing a tan work shirt with his name on a white tag above the pocket rose, opened the Big Book of Alcoholics Anonymous, and read from the first part of Chapter Five.

"Our stories disclose in a general way what we used to be like, what happened, and what we are like now. If you have decided you want what we have and are willing to go to any length to get it...then you are ready to take certain steps. At some of these we balked. We thought we could find an easier, softer way. But we could not. With all the earnestness at our command we beg of you to be fearless and thorough from the very start. Some of us have tried to hold on to our old ideas and the result was nil until we let go completely. Remember that we deal with alcohol — cunning, baffling, powerful! Without help it is too much for us. But there is one who has all power...that one is God. May you find him now!"

The older man with the toothless smile to Mark's right stretched, then got up and walked to the coffee urn, the one with caffeine, and refilled his mug. Another man from across the room did the same. Wilbur J continued.

"Half measures availed us nothing. We stood at the turning point. We asked his protection and care with complete abandon. Here are the steps we took, which are suggested as a program of recovery. Step one. We admitted we were powerless over alcohol…that our lives had become unmanageable."

Wilbur J continued reading the twelve steps, one after another. Mark had heard them many times before, but they had been only empty words to him. He thought of Daniel and how good his recovery program had been before his death. It was as if Daniel knew something he didn't. Daniel had taken the steps very seriously. Maybe there was something to them after all. Mark stretched and leaned back in the chair. Tonight the steps seemed to have been derived just for him.

Finally, Wilbur J came to the final step. "Step twelve. Having had a spiritual awakening as the result of these steps, we tried to carry this message to alcoholics and to practice these principles in all our affairs."

Then Wilbur J went back to reading from Chapter Five of the Big Book. "Many of us exclaimed 'What an order! I can't go through with it.' Do not be discouraged. No one among us has been able to maintain anything like perfect adherence to these principles. We are not saints. The point is, we are willing to grow along spiritual lines. The principles we have set down are guides to progress. We claim spiritual progress rather than spiritual perfection. Our description of the alcoholic, the chapter to the agnostic, and our personal adventures before and after make clear three pertinent ideas: (a) That we were alcoholic and could not manage our own lives. (b) That probably no human power could have relieved our alcoholism. (c) That God would and could if he were sought."

"Thank you," Oscar G said as Wilbur J took his seat. "Today, I have chosen for our topic, false pride. I know none of you have ever been guilty of that."

A chuckle spread throughout the room. For the next fifty minutes, member after member stood and introduced themselves by their first names and first letters of their last names. Then they described how false pride had caused them problems in their family lives, relationships with others, jobs, and health. And most described how their false pride had led them back to alcohol in one-way or another. It was a character defect that had to be dealt with if one were to remain sober, one of them said. As usual, the discussion was replete with AA slogans and sayings. "I had to quit drinking," one man said. "My false pride led me to the point where I had one foot in the grave and the other one on a banana peel."

Somehow, today, the AA slogans didn't seem as corny to Mark as they had in the past. He thought about the false pride he had had as a plastic surgeon, a character defect common to many doctors, and nearly all surgeons. Dr. Jackson certainly had his share of false pride. So did Eric Stottlemire. To some extent, his mother-in-law had been right. At times, he had been pretty unbearable. That had changed over the last year or so. He had learned the meaning of true humility. He wanted to share his revelation with the group. In all the AA meetings he had attended in treatment at Ridgeview Psychiatric Hospital, and those few he attended afterwards, he never had a desire to share with the group. Now, because he was a wanted man, he couldn't. He decided that the best thing for him to do was to sit quietly and take in the meeting.

Finally, Oscar G looked at the clock on the wall above the coffee urns. "It's time to pass out chips," he said. "The white chip indicates surrender…a desire to quit drinking. Are there any among you who would like to pick up a white chip?"

A half-dozen people rose and walked to the front of the room. Mark was third in line. At first, he had been reluctant to stand up for fear he would be recognized, but he felt that this was something he had to do. It would be okay, he reasoned. Since the meeting was almost over, he could get his chip, then disappear quickly into the masses of people in Atlanta.

His turn came. He took the chip in his hand, squeezed it tightly, then walked back to his table and took his seat. Apparently no one recognized him. Oscar G continued, explaining to the group that a red chip was for thirty days of sobriety, a blue chip was for ninety days, and a bronze chip was for one year. A decreasing number of individuals rose to pick up chips as the required length of sobriety lengthened. Mark thought about the Caduceus Club Daniel had urged him to join. AA seemed right to him today, but Caduceus still brought up painful feelings, reminding him of everything he had lost. Maybe someday he would go to a Caduceus meeting, but not yet. He still wasn't ready.

When Oscar G had finished passing out the chips, he requested that the group stand and say the Lord's Prayer, as was the AA custom just prior to adjourning. The group rose as one, formed a large circle around the periphery of the room, and holding hands recited the Lord's Prayer.

"Our father who art in heaven. Hallowed be thy name. Thy kingdom come, thy will be done, on earth as it is in heaven. Give us this day our daily bread and forgive us our trespasses as we forgive those who trespass against us. And lead us not into temptation but deliver us from evil. For thine is the kingdom, the power, and the glory. Forever and ever. Amen."

"Keep coming back," the man on Mark's right said, squeezing his hand…an act performed by many individuals in the circle.

Although Mark remained focused on Lisa, something in the back of his mind kept nagging him. How did Jesus and the FBI know that he would be at Charity? Dorfman knew he was in the hospital because he had told Mattie to call him after learning that Stottlemire had left the Emergency Room. Dorfman was a man who believed in following the strictest letter of the law. He could understand if Dorfman had turned him in to the FBI, but how would he have known that the agency was looking for him, unless some of its agents had been at Charity asking questions. He decided that that was a distinct possibility. Even if Dorfman had turned him in, it wouldn't explain Jesus' appearance in the Doctor's Lounge. That took place before he told Mattie to call Dorfman. Surely Mattie hadn't turned him in to Maldini. She was a friend, and a real supporter, through all this mess. If Jesus, or another one of Maldini's henchmen, had threatened to harm her grandchildren to get her to talk, she might have given in. She would do anything to prevent one of them from being hurt, as he would Lisa. Maybe Dorfman had turned him in to the FBI and Mattie had given in to Maldini's pressure. That was the only explanation that made sense.

Turning his thoughts back to Lisa, he decided that it was time to get down to business. He couldn't just barge into Maldini's stronghold unarmed. He would have to develop a plan, and he would need a weapon. Fortunately, he had one…a Smith and Wesson thirty eight-caliber revolver. The only problem was that it was still in the drawer of the bedside table in his apartment. He berated himself again for having left it behind. He wondered if his apartment were being watched. He would have to be careful. He couldn't afford to get caught. Not now. Not with Lisa's life depending on him.

He hastily slipped out of REBOS, got into the Jaguar, and headed for his apartment to get the Smith and Wesson.

Twenty minutes later, he exited the Interstate onto South Cobb Drive. Another storm front had moved in. The worst part of the storm was projected to hit Atlanta in the late afternoon. Already the rain pounded hard on the Jaguar's windshield.

Circling the block that his apartment building was located on, he carefully looked for signs that it was being watched by the police, or Jesus. Seeing none, he parked by the curb directly in front of the building and trotted up the steps in the rain. He glanced at Mrs. Grabosky's window. The curtains didn't move. He said a silent prayer of thanks and entered the building. He hurried down the hallway past Susan's door, opened the door to his apartment, and quickly passed through it. Inside, he went directly to the bedside table, took the Smith and Wesson out of the drawer, and tucked it into his belt under his shirt.

When he arrived back at the motel, he found Angela lying on the bed reading an old copy of Cosmopolitan that she had found on the shelf in the closet. She put the magazine aside and sat on the side of the bed.

"Where have you been?" she demanded. "You just disappeared."

"I told you I would be back in a little while."

"Yes, but you didn't say where you were going, and that you would be gone for so long."

"I went to an AA meeting."

"You what?"

"I went to an AA meeting. I've been to them before, but I never took them seriously."

"What about now?"

He showed her his white chip. "I've given up drinking for real this time."

"Good. You need to. You're a lousy drunk."

"I'm not just a lousy drunk. I'm an alcoholic. I haven't been willing to face up to it until now. I guess I just wasn't ready."

"What do we do now?" she asked.

He pulled the gun out from under his shirt and laid it on the bed, along with the three rounds of ammunition he had purchased on the way from his apartment. Angela didn't flinch. Guns weren't new to her. She had lived around them all of her life.

"What are you going to do with that?" she asked.

"I'm going after Maldini on his own turf," he replied. "Straight to Miami."

"You can't be serious. You're no match for Vito and his men. They'll kill you on sight."

"He hasn't given me any other choice, has he?"

"We don't have any money. How are we going to get to Miami?"

"Courtesy of Maldini's credit card."

"I thought we couldn't use it."

"That was then. This is now. He's not looking for us. We're looking for him." He patted the Smith and Wesson. "Unfortunately, this baby can't fly. It would never make it through the metal detector at the airport."

"How are you going to get it to Miami?"

"UPS. I'm going to ship it by over-night mail. We'll get there tonight. It will be delivered to our hotel room in the morning. Then we go after Maldini."

She looked at him like she thought he had lost his mind, then she handed him the credit card. He put it in his billfold and stared at the Smith and Wesson. There was no doubt in his mind that he would use it if he had to to save Lisa's life.

CHAPTER TWENTY-SEVEN

Mark called Delta Airlines and charged the tickets to Miami on Maldini's credit card, both first class. As long as Maldini was paying the bill, he didn't see any point in being frugal. He ordered his ticket in the name of Joe Williams, the name he had given coach Jarvics at Hardaway High. He ordered Angela's ticket in her own name. The police weren't looking for her, and he was sure they didn't know that she was traveling with him. Besides, he had to give her real name...she was the approved user of the card. The ticket agent he spoke with said that the tickets would be waiting for them at the check-in counter, and that they should be there at least an hour prior to flight time. When he finished talking with the ticket agent, he called the Miami Hilton and made their room reservation...a luxury suite of course. Then he made a quick trip in the rain to United Postal Service where he purchased a small shipping box and, outside of the view of the young male clerk, packaged the gun and the three rounds of ammunition. He addressed the package to himself at the Miami Hilton and returned it to the clerk. To his relief, the clerk didn't ask about the contents of the package. He would have lied if he had.

Flight time was six o'clock that afternoon. Their luggage, what little they had, was packed and sitting by the door. He would pay the motel clerk what they owed for their room right after lunch. It would take virtually every cent they had left, but that was no longer a concern. They could get all the cash they needed on Maldini's credit card, up to the $12,000 limit. He was relieved to be free of the constant worry about running out of money

He felt that he should be scared. After all, he was going after a man with a vicious reputation. A man who had killed, or ordered killed, no telling how many people. And he was going after him on his own turf. He had no way of knowing for sure how many of Maldini's henchmen would be with him. The odds would be weighted heavily in Maldini's favor, but he had to go. Maldini had left him no other choice. The feeling in his heart wasn't fear. It was more like the feeling he had experienced before the Sugar Bowl game in his senior year, the one for the national championship. The butterflies were there, but so was the confident feeling that he would be victorious, as he had been then.

His beard was getting fuller. When he wore his sunglasses, he felt like a hippie, or maybe an offbeat college professor. Angela now was wearing her hair in a ponytail bound by a small blue ribbon in the back of her head. She too wore sunglasses. To say the least, they made an interesting-looking couple. Who would suspect that they were a doctor wanted for murder and a Mafia boss' ex-girlfriend? No one he hoped.

At four thirty, an hour and a half before flight time, they headed for Hartsfield International Airport. The sky was dark, almost black, and the temperature had plummeted to seventy-two degrees. The rain hammered the windshield in a monotonous drone. The Jaguar settled in behind a long line of slow-moving cars and trucks.

When they arrived at the airport, Mark dropped Angela and their bags off at the south entrance and parked the Jaguar in the long-term parking lot. He doubted he would ever see it again. He retrieved Joanna's umbrella, the one with the bright red, yellow, and blue flowers, from under the seat, opened the car door, and let the umbrella up. As he turned to lock the door, a sudden gust of wind nearly yanked the umbrella out of his hand. He quickly grasped it with both hands and hung on until the wind momentarily died down. Then he glanced at his rain-soaked watch. The time was twenty minutes to six.

"Shit," he said aloud, angry that the traffic, slowed by the bad weather, had caused them to arrive at the airport later than planned.

Twenty minutes wasn't much time to pick up their tickets and make it to the gate. He had to hurry. They couldn't miss the plane. Too much depended on him getting to Miami. He quickened his pace, literally running across the rain-soaked pavement.

Arriving back at the terminal building, he opened the door and entered the area between the north and south terminals. Wall to wall people filled the building, all seemingly in a hurry. Angela was waiting for him just inside the door. He closed the dripping umbrella and tossed it on the floor.

"Come on, we're late," he said, rubbing his wet hands on his pants to dry them. He took Angela by the hand and led her toward the Delta counter as fast as he could maneuver through the thick crowd. When they arrived at the counter area, the line at the Delta counter was at least twenty feet long. The clock on the wall behind the counter indicated that their flight time was twelve minutes away.

He knew there was no way they could wait in line until their turn came, pick up the tickets, and make it to the gate in time. He thought about barging in the front of the line at the counter, but figured that doing so would probably start a small riot. They didn't need to draw attention to themselves. A surge of anxiety passed over him.

"Destination please?" a man of thirty or so in a blue Delta uniform asked as he walked up to them.

"Miami," Mark answered quickly, hoping that the man would let them move up to the front of the line.

The man looked at a piece of paper in his hand. "Flight 1023," he said. "No use hurrying. The flight will be late getting in. It hasn't left Jackson, Mississippi yet. It's been delayed by the bad weather. We expect it around seven o'clock."

Mark was instantly relieved. Although he hated the thought of waiting longer in the airport than he had planned, he hated the thought of missing the flight even more. He had a little over forty-two hours left to find Maldini and save Lisa. An extra hour in the airport wouldn't make any real difference.

He and Angela waited patiently in line until they reached the counter where he picked up their tickets. Then they went to the gate to wait.

Seven o'clock came and went, and there was still no sign of the plane. He went back to the counter and searched the monitor mounted high on the wall for flight 1023. Finding it, he discovered that the flight had been moved back yet another hour. He was irritated by the change, but it still didn't pose a serious problem. He would have to be patient. The plane would come, he assured himself.

Eight o'clock came and went as well. Still no boarding call. He walked to the window and looked out. The wind had picked up and the rain came down in torrents. The space on the tarmac where the plane would taxi up and stop was still vacant. More irritated than worried, he walked back to the counter and again inspected the monitor. His heart sank…**Miami Flight 1023, Canceled.** He stepped up to the desk, waited impatiently for the Delta clerk to finish talking to another would-be passenger, then pointed to the monitor.

"What happened to flight 1023?" he asked. "It was due in here two hours ago."

"Never made it out of Jackson," the man replied. "A heavy fog set in."

"Shit!" Mark said. "When's the next flight out of here?"

"Everything has been delayed because of the storm," the agent responded. "The next flight to Miami should be boarding in about six hours, but it won't do you any good."

"Why not?"

"It's booked solid. I can get you on a flight late tomorrow afternoon."

"That's too late. I can't wait that long. What about standby for the next flight?"

"Chances are worse than slim. I already have ten people on standby. Might have one or two seats open up at the most."

Mark stared at the clerk for a moment, trying to figure out a solution to his predicament. "What about other airlines?" he asked. "Do they have anything open tonight?"

"I've already checked. Not a thing. You could rent a car and drive, but that would probably take nearly as long as waiting for the flight tomorrow, given the long drive in this horrible weather."

Discouraged, Mark turned and walked back to where Angela sat. "The flight's been canceled," he said, taking a seat beside her. The thought of Lisa in Maldini's hands caused his stomach to ball up in a knot. He didn't see how he could sit by and wait until tomorrow for another flight. "Do you think Maldini would really kill her?" he asked.

Angela nodded. "Despite all of his bad characteristics, Vito's a man of his word. If he tells you something, you can bank on it." She hesitated as if she really didn't want to say what she was thinking.

"Go ahead," Mark insisted.

"I'm afraid that Lisa is as good as dead if we don't get there in time."

The knot in his stomach suddenly got bigger. He had suspected as much, given what he had learned about Maldini's past history, but he had suppressed the thought as much as possible.

"That cinches it," he said. "If there's a way to get out of here tonight, I'm going to find it."

"You can always charter a plane." Angela said. "That's what Vito does when he wants to get somewhere and it's not convenient to fly commercially."

"That's it," he said enthusiastically. "We'll charter a plane." He hugged her and kissed her on the cheek. "I'll be right back."

"Where are you going?"

"To find a telephone book."

"Not without me," she said quickly.

"You stay here with our things. I won't be long."

Reluctantly, she agreed. He stood up and went in search of a pay telephone. A few minutes later, he found one with two thick books…the

yellow pages and the white pages…hanging down from the metal cabinet by short chains. He flipped the yellow-page book open and searched
for airlines, charter. There were three listings…**Charters R Us, Atlanta
Charter,** and **Southland Air.** He settled on Southland Air and dialed the
number. A female voice, which he assumed belonged to a secretary,
answered the phone.

"Southland Air," she said. "How may I help you?"

"I'd like to charter a plane."

"Your name?"

"Joe Williams."

"Address?"

"223 South Cobb Drive, here in Atlanta," he said. Then he suddenly
realized that he had reflexively given her his correct address. He had a
sinking feeling, but quickly decided that his mistake shouldn't be a
problem. The fact that he worked at Charity had been widely broad-
casted, but he didn't remember any of the reporters giving his home
address. Who would remember it if they had?

"Social Security number?" the woman asked.

He rattled off his Social Security number. It was obvious that she was
filling out a form.

"And what is your destination?"

"Miami."

"What is the nature of your trip?"

"I beg your pardon?"

"The nature of the charter…business or pleasure?"

"Oh! Business. Definitely business."

"How many people in your party?"

"Two."

"What type of plane do you want to charter?"

"A small jet," he said, remembering his previous flights to Miami,
courtesy of Maldini. "What do you have available?"

"I'm sorry, our only jet is out on assignment. We have a Piper Navajo that's not in service right now. I could let you have it."

"I'm not familiar with that plane. Tell me about it."

"It's a two engine prop plane capable of carrying up to six passengers, not including the pilot."

"How fast will it fly?"

"You sound like you're in a hurry."

"I'm in a hell of a hurry. Big business deal. If I don't get there tonight, I could lose a ton of money."

"Its cruising speed is over two hundred fifty miles per hour. Fast enough?"

"I guess it will have to do."

"How much is it?" he asked, temporarily forgetting that he had almost unlimited funds.

"That depends on whether or not you plan on furnishing your own pilot, and how long you want the service of the plane."

"We don't have our own pilot, and we'll be gone over night, maybe two. Figure it for two."

"Will you be returning to Atlanta?"

"I'm not certain. It depends on what happens in Miami." Even if he took care of Maldini and got Lisa, he would still be wanted for murder. Atlanta wouldn't be the safest place for him. He and Angela would go somewhere, maybe to Charleston as he had contemplated earlier.

"Is that a problem?" he asked.

"Not at all. When you're ready to leave Miami, we can fly you anywhere and bill you for additional flight at that time."

He listened for a couple of minutes as she punched numbers into a calculator. Then she quoted him a figure that he thought was reasonable. He agreed to the figure, knowing that it could have been several times that amount and it still wouldn't have been a problem. The credit card still had a hell of a large credit line left. He wasn't concerned about using it up.

"What time do you wish to depart?"

"How soon can the plane be ready?"

"In thirty minutes or so. You'll have to talk to my husband about take-off time when he gets back. I expect him any minute."

"We'll be right over," Mark said. He hung up the telephone and headed back to the waiting area to tell Angela the good news.

He drove the Jaguar through the gate of the chain-link fence and parked the it next to the small building. The dripping sign over the door identified the building as Southland Air. A large hanger was located just beyond the building. A two-engine plane sat on the asphalt to their right. Gusts of wind rocked it back and forth as the downpour continued. He assumed the plane to be the Piper Navajo.

He and Angela got out of the car and ran the short distance in the rain to the building.

A stout, middle-aged woman sat at a desk behind the counter. Her sandy hair was cut short in a boyish manner. She immediately rose and approached them.

"Margaret Weathersby," she said, holding out her hand.

He recognized her voice as the woman he had talked to on the telephone. He and Angela took turns shaking her hand.

"My husband, Ken, and I own the service," she said. "We have two other pilots, but they're tied up out of town tonight. Ken will be your pilot on this trip. What kind of business are you in?"

Caught off guard, he thought quickly. "Medical supplies. We buy a lot of them in Miami."

She handed him a form to sign. "I'll need a five-hundred dollar deposit," she said.

"No problem," he responded.

He handed her the credit card. She flipped it over and read the signature on the back. Then she ran it through the machine and handed it back to him. "Sign here Mr. Petrino," she said, laying the credit card receipt and a ballpoint pen on the counter in front of Mark. He slid the receipt and the pen over to Angela.

Angela smiled at Mrs. Weathersby. "I'm Petrino," she said. Then she signed the receipt.

A few minutes later, a short, wiry-looking man wearing a yellow raincoat and matching hat barged through the door, dripping wet from the rain. His leathery face showed deep lines from years of exposure to the elements. He walked up to Mark and extended a wet hand. "Ken Weathersby," he said.

"We're ready to go," Mark said quickly, shaking his hand.

Ken didn't blink an eye. "We should be able to get off the ground in eight or nine hours," he replied. "According to the weather service, this storm's supposed to let up some by then."

"Eight or nine hours! We can't wait that long," Mark said impatiently. "Can't you fly around the storm?"

"Not possible," Ken responded. "We're right in the middle of the storm. It's going to get worse before it gets better."

"What if I double what you normally charge?"

Ken hesitated for a moment. "Still too dangerous."

"Triple it?" Mark said. After all, it was Maldini's money. He would go as high as he had to.

Ken paused again, looked at Margaret, then scratched his head. Margaret didn't respond. It was obvious that her opinion didn't count when it came to decisions about flying.

"I guess it will be okay," Ken said. "But you have to understand that it's dangerous to tempt Mother Nature."

Mark nodded. "I'll risk it."

Angela looked as if she weren't as sure about flying in the storm as he was.

"Then let's get going," Ken said. "I'll go get the plane ready. Why don't you folks wait in here out of the weather until I'm ready. When you see the steps come down, you all come running."

Ken passed through the door, back into the rain, as fast as he had come in. Mark and Angela moved to the door and followed him with their eyes through the glass until he disappeared into the plane.

"You'll need those," Margaret said, pointing at two yellow raincoats, identical to the one Ken was wearing, hanging on a coat rack by the door.

They donned the raincoats. Mark's was too small and Angela's was too large, but they would do to protect them from the rain until they got on the plane.

Twenty minutes later, Ken lowered the steps.

"Time to go," Mark said to Angela. He held the door open for her as they exited the building into the storm. Mark retrieved their luggage from the Jaguar, then locked the car doors. As they headed for the plane, the rain splattered off the pavement and soaked their feet.

"Stop! Police!" a gruff male voice yelled loudly from behind them.

Startled, Mark turned to see Sam Kincaid standing in the downpour, his light-blue suit drenched to the hilt. The business end of his gun barrel looked enormous.

"Oh hell!" Mark said under his breath. "I can't let him stop me now. Not after all this." He had a mental picture of Maldini killing Lisa because Kincaid had placed him under arrest, preventing him from getting there in time.

"Take it easy," Mark said nervously. "I'm not going to resist arrest." He was afraid that if he made any sudden move at all, Kincaid would shoot him. He would have to do what Kincaid wanted until he got a chance to escape. He prayed that it wouldn't be long.

Kincaid reached into his pocket, pulled out a silencer, and placed it on the barrel. The silencer worried Mark. Why would Kincaid need a silencer to arrest him? Then it came to him…Kincaid intended to kill him on the spot. A peal of lightening suddenly lit the horizon, followed by a deafening crack of thunder.

"You son of a bitch," Kincaid said angrily. "Do you realize how much effort I put in to get Joanna to agree to marry me? Then you ruined it all."

"I didn't kill her," Mark stated emphatically.

"Like hell you didn't. I heard you threaten her. No one else had a motive. Now I'm going to pay you back for what did to me."

The cold, steely look in Kincaid's eyes sent a chill up Mark's spine. He glanced at Angela. She was frozen in place by the side of the Jaguar. A sudden click reflexively caused him to return his eyes to Kincaid. Kincaid had cocked the hammer of the gun.

"Oh shit!" Mark mumbled. His pulse pounded hard in his temples and his chest felt tight. He watched as Kincaid's finger began to squeeze the trigger.

Suddenly, almost in a blur, a muscular-looking man in a white shirt, red tie, and dark-blue suit darted across the parking lot and caught Kincaid by surprise, hitting him with a waist high tackle. Instantaneously, the gun went off, firing a muffled shot over Mark's head. The stranger and Kincaid sprawled in a splash on the wet pavement and began struggling with each other.

"Come on," Mark said, grabbing Angela's hand and running for the plane.

As they reached the top of the steps, Mark looked back. Kincaid broke free from the stranger and ran in their direction. The stranger ran after him and tackled him from behind. Mark pushed Angela into the plane and immediately followed her. Then he pulled the steps up behind them and quickly fastened the latches of the door.

Ken looked back from his position in the cockpit. "You all have a seat and fasten your seat belts," he said. "We're ready to get this bird off the ground."

"Good," Mark said. "The faster the better."

They freed themselves from the dripping raincoats, chose a seat, and fastened their seat belts. Ken eased the plane out on the runway, then stopped momentarily and revved up the engines. Mark looked out the window back toward the building. To his surprise, Kincaid and the stranger had stopped fighting and stood side by side watching the plane as it prepared to take off.

Apparently satisfied that everything was okay with the engines, Ken eased the throttle forward and the plane began to move. It picked up speed, roared down the runway, and took off into the howling storm just as a lightening bolt blazed by the left wing tip.

The ascent was nerve wracking. The plane pitched form side to side and, at times, seemed out of control. Angela vomited into a paper sack that Ken had supplied her. Mark came close. Through it all, Ken calmly whistled Honky Tonk Woman. At ten thousand feet, the plane leveled off above the storm, and they breathed a sigh of relief. Their stomachs at last began to settle down.

"Tell me about Maldini's henchmen," Mark said to Angela who sat in the seat across the aisle from him. "I need to know as much as possible about my impending adversaries."

"Which ones?" She asked, still a little green around the eyes.

"Red-mask, blue-mask, and Willie. They're the ones I expect to encounter when we get there."

"Red-mask and blue-mask? What are you talking about?"

"The two men who abducted me from the Emergency Room. They wore ski masks. Red-mask was tall, about my height, and black. He seemed to be in charge. Blue-mask was somewhat shorter and white."

"Oh. That's Ralph and James. Ralph is definitely the leader. He's well educated. He has a college degree in something…history, I think. He had aspirations of being a high-school teacher at one time."

"What happened?"

"He discovered that he could make a lot more money working for Vito."

"Is he dangerous?"

"If he works for Vito, he's dangerous. He doesn't kill for the sake of killing like Jesus, but if Vito tells him to, or if you back him up in a corner, he'll blow your head off without hesitating. James is pretty much the same way. He's a little slow mentally, not retarded or anything. He's just not as smart as Ralph, so Ralph tells him what to do. James looks up to him, and will do almost anything for him."

"What about Willie?"

"Willie's another story. He's the proverbial schoolyard bully who grew up to become every bully's dream...a professional bully. He's big and mean, and loves to push people around. He'd just as soon kill you as look at you."

"Nice guy," Mark said sarcastically.

"Vito likes men like Willie. He's basically a bully too. He just uses other people to do his dirty work. Why do you think those three are the only ones we'll run into with Vito?"

"It stands to reason that he'll have only a few trusted men with him, since he's trying to reduce the number of people who can identify him. Willie is his bodyguard, so I figure he'll be there. Ralph and James kidnapped Lisa. I'm sure they personally delivered her to him, so they should be there too."

"What about Jesus?"

"I expect he's still in Atlanta looking for me."

"Four to one. That's not very good odds," Angela said with a worried look on her face.

CHAPTER TWENTY-EIGHT

Two and a half hours after take off, the Piper Navajo landed at Miami International Airport. After the initially turbulent start, the flight had settled down with only occasional sudden lurches of the plane due to scattered air pockets. By now the storm had passed well to the north of Miami. Mark's initial impulse was to go after Maldini in broad daylight, as soon as his gun arrived from Atlanta. Angela convinced him that Maldini wouldn't harm Lisa unless he failed to show up by the deadline. To go after Maldini in broad daylight would be too risky, possibly resulting in all their deaths, she had said. It was hard to argue with her logic. He decided to launch their assault at midnight the following night so that they would have the benefit of darkness. They would need every edge they could get.

Mark, Angela, and Ken deplaned and entered the terminal building. Ken told them where he would spend the night, and instructed Mark to call him when he knew for certain when they would be ready to leave Miami. After saying good-bye to Ken, they walked to the Avis Rent-a-Car booth and rented a black Cadillac Sedan Deville, paid for with the credit card. Angela objected to the color...she wanted a white one...until Mark explained to her that a black car would be less conspicuous at night.

"How do we get to the Miami Hilton?" he asked the young woman behind the Avis counter.

"You are here," she said, placing an X at the site of the airport on a small map of the city. "Take the expressway to the downtown area, then follow the route I've marked." She placed another X at the site of the Miami Hilton and handed the map to him.

They left the Avis counter and stopped at an ATM machine where they got a thousand dollars on the credit card. He counted the money and put it in his billfold. Then they went in search of the Sedan Deville.

After locating the car, they exited the airport drive onto Airport Expressway, which they followed to the downtown area. Despite the fact that it was the middle of the night, lights on both sides of the four-lane street made it bright as day. They passed I-95 and proceeded across Biscayne Bay on the Julia Tuttle Causeway to Miami Beach where they located the Hilton without difficulty. After checking in, they followed the tall, thin bellhop with the unruly hair to the elevator. He looked at them strangely, and treated them coolly. Clearly, in their casual clothes, they weren't the typical, classy-appearing Miami Hilton guests he was use to.

They took the elevator to the nineteenth floor and followed the bell-hop to their suite. The main room was large, elegant, and expensively decorated. The bedroom, with its four-poster bed, was even more impressive. It beat the hell out of his small, shabby apartment in Atlanta. He tipped the bellhop ten dollars. It felt good to give Maldini's money away. The bellhop's demeanor immediately improved.

"Thanks," he said, taking the money in his hand. "My name is Larry. If there's anything you all want during your stay, please don't hesitate to call me."

"Don't worry," Mark said. "We will."

The bellhop thanked him again, stuffed the money in his pocket, then left. They unpacked and put their clothes away. It had been a long day and they were both dead tired. He lay on the bed while Angela took her shower. Then he took his.

When he crawled into the bed, Angela snuggled up to him. He put his arm around her. He was glad she had come with him. Besides being able to direct him to Maldini's estate, she helped take his mind off the constant concern he had for Lisa's well being, not to mention the violent confrontation he expected. He was worried about the gun. If he had known they were going to charter a plane, he could have brought it with him. What would he do if something happened and it didn't arrive? It would be impossible for him to buy one anyway soon. He didn't need a gun five days from now. He needed one tomorrow night. It would get there, he assured myself.

He reached over to turn off the lamp on the bedside table and noticed the clock...twelve thirty. Thirty-five and a half hours to the deadline. There was still plenty of time. No need to worry, he told himself. He did worry, however...a lot. Angela went to sleep almost immediately. He finally dozed off two hours later.

At ten o'clock the next morning, a young bellhop delivered the UPS package to their room. Mark tipped him with another ten-dollar bill and thought about how much easier it was to spend someone else's money than his own. He liked the feeling. He understood how someone like Angela could have fallen into the trap of accepting Maldini's money. He felt compassion for her for having been born into a Mafia family, never knowing what everyday, hard-working, honest people were like. He wondered again about her sense of values. Where had she learned right from wrong? Certainly not from the people who surrounded her in her childhood.

Quickly returning his focus to the package, he opened it and took out the Smith and Wesson, along with the three rounds of ammunition. He visually inspected the gun, then checked to be sure the safety was on. Satisfied that it was, he flipped the chamber out, opened one of the rounds, and loaded the chamber with bullets. He wondered how many of them he would need. He had never shot anyone before. He certainly had never killed anyone. Until now his focus had been on saving lives.

He turned the gun over in his hand and stared at it. To get Lisa back safely, he would kill if he had to, and he would do it without hesitation.

Off and on the next day, he and Angela discussed their plans for the assault on Maldini's estate…first at breakfast, again at lunch, and then again over dinner. That evening she drew a map showing him how to get to the estate from the Hilton. Then she sketched out the layout of the grounds, the main house, and the guesthouse. The first floor of the main house consisted of a large marble entrance foyer. A wide staircase extended from the foyer to the second floor. The grand room with its white, marble pillars was beyond the foyer. A library was to the left of the grand room and a parlor was to the right. Immediately beyond the grand room was a formal dining room, then the kitchen and a separate breakfast area. The upstairs consisted of a large sitting area, six bedrooms, each with its own bath, and Maldini's office. The grounds were large, several acres, she didn't know exactly how many. A seven-foot-high, iron fence enclosed the entire area. He remembered the fence. He had seen it from the window of Maldini's office during his first visit there. To the best of Angela's knowledge, the fence wasn't electrified. The grounds were lit, if only dimly so, by small floodlights near the house. A near Olympic-sized pool separated the guesthouse from the main building. The quest house was small compared to the main house, consisting of a common area, three bedrooms, two baths, and a kitchen.

"What about security cameras?" Mark asked.

"Several cameras around the house monitor the grounds, but the only one at the fence is at the main gate," Angela replied.

"Then the best way to get onto the grounds would be to go over the fence behind the guest house."

She nodded her agreement.

The fact that there were two buildings on the grounds posed a problem. Which one was Lisa held captive in? His guess was the guest house. That's where Maldini's men most likely would be staying. She would probably be where they were. Angela concurred. They would search the guest house first.

A few minutes before midnight, a sleepy-looking parking attendant delivered the black Sedan Deville to the front of the Hilton. Mark tipped him a ten-dollar bill as had become his recent custom. The attendant looked at the bill and quickly perked up. Mark slid behind the wheel. Angela got in on the other side. To make them less visible in the dark, he wore blue jeans and a black T-shirt. She wore a pair of tight-fitting, black slacks and a lightweight, black blouse. Both of them wore dark sneakers.

As he eased the Cadillac out of the main entrance of the hotel into the sparse traffic, he glanced at the dashboard clock. Twelve hours to the deadline.

They had left the Hilton only once before since arriving...to get a six-foot stepladder, a flashlight, and the dark clothes. The ladder was to help them get over Maldini's fence. The flashlight was to help them find their way around on the grounds of his estate in the dark. The reason for the dark clothes was obvious. The traffic had been much heavier then, and the temperature had reached a hundred degrees. The rays of the mid-day sun had parched everyone and everything they touched. Now, thankfully, the evening air was considerably more pleasant.

The Smith and Wesson lay on the seat between them. Mark stared straight ahead in silence as he followed Angela's crude map across the Causeway, then onto I-95 South. The butterflies in his stomach began to intensify.

Twenty minutes later, Angela spoke for the first time. "Turn here," she said. "The house is about two miles down this street."

He followed her instructions.

Except for the level terrain, the area could have passed for Beverly Hills. He had been there once with his parents as a child, and had been impressed with the size of the stars' houses, the perfectly trimmed shrubbery, and the immaculate lawns. He guessed that this was the area in Miami to live if you had money, lots of it.

"Tell me when we're within a block of the estate," he instructed.

A few minutes later, Angela sat straight up in the seat "You'd better park here," she said. "The house is about two-thirds of the way down the next block."

He eased the Sedan Deville over to the curb, brought it to a stop, and turned off its lights. He sat silently in the dark for a few minutes, wondering if they would get out of this alive. Angela didn't move. He assumed that she was thinking the same thing. He looked around the area. It was deserted. A single light glared from a window of a house across the street, but no other signs of life were evident. He reached over and squeezed Angela's hand.

"Time to go," he said. Then, letting go, he picked up the gun and tucked it in his belt.

Together, they exited the car. The night was graveyard still. Not the slightest hint of a breeze filled the humid air. From somewhere far away, a dog let out a lonely sound, somewhere between a moan and a howl.

He opened the trunk and took out the stepladder and the flashlight. The ladder was made of an aluminum alloy and weighed only a few pounds. As a result, it was easy to carry with one hand. He stuck the flashlight in his back pocket, then slid his free hand into Angela's. He squeezed her hand, and then they carefully made their way down the sidewalk toward their destination. He hoped they wouldn't run into any late-night partygoers. They would have a hard time explaining the ladder. Neither of them looked much like a house painter. Even if they did, who would believe that they were out working at twelve thirty at night? He wondered if Angela noticed that his palms were sweating.

After passing three houses, Angela spoke. "The next house is Vito's," she said softly.

The corner of the black, metal fence that surrounded Maldini's property immediately came into view. They stopped for a moment to survey the area as best they could in the dim light cast by the single street light a half a block away. Through the palm trees, Mark could see a light on in an upstairs room in Maldini's mansion. He wondered if Maldini were sitting in his office working at this late hour. If so, he was going to be in for a hell of a big surprise.

"Come on," Mark said. He led Angela by the hand through the yard of Maldini's nearest neighbor, keeping the fence between them and Maldini's house. Fortunately, the neighbor's house was one of the few houses in the neighborhood not surrounded by a fence or a wall, thereby giving them easy access.

Angela followed him as he worked his way along the fence to its furthermost corner of the yard. Then the manicured lawn ran out. He took the flashlight out of his pocket and flipped the switch. Dense palmetto bushes took over from the lawn and stretched as far as he could see in the narrow beam cast by the flashlight. He raised the ladder up out of the way of the palmetto bushes and placed it horizontally on his right shoulder. The rest of the way was going to be tough going.

Led by the flashlight beam, they fought their way through the thigh-high growth, and finally arrived at the section of fence directly behind the guesthouse. He wasn't sure how far they had struggled through the palmetto bushes, but he figured it had to be at least a hundred yards. Every foot of the way, he had worried about stepping on one of the poisonous snakes that come out in the relative cool of the Florida night to feed on small rodents and lizards. He had wanted to say something to Angela about his concern, but he figured that the better part of valor would be to keep quiet so as not to scare her. He sat the ladder on the ground by the fence, and then opened it. He jockeyed it around a few inches until it was stable, then he looked back at Angela.

"I'll go first," he said. "That way I can help you over."

She nodded her head in agreement, then studied the fence with an unsure look on her face.

Holding to the vertical bars of the fence for stability, he climbed up the ladder. When he reached the top, he placed one of his feet on the top bar of the fence, then followed it with the other one. Then he bent his knees and jumped.

Landing in the soft grass on his feet, he tucked his head to his chest, pitched forward, did a perfect somersault, and came up on his feet. Then he walked back to the fence. "Your turn," he whispered to Angela through the bars.

"You've got to be kidding," She said dead seriously. "I can't do that."

"It's up to you. You can stay out there with the snakes, or you can come over the fence to be with me."

"Snakes! You didn't tell me there were snakes out here," she said loudly.

"Shhh. You'll wake everyone up," he whispered, irritated with her. Maybe he should have left her at the hotel.

She quickly looked around her feet as if she could see anything in the blackness. Then she scurried up the ladder to the top.

"Okay, jump," he instructed sternly.

She took a deep breath, closed her eyes, and jumped. He broke her fall as best he could. She landed clumsily, and lay on the ground in a pile.

"Are you hurt?" he asked quickly.

"Just my pride," she replied.

As he helped her to her feet, she looked back at the ladder sitting on the other side of the fence. "How are we going to get out of here?" she asked.

"Through the front door, one way or another."

She didn't respond.

They walked the short distance to the back of the guesthouse and located a door. He shined the light on the lock. There were two of them.

"Deadbolt," he said dejectedly. Then he looked back at Angela. "I doubt that we're going to get a locksmith to open this one." He gently tried to turn the knob. As expected, the door was locked.

"Mark," Angela whispered softly.

"Not now," he said, still looking at the locks. "I'm trying to figure out how to get into this place."

"Mark," she whispered a little louder.

"What is it?" he asked, irritated at her for her persistence. He turned back to look at her just as she thrust her hand into her pocket.

She pulled her hand out of her pocket and handed him a key. "This fits the guest house and the main house. I thought it might come in handy."

"Why didn't you tell me you had a key?"

"I tried to."

He kissed her on the cheek, took the key, inserted it into the deadbolt lock, and gently turned the key. Then he inserted the key into the regular lock and repeated the maneuver. He stuck the key in his pocket and tried the doorknob again. This time, with a slight squeak, the door opened. He entered the building. Angela followed. He shined the flashlight around the central room and studied it. It was empty. After carefully checking bedroom after bedroom without result, he came to the disappointing conclusion that the entire quest house was unoccupied.

"Lisa has to be in the main house," he said.

As they left the guesthouse by way of the front door, he suddenly noticed something that he hadn't been aware of before. He couldn't believe he had been so unobservant.

"I thought you said the grounds were lit by floodlights," he whispered to Angela who followed closely behind him. "I don't see any light at all. It's pitch black out here."

"Why would Vito have the lights off?" she responded. "I've never seen them off at night before. They're supposed to come on automatically when the sun goes down. A light sensor, or something like that, turns them on."

"I don't understand why they're not on, but I'm glad. It means that the surveillance cameras can't see us out here."

"Vito can be pretty devious," Angela said with a worried sound to her voice. "If they're off, you can bet they're off for a reason."

For the first time since leaving the hotel, he felt a twinge of fear. He quickly shook it off and put his arm around Angela.

"This key fits the main house?" he asked, holding up the key.

"I wouldn't lie to you."

"Good. Let's go."

They had taken only a half-dozen steps toward the main house when a low-pitched growl startled him. He turned the flashlight on and pointed it in the direction of the noise. His heart leaped up into his throat. A large, black Doberman in full snarl stood about ten feet from them. It had the biggest, whitest teeth he had ever seen.

"Oh shit!" he muttered to himself.

Then he heard another growl as a second Doberman, equally as vicious looking, joined the first one.

"Got any ideas?" he whispered to Angela. He reached out, took her by the arm, and pulled her close to him.

The two dogs edged menacingly closer. He stood frozen. For an instant, he thought about running for it, but he decided that running would provoke them. He had a visual image of the two dogs tearing into their hamstrings from behind to bring them down. The Dobermans continued to edge forward, their growls getting louder and louder, until they stood only a couple of feet away. He held his breath and said a silent prayer.

"Sit Durk!" Angela commanded.

The lead dog promptly sat on its haunches.

"Good dog," she said. She reached out and scratched its head.

"I'll be damned," Mark said softly.

The other dog eased up in front of them and sat by the first one. Angela stopped scratching the first dog's head, bent over, and rubbed the second dog on the nap of the neck. It promptly lay down at her feet.

"This is Gurk," she said, smiling at Mark.

"Durk and Gurk," Mark said, shaking his head. "At first, I thought they were killers."

"They are. Given the right command, they would tear you to shreds."

He didn't like the sound of that. "Come on," he said, giving the dogs one last look. "We've still got work to do." Now he was glad that he hadn't left Angela behind.

As the Dobermans returned to their resting place, he and Angela eased around the pool toward the main house. The light was still on upstairs. When they arrived at the back door, Mark tried the key. Just as Angela had said, it worked. He opened the door, then quietly entered the hallway that led to the kitchen. They had already made the decision that if Lisa were there she most likely would be in one of the bedrooms upstairs. Using the beam from the flashlight to guide them, they worked their way to the front of the house, then up the stairs. Not a soul was to be seen or heard. The silence was deafening.

They reached the top of the stairs, passed through the sitting area, and went directly to the room with the light shining under the door. From Mark's first trip to Maldini's mansion, he recognized it as Maldini's office. As they crept cautiously up to the door, he pulled the Smith and Wesson from his belt and clicked the safety off. Then he gently opened the door a crack and peaked in. The room was empty.

Disappointed again, they silently opened one bedroom door after another and checked inside the rooms. He held the Smith and Wesson at his side, the safety still off. He was ready to use it if he had to. After finding the third bedroom empty, the hollow feeling in the pit of his stomach told him that something was wrong. When he found the makeshift operating room still set up, he was sure of it…the house had been vacated.

Frustrated, they returned to the sitting area, flipped the light on, and took a seat. He held his head in his hands, trying to decide what to do next. Angela sat quietly and watched him.

"Maldini said to come and get her," he said. "He gave me forty-eight hours to do it. So why aren't they here?" Then it occurred to him. That's why the FBI was involved. Despite the fact that it hadn't been in the news, Maldini must have skipped town and they couldn't find him. Apparently they had found out that he had done Maldini's surgery. Why else would they have tried to stop him at Charity? More importantly right now, how in the hell did Maldini expect them to find him when the FBI couldn't?

He raised his head and looked at Angela. "Why would he give me forty-eight hours to come and get Lisa, then make it impossible for me to find her? It's me he wants, not her. She's just the bait. It doesn't make any sense."

"It does if you know Vito," she said. "He's like a cat. He gets a kick out of toying with his prey before he moves in for the kill."

"And I'm the mouse," he said.

"Right. And you can bet your last dollar that he's left a trail for you to follow."

Mark looked around the sitting area. "There must be a lead around here somewhere," he said.

"This is a hell of a big house," Angela replied.

"The light in his office!" Mark said excitedly. "It was the only one in the house that was on. It has to mean something. Come on. Let's search his office."

They quickly returned to the office and looked around the room…nothing unusual. Then Mark noticed that one drawer in the desk was pulled out slightly, only about a half an inch. He opened it all the way and looked in. It was empty except for a single piece of paper. He picked the paper up and looked at it. It was a receipt from a charter airline service located in Miami, dated only days ago.

"This has to be a clue," he said enthusiastically.

"Let me see it."

He held the receipt down at Angela's level so that she could see it better.

"Argentina," she said dejectedly.

"Yes, but with a lay-over in New Orleans. Look at the length of the layover."

She stared at the page for a moment. "Forty-eight hours!" she exclaimed. "It's the same length of time he gave you to come and get Lisa. He's waiting for you in New Orleans."

"But where in New Orleans? Why didn't he leave a clue as to where he would be? He could be anywhere. It's a big city, and there's a lot of places to hide. If I don't show up in a few hours, he will kill Lisa and fly off to Argentina, never to be heard of again."

"You're wrong. He did leave a clue."

"What are you talking about? I don't see a clue."

"It's me. I know where he is. Vito has a vacation house in New Orleans. He had to know I would tell you about it."

"He is playing a cat and mouse game," Mark said. "But why would he let me know that he's going to Argentina after he leaves New Orleans? It stands to reason that I'd turn that information over to the FBI."

"You have to know how Vito thinks. He likes to brag. It's his way of flaunting his upper hand."

"Or he could be setting me up again. If he gets away from me, he could go anywhere."

"Right. And he would expect you to carry the message to the FBI that he's gone to Argentina."

"And while the FBI looks for him in Argentina, he could be sitting in Paris with his feet propped up drinking wine, or anywhere for that matter, and the FBI wouldn't have a clue."

"It's a possibility," she replied.

He looked at his watch…one thirty. Ten and a half hours to the deadline. He cursed Maldini for leading them on a wild-goose chase, then he extracted a cigarette from the pack, lit it and took a deep drag.

CHAPTER TWENTY-NINE

Mark called Ken from Maldini's office. The telephone rang twice before Ken picked it up.

"Yeah. What is it?" Ken asked, obviously irritated at having been awakened at one thirty in the morning.

"This is Joe Williams," Mark said, remembering not to use his real name. "You need to meet us at the airport at six thirty. Our schedule has suddenly gotten tight. We have to leave for New Orleans. I've got an urgent appointment at noon."

"No kidding. We're going to New Orleans?" Ken said. The irritation in his voice had disappeared. "I haven't been in Cajun country for a long time. The last time I was there without Margaret I had a hell of a good time on Bourbon street."

Mark hung up the telephone. Time was running out too fast to suit him.

"What did he say?" Angela asked.

"He'll meet us at the airport. He wasn't too happy about being there so early, but he agreed to do it. Funny, his speech sounded a little slurred."

"Well, you did wake him up. Maybe he was still half a sleep."

"Maybe, but I think he was intoxicated."

They walked down the stairs of Maldini's mansion, exited the front door as Mark had said they would, and walked to the Sedan Deville. Then they drove back to the Hilton to try to get a few hours sleep.

The next morning they waited impatiently for Ken at the airport. He was thirty minutes late. Mark started pacing back and forth. The deadline now was only five hours away, and getting closer by the minute.

"Where can he be?" Angela asked. "Are you sure he understood that he was supposed to be here at six thirty?"

"He understood. I'm giving him thirty more minutes, then we're looking for another charter service."

"Do you think we can charter another plane at this late date?"

"I doubt it," Mark said, beginning to experience the helpless feeling he despised so much. The desire for a drink eased its way into his conscious mind and began to grow. He rubbed the white chip in his pocket, and the desire went away. One day at a time, Daniel had said.

After much pacing, Ken finally showed up…exactly one hour late.

"Where the hell have you been?" Mark asked, fit to be tied.

"I'm sorry I'm late. I stayed up late last night watching TV. I overslept. It was the hotel's fault. The operator was supposed to give me a wake-up call this morning, but didn't."

Mark had the distinct impression that he smelled alcohol on Ken's breath. He remembered the lies he used to tell when drinking too much had caused him to be late, or simply caused him to forget a function all together. He didn't intend for that to ever happen again. "Okay. Whatever you say," he said. "We're wasting time talking. Let's get the hell out of here."

Apparently relieved by the fact that Mark had chosen not to belabor the point any longer, Ken led the way onto the Piper Navajo. Once aboard, he cranked up the engines and they headed for New Orleans.

Mark's thoughts fleetingly turned to Billingsworth. Surely he would be safe now with a guard posted at his door. He wondered if further study of Lowenstein's data had verified the identity of the hospital's serial killer, as he thought it would. He would have to wait and see. The time was seven thirty…four and a half hours to the deadline.

"Do you think he'll come?" Willie asked, sitting in an armchair that strained under his massive weight.

Maldini stood in the center of the room lighting a cigar. "You can bet on it," he said. Then he blew a thick cloud of blue smoke toward the ceiling. "Dr. Valentine would give his life for his daughter, and we're going to give him the oppqrtunity." He walked over to the sofa and sat down.

"Are you really going to kill the girl if he doesn't show up?" Willie asked.

"What do you think?"

"I think she's as good as dead. What if he doesn't follow the clues you left him in Miami?"

"He will. He's smart."

"I can hardly wait. I haven't liked that smart-ass doctor since I first laid eyes on him. I've got a bullet just for him."

"You may have to stand in line. Ralph and James would like to get their hands on him too. The important thing is that he not get away. I don't care who kills him, as long as he's dead."

Willie nodded his head in agreement, but he still wanted to be the one who plugged Valentine.

———————

Three hours and twenty minutes later, Ken cut back on the throttle and the Piper Navajo began to descend toward New Orleans International Airport. As the plane made a wide turn to approach the runway, the massive Louisiana Superdome suddenly came into view. Mark felt a sudden surge of confidence. The dome had been the site of Georgia's national championship game nineteen years ago. They had been the underdogs. Notre Dame was favored by thirteen points. He threw three touchdown passes that day and ran for another. They were victorious, twenty-eight to seventeen. Now he was again the underdog. This time, however, the battle was for more than a trophy. It was for human to lives...his, Lisa's, and Angela's. He glanced at his watch. The time was twenty minutes to eleven...one hour and twenty minutes to the deadline. Once on the ground, they would have to move fast. Eighty minutes wasn't much time. It would pass quickly.

A few minutes later, the plane landed, taxied to the terminal, then came to a stop.

"We'll be back in two or three hours," Mark said to Ken. "Don't go anywhere."

"What do you mean, don't go anywhere? Aren't we spending the night?"

"Sorry, this is a business trip. You'll have to do your partying on your own time."

"I'll be here. I didn't build this charter service into the moneymaking business it is by putting pleasure ahead of business. I told you, I'm sorry about this morning. It won't happen again."

"Okay, just be here," Mark said sternly.

Mark and Angela left the plane and hurried into the terminal building where they located the Avis counter and rented another Cadillac Sedan Deville, a white one this time. Unlike Miami, they would have to go after Maldini in broad daylight, so the color didn't matter. He looked at the clock on the wall over the head of the rent-a-car agent...eleven o'clock. One hour to the deadline. An intense sense of urgency forced his pulse rate up. Time was rapidly running out. They had to hurry.

They quickly located the white Sedan Deville in the rent-a-car lot, then exited the airport onto Airline Highway and headed toward downtown New Orleans. The pavement was still wet in spots from the storm that had passed through the area two days before. The sun now shined brightly through the few dark clouds that remained in the mostly blue sky. Angela gave him directions to Maldini's house as she had done in Miami.

Ten minutes later, he eased into the right-hand lane and turned onto state highway 90. As they weaved in and out of the heavy traffic, the knot in his stomach grew with each mile. The knot wasn't caused by fear. It was something deeper...worry that his only child might not live through the day.

They passed the New Orleans Convention Center and River Walk on the left, with its docked gambling boats. The French Quarter lay just beyond the Convention Center. The towering International Trade Mart, with its public observation deck overlooking the city and the river, was visible in the distance.

As they passed over the Mississippi River on the Crescent City Connector, flat barges linked together end to end like dominos passed beneath them.

Ten miles later, Angela spoke up. "Get off at the next exit," she said quickly.

He slowed slightly, then exited the highway onto General De Gaule Drive and picked up speed again. Service stations, convenience stores, and inexpensive motels lined the street. Coming up behind a slower-moving, dilapidated, old Chevrolet in the fast lane, he eased his foot down on the brake pedal. The line of slow-moving cars to his right prevented him from passing the Chevrolet on that side. Frustrated by the driver's failure to move over and let him pass, Mark blew the horn. The driver of the Chevrolet, a bald-headed man with his arm around an overweight woman with dyed red hair, didn't respond. Mark thought about flashing the Smith and Wesson, which lay on the seat under a newspaper between him and Angela, but decided against it. Instead, he eased up to within a foot of the Chevrolet's bumper and blew the horn again. This time, the man removed his arm from around the fat woman and gave him the finger. Unable to control his anger any longer, Mark stepped hard on the accelerator pedal. The Cadillac lunged forward and struck the rear of the Chevrolet with a jolt.

Shaken by the sudden impact, the driver of the Chevrolet quickly looked back. Mark couldn't hear his words, but it appeared that he said something like "Crazy son of a bitch." Mark motioned for the man to merge with the slower-moving traffic in the right lane. This time he did. Then, easing his foot down on the accelerator, Mark pulled up beside the Chevrolet, returned the finger, then accelerated out ahead of it, relieved to be moving at high speed again.

"My guess is that Maldini and Lisa will be somewhere in the center of the house," he said. "Ralph or James will be watching the front of the house and the other one will be watching the back. Willie will be with Maldini."

"What do you have in mind?" she asked.

"I'm not sure. Somehow I've got to take Ralph and James out without Maldini knowing it, then go after him and Willie. If we could get one of his watchdogs to come outside, I might be able to slip up behind him and get the jump on him. Then we could go after the other one."

"James has always been crazy about me. He used to watch me all the time. Once I caught him peaking through the door when I was taking a bath. I asked him to come in and get me a towel out of the cabinet."

"Did he?" Mark asked, wondering where this conversation was going.

"Yes, but I thought he was going to have a nervous breakdown. He got me the towel and beat it out of the room as fast as he could. If I knew whether he was watching from the front of the house or the back, I bet I could get him to come out."

"If Ralph is the one in charge, you can bet that James will be watching the back."

"Why do you say that?"

"Pecking order. The front of a house is the most important part. That's where the majority of the money goes when building the outside of a house. The back is usually less elaborate."

"So the one in charge gets to pick, and he would pick the front."

"Right."

Suddenly, Angela sat straight up in the seat. "Turn right at the next intersection," she said quickly. "Vito's house is less that a block away from there."

At the intersection, Mark turned right onto General Mayer Avenue and parked just around the corner. What had been typical New Orleans middle-class dwellings now had become the fancy dwellings of the New Orleans elite. The time was eleven forty…twenty minutes to the deadline.

"Come on," he said, quickly throwing the driver's-side door open and getting out of the car.

Angela followed him.

The Mississippi River flowed toward the Gulf of Mexico a short distance beyond the neighborhood. The houses, set well back from the street, were expensive and of varied design. According to Angela, Maldini's house was typical Louisiana-Creole, plantation style. Latticework separated brick peers that elevated the porch three feet above ground level along the front of the two-story house. Four wide, brick steps led up to the porch and six white, square columns extended from the front of the porch to support the upper level of the house. Maldini had had the house built in the mid-1980s to have a place to stay the three or four times a year he visited the city to party and partake of the local Cajun cuisine, which he was especially fond of. The downstairs consisted of a living room, dining room, large family room, garden room, kitchen, utility room, and master bedroom. The upstairs consisted of four bedrooms and two baths. At the back of the house, a wooden deck looked out at a kidney shaped swimming pool. A six-foot-high, wooden fence surrounded the back yard. The front of the house was unobstructed. Apparently, 800 miles from home, Maldini didn't feel the need for the strict security of his residence in Miami.

Mark figured that Maldini had chosen the New Orleans site to hold Lisa because the openness in front made it easier for him to fall into Maldini's trap. Angela pointed out that there was a second reason, possibly the most important one. Maldini had over five million dollars stashed away in a safety deposit box in the Bank of New Orleans. He had probably already gotten it. She was sure it was his get-away money.

As they walked briskly down the street toward Maldini's house, Mark eased the Smith and Wesson out of his belt and flicked the safety off. Then he replaced the gun in his belt and gritted his teeth. He was ready.

Reaching the front of the house that sat between them and Maldini's, they stopped suddenly. A tall, black man with a shoulder holster strapped under his arm sat in a swing on the porch of Maldini's house. He appeared to be about six-feet tall and was well built. His crooked nose gave evidence that it had been broken in the past and improperly set. A cellular telephone sat by his side.

"That's Ralph," Angela said softly.

"Then I was right. James has to be guarding the back door. They're communicating by cellular telephone."

At that point, Mark wished he had a silencer like Kincaid had had at Southland Air. He would shoot Ralph without remorse to save Lisa's life, but he didn't have one, and Maldini would hear the shot if he fired the gun without it. He would have to come up with a better idea. James would be the easier of the two to take out. If he could eliminate James, maybe he could slip around through the inside of the house to the front without Willie and Maldini knowing it. Then he could take Ralph by surprise. But it would all have to be done silently. He could take them on one at a time, but he wasn't a match for them collectively.

He and Angela cut through the neighbor's yard, keeping the neighbor's house between them and Maldini's. At the back of the neighbor's house, they scurried through his yard and approached the wooden fence that surrounded Maldini's back yard. Mark looked around for something to climb on and spotted a garbage can at the side of the neighbor's house. He hurried to the can, picked it up, and carried it back to the fence. Just as he started to climb up on it, a male voice coming directly from behind startled him.

"What are you doing?" an elderly man in a red, leisure suit asked loudly as he walked in their direction.

Mark turned toward the man and put his finger to his mouth. "Shhh," he said. "They'll hear you."

"Who will hear me?" the man asked in a quieter voice.

Mark figured that this time the truth would be better than a lie. "The man next door, Vito Maldini," he said.

"Vito who?" the man said. "The owner of the house next door is Melvin Smith. He's a business man from out of town."

"That may be what he told you, but his real name is Vito Maldini. He's the head of organized crime in Miami. He's wanted by the FBI."

"I'll be damned. Are you an agent? I had a nephew who was an FBI agent for a while. His name was Harry Everstreet. Did you know him? He retired from the agency ten or eleven years ago."

Mark looked anxiously at his watch...fifteen minutes to the deadline. No time to waste. He thought about telling the man that he was an FBI agent, but decided that it would be too risky. He might ask for some identification. Mark continued the honesty approach.

"No, I'm not an agent. Maldini kidnapped my daughter. We have every reason to believe that he's going to kill her any minute if I don't stop him. Please trust me," he pleaded. "I don't have time to explain now."

"He's telling you the truth," Angela chimed in. "It's an emergency. We've got to hurry."

"I don't know," the man said, scratching his head.

About that time, the man's wife, a thin, white-haired lady in flowered Bermuda shorts and an equally colorful blouse, joined the elderly man.

"Wilbur, what are you doing out here?" she asked. "You know doctor Arceneaux told you to avoid the noon-day heat. It's bad for your heart condition."

"Martha, these people say that Mr. Smith, or whatever his name is, is a crook from Miami, and that he's kidnapped their daughter."

"The woman gasped. "I thought there was something sinister about him, the way he kept to himself, and those awful looking men who hang around the house when he's here. Maybe they're right. Nothing would surprise me anymore."

"I'll tell you what," Mark said. "If we're not back in thirty minutes, you can call the police."

Instinctively, the man looked at his watch. "I guess we could do that," he said. "What do you think Martha?"

"I think it would be okay. They look like such a nice young couple. It's hard not to believe them."

"Thirty minutes," the man said, "not one minute more."

"Thanks," Mark said, breathing a sigh of relief. He rushed to the garbage can and climbed up on it. Then he lifted his body to the top of the fence and dropped to the ground on the other side. After he helped Angela over the fence, they hurried to the back corner of Maldini's house where Mark looked at his watch again.

"Damn," he said under his breath. "It's ten minutes to the deadline. We've got to hurry. How are we going to get James outside?"

"Trust me," Angela said with a wink. "Stay here."

CHAPTER THIRTY

Before Mark could ask Angela what she had in mind, she was gone. He stayed put and watched her walk around the deck until she was in open view of the back door. Standing on the patio between the deck and the pool, she faced the house, placed her hands on her hips, and smiled coquettishly.

"James, are you in there?" she coaxed softly. "You've been wanting me for a long time. This is your chance."

"What the hell is she doing?" Mark muttered under his breath.

A minute passed, then two, then three. Nothing happened. He glanced at his watch…seven minutes to the deadline.

The knot in his stomach had reached basketball proportions. He had a sudden urge to storm the house and take his chances. Instead, he forced himself to wait.

"Want to play hard to get, huh," Angela said, still smiling. She removed her blouse, then her slacks, and dropped them in a pile on the concrete. Standing there only in her white silk bra and matching, bikini panties, she waited for the door to open.

"This is your chance," she repeated. "Don't blow it."

The door didn't move.

"Damn," she said softly. "It's all or none I guess." She slipped her bra off and dropped it on the concrete with her other clothes. Then, replacing her hands on her hips, she wiggled her hips slowly from side to side.

Mark stood silently and watched her with his mouth open. God she had a gorgeous body. The door suddenly opened and James eased out.

His eyes were as big as half dollars. He was about Angela's height and had oily-looking skin. A distinctive gap separated his two front teeth. He, like Ralph, wore a shoulder holster. He held a cellular telephone in his hand.

Mark kept his eyes on the telephone, hoping that it wouldn't occur to James to use it. If it did, they were as good as dead. James approached Angela, looking like he could hardly believe his good luck. The cellular telephone remained at his side.

"Angela. What are you doing here?" James asked, his eyes fixed on her bare breasts. "Vito said you'd run off."

"I came back to see you," she said in a sexy voice.

For some reason, Mark had the distinct feeling that she was enjoying her strip tease act.

James walked toward her, mesmerized by her nearly nude body. Mark slipped up behind him. Just as James reached out to put his arms around Angela, Mark hit him sharply across the right temple with the Smith and Wesson. James slumped to the ground in a limp pile, out cold.

"Now it's three to one," Mark said to himself. "The odds are getting better." He looked at his watch again.

"Oh shit!" he said to himself. It was four minutes to the deadline. He had to hurry. He briefly closed his eyes and prayed that Maldini wouldn't kill Lisa before he got to her. He glanced back at Angela.

"Come on," he whispered. Then he bounded up the steps to the deck.

"Like this?" she asked, holding her hands out in the air to her sides, palms up.

"No. Put your clothes on."

Not waiting for her, he hurried through the back door into the hallway that led to the kitchen and the dining room on the left and the family room on the right. He could hear voices coming from the family room. Approaching the door, he stopped and listened for a moment. Then, peering through a crack in the door, he saw Maldini and Willie casually sitting and talking to each other. A cellular telephone sat on the coffee table in front of them. He wanted to barge in and demand that Maldini tell him where Lisa was, but first he had to take care of Ralph.

Quietly leaving the cracked door, he made his way through the kitchen into the dining room, headed for the front door. Suddenly, he heard the door to the family room open. He quickly stepped back against the wall and froze, his finger on the trigger of the Smith and Wesson.

Moments later, Willie appeared in the doorway between the dining room and the kitchen. Mark held his breath. If Willie looked to his right, he would see him in clear view. He thought about Angela. He had left her in the back yard getting dressed. He hoped she wouldn't barge into the house and give him away.

Appearing preoccupied, Willie lumbered straight ahead and disappeared from view.

Seconds later, Mark heard the refrigerator door open, then close. Willie then reappeared in front of the doorway with a can of beer in his hand. Mark continued to stand motionless, pressed against the wall. Willie popped the top off of the beer, then quickly disappeared from sight again.

Wiping the sweat from his forehead with the back of his gun-free hand, Mark hurriedly made his way through the dining room to the foyer. The front door was straight ahead. Somehow he would have to take Ralph out without alerting Maldini and Willie. He could suddenly push the door open and rush him, but that would be too dangerous. The loud confrontation that was bound to follow would instantly give him away. Instead, he eased up to the door and carefully opened it a couple of inches. He could hear the squeak of the swing at the far left end of the porch as Ralph moved around in it. He would have to create a disturbance of some sort, a very quiet one, to get Ralph into a position so that he could knock him unconscious as he had done James. But how?

He looked around the foyer and spotted a silk plant in a small brass urn sitting on a table by the wall. He crossed the foyer, pulled the plant out of the urn, and tossed the plant to the floor. Then he reapproached the door and opened it a few inches more. Ralph still sat in the swing. Mark drew the small urn back and pitched it underhanded through the opening in the door. It sailed through the air and landed on the sidewalk with a clang, a good thirty feet away.

"What the hell," Ralph muttered. He jumped to his feet, quickly walked to the area of the porch that was at the head of the steps, and stared out at the yard.

To Mark's delight, Ralph stood directly in front of the door with his back to him. He took a deep breath, pushed the door open, and lunged across the porch at full speed, striking Ralph in the small of the back with tremendous force. Ralph grunted in pain as his head snapped sharply back.

Flying through the air, Mark held onto the Smith and Wesson with a strong grip, afraid it would be jarred from his hand by the impending impact. Ralph crashed head long into the sidewalk. The crunch of his facial bones made a sickening sound. Simultaneously, a sharp pain shot through Mark's shoulder as the full weight of his body landed hard on his left elbow. From the location of the pain, he knew immediately that he had broken his arm near the shoulder joint. He cursed under his breath, pissed at his misfortune.

From underneath him, Ralph, in a dazed state, struggled to free his gun from its holster. Mark quickly raised himself up and placed the barrel of the Smith and Wesson to the back of Ralph's head. A wave of nausea immediately passed over him, and his head began to swim. The pain was excruciating.

"Please God, don't let me pass out now," he pleaded.

The nausea and lightheadedness passed as fast as they had appeared. "Make one sound and I'll blow your brains out," he said forcefully.

Ralph withdrew his hand from the holster and lay dead still.

Maybe this is going to work, Mark thought. He drew his gun above his head. "Sweet dreams," he said. Then he struck Ralph in the back of the head with all the strength he could muster. Ralph's body twitched twice, then went limp.

"Two to one," Mark said under his breath. "The odds are definitely getting better." He got to his feet, his injured arm dangling limply at his side. He couldn't let the pain stand in his way. He still had work to do. He quickly glanced at his watch…five seconds to the deadline. The pain in his arm immediately disappeared, replaced by fear for Lisa's life.

He hurriedly re-entered the house and worked his way through the dining room and the kitchen back to the hallway where he had seen Maldini and Willie through the crack in the door. He again glanced at his watch…TWELVE NOON. THE DEADLINE HAD ARRIVED. He quickly peaked through the crack. Maldini and Willie still sat in the same chairs conversing.

"Well, Valentine's a real disappointment," Maldini said. "I thought sure he cared enough about his daughter to try to save her life."

"Can I kill her?" Willie asked.

"Go to it," Maldini answered. "Let's get it over with."

Mark pushed the door open and quickly stepped inside. "Don't move," he said loudly, pointing the Smith and Wesson directly at Maldini's chest. He couldn't help but admire the work he had done on Maldini's face. The puffiness had all but disappeared, and the bruises had faded considerably. The previous heavy scar now was just a thin red line, barely visible. Without his mustache, and with the streaks of gray that used to run through his now dyed jet-black hair, Maldini looked twenty years younger.

"Where's Lisa?" Mark demanded. "If you've hurt her, I'll kill you both."

Maldini started to stand up, but thought better of it. The chair springs squeaked and twanged from Willie's massive weight as he jumped to his feet and went for his shoulder holster. Mark fired a shot just above his left ear. Willie froze in his tracks.

"Now, slowly unfasten the shoulder holster and let it drop to the floor," Mark instructed.

Willie didn't move. The anger in his eyes was chilling. His teeth were clinched so tight that his jaw muscles bulged. Mark fired another shot, this time just above Willie's right ear. Willie quickly unhooked the holster and dropped it to the floor.

"That's better," Mark said.

"How in the hell did you get by Ralph and James?" Maldini asked

"I had help," Mark replied.

Angela suddenly walked into the room buttoning her blouse.

Maldini quickly turned his eyes toward Angela. "Angela, I'm so glad you came back. I've missed you."

"I asked you a question," Mark repeated, cocking the gun. "Where's Lisa? I'm not going to ask you again."

"Okay, okay," Maldini said hastily. "She's here. You don't have to worry. She's okay."

Mark nodded his head toward Willie. "Tie him up," he instructed Angela.

"With what?" she asked, looking around the room with a perplexed look on her face.

Mark pointed with the barrel of the gun to a lamp sitting on an end table. "Use the cord." A lamp cord, he had discovered in Billingsworth's hospital room, made a pretty fair substitute for a rope. Blood from his skinned elbow began to drip off the end of his fingers and splatter on the floor.

"What's wrong with your arm?" Angela asked.

"I'll tell you about it later. Just tie him up."

She walked to the table and unplugged the lamp.

"I'll feel a lot better when Willie's three-hundred pounds are out of commission," Mark said. Then he waved the gun at the floor in front of Willie. "Lie down," he instructed gruffly.

Willie grunted, then lay down on the floor. Using the lamp cord, Angela tied his hands behind his back, then she tied his feet together.

"Bend your knees," she instructed.

Willie didn't move.

"Do as the lady says, or I'll blow your knee cap off," Mark commanded.

"She's no lady," Willie said sarcastically. Then he bent his knees.

Angela looped the free end of the cord from his feet around the cord tying his hands together and gave it a hard tug, apparently in return for his ungentlemanly remark. Willie grunted at the pain, then struggled briefly to get free before becoming resigned to his fate. Angela tied the cord in a final knot.

"Okay, take me to Lisa," Mark demanded, waving the gun at Maldini.

"You don't give me much choice. I have to admit though, I'm surprised."

"At what?"

"That you're still alive. I never expected you to get this far."

"Let's go," Mark said. "I'm through talking."

Maldini stood up and took a step toward the stairs. Mark followed, relieved that it all was about over.

"Drop the gun, Dr. Valentine," a male voice suddenly growled from behind them.

Mark froze. He had heard the voice before…in the car when the gunmen abducted him from the Emergency Room. It belonged to the driver of the get-away car. Lowering the Smith and Wesson to his side, he turned to see a heavy-set, white man in a gray chauffeur's uniform standing in the doorway with a gun pointed directly at him.

"Shit," Mark muttered under his breath. He hadn't counted on another one of Maldini's men showing up. He thought of all the movies he had seen where in similar situations the hero suddenly did a somersault to one side or the other and, coming up on one knee, fired off a round to drop the enemy in his tracks. He wondered if it would work in real life.

Probably not, he concluded. He wouldn't do Lisa much good dead. He hesitated, then dropped the Smith and Wesson to the floor. In an effort to ease the pain in his broken arm, he placed his right hand under his bent left elbow for support. The pain slackened some.

"Lonnie, where the hell have you been?" Maldini demanded angrily.

"I went to get some cigarettes," Lonnie said apologetically. "I ran out over an hour ago. I couldn't stand it any longer. I had to go get some."

Maldini furrowed his brow. "Why would you leave? You knew we had to keep a look-out for Dr. Valentine."

"But boss, you said it was beginning to look like he wasn't going to show. Besides, there were four of you here. I didn't think you needed me."

Maldini shrugged his shoulders and looked disgusted. Mark had the feeling that he would deal with Lonnie later.

Angela walked to Maldini's side, put her arm around his waist, and kissed him gently on the cheek. Then she looked at Mark. "Sorry," she said. "I've got too much to live for."

Mark stood there with his mouth open…totally speechless.

"What do you want me to do with Valentine?" Lonnie asked Maldini.

Maldini glanced at Mark, then at Angela. "Kill them both," he instructed.

"Vito, you can't kill me," Angela said quickly. "I love you. You can't go back on your word. I led Mark to you like I promised."

Mark looked at her in disbelief. Now it all made sense. She was the one who informed Maldini that he would be at Charity. Maldini must then have gotten word to Jesus. He should have figured it out earlier. After all, Angela was the only one who knew that he had gotten the Porsche painted. How else would Jesus have known to plant plastic explosives in a black car? The question he had posed earlier about where she had learned her values when she was growing up had been answered. She had learned them from slime like Maldini.

"Don't look so betrayed," Maldini said to Mark. "I know Angela like the back of my hand. I'm sure she's been playing the two of us against each other. If you had won, she would have stayed with you, and you never would have known about our little deal"

Maldini looked into Angela's face, then pushed her away. "How many times did you sleep with him?" he asked gruffly.

The color drained from her face. "Vito, you know I would never do anything like that. I've always been true to you."

"Bullshit," Maldini said angrily. "Do you really think I don't know about all the other times you cheated on me?" He scowled at Lonnie. "I said kill them both. Now do it!"

Lonnie lifted his gun and pointed it directly at Mark's heart. "Adios mother fucker," he said with a sneer on his face.

Wide eyed, Mark watched him as he began to squeeze the trigger, helpless to do anything to prevent his eminent demise.

BAM

Mark was sure that he had been hit. But why didn't it hurt? He glanced down at chest, looking for blood. None was present.

With a loud crash, Lonnie suddenly collapsed to the floor, a bullet between his eyes. His gun clattered to the floor and landed at Maldini's feet. Maldini quickly picked it up.

BAM

Another bullet glanced off the gun and struck the wall near the ceiling just above Maldini's head. Maldini immediately dropped the gun. Then Sam Kincaid stepped through the door.

"Oh shit!" Mark exclaimed. "Out of the frying pan into the fire."

Kincaid pointed his police revolver at Willie who was still tied up on the floor. "Do the same for Maldini," he instructed Angela.

Angela walked to the other end table, unplugged the lamp, and tied Maldini up, leaving him on the floor by Willie. Then, with a menacing look on his face, Kincaid turned and faced Mark. Mark stood frozen in position, staring at Kincaid's cold, steely eyes. His heart skipped a beat, and beads of sweat burst out on his forehead. Then his life began flashing before his eyes.

CHAPTER THIRTY-ONE

The body bag was black and over six-feet long. Two men in short, white coats pushed it across the room on a portable gurney, then out the door. A large pool of blood marked the spot where a body had been sprawled on the white, marble floor minutes before. A yellow, plastic band encircled the entrance to the estate, declaring the area off limits to the public. The forensic crew had arrived and was now busy taking photographs and making measurements. A Miami homicide detective arrived on the scene and began questioning those who were present at the time of the shooting and recorded their answers in a small, brown notebook.

Special Agent Daryl Barnes and three FBI agents, along with an equal number of uniformed New Orleans policemen, had made their entrances immediately behind Kincaid's and placed Maldini and his henchmen under arrest. All four...Maldini, Willie, Ralph, and James...were now on the way to city jail. Lonnie was on the way to the morgue.

Mark had rushed upstairs and found Lisa safe, tied to a chair in one of the bedrooms. They had hugged each other tightly, thankful that the nightmare was over. Lisa had been so happy to see him that she cried. He almost did. She had been concerned about his arm. He had assured her that it would be okay as soon as he got to a doctor. He would have to wear a hanging cast, flexed at the elbow and supported by sling and swath bandage, for six weeks, but after all he had been through, that didn't seem so bad. Lisa helped him make a makeshift sling out of a pillowcase, then they joined the others in the great room downstairs.

"You wanted to kill me," Mark said to Kincaid who stood by the door out of the way of the forensic team. "Why didn't you pull the trigger? "

"I discovered that you were innocent. I didn't want to believe it at first, but it's hard to argue with facts. We arrested Jesus Dimaria yesterday. He had a diamond dinner ring in his pocket. Joanna's mother identified it as one she had given her as a birthday present a few years ago."

"I know the ring. I never did like it. I thought it was too gaudy."

"He also had a knife in his possession that was compatible with the one the autopsy reports said Joanna and Daniel Iverson were murdered with. And we found some plastic explosives and fuses at the place where he was staying. They matched material we found at the site of your car explosion."

"How did you catch Jesus?"

"It actually was fairly easy. Our big break in the case came when a lady in your apartment building called and said a strange man had been hanging around the area. She described him in minute detail. Even described his car and gave us the license plate number. It's the most complete description I've ever been given."

"The lady wouldn't happen to have been a Mrs. Grabosky would it?"

"Well, yes. I believe it was. How did you know?"

"It figures. Thank goodness for nosy people."

"After we picked Jesus up," Kincaid continued. "We ran an I.D. on him and discovered that he was one of Maldini's men. Then it all fell into place."

"It sounds like most of your evidence against Jesus is circumstantial, no eye witnesses."

"It's enough of a case to get an indictment. We feel certain we could have gotten more evidence by the time of the trial."

"What do you mean, could have?" Mark asked.

"He confessed. The District Attorney offered him a deal he couldn't refuse, under a considerable amount of pressure from the Director of the FBI I might add. In exchange for his confession, the District

Attorney offered Jesus life in prison without parole instead of seeking the death penalty."

"I don't understand. Why would the District Attorney be willing to do that?"

"For implicating Maldini in the murders. After all, Jesus worked for him. He jumped at the opportunity to save his own ass. We've added murder one to the charges against Maldini."

Mark smiled. "Great. The guy deserves to fry." Then he turned to the man standing next to Kincaid. "You're the guy who saved my life at Southland Air when Kincaid tried to kill me."

The man extended his hand. "Special Agent Daryl Barnes," he said. "I was just doing my job sir."

Mark shook Barnes' hand. "How did you find me?"

"We knew you were at the hospital because a nurse in the Emergency Room, a Mrs. Mattie Johnson, called you in the Doctors' Lounge."

Mark had a sinking feeling. Had Mattie indeed turned him in? "How did you know about that?" he asked.

"We still bug telephones, with a judge's approval of course," Barnes said. "We also knew you broke into your ex-wife's house and took her Jaguar. We located the taxi driver who picked you up at Charity and took you there. He had a good memory. Then we got the Jaguar's license plate number from the County Tax Assessor's office and put an APB out on it. The Jaguar wasn't difficult to locate. From that point on, we just followed you. When you started using Maldini's credit card to schedule flights and rent cars, it helped. Every time you made a charge, the credit card company immediately reported it to us."

"It was Maldini's card. How did you know he wasn't using it?"

"At first, we thought he was, but it didn't make any sense for him to be going back to Miami. Besides, he's too smart to use his own credit card. He would have known that it could be traced. Since we knew you were running around with his girlfriend, we figured the card had to be hers."

"You not only saved me from Kincaid at Southland Air, you saw to it that I got away."

"That's right. We had a hunch that if we gave you enough slack you would eventually lead us to Maldini. Captain Kincaid almost botched the whole operation. I explained everything to him after your plane took off. He was insistent that he be allowed to come with us to New Orleans, so I gave in and invited him to make the trip."

Mark turned back to Kincaid. "How did you know that I'd be at Southland Air?"

"The FBI's not the only one that bugs telephones," Kincaid said with a grin. When I learned that Walter Black had sent Special Agent Barnes to Atlanta to spearhead the FBI's investigation, I put a bug in the telephone in his hotel room."

"You what?" Barnes exclaimed. "That's against the law. I could have you arrested."

"What purpose would that serve?" Kincaid countered. "You've got what you came for."

"I guess you're right, but I still don't like it."

"When the call from the credit card company came into FBI headquarters, the agent on duty immediately notified Agent Barnes," Kincaid continued. "I heard every word. Then I beat him to Southland Air."

"It wasn't very hard for you to beat me there," Barnes said. "I hate driving in this damned Atlanta traffic, and I wasn't in any particular hurry. My mission was to find out where Valentine was going, not to stop him."

Mark turned to Barnes. "You know that I could have been killed trying to track Maldini down."

Barnes smiled wryly. "Well, all's well that ends well I always say."

"It's hard to argue with that," Mark replied. "Thank God Lisa's safe. That's the most important thing." He put his good arm around her and hugged her again. She returned the hug.

As Mark and Lisa started to leave the room, Kincaid stopped him. "I thought you might like to know that we arrested the doctor behind the hospital murders. When the hospital's computer people took a look at the data Lowenstein had been analyzing, the pattern you predicted in your call to Dorfman showed up clear as day. The excess cardiac arrest group was split almost evenly between Dr. Haynes' and Dr. Wilson's patients. Virtually none occurred in Dr. Jack Jackson's. We put pressure on Betsy Barfield, telling her that we knew the name of the doctor who put her up to causing the cardiac arrests, and that unless she got honest she alone would be charged with the murders. She immediately broke down and spilled everything. Seems that Dr. Jackson was obsessed with the fact that Dr. Haynes and Dr. Wilson were getting much larger portions of income from paying patients than he was. Before Haynes and Wilson were hired he got it all."

Mark stroked his new beard. "Because of the loss of income, Billingsworth's policy of sharing complication and death-rate data with prospective paying patients caused Dr. Jackson a tremendous amount of stress. It was common knowledge that he had the worst track record of the three. Since he couldn't improve his own record, it occurred to me that he might be trying to make Haynes' and Wilson's worse."

"Right. To level the playing field, so to speak. And when Haynes' and Wilson's records began to worsen, Dr. Billingsworth suspected that Dr. Jackson played a role, but he couldn't prove it."

"Dr. Jackson told the policeman who arrested him that he had thought about the income thing for a long time, and that causing the cardiac arrests was the only logical thing he could come up with."

"Some logic. Why would Betsy Barfield kill patients for him?"

"She was head over heals in love with the guy. They had been having an affair for almost two years."

"But Stottlemire dated her. Why would she go out with Stottlemire if she were so crazy about Dr. Jackson?"

"Another one of Dr. Jackson's brainstorms. He forced her to date Dr. Stottlemire a few times to strengthen the apparent link between the two of them. Once he had her addicted to drugs, coupled with the fact that she really loved the guy, she would have done anything for him, even commit murder."

"Or date Stottlemire."

Kincaid didn't see the humor in the statement.

"How does Stottlemire fit into all of this?" Mark asked. "He was supplying Betsy with drugs. We saw his name on the prescription bottles."

"Wrong. That's what Dr. Jackson wanted everyone to think. He was the one supplying her with drugs. She finally admitted it. He periodically stole Dr. Stottlemire's prescription pads from the Emergency Room. With a little practice, he became very adept at forging his signature."

"Why did Betsy need Dr. Jackson? Couldn't she have forged the prescriptions herself?"

"She tried that once," Kincaid replied. "Apparently she wasn't very good at it. When she took the prescription to the drug store, the pharmacist got suspicious and reached for the telephone...she assumed to call Dr. Stottlemire. She panicked, grabbed the prescription, and ran out the door. She switched pharmacies after that, but she never had the nerve to try to forge another prescription on her own."

"Did you question Betsy about how she managed to cause the cardiac arrests without being anywhere near the patients?"

"We did. It was very simple. I'm surprised you all didn't figure it out. She injected a highly concentrated solution of potassium chloride into the patient's I.V. bag. As the mixture ran into the patient, the concentration of the potassium in the patient's body gradually built up over an hour or so until it reached a critical point."

"And when that point was reached, the electrical activity of the heart went wild, causing the cardiac output to fall too low to support life and, bingo, cardiac arrest. By that time, Betsy was long gone."

"You're the doctor," Kincaid said. "I'll have to take your word for it."

"The excess cardiac arrests occurred on Stottlemire's shift. How do you explain that?" Mark asked.

"Dr. Jackson arranged it. If Betsy ever got caught, he wanted his trail to be well covered."

"Why did he target Stottlemire as the fall guy?"

"We asked him that. He said there was no reason in particular. Someone had to be chosen. Stottlemire was so arrogant it rubbed him the wrong way. Apparently he just didn't like the guy."

"Talk about irony. Dr. Jackson and Stottlemire are the two most arrogant people I know. They're like two peas in a pod."

"Oh, I almost forgot," Kincaid said quickly. "Stottlemire told me to tell you to hurry back to the Emergency Room. Everyone misses you."

"I miss them too," Mark said with sincerity. "Can you believe it, I'm actually looking forward to getting back to work there."

Kincaid continued. "He also said to tell you that Billingsworth is doing great at Emory. He's alert and off the ventilator. His heart's much stronger." Kincaid paused. "It looks like you're a free man," he said. "You've been cleared of Joanna's murder, and the FBI has decided not to press charges for obstructing justice. Where do you go from here?"

"I've got a date with a gorgeous lady in Atlanta, Mark replied. "But first I've got a Caduceus meeting to go to...just as soon as I get my arm taken care of."

Daniel had been right. He knew it now, and he was finally ready. With the support of the doctors in Caduceus, he had an excellent chance of getting his life back together and eventually getting his license reinstated.

Angela edged closer to him. "What about me," she asked, forcing a smile.

He looked at her for a moment. "You made your choice," he said. "I guess you'll have to live with it."

She hung her head and stared at the floor. He watched her for a moment, feeling sorry for her. Then she raised her head, focused her eyes on Kincaid, and slowly looked him up and down. She would be okay, he concluded. She was a survivor.

"By the way," Kincaid said. "When we picked Jesus up, he had a briefcase full of money in the trunk of his car. $100,000 to be exact. He said that he took it from your apartment. Apparently, he meant to keep it for himself."

"Well, it doesn't sound like he's going to be able to spend it where he's going."

"You're right about that. You can pick it up at the station at your convenience."

"You're kidding."

"I don't kid," Kincaid said with a straight face. "It's the responsibility of the Atlanta police department to return stolen property to its rightful owner. It's yours."

"I'll be damned," Mark said. He gave Angela one last look, then turned to leave the room. When he and Lisa reached the door, he stopped, took the nearly full pack of cigarettes from his shirt pocket, and tossed it at the wastebasket in the corner of the room. The pack hit the basket dead center. Then he turned back to Kincaid and smiled. "Two points," he said, holding up two fingers in a victory sign.

THE END

About the Author

H. Thomas Milhorn, MD, PhD is the author of numerous research papers and three nonfiction books. *Caduceus Awry,* his first novel was a finalist in the Eudora Welty Film and Fiction Festival novel contest, which is held annually in her hometown of Jackson, Mississippi.

9 780595 128839